UNBROKEN

The Protectors #12

SLOANE KENNEDY

Unbroken is a work of fiction. Names, characters, businesses, places, events and incidents are either the products of the author's imagination or used in a fictitious manner. Any resemblance to actual persons, living or dead, or actual events is purely coincidental.

Copyright © 2018 by Sloane Kennedy

Published in the United States by Sloane Kennedy
All rights reserved. This book or any portion thereof may not be reproduced or used in any manner whatsoever without the express written permission of the publisher except for the use of brief quotations in a book review.

Cover Image: © Eric David Battershell

Cover Model: Julian Ramos

Copyright © Cover Design: Cate Ashwood Designs, 2019

Copyediting by Courtney Bassett

ISBN-13:
978-1717422965

ISBN-10:
1717422969

Unbroken

Sloane Kennedy

Trademark Acknowledgements

The author acknowledges the trademarked status and trademark owners of the following trademarks mentioned in this work of fiction:

Piper
Trix
Minecraft
Captain America

Acknowledgments

Thanks to Claudia, Kylee and Lucy for the beta reading that you all have become such experts at! An extra thanks to Claudia for doing double duty as my expert on Brazil!

Thanks to Courtney for the quick and thorough proofing job! I honestly am not sure what I'd do without you at this point! Also, thank you Barb for being a second set of eyes for me!

And finally thanks to Colleen… you know what for! Hope you like what I came up with for you!

Author Note

For those of you who want to begin my Protectors series with this book, you may want to consider reading Atonement (Book 6) first.

Atonement is the story of Aleks's brother, Dante and both brothers appear in each other's books so it is helpful to know their backstories. This is just a recommendation, not a requirement… the book can absolutely be read as a standalone.

—Sloane

Series Reading Order

Several of my series cross over with one another so I've provided a couple of recommended reading orders for you. If you want to start with the Protectors books, use the first list. If you want to follow the books according to timing, use the second list. Note that you can skip any of the books (including M/F) as each was written to be a standalone story.

Note that some books may not be readily available on all retail sites

Recommended Reading Order (Use this list if you want to start with "The Protectors" series)
1. Absolution (m/m/m) (The Protectors, #1)
2. Salvation (m/m) (The Protectors, #2)
3. Retribution (m/m) (The Protectors, #3)
4. Gabriel's Rule (m/f) (The Escort Series, #1)
5. Shane's Fall (m/f) (The Escort Series, #2)
6. Logan's Need (m/m) (The Escort Series, #3)
7. Finding Home (m/m/m) (Finding Series, #1)
8. Finding Trust (m/m) (Finding Series, #2)
9. Loving Vin (m/f) (Barretti Security Series, #1)

10. Redeeming Rafe (m/m) (Barretti Security Series, #2)
11. Saving Ren (m/m/m) (Barretti Security Series, #3)
12. Freeing Zane (m/m) (Barretti Security Series, #4)
13. Finding Peace (m/m) (Finding Series, #3)
14. Finding Forgiveness (m/m) (Finding Series, #4)
15. Forsaken (m/m) (The Protectors, #4)
16. Vengeance (m/m/m) (The Protectors, #5)
17. A Protectors Family Christmas (The Protectors, #5.5)
18. Atonement (m/m) (The Protectors, #6)
19. Revelation (m/m) (The Protectors, #7)
20. Redemption (m/m) (The Protectors, #8)
21. Finding Hope (m/m/m) (Finding Series, #5)
22. Defiance (m/m) (The Protectors #9)
23. Unexpected (m/m/m) (The Protectors, #10)
24. Shattered (m/m) (The Protectors, #11)
25. Unbroken (m/m) (The Protectors, #12)
26. Forgotten: Luca (The Four, #1)

The following novellas are also available and can be read any time after book 5 (Vengeance) in The Protectors series:
Protecting Elliot (m/m)
Discovering Daisy (m/m/f)

The short story entitled "Pretend You're Mine" can be read anytime after book 7, Revelation.

Recommended Reading Order (Use this list if you want to follow according to timing)
1. Gabriel's Rule (m/f) (The Escort Series, #1)
2. Shane's Fall (m/f) (The Escort Series, #2)
3. Logan's Need (m/m) (The Escort Series, #3)
4. Finding Home (m/m/m) (Finding Series, #1)
5. Finding Trust (m/m) (Finding Series, #2)
6. Loving Vin (m/f) (Barretti Security Series, #1)
7. Redeeming Rafe (m/m) (Barretti Security Series, #2)
8. Saving Ren (m/m/m) (Barretti Security Series, #3)

9. Freeing Zane (m/m) (Barretti Security Series, #4)
10. Finding Peace (m/m) (Finding Series, #3)
11. Finding Forgiveness (m/m) (Finding Series, #4)
12. Absolution (m/m/m) (The Protectors, #1)
13. Salvation (m/m) (The Protectors, #2)
14. Retribution (m/m) (The Protectors, #3)
15. Forsaken (m/m) (The Protectors, #4)
16. Vengeance (m/m/m) (The Protectors, #5)
17. A Protectors Family Christmas (The Protectors, #5.5)
18. Atonement (m/m) (The Protectors, #6)
19. Revelation (m/m) (The Protectors, #7)
20. Redemption (m/m) (The Protectors, #8)
21. Finding Hope (m/m/m) (Finding Series, #5)
22. Defiance (m/m) (The Protectors #9)
23. Unexpected (m/m/m) (The Protectors, #10)
24. Shattered (m/m) (The Protectors, #11)
25. Unbroken (m/m) (The Protectors, #12)
26. Forgotten: Luca (The Four, #1)

The following novellas are also available and can be read any time after book 5 (Vengeance) in The Protectors series:
Protecting Elliot m/m
Discovering Daisy m/m/f

The short story entitled "Pretend You're Mine" can be read anytime after book 7, Revelation.

Series Crossover Chart

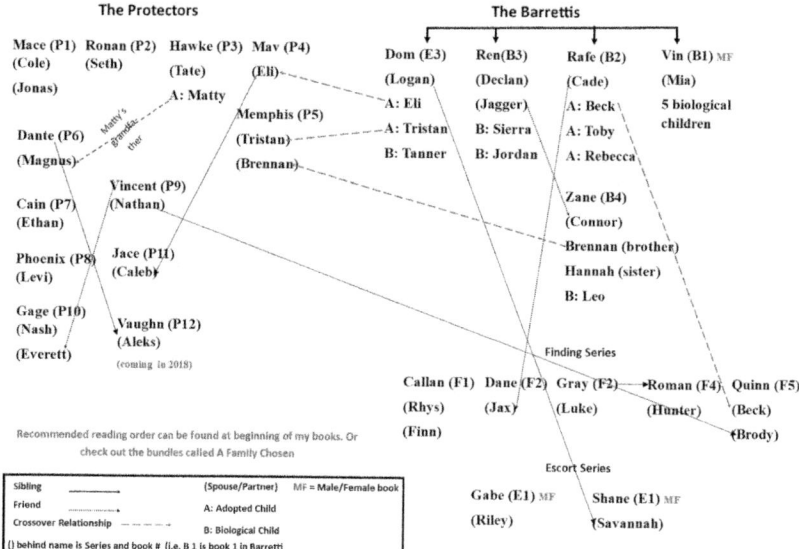

Trigger Warning

Includes references to sexual assault of a minor

Dedication

This book is for all those who've had to fight, are still fighting or are just trying to survive each day as it comes.

Always remember you are never alone and there will come a time when you stop just surviving and start really living.

And no matter what, it is okay to not be okay!

unbroken

ˌənˈbrōkən/
not broken, fractured, or damaged.

Prologue

ALEKS

"Thanks, Aleks! These are definitely getting me out of the doghouse with the missus!"

"You're welcome, Mr. Dunbar," I said as I locked the door behind the older man and flipped the *Open* sign to *Closed* and drew down the full-length blind that kept people from seeing into the flower shop after hours. I instantly felt more relaxed.

"So much for all the progress you've made, Aleks," I murmured quietly to myself.

Progress? What progress?

I told my inner voice to shut up and reached for my phone. I wasn't surprised when it rang before I could even unlock it. My brother Dante's name flashed on the screen, along with the picture of him, his fiancé Magnus, Magnus's grandson Matty, and Matty's best friends, Leo and Jamie. The picture had been taken during Matty's birthday party at our house – the *private* one.

Because I hadn't been brave enough to attend the real party he'd had with his friends or the one with the entire family. While Matty definitely hadn't minded having multiple parties, I knew Dante and Magnus had made special arrangements with Matty's fathers to give the boy a small party that I could attend that wouldn't overwhelm me. It had been both humiliating and a relief. Because I'd wanted to celebrate Matty's birthday with him, but it was pathetic that after two years of trying to adjust to my new life, I still couldn't do something as nonthreatening as attend a family gathering that would have more than a handful of people at it.

And not just any people, but ones who knew about my past and were always respectful of my boundaries.

"I'm leaving in a few minutes," I said before Dante could say anything.

"Let me guess, you stayed open late for Mr. Dunbar again. What did he do this time?"

I smiled. "He used one of Mrs. Dunbar's favorite vases as a hole for putting practice." I didn't actually know what that meant, but as someone who understood how much Mrs. Dunbar loved her flowers and the vases she put them in, the fact that Mr. Dunbar had even touched one of the vases, let alone used it for a purpose other than it was intended for, explained why Mr. Dunbar had been forced to go for one of the more expensive arrangements today.

"Idiot," Dante muttered. "Why don't I come get you?" Dante asked. "If I leave now, I can be there in fifteen minutes."

I was more than tempted to take my brother up on the offer but doing so would be yet another step backward for me.

"No, it's okay. I... I want to take the bus."

I really didn't, but most of the things I did these days were less about what I *wanted* to do and more about what I *needed* to do.

Dante was silent for a moment, no doubt torn between encouraging me and trying to change my mind. I wasn't the only one who'd been rattled by the abduction of my friend, Caleb, three days earlier. I'd been with the young man when some men from his past had shown up at the small park we'd been at. Caleb and his infant daughter had come with me to support me as I'd tried to work on being around a crowd of people. I'd done pretty well at Caleb's brother's wedding a couple of weeks earlier, so I'd been feeling confident that I could somehow magically handle being around a large group of complete strangers.

I'd been a mess.

But I'd managed not to flee.

Until Caleb had spotted a man who'd been hunting him. Caleb had shoved his daughter, Willa, into my arms and had told me to go into the nearest shop and call for help. He'd then taken off to lead the men away. It had been a horrific situation, but fortunately my brother and Caleb's boyfriend, Jace, had been able to find him.

The whole thing had set me back quite a bit, and it had undoubtedly given Dante a scare too. It had all been too reminiscent of my own abduction twelve years earlier when I'd been eight and Dante had been sixteen. Dante had been with me when I'd been taken from a mall and he'd spent nearly every moment since then looking for me.

Despite knowing the reasons I'd been taken, I had no doubt that Dante had been shocked by what he'd found when he'd shown up at a mansion just outside Chicago one night to rescue me.

I could still remember the events of that night as if they'd happened yesterday, instead of a little over two years ago. Dante and Magnus had watched in horror as I'd followed the command I'd been given to strip and bend over a desk. I hadn't even hesitated to do as I'd been told.

Because it was all I'd known.

Show this man what you are...

I flinched as the voice permeated my mind. I'd worked for two long years to get Father's voice out of my head, but every time I was certain I'd managed to silence it, it would randomly appear again.

I was coming to accept that it was a part of me.

Just like I had long ago accepted that I would always refer to Marcus Parks as *Father*, despite sharing no blood with the man. Not to mention the fact that the things he'd done to me had had absolutely nothing to do with being any kind of father to me.

Even the man's death hadn't changed that.

Father's death automatically had me thinking about another man I'd tried long ago to vanquish from my thoughts, but for a whole other set of reasons.

I only knew him as Vaughn. I wasn't sure if that was his last name or first. I shouldn't have even known that much about him, because Father hadn't liked it when the guards talked to me.

But Vaughn had done more than talk to me. He'd become like the thin stream of light that had somehow managed to break through the black paint covering the little window of the first room I'd been cast into after I'd been taken.

Sometimes that stream of light had been the only thing that had kept me wanting to open my eyes each day.

"Aleks?"

Dante's soft voice broke through the memories of the dark-haired, dark-eyed man who'd been my only source of light for the longest time…

"Sorry," I said. "I'll take the bus, Dante." I was proud of how firm my voice sounded, even though my stomach was tied in knots.

"Okay, I'll see you in a bit," Dante said.

"Okay. Love you, meu melhor…"

Dante paused for a moment, and when he said, "Love you too, irmãozinho," I could tell he was choking up a bit. I was too. I always did when he called me his little brother. I'd thought him lost to me forever for so long that it was sometimes hard to accept I had my big brother watching out for me again like when we'd been kids.

I hung up the phone and tucked it into my pocket, then hurried to finish closing the store for the night. It was already starting to get dark out and I really didn't want to risk missing my bus and being forced to wait fifteen minutes for the next one. I'd lucked out that my work was on a bus line that went directly by Magnus and Dante's house. It meant not having to deal with transfers. The bus itself usually wasn't too crowded, but on the occasions it was busier than normal, I usually stood near the back exit rather than sitting and reading a book on my phone (a concept I still hadn't gotten used to).

As I worked, I found myself reaching for the bracelet on my left wrist, only to remember it wasn't there. Touching the bracelet throughout the day had become a habit that I just couldn't break myself of.

Because it wasn't an ordinary bracelet.

My brother had designed it to include some kind of tracking device so he'd always be able to find me. He'd given it to me after I'd forgotten my phone one day about two months after Dante and Magnus had rescued me. I'd been walking the four blocks from home to the library and had gotten lost. Instead of remaining calm and asking someone for directions, I'd panicked and gotten myself even more lost. I'd ended up being missing for hours, and by the time Dante had found me, I'd been sitting in the middle of the sidewalk crying like a baby. A passerby had called the police, who'd managed to get enough information out of me to call Dante and Magnus.

After that, I'd been afraid to leave the house for weeks. It was only when Dante had given me the bracelet and told me it meant he'd always be able to find me that I'd ventured out again. The bracelet had become my lifeline to the outside world.

But I no longer had it. On the day Caleb had been abducted, I'd managed to stuff the bracelet into his pocket. It had allowed Dante and Jace to track Caleb's location and rescue him from the men who'd taken him. Unfortunately, the bracelet had gotten lost in the shuffle of Caleb being transported to the hospital, and Dante was still working to get me a new one. But I still had my phone. Not only had *I* made a point of remembering to grab it the past few mornings, but Dante and Magnus had both checked to make sure I had it on me before I'd left the house.

After making sure everything was locked down, I hurried out the back door. I only had a few minutes to meet the bus, so I didn't do my usual routine of scanning the alley behind the shop several times before turning my back while I locked the door.

As I began walking toward the northern end of the alley, I heard the sound of squealing tires. I looked over my shoulder just in time to see a green van come careening around the corner of the alley's southern entrance. I told myself not to panic, but instinct won out over reason and I began running. I kept looking over my shoulder as the van closed in on me. When I saw a figure step out of the back door of one of the other shops, I shouted, "Help me, please!"

I practically slammed into the guy. "Please, they're after me!" I yelled frantically as I pointed to the van. I wasn't completely sure it wasn't just some random, reckless delivery driver, but I wasn't taking any chances. The van was less than a hundred feet from me and coming fast.

When the man didn't respond, I tried to push past him, but he grabbed me by the upper arms in a painful hold.

And that was when I knew.

He hadn't been coming out of one of the shops because he worked there.

He'd been waiting for me.

"No," I whispered as pure terror ripped through me with violent force.

I opened my mouth to scream again when the man holding me punched me in the face. The blow left me reeling and I hit the ground hard. I tried to get my bearings as pure panic clawed through me, but I wasn't fast enough.

A second blow left me too stunned to do anything at all. Several pairs of rough hands grabbed me as the world spun. I was lifted and thrown onto a cold, metal floor. More hands, or the same ones – I wasn't sure – held me down as the van's door slid shut.

It's happening again.

Tears streaked down my face. "Please, don't!" I begged, but that was all I got out before a piece of fabric was jammed into my mouth and tied behind my head. I flailed my arms and legs, but they were bound with plastic ties within seconds.

"Get his phone," one of the men said.

I was quickly searched and let out a harsh sob when my phone was yanked out of my pocket.

"Toss it," I heard someone say and then I heard a window opening.

And with it went my only lifeline.

I began crying uncontrollably, but my captors didn't take any pity on me. Instead, one gruffly said, "Shut the fuck up," and then he covered my head with some kind of hood, pitching me into darkness.

They left me alone as I rolled onto my side and sobbed into my gag. My hands were bound in front of me, but the second I lifted them to try and get the hood off, I felt something sharp at my throat.

"Do it and I'll cut you. He said bring you back, but he didn't say shit about doing it in one piece."

I froze as the tip of the blade trailed down my throat. When I felt it snag on the first button of my shirt, I stiffened. Then it was popping the button off.

The second button followed.

Then the third.

I squeezed my eyes closed and let out a moan of denial.

"Knock that shit off, Spears."

"The order was to bring him back. Didn't say we couldn't have some fun along the way. It's a long drive to Chicago."

Bile rose in my throat. They were taking me to Chicago?

Despair had me folding in on myself, not caring about the knife anymore. There was only one reason they could be taking me back to Chicago. Father might be dead, but there were plenty of men who'd be happy to take his place.

I stopped listening as the men argued and searched out that place inside my head where I wouldn't hear them anymore. There'd be no hood, no gag, no van…

Alstroemeria… friendship.

Amaryllis… splendid beauty.

Anemone… fading hope.

I let out a sob when I realized it wasn't working. From the time I'd been handed a book with stunning pictures of all kinds of flowers, along with their meaning, I'd recited the list of flowers in alphabetical order whenever I'd needed to block out what was happening to me. But I could still hear the men bickering; I could still feel the floor of the van beneath me and the rocking motion that went with the vehicle taking turn after turn. The gag was still there, as were my bindings.

I felt a keen sense of betrayal by my own mind as I lay there and tried to accept that I would never see my brother again. Because there was no way Dante was going to be able to find me a second time. It'd been sheer luck that he'd managed it the first time.

My body began to shake violently as this new reality crashed down on me. I had no idea how long we drove for, but it felt like hours.

"What the fuck?" I heard one of the guys say. "What is this asshole doing?"

The man sounded annoyed, and I felt the van slow.

"Just go around him!" one of the men sitting near me said.

"He's in the middle of the fucking road," came the response.

"Idiot probably broke down," a third man grumbled.

There was a brief moment of silence as the van slowed even more, then someone yelled, "He's got a gun!"

A split-second later came the squealing of the brakes. I rolled forward, then back as the van careened out of control. I heard a chorus of yells and curses, along with several popping sounds. One of the guys grabbed my arm as the sliding door was opened.

"Wait… wait—" I heard the guy named Spears yell, then there were another few popping sounds and then silence.

Complete and utter silence.

I lifted my hands to try and get the hood off but froze when a hand closed around my arm. I tried to scramble back, but the hold on me was firm.

"It's okay," I heard a man say, then he was pulling me to an upright position. I could feel fingers at the base of the hood. It was removed a few seconds later and despite it being dark outside, my eyes still felt the need to adjust. There was enough light from the dome light inside the van to make out the man who was working to release the gag.

I let out a sob of relief at the familiar sight of the dark hair, brown eyes that almost appeared black, and bearded face that was just inches from mine.

Vaughn.

"It's okay, Aleks, I've got you," Vaughn murmured as he got the gag off and dropped it on the floor of the van.

The combination of terror and relief mixed in a symphony of

emotions that I couldn't control and before I could stop myself, I lifted my bound hands and looped them over Vaughn's neck. I tucked my nose against his throat and breathed him in to prove to myself he was really there.

He still had the same scent – some kind of woodsy smell mixed with musk and just a hint of butterscotch.

I wanted to laugh at that.

The brutally dangerous man loved butterscotch.

And it was how he'd gotten me to trust him when I'd first met him, because he'd shared his butterscotch candies with me.

In secret.

Because I hadn't been allowed to have candy.

Or anything else.

I couldn't form words as I clung to him. He held me against his big, warm, strong body, making me feel even safer. I could have stayed there all day, but Vaughn gently eased my arms up over his head and settled them in front of me.

And that was when I noticed the bodies.

Two in the back of the van with me, two in the front seats, and one just outside the door on the ground.

The ones whose faces I could see had their eyes open and perfectly shaped holes dead center in their foreheads. There wasn't even much blood.

I was dimly aware of Vaughn tucking the gun in his hand into his waistband and then pulling a small utility knife from his pocket. He cut through the ties at my feet, then pulled me to a standing position.

"Are you hurt?" Vaughn asked as he quickly scanned my body, then settled on my face, which was no doubt bruised from the punches I'd taken.

I shook my head and then lifted my shoulders so I could wipe my wet face on my shirt sleeves.

And that was when I realized my hands were still bound. Before I could ask Vaughn to remove the plastic ties around my wrists, he grabbed my arm and led me from the van. "We need to get moving," he said. "Someone could come along at any minute."

Wasn't that a good thing?

I felt off-balance as he steered me toward a sedan that was parked in the middle of the road. I had to lean into him to keep myself from stumbling, and I was glad when his arm went around me. He was considerably larger than me and while his bulk should have scared me, Vaughn was the exception to that general rule.

Vaughn was the exception to a lot of rules.

While I'd initially thought him to be just another one of Father's guards who'd become infatuated with me, he'd been different. He'd never once made a move on me, and when things had come to a head in Father's study the night Magnus and Dante had shown up to rescue me, it had been Vaughn who'd saved us all. I'd ended up stabbing Father in the back – literally – when he'd been preparing to shoot Dante. Dante had still gotten shot, but only in the shoulder.

But then Father had turned the gun on me.

And that was when Vaughn had appeared, and I'd watched Father's eyes go wide as a bullet had torn through his neck. Blood had spurted everywhere, and he'd collapsed onto the very desk he'd made me bend over on. Vaughn had shot the other two guards in the room before I'd even been able to process what was happening, then he'd calmly walked up to me and helped me stand from where Father had knocked me to the ground. He'd touched the spot on my face where Father had marked me, then he'd shot Father in the head.

I'd never seen Vaughn again after he'd gotten me, Magnus, and Dante out of the house.

But I'd dreamed of him often.

Almost nightly.

Strange dreams I didn't always understand.

But that I enjoyed just the same.

And now he was here, saving me again.

Vaughn led me to his car and got me settled in the passenger seat. He walked around the front of the car and climbed into the driver's seat. I turned and held out my hands as I said, "Can you… can you take me home, please? I don't want to wait for the police.

Dante will be worried… he'll… he'll help us explain what happened to the police."

Vaughn got the car started, then turned to look at me. There was enough light from the touchscreen in the dashboard to see his face.

And I didn't like what I saw.

In fact, it had fear skating through me.

Fear that turned to a sensation that I could only describe as agony as a sense of betrayal hit hard and fast.

"Vaughn," I whispered as I jutted my hands toward him a bit, desperately hoping I was wrong. "Please untie me and take me home."

Tears began flowing down my cheeks long before he turned away from me and put the car in gear. Long before he set his eyes on the road ahead of us. And long before he confirmed my worst fear with seven little words that cut through me like the sharpest of blades.

"I'm sorry, Aleks, I can't do that."

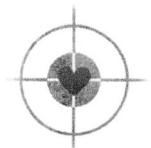

Chapter 1

VAUGHN

It'd taken me nearly two months to earn enough of his trust to get him to talk to me.

I doubted I'd ever be able to get that back after this.

Even when he'd been a prisoner in the Parks mansion, he hadn't ever flinched away from me or any of the other guards. He'd mostly just been emotionless... a breathing, walking, silent robot who'd done as he was told. I'd never once seen him cry or beg or argue.

Young Aleks, who hadn't even been allowed to possess a last name, had been the epitome of obedience.

It had made me sick.

Not because of him, though... he'd had no choice. He'd already known what I'd had yet to learn... that Marcus Parks was a twisted, cruel master who'd found as much, if not more, pleasure in mental torture than sexual gratification.

I had a sneaking suspicion that it wasn't a lesson Aleks had necessarily first learned when Marcus had purchased him like he was nothing more than a prized animal at an auction, but I had no doubt that after years as Marcus's possession, Aleks had become more than adept at doing what needed to be done to survive his master's cruel whims.

The day I'd met Aleks was still seared into my brain, no matter how many times I'd tried to will it away. I'd been sitting in Marcus's lavish study, an expensive glass of scotch in hand as Marcus had sat behind his big desk and pinned me with what probably was supposed to have been an intimidating look. I'd wanted to laugh because the man had had no clue that he was about as threatening as a kitten compared to the man who'd ruled my entire world as a child. I'd also really wanted to put a bullet through the sick fuck's brain then and there, but I'd had to remember the end game... the reason I was there.

My disinterest had probably ended up working in my favor, but hell if my mask of indifference hadn't slipped just a little when the man had summoned his "pet" into the office. Marcus had languidly gotten up from behind his desk as a teenage boy had silently entered the study, escorted by a large man in a slick-looking suit.

The boy had remained by the door, eyes downcast and hands carefully folded in front of him until Marcus had motioned to him. By the time Marcus had been sitting in the opulent armchair across from me, his own scotch in hand, the boy had been standing next to him.

I could still remember every detail about Aleks as he'd stood there as still and silent as a statue. He'd been about average height with a boyishly skinny body and naturally bronzed skin that hinted at a mixed heritage. His chocolate-brown hair had been short but there'd been just a bit of curl to it. He'd been wearing clean, pressed khaki pants and a thin shirt that had appeared a little big on him... he'd looked like the countless private-academy-attending rich kids I'd always been secretly jealous of as a teenager. I hadn't known how old Aleks had been at the time, but he easily could have passed for Marcus's son.

But there'd been nothing fatherly about the way Marcus had treated the young man. With the wave of one finger, Aleks had dropped to his knees in front of Marcus, opened his pants, and sucked his cock to the back of his throat in one well-practiced move. It was like I hadn't even been in the room.

And as far as Aleks had been concerned, I hadn't been.

He hadn't once looked at me.

Not before he'd serviced Marcus and not afterwards as he'd obediently sat at Marcus's feet while a trail of cum had dripped down his chin as Marcus had tucked his sated dick back into his pants. I'd somehow managed to not react to the whole thing, but if the glass in my hand hadn't been made of expensive crystal, I surely would have broken it with the grip I'd had on it. And no doubt if that had happened, I would have used the jagged edge that remained of the biggest chunk of glass to slice open the throat of the man in front of me.

I'd seen a lot of depraved shit in the nearly eight years since I'd first entered the underworld of trafficking kids for sex, but for some reason the sight of Aleks on his knees staring blankly at the floor as semen ran down his chin had broken something inside of me. I'd had no choice but to put up a wall between me and all the kids I'd had to ignore over the years in order to try and save one. Yes, I'd done everything in my power to eventually get those kids out, but there'd been no way to save them all and I couldn't deny the horrible things that had happened to them in the days and weeks until I'd been able to send someone in to get them out.

So that wall had been very necessary.

It'd been the only thing keeping me from killing every single man I encountered who used kids for their own pleasure. Fucks like Marcus Parks were the hardest not to kill the second I met them. Because not hours after he was using Aleks like he was nothing, he'd likely been in his downtown Chicago loft with his wife and children, listening to whatever it was the privileged family members had done with their day. Then he'd probably waved off his own supposed boring day of running his multi-million-dollar empire and advocating for less fortunate kids through his handful of charities that had made him a beloved social figure in the Windy City. What his family and closest friends hadn't known as he'd gotten up in front of large crowds of the most socially elite and convinced them to donate to his various fundraising efforts, was exactly what he did in his free time and how many men in his own social circle shared his twisted depravities.

It had taken me years to get into that inner circle of powerful men, and garnering an interview with Marcus Parks for the coveted role of protecting his dirty little secret had been the coup in my illustrious climb to the top. Every degenerate I'd served over the years had pulled me deeper and deeper into the underbelly of a culture that most were afraid to acknowledge existed. But I'd eagerly walked into that very world because it had taken one of my own and I'd quickly erected a barrier between who I'd once been and who I'd had to become.

Until Aleks.

There'd been no doubt in my mind that the whole show with Aleks had been meant as a test and what would have happened if I'd failed it. Marcus had paid well for loyalty and if I *had* given in to my instincts and sliced his throat from ear to ear, his men wouldn't have let me walk out of that study alive.

Well, they would have *tried* to stop me, anyway.

But even Marcus hadn't known how truly qualified I'd been for the position. Fortunately for him, and unfortunately for Aleks, there'd been something stronger keeping my ass in that chair as Marcus had paraded his toy in front of me.

Loyalty.

Love.

Hope.

My already rolling belly clenched when I considered everything Aleks had endured in the three months I'd ingratiated myself with Marcus Parks in the hopes I'd find the information I'd needed to bring the whole thing to an end.

A few fucking shared butterscotch candies and making sure none of the other guards put their hands on him hadn't undone any of that. And even though I hadn't been the one who'd typically had to escort Aleks to wherever Marcus was in the mansion when he wanted to play with his toy, I might as well have been the one who'd handed him over and stood outside the door and listened to the piece of shit's grunts and groans as he'd taken his pleasure.

The handful of times I *had* been forced to listen to Aleks being used by Marcus, I'd managed to not stride into the room and kill the man because I'd been *so* close to getting the information I'd needed. I'd wanted to tell Aleks that… to beg him to hang on just a bit longer, but he'd clearly accepted for some time that his survival was all about hanging on, and he'd learned on his own how to do that.

By becoming exactly what Marcus had wanted.

He'd never spoken out of turn, he'd never cried, he'd never protested; he'd obediently waited for every order to be given, no matter how long it had taken to come… it was just something so ingrained in him that there were times I'd actually come to wonder if he'd tell Marcus about my efforts to befriend him.

He hadn't, but my instincts that Aleks knew survival meant allowing Marcus to own him in every way possible had been proven right when I'd learned that the young man had told Marcus about his brother's rescue attempt. I'd only just walked into the mansion's front door when one of the guards had searched me out to inform me that Dante Thorne, Aleks's older brother, had managed to track Aleks down and, along with his lover, had tried to rescue the young man – something Aleks had been made aware of. Instead of helping in his own rescue, Aleks had immediately gone to Marcus and told him about the note his brother had managed to get to him while he'd been in the greenhouse on the mansion's expansive property. It was also the one place Aleks didn't have to have an escort with him and where the security cameras hadn't been working at the time.

From everything I'd learned, Aleks had had a good chance of being rescued that night because his brother and the man's Texas Ranger boyfriend had been more than capable of the task. But Aleks had betrayed his own flesh and blood because Marcus Parks had been God to Aleks. He'd meant the difference between life and death for the young man. I hated thinking about the things he'd had to endure over the years to learn *that* particular lesson…

Dante's timing had been pretty damn shitty because my plans to get what I needed from Marcus had been in the works for that same night. I'd been so close to coming face to face with the man I'd been searching for for years, but the meeting had been called off when

Marcus had learned of the rescue operation. I hadn't even had time to curse Dante and his lover, Magnus DuCane, because the scene I'd walked in on after killing the guard who'd come to find me to tell me that Marcus needed me to get rid of some bodies had been utter chaos, and I'd had only seconds to react.

I'd thrown open the door to the study just in time to see Marcus point his gun at Aleks, who'd looked disoriented as he'd leaned heavily against Marcus's desk. It'd taken only a split second for my brain to process the sight of the gold letter opener sticking out of Marcus's back and I'd pulled the trigger just as Marcus's own trigger finger had begun to move. My bullet had rung true and ripped through Marcus's throat. Blood had sprayed everywhere as he'd made a gurgling sound and then pitched forward onto the desk, knocking Aleks to the ground in the process. I hadn't given in to the immediate need to check on the young man as I'd turned and taken out the two guards in the room. There'd been two other men in the room, one shot in the arm, the other seemingly unharmed, but I'd ignored them as I'd hurried to Aleks. He'd let me pull him to his feet and when I'd seen the fresh bruises on his face, I'd felt that last chink in my armor break. In all the time I'd been working for Parks, he hadn't once struck Aleks because the young man had been so unfailingly obedient.

But somehow the sight of the punishment Aleks had received for his act of rebellion had shattered that wall that'd had about a million cracks in it, most of which had only started to form when I'd met the young man for the first time. It'd been wholly unnecessary, but I'd enjoyed putting that final bullet through Marcus's brain.

I'd managed to get Aleks, Dante, and Magnus out of there, but then I'd been in damage control mode. I'd had only enough time to grab the notebook where I'd often seen Marcus jotting notes and then I'd torched the mansion, not only to get rid of the evidence that would bring the authorities into a world they were ill-equipped to handle, but to cover my own trail as well. It'd been my only chance to not blow my cover. As it was, the whole thing had undone years of hard work, but I wasn't giving up. And Aleks was safe… that was all that had mattered.

Well, he *had* been safe.

Fuck, how had this all gone so wrong?

I glanced at him in the blackness of the car. He hadn't moved or spoken in a while... not since I'd told him I couldn't take him home and he'd let out the tiniest of choked sobs as tears had flowed down his cheeks. I knew I should have told him everything that was happening then and there, but there was this part of me that just wanted to spare him the truth. I wanted to pretend that none of this was happening and he was still safely tucked away in his little flower shop and living with his brother. But to tell him anything meant I needed to know what the fuck I was doing, and I just didn't.

I had no clue.

And that was so very unlike me.

But I hadn't really had the time to form a plan, either. Not only was I dealing with a betrayal I hadn't seen coming, but things had happened faster than I could have imagined. And even getting Aleks away from those men didn't mean he was safe. Taking him home to his brother wouldn't mean he'd no longer be hunted. If anything, that would just put his whole family in danger.

That's the story you're trying to sell, you coward?

I ignored the voice in my head and glanced at the clock on the dash. We'd been driving for nearly an hour. I wanted to put a lot more distance between us and Seattle, but we were far enough away from the bodies I'd left behind to at least cut Aleks loose and try to reassure him again that everything would be okay.

I took a few turns onto various backroads until I was able to find what looked like an unused service road of some kind, then drove far enough down it until I was sure the car couldn't be seen by passersby from the road. When I reached a clearing, I drove until I was in the middle of it so that if Aleks did manage to take off on me, I'd be able to see him without too much trouble... and catch up to him.

I turned off the car but turned on the dome light. I reached into my pocket for the utility knife. "Aleks, I'm going to cut you free now. I just needed to make sure you didn't try to come after me while I was getting us out of there," I began to explain, but when I reached for his hands, he jerked away from me. His body slammed into the door. He let out a loud wail of pain, but I instinctively knew he hadn't physically hurt himself.

"Don't touch me!" he cried as harsh sobs racked his entire body. He tucked his bound hands protectively against his chest. "Please, don't touch me!" he managed to get out, his throat sounding raw. Then he was reaching for the door handle and part of me actually wanted to let him go.

But I couldn't.

So I gently grabbed his arm just as he got the door open. I expected him to fight me or struggle, but he suddenly went completely still. The tears seemed to dry up on their own and even in the dim light I could see his eyes go blank. Then his bound hands were reaching for his throat and I automatically knew what he was looking for.

The collar.

The fucking collar Marcus had put around his neck to remind him he was nothing more than a possession… a pet. It'd been made of heavy chain link, the kind a large dog would wear. But unlike an animal, Aleks's collar had been designed so it couldn't be taken off. I'd seen the burn marks myself on his thin neck. He'd never told me as such, but I'd known in my gut they were the scars from when Marcus had had the links in the chain permanently welded together so the only way the collar could ever be removed was if it was cut off.

"Vaughn," Aleks whispered quietly as he rubbed the absent links that I strongly suspected still existed in his mind. "Do you think he'll finally do it this time?" he asked so softly I almost didn't hear it. His empty gaze turned to meet mine and I felt it like a throat punch.

Just like that, Aleks, the young man who loved flowers and smiled whenever he first tasted that rush of buttery, sugary flavor of the hard candies I'd snuck him whenever I could, was gone. The past two years had been wiped away as if they hadn't existed.

He didn't give me a chance to respond to him.

"I'll ask Father to forgive me, but I don't think he will," Aleks murmured. His eyes shifted so he was staring out the windshield. "Not this time…"

"Aleks…" I began, but he interrupted me. I doubted he'd actually even heard me say his name.

"It's okay, Vaughn. You should take me home now. Father is waiting."

Chapter 2

ALEKS

"*I just wanna go home.*"

"I know you do, but your parents can't take care of you anymore, Aleks. They said it was just too hard."

"'Cause they don't have much money?"

"That... and 'cause you were bad."

"I didn't mean to be bad. Please, I'll tell them I'm sorry and I'll be good. I promise!"

"Aleks, it doesn't work like that. It's too late. I'm sorry."

"No!"

"Hey, hey, calm down. Everything will be okay."

"I wanna go home!"

"I know you do, but you can't. But you can stay with me, okay? For as long as you want. Hey, don't cry, Aleks. I'll take care of you. I promise. We can be friends."

"We can?"

"Best friends."

"But... but you're a grown-up."

"I'm not that much older than you. Besides, being friends with a grown-up would be kind of cool, right? We can do lots of fun things. Like eat ice cream for breakfast and play video games all day. That sounds cool, doesn't it, Aleks?"

"Can... can I go home and we can still be friends?"

"No. Remember what I told you about your parents?"

"But... but maybe Dante can take care of me. He can talk to Mama and Papa..."

"Dante? Is that your brother?"

"Yes, he watches out for me and he—"

"He knows you're here, Aleks. Who do you think told us about your Mama and Papa being mad at you and not wanting you anymore?"

"No... no, he... he wouldn't do that. He... he loves me."

"Well, maybe he does. How about you come stay with me for a while and if he wants to come see you, he will?"

"You'll tell him where I am?"

"I will, I promise. But if you want me to do something for you, you have to do something for me."

"Wh... what?"

"You just have to behave, Aleks. That's all. Just do what I tell you. And you can stay with me until Dante can convince your Mama and Papa to give you another chance."

"Um..."

"You trust your brother, right? Then he should be able to come get you real soon. But my house is much nicer than this place. You can have your own room and watch TV and eat whatever you want. As long as you behave."

"Okay... but I can go when Dante comes?"

"Of course. But until then, we'll be the best of special friends, how does that sound?"

"Okay."

"My name's Brian, Aleks. Let's go home, okay?"

"No... no!"

"Aleks, wake up, you're dreaming!"

"No, I don't want to go with you!"

"Aleks, damn it, wake up!"

I jerked awake at the voice that was too deep and desperate to be Brian's. Brian never got angry. He punished, he manipulated, he threatened, but he never raised his voice to do it. There was a slight pressure on my upper arms as I tried to get my eyes to open, but between the pounding in my head and chest and the way my eyes felt stuck together because they were dry, I couldn't escape that moment when I'd naïvely put my hand in Brian's and let him lead me from the dark, empty room with just the one mattress on the floor. I began to cry because I couldn't even tell my young self to run.

Just run.

I'd never run.

I'd never even tried.

"Just behave, Aleks, and your brother will come soon."

"And you'll tell him I was good?"

"I'll tell him you were the best."

Meu melhor…

My best…

"Dante," I whispered as I forced my eyes open. "Meu melhor," I gasped as I sat up.

I waited for him to play the game with me. The first time I'd called him my best, he'd started making up ridiculous guesses to finish the statement and it had become our thing. Even now, we still did it and it was how I knew I was okay… that everything was finally okay.

But it wasn't Dante's gentle expression that met mine when I managed to focus. And it wasn't his big hands on my upper arms.

"Vaughn," I breathed in relief.

Until I remembered I couldn't feel relieved around this man.

Not anymore.

I scrambled back from him and he immediately released me. My back slammed into something behind me and I realized it was a headboard.

Jesus, I was in bed with him.

I lurched away from him and would have fallen out of the bed if he hadn't chosen that moment to latch onto my arm again. "Don't!" I screamed and he instantly released me. I'd regained enough of my balance so that this time I didn't fall, but I quickly got out of the bed and backed up until I was lodged into the nearest corner. I began jerking my eyes around the room to look for Father when my brain caught up to my reality.

Father was dead.

I'd seen his body for myself. I'd felt his warm blood on my skin. I'd stared into his open, empty eyes. Those eyes haunted my nightmares, just like Vaughn's eyes dominated my dreams.

Father was dead. I knew that.

Vaughn was here.

He'd kidnapped me.

I knew that too.

But that was all I knew.

I looked down at my hands and saw they were no longer bound. Not like they'd been in the car.

I fought to remember the events after he'd told me he wasn't taking me home, but there were only bits and pieces.

"Where are we?" I managed to get out, despite my ragged breaths. The room was dim, but not dark. It had old-looking wallpaper and there were just a few simple furnishings including a bed and dresser with a vanity mirror on it. There were two doors. One that was closed, either for a closet or a bathroom. And one that led out of the room. It was currently open and I wondered if I could make my escape through it.

Don't run, Aleks. Just do as you're told and you'll be okay.

I felt bile rise in my throat as Brian's voice filtered through my head. I actually had to close my eyes because I felt so dizzy. I hadn't heard his voice in years, but it was like he was standing right next to me.

"In a safe place," Vaughn responded as he slowly got up off the bed. He moved around the foot of it, his eyes wary, like he was waiting for me to try and get past him. I wanted to laugh at that because not only would my body not respond to the instinct, but I knew he'd catch me with next to no effort.

"Why?" I bit out as I looked at the bed, then myself. I was still wearing all my clothes. All except my shoes, and I could see those sitting on the floor next to the bed. I looked at the bed again. There were no restraints of any kind.

But all he'd need were plastic ties like the other guys. They could easily be in his pocket. And in truth, we both knew he didn't need them. He was much bigger and stronger than me. He'd have no problem subduing me, assuming I could even find the courage to fight back.

And since I couldn't find the guts to even try and run, I knew there was no chance of me fighting him. I had no doubt he knew it too.

"Is it you?" I asked. "Or someone else?"

"No one is going to hurt you, Aleks."

He had the audacity to actually look pained as he said the words, but I didn't believe him or the imagined emotion. I might be a coward, but I wasn't stupid. I'd long ago learned that the master manipulators were the ones who knew how to use the words you wanted to hear against you.

I took a moment to study him. He looked the same, though there was a certain tiredness to his eyes that I'd never noticed before. Like his soul had aged at a considerably faster rate than his body. I guessed him to be in his mid-thirties or so. He was taller than me by several inches and outweighed me by maybe sixty pounds. He wasn't a muscle head, but he was really well built with a broad chest and trim hips. The muscles of his thighs flexed beneath the black dress pants he was wearing as he moved a little closer to me. He was wearing a light-blue button-up dress shirt but had taken his jacket off at some point. I didn't see his gun, but that didn't mean anything. It could easily be at his back.

Vaughn's black hair was a little longer on top and trimmed short on the sides. His beard was also a touch longer than it'd been two years ago. I'd always had this weird obsession with wanting to know what the neatly groomed hair would feel like beneath my fingers. I'd only ever seen Vaughn dressed in suits, so it had always fascinated me to see the single black earring he wore in his left ear… I always imagined it to be some kind of silent "fuck you" to the world.

My gaze dropped to Vaughn's muscular forearms. He'd rolled his shirt sleeves up so I could see that his right arm had a tattoo on it, but his left didn't. Another silent act of rebellion? Or was that who he really was and the suits were the fake part?

Why did I even care?

He wasn't real.

At least not the version of him I'd imagined in my head. The one who'd saved me two years earlier.

Why had he done that?

Maybe his goal had only been to kill Father? Maybe they'd had some kind of falling out.

But he'd let me and Dante and Magnus go.

Oh God, Dante… he had to be going crazy with worry. How long had it even been since I'd been taken?

I looked at the single window in the room but the curtain was drawn. There was no light filtering in through it, so that meant it was probably still dark out.

Or dark *again*.

God, why couldn't I remember anything?

"What are you going to do with me?" I asked. My limbs felt heavy and before I could even consider the vulnerable position I was putting myself in, I slid my back down the wall and dropped to the floor. I drew my knees up against my chest and wrapped my arms around them. I was aware of Vaughn moving, but I was suddenly too tired to care. He'd do whatever he wanted. Better to let him get it over with.

Because there would be no rescue this time. Even once he got me back to Chicago, he or whoever he was delivering me to would make sure Dante could never find me again. When I'd first been taken as a child, they'd moved me around from place to place so many times I'd eventually lost count. All sense of time had been stolen from me until Brian had come and offered me a chance to go home.

And stupid kid that I'd been, I'd taken him up on it.

I'd been so damn good that I was sure I'd make my parents proud and they'd want me back.

"Here," Vaughn said, and then a bottle of water was being put into my hands.

The words, "fuck you" were on the tip of my tongue, but I bit down on the flesh rather than speak them. I wasn't someone who naturally swore, but even if I had been, it was against the rules.

There were some habits I'd eventually managed to break in the two years I'd lived with my brother and his fiancé, but so many things were so ingrained that they'd become my new normal. I had no idea if I would have been someone who swore if I'd been allowed to be a regular kid, but it didn't matter anyway.

I took the water and obediently drank a sip.

And gagged.

The water was fine, but my stomach was in such tight knots that the cold liquid made me feel all kinds of worse.

Who would have thought such a thing possible?

"Take a few bites of this," Vaughn said as he handed me some kind of protein bar.

I wanted to say no, I really did. But he hadn't been asking. He wasn't the Vaughn who'd snuck butterscotch candies into my palm when no one was looking.

My body shivered as I remembered the little sparks I'd always feel when he touched me like that. I'd only ever felt those sparks around him.

I wasn't sure what that meant.

But there were no sparks this time as I took the protein bar.

Thank God for small mercies.

Because being cold made it so much easier to deal with the bad stuff, and I always started with mentally reciting my most favorite flowers and their meanings. It was the first step in escaping into that pretty little place in my head where no one could touch me. Dante was there. The rest of my family too. It'd been a particularly brisk day, but we'd decided to go to the beach anyway and everyone, even Dante and my father, had seemed to get along. Dante and I had spent hours building the perfect sand castle and then had let our baby brother, Breno, destroy it. In that place I was warm and safe and happy. But to be warm, I had to be cold first.

And I'd never felt that around Vaughn.

Not even on that day when I'd first seen him in Father's office. I'd tried to escape into my head long before I'd entered that study, but I hadn't managed it in time and once I'd caught sight of the scary-looking dark-haired man sitting in the armchair, I'd been momentarily trapped in the present. It wasn't until Father had snapped his fingers at me that my brain had thankfully turned off. The blackness had let me stay in its peaceful grip until one of Father's men had taken me by the arm and led me back to my room. I'd tasted Father on my tongue and usually when that happened, it meant I was spared from the rest of it. Since Father never shared me with anyone, I hadn't had to worry about Vaughn that particular day. I hadn't even been sure I'd see him again.

But he'd been there a few days later and when one of Father's men had let his hand linger on my body just a little too long, Vaughn had slammed the man back against the wall and informed him in no uncertain terms what would happen if he ever touched me like that again. I'd waited for him to add the caveat that I belonged to Father, but there'd been nothing else.

Just the singular threat to never touch me like that again.

And that was when it had happened.

That little something inside of me that kept me from seeking out the blackness whenever Vaughn was around.

Like if I did, I'd miss something important. I hadn't known *what* exactly, but it hadn't mattered. That seed had been planted. Then it had gotten worse.

Because I'd begun to look forward to seeing him – even if it was while I was being taken to see Father or any number of the men who came to admire Father's well-behaved pet.

I'd still somehow managed to escape into that place in my head during the worst of times when Vaughn wasn't around, but after a while he'd started showing up on the beach with me and my family. Near the end just before Dante had come for me, it had somehow only been me and Vaughn on that beach. We hadn't been doing anything but sitting on the sand watching the sun set, but it'd been *how* we'd been sitting that my mind had craved. I'd been in front of Vaughn with his legs on either side of my body. My back had been pressed against his chest and his powerful arms had been wrapped around me, protecting me from the biting wind. Every once in a while, he'd leaned down and whispered something into my ear, but I'd never been able to make out the actual words.

But all that was gone now.

There was no safe place to go anymore… it had abandoned me when I'd finally stopped needing it. I'd been kind of glad, but now I had to wonder if maybe it hadn't been too high of a price.

Two years of freedom.

Of feeling safe.

And hoping.

All those things had had an expiration date but that safe spot in my head had been a sure thing. It had become my best friend. And I'd happily cast it aside.

God, I was such a naïve fool.

The first bite of protein bar felt like a rock as it landed in my belly. And I knew in that moment this was one order I couldn't follow. I felt tears sting my eyes as I began retching. Humiliation went through me as I threw up all over myself. It was mostly just the dreaded piece of protein bar and a little bit of water, but it felt like what little pride I had left exited my body at the same time. I began sobbing uncontrollably.

I heard my name whispered softly then suddenly I was dragged against a broad chest. I was enfolded in the warmest embrace I'd ever known and that just made the betrayal sting even more.

I told myself to push him away.

I told myself to call him every swear word I'd ever heard my brother use.

I told myself to order him not to touch me or I'd kill him.

I didn't do any of those things. To my horror, I fisted my hands in his shirt and opened my mouth against the spot on his neck where his top button had been left undone. I let out a bloodcurdling cry that didn't sound human.

I hated him.

I just fucking hated him.

Except I didn't.

And that was what was so messed up.

What I was feeling wasn't anger. The pain ripping through me was a thousand times worse than the many times my body had been stolen from me and violated in the ugliest of ways.

"I trusted you," I cried out. "You made me trust you!"

A big hand came up to clasp the back of my head. "I know, baby," Vaughn murmured against my ear.

Like how he'd whispered to me on that beach... the one in my head.

My safe place.

The safe place that no longer existed.

The endearment felt like the cruelest of violations though, and for the second time in as many years, I did fight. I shoved back from him, but he refused to let me go. I'd gotten some of my sick on him and I could still taste it in my mouth, but he didn't seem to care.

"Aleks, listen to me!"

"No!" I shouted. "I trusted—"

"Just fucking listen, Aleks! And I swear on my life, I'll call Dante for you myself when I'm done if that's still what you want!"

How many times had I heard that before? That if I just did what I was told, Dante would come and get me. It had all been a lie. I was about to tell him so when he grabbed me gently by the back of my neck and pressed his forehead against mine. "Aleks, my real name is James Vaughn Covello and I was working for Marcus Parks in the hopes of finding someone... someone who was taken just like you."

I stilled at that and sucked in a breath.

"Please, Aleks... please, just *listen*."

Chapter 3

VAUGHN

HE WAS BREATHING SO HARD I WAS WORRIED HE WAS GOING TO PASS out. I'd closed my eyes when I'd pressed my forehead against his in the desperate hope of getting him to listen. I was reluctant to open them because he was finally still in my hold and it just felt so damn good. I'd never allowed my attraction to Aleks to get out of control, not only because he was just so young, but also because he wasn't in any position to deal with any of it. But admittedly, it was hard not to respond to his closeness.

I opened my eyes and saw that he was staring at my chest. He was sucking in lungsful of air, probably to try and calm himself. I began rubbing my fingers over the back of his neck. He remained stiff for several beats, then suddenly let out a whoosh of air and closed his eyes as he relaxed a little. My other hand was on his upper arm. I moved it to his back and began trailing my fingers up and down his spine in the hopes of calming him more. I wanted to offer him the water so he could rinse his mouth out because I was certain getting sick had left behind a sour taste, but I was too afraid I'd lose him if I stopped talking. And I sure as shit didn't care that some of his sick had transferred to me during the scuffle.

"After you and Dante and Magnus left the house, I torched it. Do you remember that?"

He nodded. "It blew up," he said quietly.

"Right. I needed to destroy all the evidence. The cops passed it off as a gas leak and the whole thing was considered a tragic accident. No one knew about you except the people who hurt you."

He nodded again.

"I spread the word that you were killed in the explosion... so no one would come looking for you."

He stiffened a bit and I could tell he was battling with himself to believe me. I had no doubt his internal struggle was a brutal one. I barreled on so he couldn't talk himself out of giving me a chance to explain.

"I was worried the story about your return would eventually get out and those people would recognize you and figure out you hadn't died in the blast, so I came out here about a week after you got here and watched things for a bit."

He opened his eyes and I could see the surprise in them. "You... you were watching me?"

"From a distance," I said with a nod. "I had feelers out back in Chicago too to see if anyone found out you were still alive. I kept waiting for the reporters to start showing up..."

"Dante convinced Mama and Papa not to tell anyone back home I'd been found. They got me an emergency passport but then told the people they got it from that it had all been a mistake and that it hadn't been me who'd been found. It was a false..."

He seemed to search for the right word for a moment, so I offered, "Alarm?"

He nodded. "Yes. False alarm." He lifted his hand to wipe at his mouth. "Mama and Papa didn't want people to know what happened to me," he said softly. Color deepened his already flushed cheeks. "They... they wanted me to come home and be normal but when I wouldn't let them take the..."

Aleks's voice dropped off and he reached up to finger his neck.

He was looking for the collar.

It'd been gone by the time I'd gotten to Seattle. I'd just assumed he'd taken it off as soon as he'd been free of Marcus, but now I was starting to wonder if it hadn't been more complicated than that. I silently cursed his parents for putting that kind of pressure on him. But as much as I hated the people who'd put us in this position, I hated having to tell Aleks the truth about it.

But it couldn't be helped.

"Aleks, your parents, they did an interview with a reporter in Brazil a few days ago. Did you know they were suing both the mall you were taken from and the police department?"

Aleks's eyes went wide. "What?" he breathed.

"They filed the suit last week. They're seeking damages for the pain and suffering they endured. The suit they filed attracted the attention of reporters, or their lawyer reached out to them, but either way, your parents granted an interview to one of the bigger news anchors down there. It aired two nights ago."

Aleks shook his head. "They... they didn't say anything. Dante, he would have been so angry."

"I'm pretty sure they didn't tell your brother," I reassured him. "They probably didn't expect the story to even get out, and it didn't. But the people who took you twelve years ago are still at work down there, Aleks. They're just a small part of a bigger organization that has ties all over the world. The story showed a picture of you from earlier this year in front of your flower shop."

Aleks pulled back from my touch and I instantly missed the connection. But I could tell he wasn't deliberately trying to escape me. The shock had him leaning back against the wall and his hand came up to cover his mouth. I took out my phone and pulled up the clip of the news story. I handed it to him. "Hit play," I said, because I knew he wouldn't believe anything I said until he saw proof of it for himself.

It was a reality I'd brought upon myself by not telling him sooner what was happening. Even now I was leaving out a critical piece of information, but I couldn't bring myself to admit that piece of the story to him.

I wasn't worried about Aleks trying to make a call with my phone. Not only was my location using the phone untraceable, but he was already focused on the clip because the still image showed both his parents in what was clearly an interview of some kind. He hit the play button. The interview had been done in Portuguese, but the clip had subtitles, so even if Aleks was a bit rusty when it came to his native language, he'd be able to understand the gist of the news story. My heart hurt for him as I watched the expressions dance across his face as his parents talked about what life had been like without Aleks. I just hoped he wasn't noticing what I'd noticed when I'd seen the interview for the first time.

That everything Juliana and Pedro Silva said was about them and *their* suffering. There'd been little mention of how Aleks had suffered. But there'd been plenty of blame to go around. The interview had clearly been orchestrated to cast the mall and the cops in a negative light and help move the suit forward, probably for a lucrative settlement deal. When the interview reached the part where it talked about Aleks being settled in the U.S., I knew he was looking at the picture of himself. His parents and the reporter had been careful not to actually say Aleks was in Seattle, but they'd foolishly used the picture without cropping out the name of the flower store. It wouldn't have taken a genius to figure out the store's location.

Aleks handed the phone back to me before the interview even ended. I stopped it and watched him carefully. He looked numb.

And so very tired.

I was sitting on the floor in front of him, but as badly as I wanted to take him in my arms again, I knew he wouldn't welcome the contact. He was way too raw.

"The men who took me from that alley… who sent them?"

"I'm not sure," I hedged. "Most likely someone who was worried you'd be able to identify them." I didn't add in my second guess.

Or someone who wanted you for himself…

I didn't know a lot about Aleks's past, but I'd heard enough that he'd been a coveted prize because of both his unique looks and his impeccable obedience. Marcus had taken pride in showing Aleks off to every perverted piece of shit in his tight circle of deviants. The young man had become like a prime piece of horseflesh that everyone wanted but no one could get the owner to sell. I'd had more than one fucker comment on what a shame the loss of Aleks had been – none of those same men had even made mention of Marcus's death.

But it wasn't something I wanted Aleks to know. It was bad enough that he had to face the fact that he was considered a dangerous witness… to learn there were men who just wanted to possess him was something he didn't need to deal with at the moment.

And he most definitely didn't need to know that there might even be those who were willing to use him as a pawn…

That was a fact I myself didn't want to accept, but I knew I didn't have a choice.

Aleks let out a strangled whimper that distracted me from my thoughts. I began to reach for him, but he pulled away and backed even farther into the corner. The rejection stung. He shook his head at me. "I don't know how to believe you," he admitted.

I swallowed hard and nodded. I deserved that. I put some space between us so he wouldn't feel so boxed in. "I had to get you out of there, Aleks. I knew you wouldn't understand why I couldn't take you home and I didn't want to take the time to explain it to you. I needed to make sure those guys weren't being followed. I couldn't take the risk that you'd fight me."

Aleks let out a harsh laugh. "I don't fight," he said softly. "You of all people should know that." Before I could respond, he dropped his eyes and whispered, "So what happens now?"

The fact that he seemed more willing to believe me didn't make me feel even a sense of accomplishment. "I'm still working on that part," I admitted.

Aleks raised his hands to wipe at his wet face. As soon as he was done, he curled one long arm around his raised knees, then held out his hand. "I want to call my brother, please," he said.

My stomach dropped out at that.

So my words hadn't been enough to convince him I was just trying to help him.

Fuck, that hurt.

But hell if I'd go back on my word. And it wasn't like I could really blame him for choosing his brother over me.

I unlocked the phone and handed it to him. "Our location can't be traced so you'll have to tell him where we are," I said. "We're in Huxley. It's a small town on the southeast side of Lake Chelan. This house is a foreclosure that's about three miles north of highway ninety-seven. It's on Parkview Lane."

Aleks studied me for a moment, then dialed. I was surprised when he put the phone on speaker. As it rang, he softly said, "He's going to kill you for this."

The words weren't spoken as a threat or in some kind of vendetta-like fashion. In fact, he almost sounded regretful. I had no doubt who he was talking about.

The line rang twice before Dante answered. "Aleks? Aleks, is that you?"

Regret went through me at the sound of the man's panicked voice, but it wasn't until Aleks began crying again that I felt the bile rise in my own throat.

The sight of those silent tears streaking down Aleks's cheeks was a brutal reminder that I deserved anything his brother chose to do to me.

"Dante?" Aleks finally managed to get out on a strangled sob.

"It's me, irmãozinho."

I didn't know what the Portuguese word meant, but it had a profound effect on Aleks because he covered his mouth with one hand.

"I'm coming, Aleks. I'm coming to get you. Just tell me where you are."

"Dante," Aleks whispered brokenly. I could tell he was on the verge of losing it and I could feel my own eyes stinging.

"It's okay, Aleks. Tell me where you are, and I'll come get you and take you home and it'll all be over. I won't let anyone hurt you, do you hear me? I'm coming right now... just... just tell me where you are." Dante's voice broke and I heard him suck in a breath. "Look around the room. Tell me what you see. Can you see a window? Do you hear anything? Are they in the room with you?"

The rapid-fire questions were hard to follow and I could picture a desperate Dante clinging to the phone as he tried to stave off his panic. When Aleks didn't do anything but whisper his brother's name again, I started to reach for the phone so I could tell Dante myself where we were.

But Aleks suddenly pulled the phone closer to his mouth and with surprising strength said, "Dante?"

"I'm here, little brother. I'm here," Dante said.

"Dante, I..."

Aleks suddenly looked up at me and held my eyes. I could see the terror in them. But there was something else too. Some emotion I couldn't name. When he spoke again, Aleks kept his eyes on me.

"Dante, I can't come home right now."

"You can, Aleks. Just... just stay on the line as long as you can, okay? Magnus is having Daisy trace your call. We'll know where you are in a minute."

"Dante," Aleks repeated. "I can't come home... it's not... it's not safe."

There was a beat of complete silence that was almost deafening as Dante finally seemed to understand what his brother was saying. I held my breath as I stared at Aleks in surprise.

Was he... was he...?

God, he *was*. He was choosing me. He was choosing to stay with *me*.

"Why isn't it safe, Aleks?" Dante asked carefully.

Aleks finally dropped his eyes. "They found me. Don't be mad at Mama and Papa, Dante. They didn't know..."

"Aleks," Magnus's voice cut in. I heard some background noise, so I figured Magnus had put the phone on speaker as well. "Aleks, talk to us," the older man said, his voice calm but carrying an edge of something to it.

"I'm okay, Magnus," Aleks said. "Tell Dante I'm all right. They didn't hurt me."

"He's here," Magnus said. "He can hear you, Aleks."

"Dante," Aleks whispered, his own voice cracking a bit. "I'm sorry."

"Don't be sorry, irmãozinho," Dante said softly. "You didn't do anything wrong."

"Dante, you have to get out of the house. You and Magnus... and you have to watch out for Matty and Hawke and Tate and everybody because they might come to the house looking for me."

"Who?" Magnus asked gently.

"He doesn't know," Aleks said as he looked up at me. "I... I believe him, Magnus." There was a tremor in Aleks's voice as he spoke. "He says he took me to keep me safe and I believe him."

I released the breath I hadn't realized I was still holding.

"Is it Vaughn?" Magnus asked. "Is that who you're with?"

Aleks didn't answer. He held my gaze and chewed on his lower lip nervously. I gave him a nod.

"Yes," he breathed into the phone.

"Is he there in the room with you?" Magnus asked carefully.

"Yes," Aleks repeated. "He can hear you."

"Aleks," Dante said calmly, his voice now holding a cold edge to it. "Take the phone off speaker and give it to Vaughn," the man said.

"Dante—" Aleks began.

"Aleks," I interrupted as I held out my hand. "It's okay," I said. Aleks hesitated, then handed me the phone. I took it off speaker. By the time I had it to my ear, Dante was talking.

"Tell me where you are," was all he said.

"The second I figure out how to keep him safe, that's exactly what I'll do," I said.

"Vaughn," Magnus said. "You need to bring him back. If what you say is true, he's going to need as many eyes on him as possible."

I wanted to laugh at the man's attempt at pragmatism. Not surprisingly, I didn't get a chance to respond.

"If you even touch him—" Dante began, but then stopped and I could practically feel his fury vibrating through the phone. "I'm going to kill you for this," he finally whispered, his voice deadly.

"I know," was all I said. "I'll keep him safe. Watch out for your family, Dante. These people will use whatever means it takes to get what they want." I was about to hang up when I saw the starkness in Aleks's eyes. "Talk to your brother, Dante," I said gently, then handed the phone back to Aleks, who put it to his ear.

I watched as Aleks mostly listened as Dante spoke. I suspected the first part of the conversation was Dante trying to convince his brother to tell him where he was, but when Aleks began apologizing again and his voice cracked, something seemed to shift because Aleks began nodding and began repeating to his brother, "I will." Then he was making Dante promise to watch out for everyone… he rattled off one name after another and I felt my insides warm as I realized what all those names meant.

Aleks had people who cared about him besides just his brother and Magnus… and from the sounds of it, it was a lot of people.

I hid my smile when Aleks made some comment about reminding someone named Leo to keep his clothes on, then he was laughing at whatever his brother said in response and I wanted to kiss Dante for steering the conversation in a different direction.

When it came time to end the call, Aleks sobered and wiped at his face again. "I love you, meu melhor," he murmured.

Whatever Dante said had him smiling. After a few moments, Aleks managed to hang up the phone after saying goodbye to both his brother and Magnus. When he handed it back to me, his hand was shaking. He began crying again but before I could say anything, he was climbing to his feet. I stood as well. Aleks cowered in the corner as he crossed his arms. "Can I use the bathroom to clean up?" he asked.

"You're not a prisoner, Aleks," I reminded him, but that only seemed to make him more tense. "Yes," I finally said when he didn't move. "Down the hall, first door on the left."

He waited until I stepped aside before he hurried past me. When he reached the door, I called his name. He paused but didn't look at me.

"Thank you for trusting me, Aleks," I said softly.

He was silent for so long that I didn't think he'd answer. And I kind of wished he hadn't because his next words cut me to the core.

"I don't." He paused for a beat and added, "I said I believed you but that doesn't mean I trust you." He shook his head. "I don't... not anymore. Not ever again, Vaughn."

And with that, he left the room.

Chapter 4

ALEKS

WHAT HAVE I DONE?

I looked in the mirror and shook my head at my reflection.

"I don't know," I whispered. "I don't know what I'm doing."

Part of me wanted to race back to Vaughn and beg him to give me his phone back so I could call my brother and tell him to come get me... to fix everything, to make all the hard decisions about what would happen next.

To make all the decisions *always*...

I wanted to cry all over as I considered how badly I wanted that – for Dante or Magnus to tell me when to eat and sleep, what clothes to wear, when to speak and when to remain silent, where I could and couldn't go...

Two years of being allowed to make my own choices should have been something I fought to keep. It was a right I should have been willing to die for. But being free to choose also meant having to deal with doubt and regret.

And I'd had enough of those particular emotions to last me a lifetime, thank you very much.

One choice had ruined my entire life and had torn my entire family apart.

But when I'd finally accepted that I had no choices anymore, I'd finally been safe. Yes, there'd been pain and fear, but there'd been relief too. Giving in had meant being allowed to take my next breath. *Survival* was the one choice I'd made for myself from the moment I'd been escorted out of the mall twelve years ago under the guise of being reunited with my injured parents, and that was the only reason I was even here today. I knew that, but it didn't make it any easier to accept that I'd so easily given up what should have been my innate right to keep as mine forever.

Dante had been so proud of me for the choices I'd made for myself these past couple of years, but I doubted he realized how often I'd just wanted to beg him to make them for me. Just like I wanted him to make the choice about whether I stayed with Vaughn or not.

But it'd been like I'd told Magnus… I believed Vaughn and his reason for taking me. I'd seen enough as a kid to know that the men who'd taken me, who'd owned me or had wanted to own me, would do anything to keep their world a secret. It wasn't just my life that was in danger. They'd kill anyone who stood in their way or who they thought they could use to get to me.

And I couldn't do that to my brother and his husband-to-be. Or any of the dozens of men and women who'd become my family over the past two years. I might not have interacted with all of them as much as I would have liked, but they never failed to interact with me and always included me in their family events, even when they knew I wouldn't attend. On my birthday and Christmas I was always showered with presents, even though I wasn't able to make myself go to the large gatherings. Dante and Magnus had always chosen to celebrate those holidays with me and we'd occasionally have Matty and his fathers there too, but that had been the extent of it.

But now they were all in danger because of me.

I could only hope that the men hunting me wouldn't figure out my connection to the members of my extended family. But even if they did, I knew Dante would make sure everyone was safe. Not to mention that the men in the large family weren't exactly helpless. I wasn't really sure what it was Dante exactly did for Ronan Grisham, the man he worked for. But I'd seen enough to know that it wasn't just "security" like Dante would always say. I probably should have asked more questions, but that concept was just like the choices one.

I didn't do either well.

I sighed and stared at myself. I was still wearing the light-yellow button-up shirt with the flower shop's logo on it, but there was a big wet spot on the lower part of it where I'd thrown up and the top three buttons were gone. My khaki pants looked okay, just really wrinkled. My face was red and splotchy and my eyes looked swollen, likely from the seemingly endless tears.

Those were another consequence of having choices and freedom.

Father hadn't liked it when I cried. His punishments had proven just exactly how much it displeased him when I showed any kind of emotion. But if I was with Dante or Magnus when something caused me to lose control of myself, all I ended up with was a gentle touch on my shoulder or a strong pair of arms around me that would hold me as tight as I needed until the wayward feelings went away. Even seven-year-old Matty would hug me when he merely suspected I was on edge... of course, he had a habit of hugging me *just because*.

Magnus's grandson really was a great hugger.

He was another reason I was doing this... there was no chance in heck I'd risk anything coming even close to that little boy. Even though his fathers were more than capable of taking care of him, I wasn't going to give the people pursuing me even the opportunity to go after little Matty Hawkins. The boy had spent more than a year battling cancer and deserved a normal childhood... *I* would *not* be the reason that was stolen from him.

Spying the shower in my reflection, I turned and got it started. I waited to make sure the water would turn warm, then began unbuttoning the rest of the buttons on my shirt. I stripped it off and then quickly cleaned it using a little soap and water from the sink, then laid it out on the countertop to dry. It wouldn't be anywhere near dry enough to wear when I was done showering, but it would have to do.

I scanned the drawers and cabinets for some toothpaste but there was nothing. I didn't even see a towel, so I knew I was going to have to use my wet shirt or risk dampening my pants to dry off. I should just forgo the shower, but between the man in the van touching me, the tears that had left my eyes stinging, and the vomit clinging to my skin, I wanted that shower almost as much as I wanted to go home.

I was in the process of reaching for the button on my pants when something in my periphery caught my attention. I managed not to jump at the sight of Vaughn in the open doorway. It wasn't until that very moment that I realized I'd left the door open.

Father had never allowed me to close the door of any room I was in by myself, including the bathroom, so in the past two years I'd tried to break that particular habit. But it was something I deliberately had to do and whenever I did, it'd felt like I was disappointing Father and risking his wrath. My brother and Magnus had undoubtedly wondered what was wrong with me whenever they'd see me go into the bathroom in their house and then spend five minutes just opening and closing the door as I tried to convince myself I wouldn't be punished for putting a door between me and the outside world.

The fact that I was in a strange place and had automatically reverted to the rules Father had instilled in me made me feel sick all over. And the fact that it was Vaughn who was witnessing it all just made me want to go and crawl into the nearest hole I could find.

Vaughn's eyes skimmed over me and something warm flashed through me as I realized I was naked from the waist up.

I didn't know why that mattered because he'd seen me completely naked more than once.

"Um, I thought you could use this," Vaughn said as he remained in the open doorway and handed me something. I couldn't force myself to move, though, which caused him to frown. Then he put the little bundle on the counter. "When you're finished in here, we need to get moving again."

I managed a nod. His eyes moved from my face to my chest and I fought the urge to cover my body with my arms. I'd never been allowed to do that with Father... to hide. After a while I hadn't cared either way, but with Vaughn... with Vaughn it wasn't the same thing.

And it wasn't because I was afraid me being half-naked would spur him to do something.

No, my feelings on the matter were a lot more messed up than that.

Vaughn looked away from me and glanced at the door. "Do you want me to close this?" he asked.

Yes.

"No," I said. "I'll... I'll do it."

If he thought my comment strange considering he was *right there*, he didn't show it. He simply nodded and then turned away.

Like he couldn't get away from me fast enough. Like the sight of me disgusted him...

I swallowed hard and looked in the mirror at my skinny chest and thin arms. Dante and Magnus were always urging me to eat more, but I still hadn't gotten used to being allowed to indulge in food. Father had always decided what I was allowed to eat and how much, so having to figure that out for myself was hard. My body had long ago stopped sending signals to my head about being hungry, so these days it was about *remembering* to eat and drink. With the stress of Caleb's abduction, I'd been even less focused on food than before.

Did my appearance repulse Vaughn? Did he think me pathetic for not being able to take better care of myself? Did I remind him too much of the mindless boy who'd practically fallen on the pieces of butterscotch candy he'd handed me like a dying man would throw himself into a pool in the middle of the desert?

I let out a little laugh that sounded like more of a whimper.

It wasn't really those candies I'd been indulging in. It'd been those few seconds I'd gotten to spend with the man who gave them to me. When he hadn't been scanning our surroundings to make sure we were alone, he'd been watching me peel open the little nuggets of gold and he'd let out the smallest of laughs when I got my first taste of the buttery goodness.

Vaughn had become one big indulgence for me in the months he'd been working for Father. Besides the one trip outside the house every week Father had allowed me to pick up fresh flowers, I hadn't ever looked forward to anything until Vaughn had shown up at the mansion. He'd given me a lot more than just candy and that wasn't a good thing.

Because what he'd given me had been something Brian had made sure I'd let go of long before he'd sold me to my next owner.

Hope.

A chill swept over me. Remembering the shower, I quickly hurried to close the door, ignoring the mental warning in my head that it was against the rules. I started to undo my pants, when I noticed the bundle Vaughn had left for me. I reached for it and realized the top item was actually a towel. Beneath it was a small tube of toothpaste and new toothbrush. And underneath that was a shirt… a really big shirt.

My fingers itched to touch the material. I gave in to the need and let my fingers skim over the softness of it. I didn't know what possessed me to do what I did next, but I did it anyway.

I picked the folded shirt up and held it to my nose.

Then inhaled deeply.

Definitely his.

God, would he smell like this all over?

I remembered how hot his skin had felt when I'd hugged him after he'd lifted me up off the floor of that van.

More warmth filled my body, so much so that it felt almost wrong, so I quickly pulled the shirt back and opened it so I could see how big it really was.

Something fell to the floor and it took me a moment to find it.

And when I did, I forgot all about the shirt and the shower and my state of undress. And the fact that I'd told myself I was done crying.

The dreaded tears began to flow as I dropped to my knees and silently cursed Vaughn in my head.

"Ignore it," I whispered to myself.

Jesus, it should be such an easy thing – to ignore it, get up, shower, and leave this place.

But I couldn't move. Not to get up, not even to curl into a ball on the floor like I wanted.

All I could do was stare in confusion as a little spark of unexpected hope began to curl through my entire body as I stared at Vaughn's "gift" which glittered like gold against the stark, dingy tiles beneath me.

The jerk had brought out the big guns… and he probably didn't even know it.

Damn freaking butterscotch.

Chapter 5

VAUGHN

My shirt looked huge on him. It wasn't that I was even that big of a guy, Aleks was just so…

Beautiful.

I sighed silently at my brain's attempt to be logical. The reasonable side of me was fully aware that the now twenty-year-old Aleks had lost some weight over the years, making him look pretty lean. Although Marcus had used food as a means to control Aleks, he'd also prized Aleks's beauty and had made sure he was physically healthy, so he hadn't starved him long-term. But that didn't mean he hadn't withheld food to punish Aleks. And while I'd never seen Marcus strike Aleks firsthand, there was no denying that the man had physically abused him at one point because I'd seen the scars on Aleks's back.

His back.

Where admirers were less likely to see the marks when Marcus paraded his pet in front of them.

I felt my anger stirring at even the image my mind was conjuring up of all the things Marcus had done to Aleks, and it took all of my power to focus on the road in front of me. But of course, I couldn't stop sending glances Aleks's way, mostly because he was fingering the hem of my shirt. The move was distracting the hell out of me, but I knew Aleks wasn't even aware of it. He was clearly nervous and I couldn't really blame him. It was probably only now registering with him what he'd done by choosing to stay with me rather than go home. I half expected him to beg me to take him home.

Which I would.

As badly as I wanted to keep him safe, I hadn't considered what my actions would do to him. I also knew he'd only chosen me over his brother to keep Dante and the rest of his family safe.

I said I believed you but that doesn't mean I trust you. I don't... not anymore. Not ever again, Vaughn.

Fuck, that had hurt.

Still did.

We'd gotten back on the road nearly an hour earlier and Aleks had yet to speak to me. He hadn't even asked me what was going to happen next. I thought maybe it was because he didn't trust me to tell him the truth, but I was starting to wonder if there wasn't another reason for his silence.

Just like he'd reverted to believing Marcus was alive when I'd tried to untie him earlier, maybe he was relying on the behavior that had kept him alive in the past.

Don't speak unless spoken to.

Don't ask questions.

Don't talk back.

It was likely an endless list of hard-learned lessons and I hated that he was associating any of them with me.

Another hour passed in silence. The sun was just starting to come up over the horizon when we reached the interstate.

"Do you want to stop for something to eat before we get on the interstate?" I asked. "I need to get gas anyway."

Aleks's right hand moved to his mouth so he could chew on his fingernail. He shook his head. "No, thank you... sir."

I actually jerked the wheel a bit when he called me that. If he'd called me "sir" in a snide tone to prove he was pissed at me, I would have been relieved because it meant he felt *something*. But he'd added it so naturally... like when he'd addressed any one of Marcus's colleagues that he'd either encountered at the mansion or at one of the few outside events Marcus had taken him to.

I found myself pulling the car over to the side of the road because I was so disturbed I found it hard to breathe. I wrapped both hands around the steering wheel and held on like it was my lifeline.

Because if I didn't, I'd take my anger out on the damn thing and Aleks didn't need to see that.

I had no clue how long we sat there for because I lost track of things. My mind was reliving every moment where I could have gotten Aleks out of that fucking mansion sooner. I could have done it the very night I'd spoken to him for the first time.

But no, I hadn't been able to risk it back then.

What if I had? Would we even be here now? Would things have been better for Aleks if I'd just given in to the temptation?

"Vaughn."

I startled as I realized Aleks was calling me, his voice sounding strangled. I turned to look at him. I expected to see him cowering against the car door, but he wasn't. His hands were in his lap and he was watching me, a look of concern on his face.

Concern?

For me?

At least he'd called me by my name.

The rage and regret were still too strong to make it possible for me to respond to him.

"I'm sorry, Vaughn. I shouldn't have called you that. You... you don't deserve that. It's a habit—"

"Aleks," I practically croaked.

He stopped talking and dropped his eyes. I couldn't help but reach for his face, though I only touched his chin briefly so that he'd look at me, because I didn't trust myself to have any kind of extended contact with him. Not to mention I didn't want to cause any kind of discomfort by coming into contact with the bruises the men who'd abducted him had left on him. "You don't owe me any kind of explanation... or apology," I said firmly.

He held my gaze a moment and it looked like he wanted to say something, but as soon as he opened his mouth, he closed it again. My eyes fell to his fingers.

"What happened here?" I asked as I motioned to the small cuts on his fingers. I already knew what they were, but I needed something, *anything*, that would get him talking. And there was one thing I knew Aleks would talk about without fail.

"They're, um, from working with the flowers," he said as he studied the nicks on his fingers. I could see a little bit of dirt on the pads. It was the perpetual plight of someone who worked in any kind of gardening job, but for Aleks, those little flecks of dirt were new. Although Marcus had rewarded Aleks by letting him work with flowers and plants in the greenhouse on the property's mansion, he hadn't tolerated dirty hands. I'd seen Aleks scrubbing his fingers until they were raw on more than one occasion to get the grime completely off before he met with Marcus. His hands had been so clean, he might as well have been wearing gloves when he'd worked with his beloved plants. I'd once asked him why he didn't wear gloves, but all he'd said was then it wouldn't feel the same. I hadn't been sure if it'd been a literal reference to not being able to work with the plants and flowers as well, or if it'd been something else... like touching that dirt had somehow made him feel free and safe and... *normal*.

"Father would be so angry," Aleks whispered when he fingered some of the dirt.

God, I wanted to kill the fucker all over again.

"Not possible," I said as I put the car in gear. "He's too busy burning in hell."

I got us moving and found a gas station. I didn't even bother to remove the keys while I filled the tank. Even if Aleks hadn't been with me willingly, I was starting to realize he wouldn't have tried to escape.

He was too afraid of angering me.

My phone dinged just as I was rounding the trunk of the car. I pulled it out and saw who the text was from. Relief went through me when I saw both a time and address listed in the text.

Thank fuck I wouldn't need to do this on my own.

I sent a quick text back, then got into the car. Aleks was sitting quietly with his hands in his lap. He was still staring at his fingers. I almost covered his hands with mine but decided against it. He'd probably let me touch him, but not necessarily because he wanted me to.

I went to start the car but didn't turn the key. "Aleks," I said softly.

He didn't look at me.

If I wanted him to, I'd have to ask him.

No direct eye contact unless otherwise instructed.

Another fucking rule that I wanted to send Marcus and the others to hell all over again for.

"We're going to be driving for most of the day. Are you sure you don't want to eat something?"

"No, thank you," he said.

Thank fuck he left the "sir" off this time.

It was all I could do not to order him to eat something. But when I went to start the car, he whispered my name so softly that I almost didn't hear him. I pulled my hand back from the ignition and waited. If it took him all day to speak again, I'd happily sit there and tell anyone who needed to get gas to fuck off.

"How… how long since… since they took me. Was it… was it last night?"

More guilt went through me as I realized the trauma had left him without any sense of time. I had to wonder exactly what he did remember about the night before. His memory appeared completely clear up until the point where he'd asked me to take him home and I'd told him no. But he didn't seem to remember thinking Marcus was still alive.

"It's been about ten hours since they took you from the alley behind your shop," I said. "After I…" I paused because I most certainly didn't want to verbalize the next part.

After I took you and refused to take you home…

"After I got you out of the van, we drove for a little over an hour. You were… tired," I said lamely.

He'd been a lot worse off than "tired."

"I found the abandoned house and carried you inside because you'd fallen asleep. I took your shoes off and put you in the bed."

"Did you sleep with me?" he asked.

I had no idea if he was asking me if I'd had sex with him or if I'd slept in the same bed with him, and the fact that I couldn't make that distinction made me feel like the lowest form of life on the planet. It was a question he never would have asked me in the final weeks in the Parks mansion where I might as well have been his jailer.

Because he'd trusted me then…

"I sat in the bed next to you, but I didn't touch you. I worked on my computer while you slept and when you had a bad dream, I just called your name to wake you up… until that last one. I had to touch you that time because you weren't responding to just my voice."

Aleks pulled in a deep breath and nodded.

"You slept for about eight hours."

He nodded again. "I forget to eat," he said softly. "I have to set a reminder on my phone because I'm not used to…" He shook his head and then said, "I would like to eat something, please."

If he'd asked me to hand him the sun, I gladly would have found a way to do it. And while stopping at a restaurant to eat wasn't exactly the most conducive behavior to trying to fly under the radar, no way in hell was I going to make him eat shitty food from a fast food place.

"Okay," I said quickly, then got the car started. It took just a few minutes to find a little hole-in-the-wall, no-name place that claimed to have the best omelets in town and looked busy enough to mean the food probably wasn't completely terrible, but not so full of people that I'd have to watch our backs the entire time.

Though I'd probably end up doing that anyway.

The waitress seated us quickly but when she asked Aleks if he wanted coffee, he clammed up.

"Could we have two coffees, some tea if you have it, a hot

chocolate, and a couple of glasses of orange juice? And some water?" I asked.

The woman sent me a friendly smile. "You got it, hun." She left the menus on the table in front of each of us, then left to get our drinks.

She was back within a couple of minutes, but Aleks didn't even look up from his menu. As small as the restaurant was, the thing was pretty lengthy and had several variations of every breakfast food imaginable.

"You all need a minute?" the lady asked when she saw how intently Aleks was staring at his menu.

"Please," I said with a nod. She left again. I prepared my coffee and then pretended to skim my menu as I watched Aleks. He'd managed to make it to the second page, but his distress was only building. He looked like he was on the verge of tears.

"Aleks," I began, but he shook his head and then discreetly wiped at his eyes. I snapped my mouth shut, but I couldn't just sit there and do nothing. So I used my foot to brush against his beneath the table. He let out a little whimper and I was sure he would pull his foot away, but then he was moving his foot so it was completely lined up with mine.

And he left it that way.

"Talk to me, Aleks," I urged. I put some sugar in the tea as well as the coffee and pushed both of them plus the hot chocolate toward him. I was relieved when he put his hands around the mug of hot chocolate.

He didn't answer me. He just stared at the mug.

"Is there nothing on the menu you like?" I asked.

He shook his head, but I wasn't sure if he was telling me there was nothing that appealed to him or the other way around, so I was about to ask him the question a different way when he looked up at me, his eyes shimmering with tears.

"It should be easier by now, shouldn't it?"

"What?" I asked gently.

He spoke the next word so softly that if I hadn't been leaning across the table, I definitely wouldn't have heard him.

"Choosing."

With any other person, the single word would have been their way of conveying that there was too much on the menu to pick from. But that wasn't what he was saying at all.

I managed to keep my expression soft despite the rage burning inside of me. What kind of mental torture had this young man endured to get to this point where the mere act of making a choice hurt so fucking much?

And he *was* in pain.

With his back hunched and his fingers biting into the ceramic mug, Aleks looked so damn broken.

But I knew he was anything but.

The fact that he was sitting there with me was proof of that.

I almost offered to choose something for him because I thought it would be easier for him, but I caught myself in time. "Tell me about breakfast at home," I said instead.

"What?" Aleks asked in surprise.

"What are breakfasts like at home with your brother and his boyfriend?"

"Fiancé," Aleks automatically corrected.

"Dante and Magnus are engaged?" I asked, relieved at the opportunity to momentarily take Aleks's mind off the topic at hand.

"Magnus asked Dante about a month after…" Aleks's voice dropped off.

"After you came home?" I asked.

"Yeah," Aleks whispered. "Dante was so surprised when Magnus asked, he said no," Aleks said, a rare smile forming on his lips. He pulled in a breath and I saw the sheen of tears start to fade. "He said yes about two minutes later but he yelled at Magnus first. Told him that he was crazy and it was too soon."

"What did Magnus say to that?" I asked as I took a sip of my coffee.

"Nothing. He just asked him again. And again."

"So when's the wedding?"

Aleks sobered and shook his head. "Dante won't commit to a date."

I frowned. Things had happened pretty quickly the night I'd shot Marcus and gotten Aleks, Magnus, and Dante out of the mansion before blowing it up, but I'd seen enough to know that Magnus was crazy for Dante. Maybe his feelings weren't being returned? "Your brother has cold feet?" I asked.

Aleks chewed on his lip for a moment, then seemed to catch himself and wiped at some invisible spot on his mouth. Like he was trying to make sure he hadn't left any kind of mark behind.

Fucking Marcus and his continued hold on Aleks. I suspected the majority of little nervous behaviors Aleks exhibited were ones he didn't even realize he had.

Aleks took a sip of the hot chocolate, which made me feel a bit better. I so badly wanted to get some calories into him. He wasn't scary thin, but he could definitely use some meat on his bones.

"Dante doesn't think he's good enough for Magnus," Aleks said with surprising bluntness. There was also a certain ferocity in his expression, like he was daring me to somehow agree with that statement.

"Why not?" I asked. "Anyone can see that Magnus loves your brother," I added.

That last part seemed to ease some of the tension in Aleks's expression. He nodded. "He does," he said. "And Dante loves him... he tells him so every day. Shows him too."

"So why does he think he isn't good enough?"

Aleks hesitated and I realized why... he was potentially sharing something very personal with me about his brother. "It's okay, you don't have to tell me," I quickly said. My goal had been to get him talking, not betray his brother's confidence. But amazingly, he continued on his own.

"Mama and Papa weren't kind to him," Aleks said. "Even before I... before I...was gone..." he said awkwardly. "Papa said mean things to him and Mama didn't put a stop to it." Aleks leaned forward a bit and began tapping his finger on the edge of the mug. "He tried so hard, Vaughn... to please Papa. But nothing he ever did was good enough for him."

"Did your father treat you that way too?" I asked, my anger on behalf of both Dante and Aleks growing by the second. Some assholes just didn't deserve to have kids.

Aleks shook his head. "Only Dante," he said. "I... I tried to make up for how mean Papa was—"

"How?"

"What?" Aleks asked, startled by my interruption.

"How did you try to make it up to Dante?"

"I told him what Mama and Papa should have," he responded, as if the answer should have been obvious to me.

"And what was that?" I asked with a smile.

"That he was perfect... the best... meu melhor... *my best*," Aleks whispered. "He turned it into this game where he'd guess what he was best at. He did it to make me smile. He always wanted me to be smiling." Aleks's smile turned wistful. I loved seeing him like this... so open, so free to say what he was actually thinking. He'd dropped his eyes at some point, like he was lost in the memory of his brother and himself playing the game. When he lifted them, I was sure he'd continue with the story, but something in his expression shuttered and his slightly parted lips snapped shut.

He doesn't trust you...

The reminder along with the obvious proof of that fact gutted me, but I managed not to react. I still had a goal I needed to accomplish. Everything I did with Aleks going forward would be about baby steps.

To what end? What exactly are you trying to accomplish?

I ignored my inner voice and said, "Tell me about breakfast at home."

Aleks's eyes lowered to the menu and he seemed to remember where we were and why we were there. The distress came back quickly but didn't seem as intense this time around.

"Magnus cooks when he isn't working. If he is, Dante and I eat cereal. Neither of us can cook very good."

"What does Magnus make?"

"Everything," Aleks responded. "He's good at cooking."

"Is there one thing in particular that you look forward to when he's cooking?"

Aleks nodded. "On Sundays... he makes grits. I don't know what it is, but I like it. I always eat too much. It's very hot, I don't mean warm... he puts something green in it. A pepper, maybe?"

I smiled. "Jalapeño peppers?" I asked. "Small and green?"

Aleks nodded and smiled. "Yes, that's it. He makes eggs and bacon too, but I eat so many grits I can't eat anything else. When Dante and I are done eating, we do the dishes and then we just lay on the couch until we can move again."

I chuckled at that, then reached for my menu. I scanned it and said, "Look here." I handed him the menu and pointed to one of the items. "They don't have jalapeños in them, but I bet they're still good. And if not, we'll get you something else."

"Oh no, I will eat them no matter what," Aleks said with a frown. Like wasting a little bit of food was the worst thing in the world.

To him, it probably was, since food had been such a commodity for him.

I didn't respond and instead waved the waitress over. I was pleased when Aleks ordered for himself. When it was my turn, I grabbed the menu and began rattling one item off after another. Aleks's eyes went comically wide as I ordered enough dishes to feed a dozen people. When the waitress left with a broad smile on her face, Aleks eyed me.

"What? I'm hungry," I said.

He shook his head at me. Our feet were still touching beneath the table so I shifted my body until our knees were in contact. Aleks actually let out a little gasp before he caught himself.

In all seriousness, I murmured, "Some choices you have to live with. But others," – I motioned to the table – "you're allowed to change your mind on as many times as you want." I waited until I was sure he'd heard me before I added, "And Aleks, as long as we're together, take five minutes or five hours to choose – you've more than earned that right." I brushed our knees together again, then pulled my leg back so I wouldn't overwhelm him.

He was quiet for a long time... long enough that I thought I'd royally fucked up – that I'd somehow undermined him. But when the waitress passed us, he softly called out to her. If that move alone hadn't been enough to shock me into silence, his next words did the trick.

"Excuse me, I saw that you have chocolate milk on your menu. May I please have a glass of that?" Aleks's gaze shifted to me as he quietly added, "It's my favorite."

The waitress nodded and left, and I quickly turned my attention to scan the other patrons of the diner so I wouldn't make the young man across from me uncomfortable. When the chocolate milk came, I couldn't manage to keep my eyes averted as he drank down the contents of the small glass in a few large gulps. And when he hesitantly asked the waitress for another, I barely suppressed a smile.

It was a tiny step forward, but what a great fucking step.

Now how the hell did I make sure he had a million more just like them in the time we were together? And how the fuck was I going to keep him safe long enough to make sure all those steps turned into something more?

Chapter 6

ALEKS

It was the most logical question on the planet.

Where are we going?

But I was afraid to ask it. And not only because my instinct was reminding me that asking questions was forbidden – but also because I didn't want to know the answer.

It was the coward's way out, to just remain silent. But it was what it was.

I was a coward. Always had been.

Even when I'd been little and long before I'd been taken, I'd hidden away from the scarier parts of life. For all the mean things my father had said to Dante, for all the names he'd called him, I'd never once spoken up for my brother. I'd tried to make up for it by showing Dante that Papa was wrong in other ways, but I'd never stood in front of my father and told him not to talk to Dante that way. On the rare occasions Papa had yelled or Mama had been disappointed in *me*, I'd let Dante comfort me and tell me everything was going to be okay. If the shadows on my ceiling took on the form of monsters or I heard a noise in the darkened house in the middle of the night or one of the boys in my class called me a name because I was too small or my family didn't have enough money, I'd always gone to Dante. No matter what he'd been doing, he'd either made room for me in his bed or he'd taken me by the hand to check all the corners and closets in the apartment or warned my tormentors to leave me alone.

I'd never been brave because I'd never *had* to be brave.

After I'd been taken, Brian had made sure I hadn't *tried* to be brave.

And now, with a full belly and tired eyes, I just wanted to pretend for a little while longer that Vaughn was taking me home.

I knew we were headed south… the signs on the interstate had indicated as much.

South.

So not to Chicago, apparently.

Of course, since I really didn't know much about the layout of the United States, I couldn't actually be sure that we weren't headed to Chicago. After I'd been taken, my education hadn't exactly been a priority. I'd only been able to speak English because my mother had dreamed of me one day going to the same college in the U.S. my real father had attended. He'd been an engineer and had died shortly before she'd learned she was pregnant with me. Although my stepfather had adopted me and given me his last name, something he hadn't been willing to do for Dante, my mother had made sure from an early age that I knew about the father I had in heaven.

I couldn't help but wonder once again if what my mother had believed was true… that my father had been watching out for me and Dante from heaven. Part of me didn't think so because surely that would have been a cruel jest… for him to have to watch his son get stolen away and not be able to do anything about it. What kind of heaven was that? But admittedly, when I'd first been taken I'd begged my father in heaven to help me. After a while, I'd started to accept that my mother had been wrong about heaven. When Dante had found me, that in itself had seemed like a miracle, so I just wasn't really sure what was true anymore.

"You okay?"

Vaughn's voice jerked me from my thoughts and I quickly glanced at him. His eyes were on the road, of course, but he kept shooting me quick looks. His brow line was furrowed like he was worried about something.

I nodded.

I saw his mouth tighten a bit and I wondered why. He looked... disappointed?

That couldn't be right, could it?

Why would he be disappointed?

Had I done something to upset him?

I'd tried to be quiet and I hadn't asked questions. Maybe I'd eaten too much at breakfast? But he'd seemed pleased about that when he'd asked me if it was good after I'd pushed my second helping of grits away. When he'd asked me if I needed to go to the bathroom before we'd gotten on the road, I'd dutifully gone and I'd tried to hurry. Once in the car, I'd remained silent so as not to distract him.

So why was he upset?

Was he upset?

God, I missed Dante and Magnus. I could always ask them questions like this. If I didn't understand something someone said or did, Magnus or Dante would help me make sense of it.

I could ask Vaughn if he was angry with me, but did I really want to know the answer?

I shook my head and then looked down at my lap. I stilled when I saw how jagged my nails looked.

And how dirty my fingers were.

Not fresh dirt, but the kind that got beneath the skin and didn't come off with just one or two washings. I'd had to use a special scrubber when I'd lived with Father to get the dirt off every day so he wouldn't be angry with me or tell me I couldn't have the flowers anymore. And if he'd caught me chewing my nails...

A shiver ran through me.

He's dead.

"What?"

I jumped at Vaughn's question.

"Did you say something?" he asked gently.

Oh God, had I said the words out loud? About Father being dead?

Since I didn't want Vaughn to know my train of thought, I blurted, "Do you know where MIT is?"

If I'd wanted to distract Vaughn, I'd definitely managed it because he looked completely caught off guard. "MIT? The school?" he asked.

I nodded.

"Um, yeah, it's in Massachusetts. It's not far from Boston," he answered.

"What does it mean?" I asked.

"MIT?"

I nodded again.

"It stands for Massachusetts Institute of Technology."

"Do you have to be really smart to go there?" I asked.

"Yeah, pretty smart," Vaughn acknowledged. "It's one of the best engineering schools in the country." When I didn't respond, Vaughn asked, "Why? Are you hoping to go there someday?"

I laughed at that.

The sound felt foreign and I automatically covered my mouth to stifle the noise. I sent Vaughn a sidelong glance, but he didn't seem irritated by my outburst. I'd gotten used to laughing around Dante and Magnus, but I was careful about doing it around other people. Granted, I wasn't really around other people enough to even have the opportunity to laugh. The exception was Matty... and of course, his besties, Leo and Jamie.

And it was hard *not* to laugh when a very naked Leo would go streaking down the block with one or both of his beleaguered fathers chasing after him with a handful of clothing.

I felt my mouth tug into a smile.

"What?" Vaughn asked.

I looked at him and saw he was smiling in that way that people did when they saw something they liked.

"Nothing," I said quickly.

His face fell and I felt my stomach drop out.

"I was thinking about something," I added. "Someone, actually."

"Who?"

I could see he was really interested so I said, "Magnus has a grandson named Matty. He's seven. His best friend is Leo. Leo doesn't like to wear clothes so he usually takes them off as soon as he gets the chance. His fathers live on the same block as Matty and his fathers. Magnus and Dante just bought a house a few doors down earlier this year... anyway, every once in a while I'll see Leo running down the sidewalk, completely naked. His fathers are usually chasing after him. Their neighbor, Mrs. Finney, she's in a wheelchair and she and Leo and Matty and Jamie race each other down the street, but Leo says he runs fastest with only sneakers on so he gets undressed first..."

I felt my cheeks heat when I realized how caught up I'd gotten in telling the story to Vaughn... he'd asked a simple question and I'd basically given him a book's worth of an answer.

"Leo's poor fathers," Vaughn said with a smile, which made me feel better. At least I hadn't annoyed him.

"He's finally taken to wearing underwear recently," I explained. "But Connor thinks it's only because it's been so cold out."

"Connor?"

"One of Leo's fathers," I said. "He's also one of my tutors."

"Is Connor helping you get ready to apply to MIT?"

"What? No," I said, horrified. "I'm not... I could never..."

I snapped my mouth shut because I hadn't been expecting the topic change.

"You could never what?"

I shook my head.

"Aleks," Vaughn said softly and I couldn't help but look at him. His eyes were so dark they looked almost black, but there was such gentleness in them.

Like there'd always been when it'd just been him and me...

"I can't... I can't go to college," I stammered.

"Why not?"

I looked down at my fingers and began picking at the sharper edges of some of my nails. I needed a nail file, but I didn't have one. I used the edge of my thumbnail to try and fix one of the worst of the broken nails but then suddenly a big warm hand closed over both of mine. I sucked in a breath as a jolt of electricity fired up my arms.

"I have a nail file in my bag," Vaughn said. "I'll give it to you next time we stop." He paused then added, "They don't bother me, Aleks."

I let out a whoosh of air as I realized what he was really saying.

You won't be punished for messy nails, Aleks.

"Okay," I managed to say.

He gave my hands a squeeze and I felt warmth shimmy throughout my entire body. Then something in my groin tightened and I barely stifled a groan at the strange sensation that wasn't entirely bad.

Vaughn removed his hand and I actually missed the contact.

Why?

"Why can't you go to college?" Vaughn asked.

"I can barely leave the house," I muttered.

Vaughn was silent for a beat and I was half-tempted to look at him to try and figure out what he was thinking. But I also kind of didn't want to know.

"It won't always be like that, Aleks," he said.

I wanted to laugh at that but managed not to. He said he'd watched me for the first week after he'd saved me two years ago. So he'd have no idea how little progress I'd made since he'd last seen me. And I definitely didn't want to tell him.

"I'm too far behind," I hedged. "Connor and Miss Savannah – she's my other tutor – think I could take some college courses on the computer now, but the GED stuff was so hard. And I... I like working at the flower shop."

I did look at Vaughn briefly, but to my surprise, he wasn't looking at me with anything but curiosity. No pity that I could see.

"Why'd you ask about MIT?"

"My father went there."

"Your father is from the U.S.?" Vaughn asked.

I nodded. "But Papa isn't."

I almost smiled at his look of confusion. "I have two fathers," I clarified. "Mama was married before she had me. Dante and I have the same father, but he died before I was born. He was very smart and went to MIT. Mama always hoped I'd go there someday. Mama said it was my… legacy?"

Vaughn nodded, and I relaxed a little when I realized I hadn't messed up the word. "Mama made sure I knew English because she wanted me to come back here and go to my father's school and be just like him."

"Your English is excellent," Vaughn said.

I knew he'd meant the words as a compliment, but a chill snaked down my spine. The next thing I knew my name was being called from far away.

"Aleks, sweetheart, just focus on my voice."

I felt my skin grow warm. First on my cheek, then my arms. Someone was rubbing my upper arms but not in a bad way.

"Aleks, open your eyes."

When had I closed my eyes?

I did as he said and forced my lids open. Bright light was everywhere, but it wasn't anything more than the sunlight filtering through the car like before.

Only now the car wasn't moving.

And Vaughn didn't have his hands on the wheel. They were on me, rubbing my arms. My shirt sleeves had ridden up on my forearms and every once in a while he'd give my muscles there a gentle squeeze.

"Breathe, baby," Vaughn whispered.

I automatically sucked in a breath, then another. My brain began to feel less fuzzy. As my mind started to focus, I realized we were sitting on the side of the road, but not on the interstate anymore. We were on the shoulder of an off-ramp.

"What… what happened?" I asked.

"Here, drink this," Vaughn said as he handed me a bottle of water. It was warm, but it gave me something to focus on as I tried to get my bearings.

My fingers were shaking as I tried to put the cap back on the bottle, so Vaughn took it from me and closed it, then set the bottle in the cup holder between us.

"What happened?" I asked.

"Aleks, have you ever lost time before?"

"What? I don't know what that means," I said.

"Have you ever blacked out and woken up minutes or hours later or in a different place… after you left Chicago?"

"No, I—" I began, but then fell silent. Then I was nodding. "A few times," I whispered. "After I began living with Magnus and Dante… they, um, they'd find me asleep in strange places sometimes."

"What places?"

I shook my head because I didn't want to say.

"What places?" Vaughn gently repeated. He was still rubbing my arms. My entire body started to get warm.

"My closet mostly. Sometimes the basement."

I could feel his eyes on me but refused to look up. "I don't know about the other…"

"The losing time?" Vaughn asked.

I nodded. "I guess sometimes I'd feel confused for no reason… like I couldn't remember how I'd gotten someplace or what I'd been doing."

"We were talking about how well you speak English," Vaughn said.

"I remember," I said.

"Do you remember anything after that?"

Fear began to engulf me as I realized I couldn't. "No," I said softly. "No, I just… we were talking and you said *that* and then you were calling my name and telling me to open my eyes." I looked up at him in confusion. "What happened? Did I pass out or something?"

The entire car shifted when a huge semi flew past as it got off the interstate. I jumped and felt my breathing tick up.

"Aleks, look at me," Vaughn demanded. My brain instantly responded to the command and I did as he said. "I'm going to get us to someplace quieter so we can talk. I want you to hold my hand and not let go," he said. He quickly put the car in gear, then curled his fingers around mine. I unashamedly clung to him. "I want you to tell me a funny story about when you and Dante were kids and I want you to keep your eyes on me the whole time, okay?"

I couldn't breathe well, but I managed a nod. The car began moving but Vaughn had to give my hand a squeeze. "Aleks," he said softly.

Right, the story.

"When I was seven and Dante was fifteen, our grandmother was cooking dobradinha… it's, um, part of the cow's stomach," I began. "Anyway, Dante and I both hate dobradinha but Mama always made us eat it. Our Vó used to take her wedding ring off when she was cooking it, so Dante came up with this plan. He told me to pretend to color a picture of our Vó—"

"Vó? Does that mean grandmother?" Vaughn asked.

"Yes. Grandfather looks almost the same when you spell it, but it is pronounced Vô."

Vaughn nodded in understanding. "Anyway, Dante told me to pretend to color her por… por…"

"Portrait?" Vaughn offered.

"Right, portrait," I said awkwardly because I'd known that word but wasn't sure why I was having so much trouble matching it to my thoughts. Vaughn gave my hand another gentle squeeze and I couldn't help but look down. His thumb was rubbing over mine and while it was both relaxing and soothing at the same time, there was something happening in my belly… a tenseness I didn't understand. I wasn't exactly nervous. It was more like I was waiting for something… but I didn't know what exactly.

"So Dante had you pretend to draw your grandmother's portrait…" Vaughn reminded me.

"Um, yes," I stammered as I realized I'd been staring at where his finger was stroking mine. "So I made her sit at the kitchen table while I was drawing. Dante came in but someone kept coming into the room so he couldn't take it... I had to keep distracting her. I, uh, don't know the word..."

"You stalled," Vaughn suggested.

"Right. I had to stall her. She was afraid her food would burn but I kept telling her I was almost done. Dante was taking the ring right when she said she was done sitting for her portrait. I screamed her name and then jumped in her lap and showed her the picture. It was... it was a terrible picture," I said with a smile. "Even for being seven, I did a really bad job. It didn't even look like a person... it looked more like a pig."

I couldn't help but smile as I remembered my grandmother's expression when I'd shown her the picture.

"She finished cooking and when we all sat down to eat, Dante casually asked her when she'd stopped wearing her wedding ring. She looked at the food and let out this cry... Papa had already started eating so she slapped him on the back to get him to spit the food out and made him look through it for the ring. Then everybody had to look through what was on their plate."

"How did Dante get the ring back to her?" Vaughn asked. His expression was soft and relaxed, which helped calm me even more.

"He left it in the soap dish by the kitchen sink. Beneath the soap. He let me 'find' it and our Vó was so happy she gave me an extra helping of dessert."

"Did anyone ever find out?"

I laughed. "Our Vô... he was always good at being able to tell when me and Dante were up to something. When he asked us about it, I... what's the expression... sang like a...?"

"Canary," Vaughn said with a chuckle. "You sang like a canary."

"I did," I admitted.

"Did he turn you in?"

"No." I began laughing so hard it was almost difficult to breathe. When I could finally speak, I said, "Turned out our Vô hated dobradinha too! He kept our secret and whenever our Vó said she was going to make dobradinha, either me or Dante or our Vô would ask her to make our favorite food instead and we'd give her the dog eyes."

Vaughn's laughter was a soft rumble in his chest that I itched to feel beneath my fingers.

"Puppy dog eyes," he corrected.

I nodded. "It usually worked. I never had to have dobradinha again…"

I sobered when I realized the real reason I hadn't had that terrible dish ever again… because I'd been abducted less than three months later.

The lead weight was back in my stomach.

"Hey," Vaughn said, and then I felt his fingers under my chin again. "You're safe, Aleks. Just take deep breaths and focus on my voice." When I could breathe again, I realized Vaughn had stopped the car again, this time on the side of the road beneath an overpass.

I managed a nod. "Did… did you ever play tricks like that?" I asked.

"No… pranks didn't go over real well in my house," he hedged. "But my brother and I did once convince a gardener that the lawnmower was possessed."

"What?" I asked with a laugh.

Vaughn shrugged and said, "I was always mechanically inclined. A few crossed wires and a few stories here and there about the previous gardener being horribly maimed by the thing were enough… power of suggestion and all." He winked at me.

Actually winked.

My heart almost stopped.

And I couldn't stop staring at him.

In case he did it again…

"Aleks," Vaughn said softly, and I forced myself to focus on his entire face rather than one rogue eye.

"You have a brother?" I asked, hoping to stall.

"I do," was all he said, then he was grazing my cheek with the backs of his fingers. "You don't remember what happened back there, but you know what caused it, don't you?"

I wasn't sure what "it" was, but I did know what the cause was. I wanted to deny it, but I couldn't make myself tell the lie. Even if it hadn't been against the rules, I didn't want to lie to him.

I may not have trusted him, but God help me, I didn't want to lie to him… I couldn't.

And just like with everything else when it came to Vaughn, that made absolutely no sense whatsoever.

Chapter 7

VAUGHN

I WAS RELIEVED WHEN HE STARTED TALKING, BECAUSE I HADN'T expected him to. I was still tense about the blackout he'd had while right in front of me. It'd been almost identical to the one he'd had the day before when I'd tried to remove the zip-ties from his hands.

"My English, it was okay when they took me, but not great, and I often spoke to the people who took me in Portuguese. They'd get angry and tell me to speak English, but I was just too scared."

Aleks began to shake violently and his breathing once again started to tick up. He was holding my hand with both of his and was squeezing so hard he was actually hurting me.

But I didn't even think of asking him to loosen his fingers... If there was a way I could have taken *all* his pain and felt it for myself, or better yet, *taken* it from him, I would have in a heartbeat.

"The first man who bought me... he... he pretended to be my friend and I was able to talk to him in English. He said things that I eventually started to believe. He just kept telling me the same things over and over," Aleks said with a shake of his head.

"Like what?" I interjected as quietly as I could in the hopes my voice wouldn't ratchet up his panic.

"That Mama and Papa didn't want me back because I'd been

bad. That Dante would come if I was good." Tears started to slip down Aleks's face, but I doubted he noticed. "He never came, no matter how good I was. I… I believed the man at first… that Dante knew where I was but refused to come get me." Aleks lifted his shoulders to wipe at his face, since he didn't seem to want to let go of my hand. He'd managed to calm down a bit.

"Your brother wouldn't have let anything or anyone stop him from coming to find you," I said. "You know that, right?"

Aleks nodded. "I believed he would come for me for a really long time but after a while it got too hard. It made it hard to always be good…"

"What do you mean?"

Aleks hesitated and then wiped at his face again. He tried to pull his hands free, but I gently held on to one and intertwined our fingers and began rubbing the pad of my thumb over his skin.

"When the man would do things to me that really hurt or that I knew were wrong, I'd tell him Dante was going to punish him. I… I actually started dreaming of Dante showing up just as the man was about to hurt me again and stopping it, and when he didn't…"

I used my free hand to wipe at his face.

"He would have if he could have, Aleks."

Aleks nodded. Tears kept slipping down his face. I couldn't help but lean across the console as I pulled him against me. I brushed my lips over his damp cheek, the shell of his ear, and his forehead and just whispered soft words to him, mostly about how I would have stopped the man from hurting him and that he was safe now.

But even as I said the words, bile crawled up the back of my throat. I'd had the chance to save Aleks so he wouldn't be hurt anymore and I hadn't done it… not quickly enough, anyway. And he most certainly wasn't safe now.

Aleks held onto me for a while and when he began speaking to me again, he did it against my chest, which was just fine with me.

"The man didn't like that my English wasn't better, so he brought in a woman to teach me how to read and write it. But no other subjects. I didn't understand why."

I did. The men who dealt in kids like Aleks viewed them as the most luxurious of amenities. Being able to understand and respond to his tormentor in English would have added value just like adding leather seats or specialty tires on a car did.

"Her name was Miss Penny. She always looked so... *scared*," Aleks murmured. "The man, he told me what would happen to me if I asked her for help or told her he wasn't really my cousin like he'd said. But..."

"But?" I encouraged when he fell silent.

"I think she knew," he finally admitted. "We weren't left alone very often but when we were, she'd quietly ask me questions about my 'cousin.' But I never said anything. Until one day when she... she brought me a book about flowers. I wasn't allowed to have any toys or books and that's what I told her."

"How old were you?" I asked.

"Um, I'm not really sure... ten maybe. I'd been with Brian for a while."

Brian. Finally, a name I could attach to the bastard. I automatically vowed to kill any fucker in my dark world named Brian. Even if he wasn't the one who'd hurt Aleks, he was hurting some kid somewhere.

"It wasn't a big book and I really wanted it, so I accepted it and hid it. I... I didn't know Brian had found it."

Aleks began to shake violently and since his body was against mine, I could feel his skin grow chilled. I pushed him back a bit so I could look at him. His eyes were starting to go blank.

"Aleks, stay with me," I urged as I cupped the side of his face with my hand. "Aleks," I said firmly when he began to drift away even more. It wasn't until I practically yelled his name that I saw him come back to me. "Breathe," I commanded. He took in a huge breath and slumped in my hold, like he'd been holding his breath for minutes, not seconds.

"What happened to Miss Penny, Aleks?" I asked, since I knew the woman was a part of this. I also instinctively knew what had happened to her... it wasn't hard to guess. As bad as what had happened to Aleks had been after he'd been taken, it was likely the events surrounding the teacher that had jump-started the extreme coping method he'd come to rely on so heavily.

Aleks began shaking his head violently. I grabbed him by the upper arms. "What happened to her, Aleks?" I repeated firmly. If he didn't start getting some of this shit out, he'd never be able to start dealing with it.

"Brian came into the room during our lesson. He had the book. He asked me if Miss Penny had given it to me. I... I..."

"What, Aleks? What did you do?"

"I lied to him. I told him no." Aleks squeezed his eyes and suddenly yelled, "But he *knew* and he said Miss Penny would have to pay for my lies! He let one of his men hurt her! I yelled at Brian to make it stop... that I was sorry, and I'd never lie again but the man just kept hurting her and she was crying and begging him to stop."

Aleks began sobbing. As badly as I wanted to end this, I knew I couldn't. "Finish it, baby," I whispered as I stroked his hair with one hand. His face was covered in tears, and snot and spit were sliding down his mouth and chin. He could barely get the words out.

"Bri... Bri... Brian asked me again if Miss Penny gave me the book and I said yes. Miss Penny was sitting in the chair on the other side of the table and she looked at me. I started to tell her I was sorry, but then there was a bang and blood was everywhere and I couldn't see her eyes anymore."

Aleks slapped a hand over his eyes. "He left me in the room with her all night... he... he left the book. He said I could keep it. I... I kept telling her I was sorry and then I started reading the book to her because I knew she was probably cold and scared..."

I couldn't understand his words after that so I pulled him back against my chest. I let my hand pass over his hair as I whispered to him that it wasn't his fault. When he'd quieted, I asked, "Were there other teachers after that?"

He nodded against me.

"Did he hurt any of them?"

Aleks shook his head. It took a good fifteen seconds before he whispered, "No... because I was good."

I let out a soft rush of air as I realized that moment had defined his thinking going forward. If he wanted to live, if he wanted others to live, he needed to be good, he needed to listen and do as he was told.

I held him until *he* was the one to pull back. He wiped at his face but refused to look at me. "What's wrong with me?"

I used my fingers to lift his chin. "Absolutely nothing," I said softly. His eyes shifted to meet mine and I couldn't help but hold his gaze as I trailed my thumb over the softness of his lips. He was a mess, but he was still the most beautiful thing I'd ever seen.

And even more off-limits to me.

I needed to remember that and I needed to make this about him and not my ill-timed bout of desire.

"Aleks, have you ever talked to someone about what happened to you?"

He seemed to know what I was talking about because he dropped his eyes and then carefully pulled away from me. He turned so he was facing forward in the seat. He shook his head but said nothing.

"Do you know what PTSD is?" I asked.

That got his attention.

"Like what the soldiers go through when they come home?" he asked, his expression lifting in surprise. "I… I don't have that. They see terrible things… they're forced to do terrible things. Magnus said that they can't always relate to civ… civ…"

"Civilian life," I said.

He nodded.

"Magnus says that their minds play tricks on them when they come home but that it isn't their fault and it's okay for them to ask for help."

So Magnus had suspected what Aleks was suffering from and had tried to tell the young man in a roundabout way…

It took Aleks a moment to figure things out. His mouth pulled into a frown. "I don't have that," he repeated. "You're wrong. I've… I've been doing normal things since I left Father's house."

"Yes, you have, and you've done an incredible job. But PTSD isn't something you can just will away, Aleks. Talking to someone will help you figure out what your triggers are and how to cope—"

"No!" Aleks shouted, then seemed to remember shouting wasn't something he was allowed to do. "No," he repeated as his agitation grew. "I'm fine. I'm okay… Dante… he's proud of me because I'm doing so good…"

I fell silent as he pretty much answered all of my questions with that one statement.

He doesn't want to disappoint his brother.

It made me wonder how much he was still hiding from Dante. And if he was pushing himself too hard in an effort to make his brother proud.

So his brother wouldn't regret coming to get him.

"Can we please just go, Vaughn?" Aleks asked as he turned away from me and stared out the window.

"Aleks—"

"Please," he repeated, his voice sounding hoarse.

I sighed and reached out to graze his cheek with my fingers, but he seemed to be expecting the move and pulled away.

So we were back where we'd started before we'd stopped for breakfast.

Fuck.

Chapter 8

ALEKS

I'M SORRY, MISS PENNY.

Aleks, if you'd only been good they wouldn't have hurt me...

I jerked awake at the sound of Miss Penny's voice. She hadn't spoken after Brian had left the room. I'd apologized dozens of times, but she'd never once spoken. I'd known why, of course, but my mind had tried to convince me she'd just been sleeping. Even when the man who'd worked for Brian had come to take her away, I'd kept right on reading. When Brian had come to get me later that morning, he'd led me to his bedroom, washed me off in his big bathtub and then had tucked me into his bed and told me how much he would have missed me if Miss Penny had tried to take me away from him. When his touch had stopped being about comfort, I'd silently begun repeating the names of the flowers and their meanings from Miss Penny's book and within seconds I'd slipped away to my safe place on the beach with my family. After a long day spent building that epic sand castle, I'd fallen asleep on the sand and when I'd awoken, I'd been alone in Brian's bed.

And Miss Penny had still been gone.

As the present returned full-force, I tried to catch my breath and immediately reached across the console to look for Vaughn's hand. But it wasn't there.

Because we weren't in the car anymore.

There was no console, but Vaughn *was* next to me. Only, we were in bed.

Together.

Again.

Like the night before.

This time, though, Vaughn was asleep. Whereas I'd been lying flat and under the covers, Vaughn was sitting up, his back against the headboard. His hands were folded in his lap. On the nightstand was a gun sitting on top of a laptop computer.

Had I blacked out? Was Vaughn actually right about all that?

I shook my head.

No, I was okay… I was on my way back to being normal. Well, normal enough.

Dante was so proud of how well I was doing. I could see it in his eyes every time I did something like leave for work or make a decision about something.

Vaughn was wrong.

He just had to be.

I struggled to remember the events of the day. It took a moment but things finally became clearer as my breathing evened out. I'd stopped talking to Vaughn after he'd said those things to me. I wasn't sure how many hours we'd driven for after that, but when he'd asked me what I wanted to eat for lunch, then eventually dinner, I'd politely told him I wasn't hungry.

Fortunately, he hadn't tried to make me eat because I wasn't sure I would have been able to survive the humiliation of throwing up in front of the man twice in twenty-four hours.

It had once again been dark when he'd pulled off the interstate. I'd had no idea where we were and I'd been too tired to care. I'd only heard Vaughn briefly say the house belonged to a friend of his and that we were safe there as he'd shown me to the bedroom. I'd made use of the bathroom and then I'd crawled into the bed and couldn't remember anything after that.

But luckily only because I'd been asleep.

Not because I'd blacked out.

Because I was normal... I didn't have that thing Vaughn said I did.

He was wrong.

He just was.

I glanced at him, then the clock on the nightstand. It was just after three in the morning. There was a small lamp on the nightstand that was turned on, but it didn't offer much light. I could see that the room we were in seemed a little more modern than the room we'd spent the previous night in, but it didn't look particularly fancy. There was what looked like an old-fashioned fan on the dresser that was turned on and made a soft whirring sound that broke up the silence of the room.

I turned to look at the nightstand on my side of the bed and stilled at the sight of a small bottle of chocolate milk sitting there.

It was open and empty.

I vaguely remembered Vaughn stopping at a gas station shortly before we'd gotten to the house, but I hadn't noticed him buying the milk.

And when had I drunk it?

I couldn't remember that.

God, what was wrong with me? Why did everything seem so muddled in my head?

I glanced at Vaughn again. I wanted to ask him if things would ever just go back to the way they'd been before those men had grabbed me. I hadn't exactly been living a dream life but considering all that had happened and compared to what I was going through now, I might as well have been on top of the world.

I missed Dante.

And Magnus.

And Matty.

I felt tears threaten but refused to let them fall. My eyes hurt so bad from all the crying that if I shed even one more tear, I'd probably never be able to close my eyes again.

I wondered if Vaughn would let me call Dante again in the

morning. My brother had to be going crazy with worry and Magnus would be doing his best to keep Dante calm. Vaughn shifted slightly but it wasn't until he whispered, "I'm sorry, Aleks" that I turned to look at him, fully expecting him to be watching me.

But he was still asleep.

Which meant… God, was he dreaming about me?

He'd turned his head so one side was pressed against the headboard and he was facing in my direction. My eyes fell to his mouth, which was slightly open.

Why was he even in bed with me again? Had I been having bad dreams again? Before the one that had woken me up?

"Aleks…"

He said my name on a soft sigh and my body responded to it. I didn't really know what was happening, but I couldn't say it was a bad feeling exactly. But I didn't like how my lower half was reacting. My penis was tightening uncomfortably in my pants. It wasn't the first time it had happened, but it was the first time the sensation kept getting stronger and the urge to touch myself started filtering through my head.

I wasn't completely naïve – I knew what it meant when that part of a man's body hardened. But I knew also that that kind of a reaction usually meant *I* would be the one to pay for it. I didn't know what it meant that I was the one experiencing that particular thing. I did know it had only ever happened around Vaughn, though.

After Dante had gotten me back to Seattle, he'd explained to me that he and Magnus planned to spend the rest of their lives together, just like Mama and Papa. I'd known my brother liked both boys and girls when we'd been younger, and it hadn't ever bothered me, but admittedly, after all the things that had been done to me, I couldn't imagine why my brother liked being with another man.

Maybe it didn't work the same when two people loved each other?

I'd never been brave enough to ask Dante, because then I would have had to answer questions. I knew that he knew what had happened to me but that didn't mean I wanted to talk about it in detail.

Besides, not everybody had to want that kind of thing, right? Brian and Father and all the other men had used their bodies to hurt mine, so any man who wanted to be with me like that again would just do the same, wouldn't they?

Did Vaughn want me like that?

If he did, would he care that I didn't want it? Would he hurt me anyway?

My head began to hurt as I tried to make sense of things. I willed my body to go back to being normal but when Vaughn's hand slid over his own stomach, drawing up his shirt a little in the process, my mouth suddenly felt like it had been stuffed full of cotton. He wasn't pale and soft like Father had been. His skin was darker, but not as dark as mine, and there was just a little bit of black hair that trailed down his body and disappeared into his pants. Would the hair feel the same as the hair on his beard? I automatically looked up at his face again. A strange itchiness began running through my fingers, then up my arms and out to the rest of my body.

I knew I should get up and go to the bathroom, so I could wash my hands and face with cold water to help clear my mind, but my body wouldn't listen to the silent command. Instead, I found myself shifting so I was sitting cross-legged at the head of the bed. I leaned my upper body against the headboard so I could see Vaughn's face straight on. I actually found myself waiting for him to say my name again.

I couldn't stop looking at his mouth. Even with the beard, his lips looked really full and soft. I dropped my eyes to the spot on his chest where the top couple of buttons on his shirt were undone. There was some black hair there too. I chanced a look at his forearms which were exposed by drawn-up sleeves. The tattoo on his right arm looked like a cross, though it was very intricate in its design and it looked like there were angel wings coming out the two shorter sides.

Before I could even ask myself what I was doing, I ran my finger along the arm he had resting on his stomach. When I realized what I'd done, I jerked my hand back. But he didn't wake and the memory of how warm his skin had been was already etched into my brain. I wanted to touch him there again, but I knew it was wrong, so I didn't.

I told myself to just go back to sleep, but something about watching him sleep calmed me. Maybe because *he* looked so calm. It wasn't that he seemed out of control or anything like that when he was awake… more like he was always too much in control. At first, I'd thought him more like Magnus in that he seemed like someone who was naturally relaxed and laid back, but the more I thought about it, Vaughn seemed like he was always looking for something. And that the calm demeanor was a mask.

So he was calm, but not relaxed.

I thought back to the night he'd shot Father. He'd killed so easily, like he'd been born to it. But for some reason, my mind was trying to convince me that wasn't who he was.

He reminded me of Dante in that sense – like he wanted to appear one way on the surface, but beneath was someone else entirely. And if you didn't look hard enough to get past that hard shell, you'd miss what was inside.

"Should've stopped it," Vaughn suddenly whispered, and his expression drew into a frown. "I'm sorry, Aleks. So sorry."

He actually began whimpering deep in his throat and the fingers he had resting on his stomach began twitching.

He was having a nightmare.

And I was part of it.

When he said my name again, it sounded like he was suffering the worst kind of torment.

I knew that torment.

I'd lived it.

I reached my hand out to settle it on his cheek. "Vaughn," I said softly as I leaned into him, so I could talk to him without waking him up. "I'm safe. It's okay."

"Aleks," he breathed again. The creases in his forehead relaxed just a bit, indicating he'd heard me. I began rubbing my thumb across his cheekbone to try and soothe him. The wiry but still soft hairs of his beard brushed against my palm in the most intriguing of ways.

"Sleep, Vaughn," I said softly.

"Gotta get you out," he responded.

Something inside my chest twisted, then exploded. I didn't understand this man and his words and I needed to stay angry so I wouldn't do something foolish and start trusting him again.

But who was I kidding?

Just like the first time he'd handed me a piece of butterscotch and told me everything would be okay, I knew he wasn't doing any of this to hurt me or manipulate me or trick me. I didn't understand how I could so easily give so much of myself to this virtual stranger, but it was in line with the same feelings I'd had as a child when Brian had tried to convince me that Dante didn't love me and he wasn't coming for me. I'd eventually allowed myself to stop waiting for Dante, but deep down, I'd always known he would come for me. I just hadn't believed he'd be able to actually find me.

That same strange faith kept me tied to Vaughn. All the facts said I shouldn't trust him and that I should call Dante and just go home, but it wasn't just the inevitable danger I'd be putting my brother and my family in that had kept me with Vaughn.

It was something... *more*.

The warmth in my chest began to spread throughout my limbs and for the first time in forever, I felt like I was really okay. The past fell away, so did the future – it was just me and Vaughn and this one moment and I wanted to enjoy it.

"Vaughn," I repeated softly until his body stopped moving. He sighed and completely relaxed. I lifted my hand to smooth out the last of the creases on his forehead. My finger moved of its own accord over one perfectly shaped eyebrow, then down the bridge of his nose. The hair beneath his nose tickled my finger and I found myself smiling for no reason at all. Then I was touching his lips and the humor died off as my insides got all tight and hot. My groin ached as my penis grew harder.

Cock.

That was what the men had always called that part of themselves.

They'd made the word vile and ugly. I wondered if it would be the same with Vaughn if he told me he was going to stick his cock inside of me.

Did I want that?

No, definitely not.

Did *he* want that?

I wasn't sure.

Would it change things if he did? I'd suffered through it before with other men because I'd had to. I'd had no choice. But if Vaughn gave me a choice? If it meant I could have moments like these where I felt normal and safe, and something as simple as touching the little hairs under his nose made me smile, would it be worth it? And what did it mean that *my* body was reacting? Did that change anything?

The confusing thoughts swirled around in my head as I let my eyes follow the line my finger drew along the seam of Vaughn's mouth.

What would it feel like against mine?

I knew what a kiss was. I'd seen Mama and Papa do it… Dante and Magnus too. But it wasn't something I'd ever done or even wanted to.

Had that somehow changed too?

Vaughn's mouth moved almost imperceptibly beneath my finger and I immediately looked up. The second that I saw his eyes were open, I went to snatch my hand back.

"I'm sorry!" I cried.

Vaughn grabbed my wrist before I could draw my hand away from his face.

"It's okay," he quickly said. He didn't move even a little, but his hold on me was firm. I could have gotten away if I'd wanted to, but I would have had to put some effort into it.

And something about the way he was looking at me had me forgetting I was supposed to be doing just that.

He held my wrist but didn't try to force me to touch him.

I did that all on my own after about fifteen seconds of the two of us just staring at one another. I didn't go for his lip right away, but my finger eventually found its way there anyway. And it was so much more intense with Vaughn staring at me like he was.

I couldn't look away from him.

Between touching him and his eyes refusing to let me go, I was completely ensnared and I didn't care.

"I'm sorry," I said softly.

"For what?" he asked just as quietly, his mouth moving against my finger. I slid the pad down his chin.

"It was wrong to touch you while you were sleeping," I said. Despite my apology, I couldn't force myself to pull my hand away. He was still holding my wrist but wasn't guiding my hand at all.

More like following it.

And his thumb was doing delicious things to the inside of my wrist.

My hand made its way to his throat and he let out a rush of air. "For future reference," he said with a slight smile. "You can touch me anytime you want."

His words surprised me.

"Why?" I blurted.

Vaughn's eyes held mine for the longest time. "Don't you know, Aleks?" he asked.

The intensity with the way he said my name made me shudder. "Because it feels good?" I asked dumbly, because I honestly didn't have any other answer.

Something flashed in his gaze and then he smiled again. "It does," he said. "But that's not why."

I managed not to pull back when his left hand came up to settle on the back of my neck. He used his thumb to tip my chin up just a bit so I was forced to look at him. I didn't realize I'd dropped my eyes at some point.

The smile faded and he just stared at me for the longest time. I forgot what we were even talking about until he said, "Because I would give you anything, Aleks." His fingers tightened on the back of my neck just the tiniest bit. "Anything," he repeated, his voice growing thick.

Something inside of me went off like a bomb and my already

tingling body grew hot and heavy. And then his mouth was moving toward mine. Fear and anticipation warred as I waited for him to kiss me.

But when his mouth bypassed mine and settled next to my ear, I felt a keen and completely unexpected pang of disappointment.

"Go to sleep, Aleks. I'm going to fix everything tomorrow, I promise."

He turned my head just a tiny bit and then his lips settled on my pulse point, which had to be hammering since my heart was racing like nobody's business. I gasped when his warm mouth pressed the gentlest of kisses against my skin.

"Aleks," he breathed as he lifted his mouth to my ear. "Please... would you... would you call me James... just this one time?"

James.

His first name.

I'd never heard anyone call him that. What did it mean that he wanted me to? And why just this once?

I wanted to ask him those things but found myself pressing my forehead against his instead. "James," I said in the barest of whispers.

He sighed – actually sighed – and then kissed the shell of my ear. But somehow just saying his name the one time wasn't enough for me.

"I trust you, James."

He let out a little gasp of air, then he was drawing me into his arms. His hand came up to cradle the back of my head. I loved how his arms were so big that they just completely enveloped me.

"I won't let you down, Aleks. I swear it."

And with that, he shifted us until we were both lying flat on the bed. He pulled me against his side and even though I'd never once slept with another soul in a bed besides my parents and Dante, I'd never felt more comfortable. Vaughn's fingers played with my hair, putting me to sleep within minutes. When I woke up, the clock showed that it was just after eight in the morning and both Vaughn, his gun and his computer were gone and just the utility knife was on the nightstand. But I knew in my gut he hadn't left me. I quickly got out of bed and made use of the bathroom. It took me a moment to figure out that I was actually on the second floor of a two-story house, but I had no trouble confirming Vaughn was still indeed there.

Because I could hear his raised voice and the anger in it was clear as day.

As was that of the anger in the voice of whoever he was arguing with.

Chapter 9

VAUGHN

I HEARD THE CAR COMING UP THE DRIVEWAY AS I WAS LEAVING THE bathroom. I'd ended up sleeping through the alarm I'd set, which was extremely unusual for me. Of course, I'd never had the pleasure of sleeping with Aleks before, so I couldn't exactly be upset about it. But oversleeping meant I hadn't been able to enjoy the sensation of just lying there with Aleks in my arms. I would have expected him to move away from me at some point during the night, but he'd been wrapped around me like a vine. Fortunately, my body hadn't had too much time to react to that fact other than my normal morning erection. But as soon as I'd awoken to Aleks's soft breath against my neck and his fingers pressed into my side, my dick had responded accordingly.

The night before had been both a near disaster and a nightmare. The nightmare had come first. Aleks hadn't spoken to me most of the previous day as we'd made our way south and he'd refused to eat or drink anything. When we'd gotten to our destination, he'd been so exhausted he'd been on autopilot and he'd been out cold within seconds of his head hitting the pillow. I'd actually had to take his shoes off. It'd still been pretty early, so I'd gone to the kitchen to eat the sandwich I'd bought for myself from the gas station, though I hadn't been particularly hungry. I'd also returned a couple of phone calls to some sick fucks who were in the market for "protection," but I hadn't done more than tell the assholes I wasn't currently available. In a world like mine, that just made me more attractive and coveted. Even if I hadn't been dealing with the situation with Aleks, my answer would have been the same. By being seemingly unavailable, my reputation actually strengthened because the assholes were making up their own reasons for what I was up to. As far as they were concerned, I was getting rid of witnesses or rivals for whatever degenerate I was working for. Little did they know it was all smoke and mirrors and it'd all been carefully constructed to catch a much bigger fish than any of them.

But all that was in jeopardy now because I needed to make sure Aleks was safe first.

I asked him to call me James…

What the fuck had I been thinking?

About any of it?

I hadn't been thinking and fuck if that hadn't been amazing. I'd just been feeling.

Just.

I almost laughed at that because that word made it seem like such a simple thing.

After the nightmare of Aleks once again hating me, I'd woken up to my dream come true because Aleks had been touching me and he hadn't seemed scared. Then it had been a near disaster because I'd almost kissed him.

I'd only managed to come to my senses at the last second. Then I'd gotten all vulnerable and needy and asked him to call me by my first name.

No one ever called me James.

The last and only person had been my stepmother and that had been a lifetime ago.

I'd always been Vaughn… just Vaughn.

I sighed as I tucked my gun into the waistband of my pants. I needed to get this thing with Aleks under control. He wasn't in any position to deal with any of this. I'd only ended up in the bed with him again because he'd had another nightmare. I'd managed to get him to drink some chocolate milk that I'd bought him from the gas station and then he'd fallen back asleep. I'd stayed in the bed to work on my computer for a bit until I was sure he was okay, but instead of going to sleep in one of the other rooms, I'd fallen asleep myself.

And woken up to Aleks's gentle touch.

I was just entering the kitchen when the side door opened. I felt relief at the sight of the man who entered, but as soon as I saw who was behind him, I drew my gun and pointed it at both men. The betrayal sliced through me like a knife, but I didn't have time to focus on any of that because I knew they wouldn't be alone.

"Hey, hold up," Con said as he put his hands up. My friend had his long black hair pulled back like he normally did and I could see bruises on his face from his most recent match. But I wasn't interested in him. It was the other man that I pointed the gun at. "We're just here to talk," Con said.

"Is that so?" I asked coldly as I tracked the moves of the man behind Con. His eyes were dark with anger and his expression was pulled into the familiar frown that had become his new normal in the past eight years. "Is that what your men were doing in Seattle?" I asked him, ignoring Con in the process. "They were there to just *talk* to Aleks?"

"Don't act like *I'm* the one who betrayed *you* in all this," he responded, his voice ice cold.

"Luca," Con said as he stepped between us. Not surprisingly, Luca was completely lacking in concern when it came to the gun I had pointed at him. To me Con said, "Vaughn, it's just me and him. I made sure he left his phone in Vegas and I've been with him ever since. He's not armed, and he hasn't been able to call anyone and didn't know why we were coming here until we were in the driveway and I told him."

"And I'm supposed to just believe that?" I asked.

"Yes, you are," Con responded tightly. "Because *you* called *me* for help, remember? Because you knew you could come to me out of everyone!"

"And this is how you help? You bring *him* here? You bring him straight to Aleks? Did he even tell you what his plans for Aleks were?" I snarled.

"He doesn't need to!" Con snapped. "Because I know him and I know you and I know *this* is not what you're about!" He waved at the combative stances Luca and I had each taken and I felt a sting of regret along with my fury.

Luca suddenly pushed past Con and walked right up to me, putting his chest against the gun. "You started this when you fucking lied to me and chose *him* over your own blood!"

I dropped the gun and punched Luca. He didn't go down but he did stumble backward. He didn't look overly surprised that I'd hit him.

"And you knew he was off-limits! I never asked for one goddamned thing from you, Luca! Not once in the eight years I've been doing this! All you had to do was leave him the fuck out of it!"

I didn't try to avoid Luca's fist. Not surprisingly, Con didn't intervene. It wasn't what any of us wanted. As close as Luca and I had always been, sometimes we'd resorted to making our point with our fists.

"Don't act like I forced you into any of this!" he bit out. "Two years, Vaughn! Two years you've been lying to me! And who's paid for that, huh?" he spat. "My son, that's who!" Luca took another swing at me but this time Con got between us and shoved Luca back. "Every day you protected that boy was another day my child suffered! Was he really such a good fuck that—"

I was on Luca before he could finish the question. By the time Con managed to pull me off, Luca and I were both bleeding. I'd dropped my gun in the melee, but despite what Luca had done, he and I both knew I wouldn't use it on him.

"We're no longer brothers!" I said softly. To Con I said, "Get him out of here."

"So you would just abandon your own nephew?" Luca asked as he wiped his face on his sleeve. He sounded uncharacteristically uncertain. He was one of the strongest, most ruthless men I knew, but I almost didn't recognize him in that moment.

"No, you asshole," I responded. "I'll find Gio no matter what it takes. But I'm not sacrificing Aleks or any other victim to do it! But when we get your son home, you and I are through!"

I looked at Con and said, "I hope trying to play peacemaker was worth it."

"Vaughn," Con began, but I turned away.

"Get out," I said quietly, then headed for the entrance so I could go upstairs and get Aleks. We needed to get the hell out of there before Luca could find a way to get reinforcements.

But I didn't need to head upstairs to find Aleks.

Because he was standing in stunned silence in the entryway to the kitchen. And I knew instantly that he'd heard everything.

Chapter 10

ALEKS

"Aleks—"

When he reached for me, I couldn't help but step back. The trust I'd so unfailingly given back to him the night before felt like it had been obliterated in the last two minutes.

They were brothers.

Vaughn's nephew was the one who'd been taken just like me.

And Vaughn's brother had been the one who'd had me kidnapped again.

"Oh God," I whispered as I took another step back. I ended up in the front room of the house. The door was *right there*. Thankfully, for once, my body overruled my brain and I did something I hadn't done enough of in my life.

I ran.

But Vaughn caught me before I could get the door open.

"No!" I shouted.

"Aleks," he began as he grabbed my arm. Then the gun was suddenly in his hand, but he didn't point it at me. Amazingly, he pointed it at the other two men who had followed us into the front entryway. "Don't either of you fucking move," he practically snarled. I'd never seen or heard him so angry.

Until a few seconds ago when he'd been fighting with the one named Luca.

His own brother.

I tried to catch my breath as bits and pieces of that argument came back to me.

You knew he was off-limits! I never asked for one goddamned thing from you, Luca! Not once in the eight years I've been doing this! All you had to do was leave him the fuck out of it...

What did that mean?

"Aleks—"

"Talk fast, Vaughn," I said. "Because you're scaring me and you promised me last night you wouldn't let me down and I believed you—"

"The men who took you from the alley the other night weren't his men," Vaughn interrupted.

"But you said he had plans for me."

Vaughn's eyes remained on Luca and the other man as he spoke. "His men were there too. That's why I couldn't get to you before the men in the van grabbed you."

I shook my head. "I don't understand," I admitted. My head felt like it was going to explode. I could feel the chill settling over my skin, beckoning me to the darkness. It would be so easy.

"No, Aleks, stay with me," Vaughn said desperately as he gave me a little shake. I felt his hand cup my cheek. "Baby, please, just stay with me."

I forced myself to take several deep breaths in order to stave off the blackness that was lining the edge of my vision. I managed a nod.

"When I got to Seattle, I recognized Luca's men sitting in a sedan on a side street near your shop. I wasn't expecting to see them there," he said, his eyes going dark as he snapped his eyes back to his brother. "I disabled them, but I didn't know what was happening in the alley."

"Disabled... like you did with the guys in the van?" I asked. Bile churned in my belly. As much as I'd hated those men and I was grateful to Vaughn for saving me, it had been a gruesome sight.

"No," Vaughn said. "I knocked them out. I know both men and I know Luca… he wouldn't have let them hurt you."

I didn't miss the fact that there was more to that sentence than he was saying. He clearly believed that his brother's men had been given orders to take me just like the men in the van.

"I managed to catch up to the van, but I needed to wait until it was far enough outside the city to make sure those men were alone. Then I pulled ahead of them and parked my car in the middle of the road to force them to stop. You know the rest."

I nodded. I hesitated and risked a glance at Luca, whose face was as bloody as Vaughn's. But despite the cuts and bruises, he looked unaffected.

And very dangerous.

I automatically sidled closer to Vaughn.

"They took his son?" I whispered.

"Yes," Vaughn said. "Gio. It happened eight years ago. Gio was seven."

I felt my knees go weak.

A whole year younger than me.

"And you're trying to find him?"

Vaughn wiped at his face with his gun hand, smearing the blood. The second he was done, the gun was trained on the two other men again. "Yes. We knew our only chance of finding Gio was by getting in on the ground level."

"I don't know what that means."

"Vaughn went undercover," the other man who wasn't Luca said. He was nearly the same size as Vaughn and Luca and had the same dark hair, but it was long on top and pulled into a ponytail. The sides of his head were shaved. He had a little bit of dark stubble. Unlike Luca and Vaughn, his skin tone was darker, though. His jeans and dark blue T-shirt were a stark contrast to the dress clothes both Vaughn and Luca were wearing.

"This is Con," Vaughn said as he motioned to the man. "Constantine. Luca and I grew up with him and his brothers, King and Lex."

Con sent me a small nod and said, "Vaughn was the best

equipped of all of us to look for Gio from the inside. Luca's name was too recognizable."

I didn't know what that meant, but I didn't care either. To Vaughn I said, "What does he mean 'you looked from the inside'?"

"I started pawning myself off as hired muscle," Vaughn said.

I felt like I was going to throw up. "You... you helped men like Father keep their secrets?" I whispered.

"Yes," Vaughn said.

"No," Luca cut in at the same time. "It was an act," Vaughn's brother said. "He never directly hurt any kids and he'd pass the information about the kids back to me. I'd send someone in to get them out as soon as Vaughn had moved onto the next client."

It took me a moment to process what Luca had said. When I spoke, it was to Vaughn and only Vaughn. "But you had to wait to get them out until you'd gone to work for someone else?"

"Yes," Vaughn whispered, and I could tell he knew where my mind was going.

I pulled away from him because it was hard to think when he was touching me. "So, when you worked for Father all those months, you weren't really working for him. But you didn't try to help me..."

My voice dropped off as everything clicked into place.

"I'm sorry, Aleks," Vaughn said softly. "I didn't have a choice."

I let out a harsh laugh. "Yes, you did. *I* was the one who couldn't choose, Vaughn." I shook my head in disbelief. "All those weeks you knew what he was doing and you had the power to stop it but you didn't. You... you..."

I couldn't even put words to what he'd done. "I want to go," I said as I reached behind me to try and find the knob for the door. But to my own horror, I'd moved in the wrong direction and was closer to the stairs than the door.

And Vaughn was between me and the only way out.

"Aleks," he began.

"No," I said, shaking my head violently. "I want to go home." I backed further toward the stairs. "I want to go home. To Dante."

I was on the verge of having a complete breakdown. I wanted to believe Vaughn wouldn't hurt me or turn me over to his brother, but I didn't know what to think anymore. If I'd been looking at the blue sky and Vaughn had told me it was red, I would have believed him.

He'd done that to me... played me so well I didn't even know which direction was up and which was down.

Aleks... please... would you... would you call me James... just this one time?

I clapped my hands over my ears and began shaking my head. "No," I shouted. The darkness came for me and this time I let it in.

"Don't fucking touch him!" I heard Vaughn shout and then there was more yelling, but I couldn't make out the words. A hand closed painfully around my wrist.

"Aleks, open your eyes, damn it!"

Not Vaughn's voice.

"Get your fucking hands off him, Luca!"

Vaughn sounded so distressed that I opened my eyes to look for him. He was trying to get Con to let go of his gun arm. The one holding onto me was Luca and I was no longer by the stairs but in the kitchen. There was blood on my shirt... Vaughn's too-big shirt, actually, because I hadn't put my own shirt back on yet.

Had I been shot? Was that why I was so cold?

"Vaughn?" I whispered in confusion.

"Aleks, put the knife down." The order came from Luca.

Knife? What knife? I looked at the arm he was holding the wrist of, but my hand was empty.

But my other wasn't.

I gasped at the sight of Vaughn's utility knife in my right hand. I'd grabbed it off the nightstand when I'd left the room earlier. My intent had been to give it back to Vaughn, but I'd forgotten all about it when I'd heard him, Luca, and Con fighting.

Hadn't that been a few seconds ago?

I shook my head to try to clear it. Vaughn was shouting at me and Luca. I watched in horror as he slammed his fist into Con's jaw. I was so distracted that I didn't notice Luca move until he grabbed for the hand that was holding the knife. Everything happened so fast I couldn't keep up. One second Luca was grabbing my wrist, the next Vaughn was standing over us, his gun pressed against the side of Luca's head.

"Take your hands off him!" he snarled.

But Luca didn't release me.

That was when I registered the blood pouring from Vaughn's forearm.

The blood that was also on the knife I was still holding.

"Look, Aleks!" Luca yelled at me. "Look at how far he will go for you, no matter what! He's never betrayed you! You could put that thing in his fucking gut next time and he'd still lay down and die for you!"

"Luca!" Vaughn warned.

I looked between Vaughn, Luca and the knife.

And then dropped it when an image flashed through my head. "No," I cried in a broken whisper as I realized what I'd done.

The knife clattered to the floor and then Luca was pushing it away before completely releasing me and backing away, both hands in the air as he faced his brother. Vaughn was on his knees in front of me a second later. "Aleks, it's okay," he said. "You're okay."

I wasn't okay.

I'd hurt him.

I'd cut his arm open with the knife and I barely remembered any of it.

"I'm sorry," I cried as I tried to get away from him.

I really was going crazy.

"Nothing to be sorry for," Vaughn said gently as he tucked the gun into his waistband. "It's barely a scratch."

I let out a hoarse laugh that wasn't really even a laugh. Blood was still gushing from the wound, but he barely even seemed to notice.

"Vaughn," I said with a shake of my head.

"It's okay, baby," Vaughn said, then he was pulling me against his chest. "We're both okay," he repeated over and over. I was dimly aware of Con tying something around the arm Vaughn had wrapped around me, but he didn't let me go during the process.

"I don't know what's happening to me," I admitted.

"I do," Vaughn said as he put just enough space between us so he could cup the sides of my face. "Your mind's finally ready to start fighting back," he murmured softly.

I didn't know what that meant, but I was too tired to give it much consideration. I leaned back into him. "I think the blood loss has made you as crazy as me," I whispered.

I swore I felt him smile against me right before he kissed the top of my head. "I'm good with that."

Chapter 11

VAUGHN

"Knock it off, Luca," I snapped as I eyed my brother. Aleks jumped at the sound of my voice and his eyes flitted from where Con was stitching up my arm to where Luca was sitting on the opposite side of the kitchen table. Luca shot me a brittle look before he stood and began moving.

Pacing.

Not something he did often.

That would have meant showing actual emotion and my brother just didn't do that.

Showing emotion was like exposing one's throat in our world.

It was a trait that had only worsened for him in the years since Gio had been taken.

"Stay on that side," I said as Luca looked like he was going to expand his movements to the side of the table Aleks and I were sitting on. I still had my gun out and while I wasn't pointing it at Luca, it was lying on the table in front of me and aimed in his general direction. Despite the fact that he hadn't tried to grab Aleks and use him against me when he'd had the chance, I didn't trust him for even a second.

Luca frowned at me like he was surprised by the command but

remained on his side of the table. The fingers on his right hand were twitching and I knew why.

Yeah, he was definitely in a bad way.

But any pity I normally would have felt for him had been made obsolete the moment he'd sent his men after Aleks.

I glanced at the young man next to me. He was trembling, but I didn't dare reach for him. I was still reeling from his attack on me. I didn't care that he'd cut me – I was actually happy he'd finally defended himself. But to know *I'd* pushed him to a place where his psyche had felt the need to lash out so violently was heartbreaking. Even with all Marcus had done to him, I'd never heard of Aleks ever blacking out and fighting back against the man. But when *I'd* backed him into a corner, both literally and figuratively, he'd responded in the most unexpected way.

"Does it hurt?" Aleks asked softly when my eyes met his. He glanced at where Con was putting in the final stitches. The cut wasn't overly long or deep, but it was bad enough that it wouldn't have stopped bleeding on its own.

"Just stings a little," I said. It wasn't exactly the truth, but Aleks was already feeling a shitload of guilt for what he'd done, and I didn't want to add even another ounce to that.

"He did worse climbing trees in Central Park as a kid," Con said.

Aleks looked briefly at Con, then back at me. "You liked to climb trees?" he asked.

"He loved it," Luca cut in. He was still pacing but wasn't looking at us as he spoke. "He doesn't have a lick of sense when it comes to heights," he muttered. "Our mother called the fire department the first few times he did it because she was sure he couldn't get down. He'd wait until the firemen got all the way up to him with their ladders and then he'd climb right back down the same way he'd gone up... on his own." Luca waved his hand impatiently. "The neighbors actually used to ask him to go up after their damn cat because he could climb higher than any fireman, or anyone else for that matter."

My brother's voice was gruff, but I didn't miss the admiration in it. It made his betrayal just hurt that much more.

"You weren't scared?" Aleks asked me.

I shook my head. "Getting to the top of a tree always made it feel like the next step would be to start flying," I said softly.

"Central Park… that's in New York City, right?" Aleks asked. "I saw it in a movie once and Dante said he and Magnus would take me there one day. They say it has a little bit of everything."

"It does," I acknowledged and was about to offer to show him around someday when I realized he and I would never have a someday. When I figured out how to get him out of this mess, he'd go back to his life and I'd go back to mine. Even on the off chance I found my nephew, I knew I'd never truly be able to get out of the world of kids being trafficked for sex – there were just too many kids like Aleks out there waiting for help to come.

Not to mention I'd never be able to get Aleks's trust back now. I didn't deserve it anyway.

The look on his face when he'd put two and two together and realized I'd left him to Marcus's cruelty, even though I'd had the power to stop it…

Right after that his eyes had gone blank. I'd been trying to talk to him to get him back at the same time that I'd been keeping an eye on Luca and Con, so I hadn't seen him pull my knife from his pocket. When he'd suddenly darted past me, I'd grabbed him because he'd been heading right for Con and Luca. I'd been so stunned by the knife slicing through my skin that I'd released him and he'd run at my brother and friend.

But I suspected he hadn't really even seen them in his altered state of mind. Con had rushed to aid me as I'd tried to catch up to Aleks but when I'd closed my fingers over Aleks's, he'd swung at me with the knife again and I'd barely stepped back out of the way to avoid getting nailed in the side with it.

That was when Luca had intervened.

During the scuffle, Con had grabbed me to keep me from aiming my gun at Luca, probably because he hadn't been certain I wouldn't shoot my own brother to protect Aleks – a fact I hadn't been so sure of myself in that moment – and Luca had grabbed Aleks's arm from behind. Aleks had lashed out at him and the move had taken both men to their knees. Luca had managed to get a hold of the hand Aleks had been holding the knife with.

I'd been certain he'd do what we'd both been trained to do – snap the wrist to disarm Aleks.

That was why I'd knocked Con off me and put my gun to Luca's head.

But unlike Con, my brother had seemed pretty certain I wouldn't shoot him, because he hadn't followed the order. Instead, he'd merely held onto Aleks until he'd managed to talk him out of the blackout that had so disoriented him.

Look at how far he will go for you, no matter what! He's never betrayed you! You could put that thing in his fucking gut next time and he'd still lay down and die for you!

They weren't words I'd ever spoken to my brother, but he'd clearly figured it out from my actions.

I wasn't sure how I felt about that. Aleks had been my weakness from day one and I knew what happened when you had something of value.

You lost it... usually because someone took it from you to use against you.

I'd learned that long before I'd been sucked into the world that had first taken Aleks, then Gio.

But I'd never thought I'd have to worry about protecting something I cherished from my own brother.

Luca and I had a relationship that was anything but traditional, but somehow, despite our father's intent to keep us emotionally disconnected, we'd become closer than any blood bond could have predicted.

I couldn't help but look at Luca again as he paced. Normally, I would have been giving him some kind of reassurances that we'd find Gio and he'd be okay and we'd bring him home. But the words got caught in my throat this time.

He went after Aleks, I reminded myself.

"You're all set," Con said as he tied off the last stitch. I eyed the fresh bruise on his face but before I could apologize, he patted me on the shoulder. Con wasn't my blood, but he might as well have been because my bond with him, King, and Lex was just as strong as it was with Luca... well, *had been*.

I didn't know what the fuck we were now.

Con went to the opposite side of the table after washing his hands and then stepped in Luca's path. He said something softly to my brother that I couldn't hear, then put his hand on his shoulder too. Luca remained stiff for several beats, then nodded. Then he was returning to the chair across from me and Aleks.

Con... ever the peacekeeper. He'd played that role when we'd been kids too. He'd usually been the first to get between me and Luca to break up a fight on the rare occasions when Luca and I hadn't stopped on our own. And since he'd known how to kick ass better than the rest of us, the irony had never been lost on us... and we'd learned early on that when Con told us to knock it the fuck off, we needed to listen.

God, as shitty as my childhood had been, I'd take those days back in a heartbeat.

My eyes met Con's and I said, "If you really want to help me, you'll keep him here until Aleks and I are long gone."

I held Con's gaze, even though I could practically feel Luca's eyes burning a hole through me.

"So you're going to keep running?" Con asked. He looked at Aleks. "Is that what you want, Aleks?"

I managed not to answer for Aleks, despite my instinct to tell Con that what Aleks wanted was his life back.

I looked at Aleks, who seemed surprised at the fact that Con was actually waiting for a response.

"I... I want my family to be safe."

"They will be," I said automatically.

"No, they won't," Luca interjected.

I snapped my eyes to Luca and was about to rip him a new one when Con put his hand on Luca's where it was resting on the table, likely in the hopes of silencing him. But Luca was Luca and said exactly what was on his mind.

"He won't ever be safe, and neither will his family as long as they're still looking for him!" Luca said impatiently to me.

"And you expect me to believe that's why you sent your men after him?" I bit out. "To keep him *safe*?"

"No, I…"

"What?" I yelled when his voice unexpectedly dropped off. "You what?"

Luca opened his mouth to say something, then snapped it shut. His look was icy as he eyed me. Then he shifted his gaze to Aleks. I put my hand over Aleks's where it was resting in his lap because I knew the fear Luca could instill in a person with just a look. I half expected Aleks to push my hand away, but he curled his fingers around mine instead.

"Luca," I warned, but my brother only looked at me for a split second, then his eyes were back on Aleks.

"They had orders not to hurt you," he said, his voice surprisingly soft.

I was about to speak when Aleks's fingers squeezed mine hard.

The silent message rendered me speechless.

"And that makes it okay?" Aleks asked, his voice sounding stronger than I'd ever heard it.

Luca had the grace to look momentarily ashamed. Then he shook his head slowly. "Do you know what was supposed to happen the night you supposedly 'died'?" he asked.

Before I could tell my brother to shut up, Aleks said, "No… what?"

"Marcus was meeting a man who knew where my son was," Luca declared.

"We don't know that for sure," I reminded him.

Luca ignored me and continued. "Vaughn had already made arrangements to get you out the moment that meeting ended and we had the information we needed."

"What information?" Aleks asked.

"The man's identity," Luca said. "Fuck, we didn't even need that… we just needed him to show up somewhere so we could put a tail on him and track him back to whatever hole he crawled out of.

The son of a bitch was a ghost… but he agreed to meet Marcus Parks at his place for one reason and one reason only."

"Luca, don't," I snarled.

"What reason?" Aleks asked, his voice thick with fear.

He already knew the answer.

"You," Luca whispered.

"Jesus, Luca, just shut the fuck up!" I snapped as I got to my feet. I grabbed the gun and suddenly I was the one pacing. "Con, get him the hell out of here!" I shouted. When Con didn't move, I dropped down into a crouch next to Aleks. "Aleks, please, just come with me now. It's not safe to stay here."

Aleks didn't move at first. When he did, he turned just a little so he could look me in the eye. "Why was the man meeting with Father?" he asked.

"It doesn't matter. It's in the past," I said quietly, wishing like hell he would drop it.

"Was Father going to sell me to him?" Aleks asked.

I lowered myself to my knees. "It looks that way," I finally said.

"Why didn't you want him to tell me that?" he asked as he glanced at Luca.

"Because I knew what it would do to you," I answered as I dropped my eyes to his lap. His fingers were lax, but I knew that didn't mean anything.

"What will it do to me?"

"Even though you're safe, you won't be able to stop thinking about what it would have been like… to have to start over with someone new… to think about that fear of needing to learn how to please someone new, to obey them so they wouldn't hurt you. You'll think about how close you came to never seeing your brother or family ever again."

"That's not all," Aleks whispered. "Is it?"

I shook my head.

"Is he… do you think he's the one who sent those men after me?"

When I didn't answer him, I felt his fingers stroke over the back of my head.

"I'll keep you safe, Aleks. That's all that matters."

I knew Aleks was no longer talking to me when he asked, "So you wanted to use me as bait?"

I willed Luca not to answer.

He didn't.

But whatever Aleks saw on his face was answer enough because he pulled his fingers from my hair and asked, "Can I please go to my room now?"

I wanted to tell him we needed to go, but I knew he wasn't in any shape to do anything but escape. I was half-tempted to ask him if he wanted to call his brother, but I was afraid of his answer so I merely nodded. He got up, making sure to get off his chair on the opposite side so he wouldn't touch me even by accident. I stood with my gun in hand to make sure Luca didn't try to make a grab for him. Despite my brother not being armed, he had the skills to hold Aleks in such a way that I'd have no choice but to put down my weapon.

I watched Aleks go to the stairs and head up them. There was no way for him to escape from the second floor so my biggest concern was keeping an eye on Luca and Con so neither tried to take him from me while the other distracted or disabled me.

The reality was that if they really wanted to, it wouldn't take much for them to incapacitate me. The only thing protecting me was my gun, and the idea of shooting either man, despite my need to protect Aleks, left a dead weight in my belly.

"Vaughn, sit," Con said. "I've got some steaks in the freezer that I can defrost. There aren't any eggs but I can fry up some canned potatoes—"

"I'm not hungry," I said.

Con sighed and Luca shook his head.

"We were so fucking close," my brother finally whispered, his voice full of bitterness.

I knew what he was talking about, of course. "What was I supposed to do, Luca? Let them all die? The meeting had already been fucking canceled!"

"And why didn't you know about that?" Luca shot back. "That kid's brother—"

"His name is Aleks and he's not a kid!" I bit out.

"That fucking brother of his told him of his little escape plan hours before it actually happened! If you'd been there, you could have found a way to stop it… to make sure the meeting still happened."

I laughed harshly. "God, you give me way too much credit, little brother." I leaned back in my chair. "I was still just the goddamned hired help, Luca! Even if I'd known Dante and Magnus would show up, how would it have looked to Marcus if I'd suggested he keep that meeting? That's why *I* went in eight years ago and you didn't," I said as I pointed at him. "You have all the finesse of a bull in a china shop when you decide you want something. They would have made you on day one!"

Luca leaned forward across the table, his eyes glittering with anger. "Then explain to me how a *kid*, who was and still is our best hope of finding my son, is alive and well two years after he was supposedly killed during a scuffle inside the Parks mansion before it blew up? Explain to me what fucking hold he has on you that you would choose him over the child you loved like your own son!"

Con put his hand on Luca's arm to draw him back into a sitting position, since he was practically in my face by the end of his rant.

"You want to know why, Luca?" I asked. "Because I just couldn't do it anymore," I said. "I couldn't leave one more victim behind, even for a day, a minute. You all say I was the best equipped to go in after Gio, but not one of you knows what it's really like in there." I shifted my eyes to Con briefly, then pinned Luca with the harshness of my gaze. "*I'm* the one who listened to their screams every day as they were being violated. *I'm* the one who had to look in their terrified or dead eyes day after day as they tried to find a reason to take their next breath. *I* had to listen to them cry every night for their mom or their dad or whoever was out there in the world looking for them. You got them out after I told you about them, Luca. That's fucking fantastic. But I never got to see any of that because I was on to the next monster trying to find Gio. Every day for eight fucking years I've watched kids suffer and I blocked it off so I could remember that Gio was the one waiting, the one who needed saving."

I paused to pull in a breath and automatically glanced at the stairs Aleks had disappeared up. Then my eyes were back on my brother and my friend. "So yeah, I saw an opportunity and I took it. I set Aleks free because I knew you'd want to use him. You wouldn't have just sent him home or found him a new life like the others. You've become so fucking blind to everything in your desperation to find Gio that I couldn't trust you to let Aleks go." I pointed at the stairs. "His family came for him! Just like we're coming for Gio. Aleks and his brother had a right to put their lives back together. And the fact that you can't see that…"

Luca's mouth was set into a firm line and he didn't even move a muscle as I spoke. But I saw something flash in his eyes the moment I accused him of not letting Aleks go… of choosing his son over Aleks's freedom.

I was surprised when he finally lowered his gaze and stared at his hands.

"What would you have me do, Vaughn? Every second that passes, my son waits for me to come for him. Eight years… eight years of sick fucks hurting him and him calling for me."

Con settled his hand on Luca's shoulder, but Luca pulled away.

He lifted his eyes to meet mine and I saw a moment of agony before he hardened his jaw. "Yes, I would have taken advantage of having Aleks in my hands, but he would have been safe. And I would have made sure he made it home, both then and now. I did some unforgivable things in those early days when I was trying to find Gio, but I'm not… I'm not a fucking monster. If anyone should know that about me, it's my own goddamned brother."

With that, Luca stood and headed for the front door. I reached for my gun with the intent of calling him back so I could keep him in my sights, but Con reached across the table and grabbed my arm. "Don't," he said softly. "Let him go… he can't go anywhere and there's no way for him to call anyone."

I sighed and lowered myself back down to my seat. "What did

he mean about that unforgivable part when he first started looking for Gio?" I asked.

Con shook his head. "I don't know. You know he doesn't talk about those first couple weeks where he tried to find Gio on his own. Maybe he just meant the guilt about not asking us for help sooner."

I stared at the door my brother had walked through. Con could be right, but I wasn't so sure. My brother wasn't one who dwelled on the mistakes of the past. He put them behind him and moved on; he focused on the task at hand.

But then again, Luca wasn't someone who spoke about what he was feeling, no matter what. Neither of us did. Our father had been a good teacher when it had come time to instill that particular lesson.

Covellos didn't feel.

Even fake Covellos like me.

"We need to figure this shit out together, Vaughn," Con said. "Otherwise it will just be you and him running."

"We?" I asked. "Do you actually expect me to believe Luca suddenly only has Aleks's well-being in mind? Because you know him as well as me, Con. He's going to put Gio first, no matter what. And I get why... I've been doing that for eight years now! I love Gio and I hear the same screams and pleas from that boy that Luca does. But I will not use Aleks like that! Hell, it's not even a sure thing... it never was!"

"King was able to confirm those were Stylianos's men," Con said quietly as he lowered his eyes.

My stomach dropped out. I'd suspected as much, but somehow hearing it out loud just made it all the more real. For whatever reason, the man was obsessed with Aleks, even though there was no evidence he'd ever even met Aleks. The rumor was that Stylianos and Marcus had gotten into a contentious bidding war over Aleks when his previous owner had sold him, but there was no proof of that. But if the bastard really had sent five men to get Aleks within hours of Aleks's parents airing that picture and giving away both the fact that he was alive and where he was in the U.S., it was pretty telling how desperate the man was to get his hands on him.

"Is King on his way here?" I asked.

"No, he's still cleaning up the mess you left behind," Con said. "You can't leave five bodies in the middle of nowhere and expect it to just get swept under the carpet... at least not without a little help."

While King himself wouldn't be doing the actual sweeping, since he was a more hands-on type, he employed enough people who had the skills to make things disappear, at least on paper.

"He's heading to Chicago to see if he can pick up on anything... maybe there's something we missed with Stylianos or one of our informants has heard something about Gio."

I nodded, even though I knew King's search would likely be fruitless. In the two years since we'd almost found the man who was only known by the name Stylianos online, we hadn't had any real clues leading to him or Gio. That fact explained some of Luca's uncharacteristic show of desperation.

He's starting to lose hope.

I covered my eyes with my hands and felt a sharp pain shoot up my arm from the wound Aleks had inflicted on me. It was a reminder of why I was doing all this.

"This is undoing everything Aleks has accomplished in the last two years, Con," I said softly. "The blackouts... he never had those with Marcus and the few he's had since I got him out weren't violent ones. His mind is so fucked up right now and his brain is trying to protect him in the only way it knows how. How am I supposed to ask him to be a part of something that did that to him? How am I supposed to ask him to give up what little bit of a normal life he managed to find in the last two years?" I shook my head and dropped my hand. "I can't... I won't."

Because I knew that was the real reason Con had brought Luca here. He wanted us to find a way to accomplish both things – protect Aleks and find Gio. But the latter meant making Aleks relive every terrible moment he'd already had to survive once.

I couldn't do that to him.

I loved Gio and I wanted him back, but it couldn't be at the cost of Aleks's sanity.

No, I'd find another way. I just needed to make sure Aleks was safe and out of reach from those fuckers and then I'd go back in and I'd find a way to get even deeper into the secretive network. Gio was there, somewhere in its bowels. I'd find out who Stylianos really was and I'd make him suffer a thousand times worse than any kid he'd ever put his hands on, and then he'd tell me where Gio was and I'd watch the fucker die a long, slow, painful death.

"I'm sorry, Con," I said as I stood. As I went to move around him to head toward the stairs, Con stepped in my path.

"At least let me make you guys something to eat. Take the day to rest because I know your arm hurts like hell and Aleks looks like he hasn't slept in years. Luca and I will stay here until you guys leave. I'll make sure he can't call anyone and I'll keep him away from both of you."

I began shaking my head.

"You can trust me, Vaughn. I know how you feel about him," he said softly. "Aleks doesn't know it and you might not believe it, but he's family now and above all else, we protect our family."

Con's words were fierce and I wanted to cling to them because I felt so fucking adrift. I looked at him to try and find any proof that he was lying to me.

But Con didn't lie and on the rare occasions he even tried, I could see it in his eyes. And I didn't see even an ounce of dishonesty in them now.

He was telling the truth.

"Aleks likes grits. Do you have any of those?"

Con smiled. "My grandmother made them for my grandfather every morning for fifty years. If there isn't a box of them in the pantry, I'll throw my next match."

I let out a little chuckle. We both knew he'd never intentionally let someone best him in the ring, so he had to be pretty sure about the contents of the pantry.

"I'll bring them up in a bit," Con said.

I nodded and moved past him, then went upstairs to the bedroom which, thankfully, wasn't locked.

But it was also empty.

Chapter 12

ALEKS

HE FOUND ME PRETTY QUICKLY AND I FELT BAD WHEN HE THREW open the bathroom door (which I'd actually managed to shut on my own this time) in a panic.

Vaughn took a few deep breaths when he saw me.

"Sorry," I murmured. "I wanted to try and get the blood out," I said as I motioned to the shirt in my hands. I'd put my own shirt back on so I could wash Vaughn's out in the sink and while I'd managed to get the worst of the stains out, I actually missed wearing it. And it didn't smell like him anymore.

I'd checked.

"Nothing to be sorry for," he finally said. I almost smiled because it was something Dante would always say to me when I apologized for something.

Instead of leaving, he came into the small room and shut the door behind him. "Can I lock this?" he asked as he motioned to the lock. My eyes fell to the gun in his hand.

So he still wasn't certain we were safe from his brother.

I nodded.

Vaughn flipped the lock, then came and sat down next to me on the floor. I was leaning against the side of the small bathtub.

"Con's making something for us to eat... he thinks he's got grits."

"This is his house?" I asked.

"It belonged to his grandparents."

I nodded. "I recognize him," I said. "Dante and Magnus like him... he does that fighting... not the boxing kind."

"MMA... martial arts," Vaughn said with a nod.

"He's very good," I said.

Vaughn laughed. "That he is... it's funny because he's one of the least violent and most levelheaded people I know. When Luca and I used to get into it as kids, Con was always trying to talk us through our argument before the fists started flying. King used to tell him he should be a shrink."

"King is his brother? And Lex too?" I asked.

"Yeah. They're not actually brothers, but they grew up in foster care together and became really close... even when they were split up and moved to different homes in the city, they never lost that bond."

"You and Luca, were you foster kids too?"

Vaughn shook his head and looked at his hands. He tilted the gun back and forth. "No... that's more complicated," he finally said.

I was certain he wasn't going to say anything else and I was actually smarting from the knowledge that he didn't want to share something like that with me when he suddenly said, "We're half-brothers... same father, different mothers."

"You're older than him?" I asked. "You called him little brother."

"By a couple of years. His mother was the one to raise me."

"What happened to your mother?"

I could see he wasn't comfortable talking about the subject, though he didn't fall silent. But he also wouldn't look at me while he spoke.

"She died when I was two. But I'd already gone to live with Vidone and Theodora Covello by then."

I shifted closer to him so our bodies were just barely touching. "Why?" I asked. "Your mother couldn't care for you?"

Vaughn shook his head. "She was a showgirl… in Atlantic City. Do you know where that is?"

"No," I said. "But it's like Las Vegas, right? People go there to lose money so they can try and win more money."

Vaughn smiled and I felt it ease some of the pressure in my chest. I was scared to death about what was going on around me, but having this moment where we talked about normal things and he looked at me like I hadn't just cut his arm open with a knife gave me the few minutes of quiet I needed to keep from escaping into my head.

"Exactly," he responded. "My father was already engaged to Luca's mother when he went to Atlantic City for what was supposed to have been his bachelor party. He drank too much and when his friends brought in the *entertainment*, he indulged."

"Entertainment," I repeated as I tried to make sense of the word.

"Being a showgirl didn't pay *all* the bills," Vaughn said softly.

Understanding dawned and I dropped my eyes. "Oh… I'm sorry, Vaughn."

I shot him a glance from the corner of my eye and saw him shrug. "It was what it was. When my mom found out she was pregnant, I guess she saw a chance to fund her showgirl stint for a bit longer."

"What does that mean?" I asked.

"Luca's dad was pretty well-known around New York and New Jersey, just not for the right reasons."

I must have looked confused because he clarified, "His business dealings weren't always aboveboard."

I realized what that meant… his father had been a criminal.

"Anyway, my mother saw the chance to make a buck and took me to his house in the city. His new wife answered the door."

"Oh," I whispered in disbelief.

"My mother proceeded to tell Theodora Covello all about her husband's indiscretion the weekend they'd gotten married nine months earlier. She told Luca's mother if she wanted it to stay quiet, she'd pay her ten thousand dollars. Want to know what Theodora did?" he asked me.

I nodded.

"Gave her twenty thousand, took me from her and told her to get the hell out of there... though I'm sure she used the word 'heck' – she wasn't big on swearing."

"Me neither," I whispered.

"I know," Vaughn said softly. I looked at him and immediately got lost in his eyes. That strange tingling sensation returned and I wanted to yell at it for having the worst timing ever.

"So she took you in," I prodded.

"She did," Vaughn said. "Raised me as her own. Loved me as her own," he added, then looked at his gun again. "Luca came along a couple years later. You'd think that would have changed things, but she treated us like real brothers. I wasn't suddenly disposable or sloppy seconds... at least not to her."

I wasn't sure what "sloppy seconds" meant, but I had no doubt it wasn't a good thing. And the last part meant someone *had* treated him that way.

"Your father?" I guessed.

Vaughn nodded. "He was not happy about his wife taking in the proof of his indiscretion. He actually loved Theodora quite a bit and he'd told her about the indulgence with the showgirl from Atlantic City before they'd married. They'd worked it out and wed as planned. My father was a bastard with everyone but her," Vaughn said quietly. "He would have given her anything she wanted, and for some reason, she wanted me."

"She sounds like a very good woman," I said.

"She was."

Was.

"You lost her?"

Vaughn nodded. "When Luca and I were still little. I was twelve, he was ten. Everything changed."

"How so?"

He shook his head a little. "My mother must have known Vidone would get rid of me if he had the chance. He told me once that she'd made him swear that if anything happened to her, that he'd keep me. He kept his word."

"But he wasn't a father to you," I guessed.

Vaughn sighed and looked at me. "She made up for it," he said.

"And you had your brother," I offered.

He chuckled. "God, he was such a little shit," he said affectionately.

I felt my stomach drop out at that because that little laugh and that small smile told me everything I needed to know. Whatever had happened between them was more recent. Either after Vaughn's nephew had been taken, or worse, after Vaughn had chosen to save me rather than use me to find the man who knew where Gio was.

All the anxiety I'd been feeling came rolling back. "Is he going to let me go?" I asked.

"Luca?"

I nodded.

"He doesn't have a say in it," Vaughn practically growled.

It should have made me feel better to know he was still choosing me for whatever reason, but I couldn't stop thinking that in all likelihood, *I* was the reason the two brothers were at each other's throats.

What if that were me and Dante? How would I survive such a rift?

"Vaughn…"

"Don't, Aleks," Vaughn said softly, then he leaned into me just a little so I could feel his touch. "None of this is your fault."

I didn't respond to that because I didn't know how. It wasn't like I wanted to throw myself to the wolves to save their relationship. And if Luca had been willing to take me off the street just like those other guys had, did that really make him any better?

He's trying to get his son back.

My thoughts shifted to Gio… a topic I'd been trying to avoid from the moment I'd heard his name. I felt cold run throughout my entire body as I thought about what the little boy would have gone through. What if I'd seen him at some point?

"Do you really think you guys can find him?" I asked.

It was eerie how Vaughn seemed to know exactly what I was talking about.

"I don't know," he admitted. "It's been a while since we've had a credible lead."

"Credible?"

"It means valid... substantial."

I nodded, feeling foolish.

"They took so many kids, James," I whispered. I wasn't sure why it was so important to use his first name.

Yes I did.

It was my way of telling him something he probably didn't want to hear. And I didn't actually want to tell him, especially considering that I'd been found after so many years. But I also knew my situation wasn't typical. I'd seen the parties the men had had where they could trade and buy kids, or just show them off to one another... or even share them. There was no way Vaughn and his friends could have saved them all. Not all the kids had even lived long enough to be found by their loved ones. Some had even resorted to taking their own lives...

"I know," Vaughn acknowledged. "But we can't stop looking... not until we know for sure."

"You shouldn't," I said. "It's just..."

"Yeah," Vaughn whispered.

So he knew what I was trying to say. They needed to keep looking because if Gio was alive, he was waiting for them. But they needed to be prepared to not find him, or worse...

I felt sick to my stomach as I considered how Vaughn, and especially Luca, must be feeling. My own brother had been through everything these men were experiencing and I knew it had changed him forever. My abduction had also meant he'd been stuck in time. He'd been lucky enough to find Magnus, but if he'd had to choose between spending his future with Magnus and continuing the search for me, he would have chosen me each and every time.

I rubbed my temple because my head began to hurt. I didn't want Vaughn in that world anymore. It was dangerous and the things he had to witness...

But I didn't want him to stop looking for Gio either. The boy would be a teenager by now... not much younger than me when Vaughn had saved me. God, what if Luca was right? What if Dante showing up to save me had ruined any possibility of Gio being found? What horrible things had the boy suffered through in the days, weeks, months, and years after that one chance had been stolen away?

Every day I'd been trying to live a normal life, Gio had been waiting for his own rescue.

"Hey," Vaughn said as he put his hand on my back and began rubbing circles into it. "Nothing about that night was guaranteed except that you, your brother, and Magnus would have died if I hadn't done something. It wasn't even a choice for me."

I wanted to believe him... that he hadn't had a choice in choosing to save me versus finding his nephew. But I didn't. Luca had said it himself... Vaughn would lay down and die to protect me. What if that were true? What did it mean? Why was I different? He would have met so many victims in the years he'd spent in that world... would he have done for them what he was currently doing for me? Would he have chosen them over his own flesh and blood?

"I... I need to lie down," I whispered. "I don't feel good."

That was the absolute truth. Of course, if I could have found a way to just lie down there on the floor in front of the toilet, I would have. But not surprisingly, Vaughn's arm went around me to help me stand. I still had his wet shirt in my hands but when he went to take it from me, I held onto it. He let me keep it and unlocked the door. We ran into Con in the hallway. He had a serving tray with food on it and the smell instantly had me turning back into the bathroom. I threw up into the toilet until there was nothing left in my system, but my body wouldn't stop trying to expel something that wasn't there.

It could have been minutes or hours before a cold washcloth was pressed against my face. I could hear Vaughn and Con talking, but I couldn't make out the words. Then my body was moving, but my legs weren't. It wasn't until I was laid in a bed that I realized Vaughn had had to carry me there.

I wanted the darkness to claim me because it was easier there and that made me ashamed. I wondered if Gio had found something that brought him peace when he needed it.

"Alstroemeria… friendship," I whispered.

God, I was such a coward.

Cool fingers drifted over my temple. "It's okay, Aleks, just rest."

Vaughn.

I felt tears building in my eyes because I knew he was giving me permission to let go. And that he'd take care of me no matter where I went this time or how long I was gone for.

"Amaryllis… splendid beauty," I croaked, my voice sounding thick even to my own ears.

"That's it, baby," Vaughn whispered in my ear.

"James," I breathed.

"It's okay," Vaughn responded when I couldn't continue. "What's the next one?"

"Anemone," I managed to get out as the darkness began to beckon to me. My lids blessedly began to drop and Vaughn's worried expression disappeared. Along with the vision of the two men standing just behind him, one looking concerned. But it was Luca's expression that stayed with me as I whispered the flower's meaning. Poor Luca just looked completely confused and lost.

And I couldn't help but think how the anemone would be the perfect flower for him and probably his son, because both were likely dealing with the same exact emotion.

"Fading hope," I managed to get out.

I tried to tell Luca and Gio I was sorry, but I had no clue if I managed it or not and, thankfully, the blackness made it so I didn't have to care either way.

I WAS WARM WHEN I WOKE UP… HOT, ACTUALLY. AND IT WAS ONCE again dark out. But I didn't know what day it was. I glanced at the clock on the nightstand on my side of the bed. It was just after two.

Which meant I'd been out for more than eighteen hours…

unless more than a day had passed. I'd never lost *that* much time before but I also hadn't attacked someone with a knife before either, so I wasn't sure of anything anymore.

Unlike the last time I'd woken up, I wasn't alone. I could feel Vaughn at my back and his arm was wrapped around my waist. I could also feel his even breath on the back of my neck so I figured he was likely asleep. A small, lit lamp on the dresser afforded me enough light to see several plates of food next to it.

All untouched.

There was more than enough food for one person, so if I'd been forced to guess, I would have said neither I nor Vaughn had eaten any of it. But again, I couldn't be sure because I couldn't remember drinking the chocolate milk the previous night when Vaughn had brought it to me.

I wasn't particularly hungry, but I knew I needed to eat something because if I hadn't eaten whatever Vaughn had offered me, it meant the last time I ate actual food was the morning at the restaurant when I'd had two orders of grits.

That had been almost forty-eight hours ago.

But one need was more pressing than food. I shifted my body so I could look over my shoulder at Vaughn to see if he was actually asleep or not.

He was.

And he looked exhausted.

Even in the dim light, I could see the dark circles beneath his eyes.

I glanced around the rest of the room but it was empty.

Did that mean Con and Luca had left?

It didn't seem likely since Vaughn had seemed certain that Luca would call for reinforcements the second he got the chance. But Vaughn was also sleeping, which didn't seem like something he'd do unless he felt safe.

I was about to ask him if it was safe to leave the room, but when he snuggled up against me and let out a soft sigh, I held my tongue. But my bladder refused to be ignored, so I carefully lifted Vaughn's arm from my waist and slipped out from beneath the heavy weight.

I replaced my body with my pillow and smiled when Vaughn accepted it. The fact that he hadn't woken up was proof that he was as exhausted as me… more so, probably.

I went to the bedroom door and found it locked.

So Vaughn *wasn't* feeling completely safe.

I unlocked it and left it open so Vaughn would be able to hear me if I called for him. The bathroom was just down the hall so I hurried to it and locked myself in, then took care of business. Vaughn's shirt was lying folded on the counter. It looked dry and clean, and when I picked it up it smelled laundered. I was both disappointed and relieved at the same time.

I glanced at my reflection, hoping to find some stain on my own shirt so I'd have a valid excuse to put his back on.

I didn't recognize myself.

I looked pale, gaunt and very sickly. My skin had a gray tint to it and my hair was all over the place.

No wonder Vaughn was always looking at me with concern.

I looked like one of those dead people who came back to life on Dante's favorite TV show. I personally couldn't watch it because it was too violent for my tastes, but I'd caught glimpses of it now and again.

A zombie.

That was the word.

Dante would be so disappointed in me.

I needed to call him… even if it was just to tell him I was okay. He and Magnus had to be worried sick that I hadn't checked in.

But did I want them to come get me?

I didn't even know where I was. I hadn't been paying close enough attention on the ride from the first house to know what state we were in.

First things first. I needed to take care of myself so I wouldn't worry Dante and Magnus when they saw me.

Or Vaughn.

I cursed myself for that silent addition to my thoughts.

I went back to the bedroom to wake Vaughn up but when I saw him hugging my pillow, I kept my mouth shut. I considered the food on the dresser. I didn't care that it was cold, but I knew the meat and mashed potatoes would be too much for my stomach and would likely just make me sick again. I needed something light. Dante had always given me toast or crackers when I hadn't been feeling well at home. Maybe I could find something like that downstairs.

If Luca and Con were still here, surely they were asleep. And if not, I wouldn't go to the kitchen… I'd get Vaughn. But if there was no reason to wake him up, I wouldn't… after all, I knew how to be invisible.

I left the bedroom and quietly padded down the hall to the stairs. The house was quiet. There was no TV on and I couldn't hear anyone talking. I took my time making my way down each stair, prepared to flee back upstairs at the slightest sound.

But there was nothing.

Maybe the men had left?

There were a few lights on downstairs. When I made it to the front entryway, I could see that the kitchen was empty. To my left was the living room and I could see Con propped up in an armchair by the fireplace. He was asleep.

I didn't see Luca.

I held my breath as I listened.

I should go back upstairs.

Or call for Vaughn.

Man up for God's sake, Aleks.

I nodded to the voice in my head. I could do this. Even if I came across Luca and he tried something, I'd yell for everything I was worth. If I could attack Vaughn to protect myself, surely my brain would react in a similar manner around a man who wanted to harm me.

But was that what he really wanted?

He'd said he wouldn't have hurt me.

It wasn't something I wanted to find out for sure, so I hurried to the kitchen and began scanning the counter for a bag of bread, then realized there probably wouldn't be any because no one appeared to currently be living in the house. The little food I'd seen upstairs had looked like it could have come from the freezer… Dante often made potatoes like that from a bag that he just had to put in the microwave. And there was always some kind of meat kept in our freezer.

I moved silently to the cabinets and began carefully opening them to see if there were any crackers. I hadn't thought to check if there'd been glasses of anything to drink on the dresser where the food had been, so I grabbed one during my search. I'd be able to fill it with water from the bathroom faucet.

I was in the process of opening one of the long cabinets by the refrigerator when I heard a slight cough. I froze, then began frantically searching the kitchen to see who'd managed to sneak up on me. But there was no one. When I heard the sound again, I realized it was coming from outside. I'd somehow missed the fact that the kitchen door was open but the screen door was closed. There was a little bit of light out on the porch off the kitchen, but I didn't see anyone.

It could only be Luca out there... or one of his men.

I carefully closed the cabinet and gripped the glass in my hand so I could use it as a weapon if someone came rushing through the door to grab me. Then I began backing away from the door and back toward the front entryway and stairs... and the safety of Vaughn.

Then I heard it.

This time it wasn't a cough.

I stilled as I acknowledged what it was.

A sob.

I shook my head because it couldn't be. Guys like Luca didn't cry.

It was a trick.

He knew I was in here and was trying to draw me outside so he could grab me.

I took another step back and heard another sob, softer this time... muffled.

Guys like Luca didn't cry... *but fathers who'd lost their sons did.*

I moved silently forward, the glass still in my hand. I listened for any creaking of the floorboards that proved he was moving around, but there was nothing but the sound of crickets.

And that occasional muffled sound that I could barely make out now.

I saw him almost immediately when I reached the door. He was sitting on the steps leading to the grass. His back was to me and he was wiping at his eyes.

If he was aware of me, he was really good at pretending he wasn't. There was something in his hand that he put to his mouth, and a moment later I smelled a hint of smoke.

He was having a cigarette.

Brian had smoked. The smell had always made me sick because he'd smoked almost nonstop and I'd smell it on his hot breath while he was making me his special boy.

Fucking you.

I closed my eyes at the voice in my head. Brian had never called what he'd done to me that but some of the other men had. They'd liked that word.

Brian hadn't.

He'd said it was crude and uncouth. I hadn't known what those things meant, but I'd known that nothing about what he'd been doing had been special.

I felt nausea roll through my belly as the memories of the first time he'd hurt me threatened to steal into my mind.

No, not here. Not now.

Not anymore.

I willed the blackness away and opened my eyes. I was startled to see Luca watching me.

I automatically stepped back, but he didn't make a move to get up. I told myself to run, but his eyes were like Vaughn's... something about them made it impossible to move. But with Vaughn it was more like I didn't want to. With Luca it felt like I was staring into the eyes of a predator... moving would just cause it to hunt me down.

I was surprised when he turned his attention from me. He took another puff on the cigarette. "Don't tell Con, okay?" he said as he held the cigarette up briefly. "He thinks I quit."

I didn't respond to him, but I took advantage of the fact that he wasn't looking at me to check the screen door for a lock.

It had one so I flipped it.

If he noticed, he didn't say anything. I started to back up.

"Aleks, can I ask you something before you go?"

His voice was so different than it had been earlier. The fury and rage were gone for the moment.

"You don't have to answer," Luca added.

"Okay," I finally said when he didn't make a move to even *look* in my direction again.

"The blackouts... did they... did they start when you first got taken?"

I wasn't expecting the question so it took me a moment to find my voice to answer. "I'm not sure."

He continued to stare into the inky darkness. It was several long seconds before he took another puff. "Did they make it easier?"

I tensed because I started to understand what he was asking me and more importantly, *why*.

"Yes," I said. "The first time I went into my head, it was more like I was just in a dream. I knew what was really happening to me, I just didn't feel it. Does that make sense?"

Luca nodded. "So not blackouts then," he said.

"No... I guess not. I think those are more recent."

God, that was hard to admit to. But I had no choice but to accept it. The proof was on Vaughn's arm.

"I don't know why, though," I admitted.

"Because your mind feels safer now," Luca said.

I shook my head. "That doesn't make sense."

He finally cast me a glance over his shoulder. "There was no one to take care of you when you were with those men. If you'd done what you did to Vaughn today, they would have killed you for sure. Somewhere in your mind, you knew that. To escape that completely, that fully, you had to be certain you'd live through it. That there'd be someone to watch out for you. Back then you had to survive. Now your mind is trying to figure out how to… live."

I didn't know what to make of that. But he was right about one thing… if I'd lashed out at Father like I had Vaughn, he would have killed me. He'd tried to do exactly that the one time I *had* fought back.

"I don't know what I want for him more," Luca whispered.

I knew he was talking about his son. Gio would have been faced with the same choice as me.

"You want him to survive," I said. I found myself flipping the lock on the screen door and opening it. I had a good view of Luca's profile as I moved out onto the porch. He shook his head slightly and swallowed hard.

"I didn't really understand," Luca said softly. "Or maybe I didn't want to."

"Understand what?"

"The suffering those kids we got out went through." He took another drag on his cigarette. "We saved them… I wanted that to be enough. It had to be enough. And the ones we couldn't… I forgot about those. I *had* to forget… we all did."

"So you could keep looking for Gio," I said.

He nodded almost violently. "Vaughn thinks I didn't see what he did and in some ways he's right. But when they first took Gio, I went after him on my own and I did see things. There was this one boy… he… he…"

Luca just shook his head. "I had to forget about him," he whispered. "I had to find my son."

I felt myself softening a bit as I realized like Vaughn, this man was haunted.

And not just by the loss of his son.

"Will you tell me about your son?" I asked as I moved to stand next to one of the pillars that bracketed the steps Luca was sitting on.

Luca stubbed out his cigarette, then pulled out the pack from his pocket, along with a lighter. I flinched when he reached into his pocket again. He must have noticed my reaction because he said,

"It's a picture of Gio. Most of them are on my phone but Con took that when he searched me. I found the cigarettes in the pantry – I guess one of Con's grandparents was a secret smoker. Vaughn made Con remove all the knives and anything else that could be used as a weapon. They're with Vaughn in the room you guys are in. So even if I wanted to do something to you, which I don't, I couldn't."

Luca kept talking as he pulled a small picture from his pocket. I didn't actually believe him about not being able to hurt me if he wanted because he didn't seem like the type of guy who needed to have a weapon to subdue someone – hadn't he proven that when he'd kept me from striking out with that knife for a second time?

"Gio gave this to me the day he was taken... school picture," Luca said as he reached his arm out to hand me the picture.

I was shocked by how the boy in the picture looked nothing like Luca. His hair was a startling shade of blond...it actually looked white. And his eyes were a crisp, pale blue. A big, toothy grin spread across his features. I looked at Luca in surprise.

"I know," he said. "He doesn't look like me even a little bit... that's all his mother," he added as he motioned to the picture.

I understood now why Vaughn, Luca, and their friends believed the leads they'd been given about Gio. His unique look would have made him very valuable. The people who'd taken him might have temporarily colored his hair after first kidnapping him, but they would have let the natural color grow back as soon as they'd moved him some place he wouldn't be recognized. It wouldn't have surprised me if they'd never even colored it, because that would have meant having to wait to sell him.

"He has your chin," I finally said. "It looks very stubborn."

Luca actually chuckled. "I wish I could say that was the first time I'd heard that. About my chin... and his. He was... *is* a really good kid. Never gave his mother or me any kind of trouble. But he's a fighter too. He... he..."

Luca's voice dropped off before he whispered, "He's a fighter."

My heart broke for him because I knew what he was thinking.

Fighters in the world I'd grown up in suffered more. I'd seen it myself. The kids who'd tried to stop what was happening to them or escape it had been punished in the worst ways. My friend, Remy, had been one of those boys. He'd fought tooth and nail to escape the life and he'd suffered so much more than me. He was also the reason Dante had found me.

"My friend is a fighter," I said quickly. "He survived, Luca. The things they did to him were terrible, but he got out and he's got a good life now. And he saved me. He's the only reason my brother even found me. He had the chance to get out and just run, but he called Dante and told him where I was. If your son is anything like my friend, Gio will make it through this and you'll get him home and he'll keep fighting."

Luca turned away from me as he nodded and lit up another cigarette. I saw him wipe discreetly at his face and I quickly looked away so he wouldn't feel as embarrassed about the show of emotion.

I thought about Remy and the day I'd met him. Though I hadn't actually "met" him – I'd encountered him in a bathroom. He'd been badly bruised and I'd learned later he'd been violently assaulted just moments before I'd walked into that bathroom. We'd talked for less than fifteen seconds. He'd recognized a birthmark I had on my collarbone, the same one Dante had, and he'd called Dante as soon as he'd been able to.

I hadn't known then that Remy and I had met once before... he and I had actually been kept in the same house when I'd first been taken. He'd remembered the birthmark from that first time and when Dante had initially come to Chicago to search for me, he'd encountered Remy who'd told him he'd seen me when we'd both been little. When Remy and I had run into each other in that bathroom years later, he'd reached out to Dante afterwards.

He hadn't had to do that.

He'd chosen to help me. He'd had no reason in the world to do what he'd done other than it'd been the right thing.

You gave me hope when I had none left, Aleks. I couldn't leave you behind.

That's what he'd told me when I'd once asked him why he'd helped me. My aim had just been to comfort him when I'd given him one of the flowers from the ornate arrangement in the bathroom and had told him what it meant.

He'd never really explained how that had given him hope, but I'd never asked him to, either.

There were just some things that neither of us wanted to remember and that night was definitely one of them.

My heart began to pound in my chest as a thought took form in my head and wouldn't let go.

"Luca," I said quietly.

He turned to look at me.

"The man you're looking for… the one who might know where Gio is…"

"Stylianos," Luca supplied.

I startled at that. "I… I thought you didn't know his name," I said. Oh God, had they lied to me about all of it? Was this all just some elaborate scheme to mess with me?

"It's not his real name, Aleks," Luca said gently. "We didn't lie to you."

I managed to calm down a bit.

"Most of the dealing in kids happens online nowadays – in private chat rooms and forums on the dark web where it's hard for the authorities to track. Stylianos is the name this guy started using online and so that's what he's known as. No one knows his real name."

"Maybe Stylianos is a real name… Dante uses our father's last name while I have Papa's," I suggested.

"It's not," Luca responded. "Stylianos is the name of a saint known as the Protector of Children. We've seen the fucker's chat transcripts… he actually believes he and guys like him are helping kids to be in their purest state. Some of the guys like Marcus Parks know what they're doing is wrong and just don't give a shit. And then you've got guys like Stylianos who actually believes he's doing God's work by creating a world where adults and children are free to love one another. He's become quite a power player in the past few years and that's made him be even more careful to stay in the shadows."

My knees almost gave out as nausea swept through me. "Why me?" I asked. "I'm… I'm no one."

"He's fixated on you, Aleks. There's no rhyme or reason to it. Our theory is that he saw you at some point and became fascinated with you. He probably tried to buy you but whoever…"

Luca's voice dropped off suddenly and I knew why.

"Owned," I said. "Whoever *owned* me…"

"Right," Luca murmured. "Whoever that was wouldn't give you up. It's possible he missed out on you during a bidding war… Marcus had a lot of money and there's no proof that Stylianos is wealthy, so losing you a second time could have just strengthened that obsession. When word got out you were still alive, it would have been like some kind of 'meant to be' thing with him. He sees you as his and he wants you back… it's like those celebrity stalkers who invent entire relationships with the famous person, even though they've never even actually talked to them. When they don't get what they want, they can turn desperate… and violent."

I leaned heavily against the pillar as Luca spoke. If the man was as sick as Luca believed, he'd never stop coming after me.

I'd have to completely disappear again.

"Do you think this man has Gio?"

"We don't know for sure. Two years ago there was online chatter about Stylianos being willing to arrange a trade. He knew of a boy that was closer to the age Marcus liked. A boy with hair that was almost white and blue eyes that were so light they seemed clear sometimes. If Stylianos didn't have Gio himself, he knew who did. Two years ago, Gio would have been thirteen. That's around the age Marcus acquired you, right?"

I managed a nod, but nothing else.

"These men, most of them want boys or girls to be a certain age. Some want them before puberty hits so they're more childlike, others want them after puberty so they're more sexually developed."

I nodded in understanding. I'd been bought and sold a few times but I'd been with Brian and Father the longest. Brian had stopped touching me more and more as I'd gotten older. Father had been the same way. But I'd never made the connection before that I was being bought and sold based on my age.

"Two years ago, Stylianos was talking about having access to a boy who looked like Gio. Gio would have been the right age for Marcus. But it was never clear if Stylianos had Gio himself or if he would have had to trade a boy he did have to get Gio for the trade with Marcus."

"So you don't know for sure if he has Gio anymore, or knows where he is?" I asked.

Luca dropped his eyes and shook his head. "We haven't been able to find any recent chatter relating to a boy fitting Gio's description. Stylianos seemed to go underground too... until a few days ago."

When my parents had done that interview.

Luca fell silent and took a few drags on his cigarette. "It's late, Aleks. Get some sleep." He flicked the cigarette a few times, then stood. I jumped when he approached me, but with the pillar and porch rail at my back, I had nowhere to go.

He paused and held my gaze for a moment. He actually looked... hurt.

I waited for him to grab me and told myself to open my mouth and call for Vaughn, but that need to protect myself by being as quiet as possible kicked in. To my surprise, Luca stepped past me and opened the screen door. "Go inside, Aleks."

I made my body move, even as my mind tried to accept that he was going to grab me. But he didn't. When I was nearly in line with him he whispered, "You've got nothing to fear from me, Aleks. I swear it on Gio's life."

With that, he carefully released the door so my shoulder was holding it open, then he turned and went down the porch steps and disappeared into the darkness.

"He'll be back."

I jumped at the sound of the voice coming from inside the kitchen and dropped the glass I'd been holding.

"Sorry," Con said as he approached me.

The glass hadn't broken, so Con picked it up and handed it to me. "Can I get you something to eat or drink?" he asked.

"Um, something light for my stomach," I said as I forced myself to move into the kitchen.

"Sure," Con said. "We use this house as a safe house every once in a while so it isn't typically stocked with perishable food, but I try to make sure there's plenty of snacks and stuff. It's been a while since we've used it, but there should be something."

Con went to a closet on the far wall and opened the door, then pulled the string for a light hanging from the ceiling. I followed him to the small room but stayed outside it. The shelves were full of a variety of food.

"What's your fancy?" Con asked.

"Do you have any crackers or cereal?"

Con grabbed a couple of boxes and handed them to me. "These okay?"

I nodded, then he was snagging some bottles of water from the refrigerator. He grabbed two more bottles of something else… it looked like colored water.

"Sports drink," he explained as he handed me the bottles. "You're pretty dehydrated. These will help."

"Thank you," I said with a nod.

Con moved past me to shut the screen door and the main door but he didn't lock them.

"Don't worry, he can't call anyone or anything. The nearest neighbor is more than ten miles away. He just needs to keep moving… probably wants to smoke a bit more."

"You know about that?" I asked.

Con smiled. "I know everything there is to know about all my brothers, Aleks. Who do you think left that pack of cigarettes for him to find?" He looked at my full arms. "You need help with any of that?"

I shook my head. "No, thank you."

I quickly turned and headed for the stairs.

"Aleks," Con called just as I reached the first step.

I barely managed to not flinch. "Yes?"

"Everything will be okay, I promise."

I held the good-looking man's eyes and saw only truth there. I nodded and went up the stairs. I didn't doubt Con's honesty, but the "everything" he was talking about was only about me. And I couldn't help but wonder if maybe it needed to stop being about me and needed to start being about someone else who was in the same place I'd been two years ago.

Wanting to go home.

Chapter 13

VAUGHN

I WOKE UP TO THE SOUND OF CRUNCHING. IT WASN'T PARTICULARLY loud, but it was one of those sounds that my brain knew didn't fit. I was alone in bed with just a pillow tucked up against my body, so I lurched upright.

"I'm right here," I heard Aleks say.

My heart slammed against the wall of my chest as I quickly scanned the room. He was sitting on the bench that was built into the picture window that overlooked the front yard. There was a box of something between his legs.

"Sorry," he murmured. "I didn't want to get crumbs in the bed." He held up the box.

"It's okay," I said. My arm felt like it was on fire, but I ignored the sting and got out of bed. I snagged the gun off the nightstand and then went to make sure the bedroom door was locked.

It was.

I went around the bed to the bench and sat down on the opposite side. The window wasn't big so Aleks's legs were touching mine as I made myself comfortable. I was glad he didn't move his legs when I was finally settled.

"What is that?" I asked.

"Con gave it to me," Aleks said. "I needed something light for my stomach. It's cereal."

"You talked to Con?" I asked.

How the fuck had I managed to sleep through that?

"I went downstairs."

"Aleks—"

"I was careful, Vaughn. I would have screamed for you if I'd needed you."

His voice sounded surprisingly strong. As proud of him as I was that he'd ventured out on his own, now was the absolute worst time for him to exert more independence. Before I could tell him so, he said, "Why is there a rabbit on this box when all the cereal pieces are shaped like fruit or flowers? Is it because rabbits eat those things?"

I laughed as he held the box out to show me the front of it.

"I think they just needed a memorable spokesperson... or rabbit, in this case. I don't think the cereal was always shaped like that. The more colorful and fun they can make both the cereal and the box, the more likely they are to sell it."

"It's good," Aleks murmured. "Magnus only buys the cereal that has regular-looking flakes in it. Or the stuff that has nuts and raisins. He tells Dante he needs more fiber. I don't know what that means but this is much better," he said as he took a few more bites of the cereal.

"You should definitely try it with milk, then," I said.

Aleks leaned back against the wall and slowly closed up the box. He seemed both relaxed and tense at the same time.

"What are you thinking?" I asked.

"I'm wondering what you're going to do after you guys find Gio."

It wasn't a topic I was expecting.

"I'm not sure yet," I hedged.

"Yes, you are," he said softly as his eyes met mine. "I'm good at figuring you out too, James."

The use of my first name was definitely a sign. He wasn't asking just out of curiosity.

"You're not going to go home, are you? You're going to stay in," he ventured.

I dropped my eyes because I hadn't expected him to be so up front about it. I wondered where the show of strength had come from. I loved it but being the focus of it was a bit disconcerting, especially since he was bringing up a topic that I hadn't thought through much yet.

"There's no way to stop it, Aleks. Kids, women, even men – they'll continue to be forced into a life they can't escape. Not everyone has friends or family looking for them, and even if they do, most don't have the resources to find them. You were lucky in that you had a brother who both wouldn't give up and who had the skills to find you. Gio has an entire family with those skills and it's not a guarantee we can get him out." I shook my head. "I can't save them all but I'm damn sure going to help as many as I can."

"And your family?"

I sighed and looked at him. "We should get some more sleep. We need to get back on the road tomorrow."

I expected him to ask me to where – it was a question I didn't have an answer to – but instead, he leaned his head against the window.

"Where's home for you, James?"

I almost blurted that it was here, with him. Luckily, I caught myself and said, "You look tired, Aleks. Let's go back to bed."

It wasn't a lie. He did look sleepy. His lids were drooping and he was hugging the box of cereal to his chest. I could see an empty bottle of water sitting next to him. There was also a half-empty bottle of some kind of sports drink.

I knew I owed that last one to Con.

I got up and helped Aleks to his feet, taking the box from him and setting it on the bench. I grabbed the sports drink and took it with us as I led him back to the bed. When I made a move to step away from it after getting Aleks settled under the covers, his fingers reached out to grab mine.

"Stay with me," he said softly. "Easier to sleep next to you."

That had been my plan anyway, but for him to actually ask me and to make that physical contact with me was new.

My heart thumped in my chest and my dick reacted with anticipation.

I climbed over him and onto the bed so I wouldn't have to let go of his hand. I faced him on the bed and expected him to just close his eyes and go to sleep. But to my shock, he released my hand and then reached up to touch my face.

"I don't want you to give them up for me," he whispered.

"That's one choice that isn't yours to make," I said after a moment. "A lot has changed in the last eight years, Aleks. You can't just come back from that… none of us can."

He closed his eyes and was quiet for so long I was sure he'd fallen asleep.

"James?"

"Yeah?"

"Are you ever going to kiss me?"

My mouth went dry at that. Had he actually been thinking about that?

Clearly, he had.

"Do you want me to kiss you, Aleks?"

Aleks let out a soft sigh. His fingers were still on my face. He was toying with the hairs of my beard.

"I don't know. No one's ever done it before. What if I don't like it?"

"Then I won't ever do it again."

He opened his eyes and stared into mine. "Would you still be my friend even if you couldn't kiss me?"

This time it was my turn to touch his face. "Yes."

"Good," he said. He was about to close his eyes when I tipped his face up just a bit. He sucked in a breath and I knew it was because he thought I was going to kiss him then and there. The thought had crossed my mind, but I knew he wasn't ready.

"Aleks," I whispered. I could tell he was on the verge of drifting off.

"Yeah?"

"I'm going to make sure you like it, okay?"

A little smile drifted over his mouth and I found myself touching it. "Okay, James, I believe you."

It was my turn to smile. His eyes drifted shut and then he was pushing against me. I wrapped my arms around him.

"James?"

"Yeah?"

"I think I'm going to like it too."

I kissed the top of his head.

"James?"

"Yeah?"

"Don't wait too long, okay?"

"Okay, Aleks, I won't."

"Good," Aleks said on a sigh.

"James?"

"Yeah," I said, unable to stop the smile that spread across my mouth. My name on his lips was heaven.

"You'll always come for me, won't you, James?"

I hugged him tighter. "Always," I assured him.

"Okay."

We were both silent for a long time and I was sure he was out until he suddenly whispered, "I'm sorry, James."

"For what?" I asked, but he didn't answer. I assumed he was apologizing yet again for cutting my arm with the knife, but it wasn't until I woke up a few hours later to a very cold, very empty bed that I knew what he was really sorry for.

Because lying on the pillow where his head should have been was a note with just nine neatly written words on it.

Nine words that sent pure terror ripping through my system all at once and had me screaming Aleks's name in denial.

It was my choice to go with him, James.

Chapter 14

ALEKS

"He'll be here soon, Aleks. Everything will be all right," Con said from where he was sitting on an armchair that looked like it cost more than my brother's car. I was sitting on a couch made of the same fabric, so I was afraid to move for fear that dirt would transfer from my clothes to the fine material.

I wanted to ask Con how he was so sure he was coming, but I was too afraid to open my mouth.

Because then I might ask the three men staring at me like I was some bizarre-looking animal at the zoo to take me home… or back to that little house in the middle of nowhere so I could get rid of that note and just crawl back into Vaughn's arms.

What the hell had I done?

"No," I whispered so the men around me wouldn't hear. "I did the right thing."

"Did you say something?"

I jumped when the man named King spoke.

"Um, no, sir… sorry," I croaked.

I chanced a glance at him and saw that he was watching me with a mix of pity and understanding. He was a really big guy… bigger than both Con and Luca. He wasn't classically handsome and had lighter features, but he scared me the most. A dark green T-shirt was pulled across his broad chest. His arm muscles were stretching the thin material to the brink and I could see a tattoo on his bicep, another on his lower arm and even on his hand.

I told myself just to take deep breaths. Vaughn would come. He had to.

Unless I'd angered him so much that he wanted nothing more to do with me. He'd said he'd always come, but maybe *always* didn't really mean the same thing when you defied someone.

"Can I get you anything to eat or drink, Aleks?" Con asked. If I hadn't been so nervous I would have smiled at how the man always seemed to be wanting to feed me.

I shook my head. "No, thank you."

No way was I going to throw up in front of these men, and that was exactly what would happen if I tried to put anything in my belly at this point.

Where was Vaughn?

Luca and Con had said he'd probably be right behind us… that it would be only a couple of hours at the most until he arrived. But it had already been three hours since we'd arrived at the too-big house. The drive to Vegas had taken a couple of hours and the flight had taken almost five, so it was nearing the twelve-hour mark since I'd last seen Vaughn.

"He never picked up the ticket," Luca said as he hung up his phone, his face pulled into a mask of irritation.

"Ticket?" I asked.

Luca sat down in the other armchair. To say I'd shocked the man when I'd found him early this morning and told him I'd help him find his son was an understatement. The man continued to look at me like he couldn't believe I was there.

I couldn't believe it either.

"I left a ticket for him at the airport. It was an open ticket so he could grab the next available flight to New York as soon as he realized we were gone. I had Con text him the information when we left Vegas."

I nodded. I'd finally discovered we were in Nevada when Luca,

Con, and I had left the house in the early morning hours. We'd flown out of the city on a private jet, but I hadn't thought to ask where we were going or how Vaughn would get there. Admittedly, I'd been too numb to do much but sit there and stare out the window. It had taken every ounce of control I'd had not to lose myself to a blackout.

Or to beg Luca to turn the plane around and take me back to Vaughn.

I hadn't actually made the decision to help Luca find his son until I'd been lying in bed with Vaughn and he'd talked about staying in the life he'd had to take on to look for the boy. It was the part when he'd admitted he and his family couldn't come back from what they'd been through that I'd known what I needed to do. I'd already been mulling over what it would mean to try and help Luca find Gio but knowing Vaughn would go back to that life and do it alone, without his brother and friends, had made me realize Gio wasn't the only one who needed to go home.

They all did.

Just like Dante had needed to go home.

My brother had been lucky because he'd had Remy to help him and me. And of course, Vaughn had saved us all.

I needed to give that back to Vaughn and his family, and I needed to help Gio because I was Gio and Gio was me. There were hundreds of Gios out there, thousands even, and they were all waiting for someone to come for them.

I couldn't save them all, but I wouldn't let my fear keep me from trying to save at least one.

Would Vaughn understand that?

Would he forgive me?

Was he even going to come?

"He knows we're here?" I asked, my voice cracking a bit. "Not in the city?"

Luca nodded, his expression softening a bit. "He knows we're in the Hamptons and he knows how to get here. We spent most of our childhood in this house because our mother preferred it to the city."

I managed another nod. I couldn't stop shaking so I tucked my hands under my legs so it wouldn't be as obvious.

Then I remembered the dirt on my fingers. "I'm sorry," I cried as I yanked my hands from beneath my legs and jumped to my feet to see if I'd stained the pretty fabric.

"Aleks—"

"I should have washed my hands better," I said, completely horrified. "Those men took me from work so my hands were still dirty and I was too upset to really scrub them but I should have when I got here—"

Terror began to skate through my system. What kind of punishment would I have to endure for staining the cold man's expensive couch?

"Aleks!" Luca called and I snapped my eyes to him. King and Con were both standing now. They looked worried.

"Aleks, the couch is fine and your hands aren't dirty. Even if you rolled around in mud and then on this couch, I swear to you, I wouldn't care. It's okay."

Luca seemed tense and I realized he was probably waiting for me to slip into another one of my blackouts.

Part of me kind of wished that would happen. I forced myself to take several deep breaths as I tried to accept that I wasn't in trouble. But I couldn't find any sense of calm.

Oh God, I couldn't do this.

"Where's Vaughn, Luca?" I whispered.

Luca carefully reached out to touch my upper arm. It was all I could do not to pull away. "He's coming, Aleks. I swear he is."

"He's here," King said softly. I jerked my head to look at him and saw him holding his phone out so Luca could see the screen. "My guy says he just pulled up."

"Make sure your guys stay out of his way," Luca said as he stepped back from me.

"Luca, not even *you* could pay them enough to get in his way," King said as he put his phone away. There was a hint of humor in his voice, but I didn't understand it.

Vaughn was here.

He'd come.

Luca moved away from me and then Con was at my side. I was shocked when he actually put his body between me and the big door that led into the hallway.

"Con?" I said softly in confusion.

"He's gonna need a minute, Aleks. Just stay behind me, okay?"

"I should tell him I'm sorry," I said. "I… I should take my punishment without argument."

Con looked over his shoulder at me. "Aleks, the only thing you need to worry about is him hugging you a little too tight," he said with a little grin. "You're not the one whose ass he's going to kick." He motioned to King. "Why do you think I called King in for backup?"

I looked toward the other two men and saw that King was standing just a few feet from Luca. And Luca actually looked a little nervous.

"Vaughn said you try to make them talk things out before they fight," I said.

Con chuckled. "Even I'm not *that* good," he said.

The huge door suddenly flew open with violent force. Vaughn's eyes swung to mine and I swore I saw the slightest bit of relief in them. Then it was like he forgot all about me and he was on Luca without a word.

It was a violent encounter and Luca didn't seem to be doing more than trying to defend himself. I didn't actually see him throw a punch.

I shouted Vaughn's name a couple of times, but he completely ignored me. King finally intervened, but Vaughn turned on him instead.

"Get your fucking hands off me!" he snarled as his rabid eyes remained on his brother.

"He's had enough, Vaughn!" King said.

"I'll say when it's enough!" Vaughn responded. "You're no longer my brother!" he bit out, then his eyes were on King, then Con. "We're no longer family!"

"Vaughn, it was his—" Luca began, but Vaughn hit him hard.

"Shut the fuck up! Don't tell me it was his fucking choice because you guilted him into it!"

When Vaughn slammed his fist into King's face, I felt the tears start to fall.

"Vaughn," I said softly, though I knew he wouldn't hear me. Con moved away from me and toward the struggling men. All four men began shouting so loud at one another that I knew I'd never be able to get Vaughn's attention. I looked around desperately, then grabbed a large sculpture that looked like a green rock. It was heavier than I would have thought, but I didn't care. I also didn't care what punishment damaging it would earn me.

I pulled my arm back and with every ounce of strength I had, I let the thing fly. I'd expected it to just make a hole in the window and figured the breaking glass would make enough of a sound to be heard. But to my horror, the entire floor-to-ceiling window shattered and the sound was deafening as glass flew. Fortunately, none of the glass hit me or any of the other men.

There was a beat of silence as we all looked at the window.

And then everyone was looking at me.

Luca's face was covered in cuts and bruises and his lip was bleeding.

King had a fresh bruise on his cheek.

Con and Vaughn both seemed unhurt.

"James," I whispered as my eyes met Vaughn's.

"Get out," he practically snarled, but I knew he wasn't talking to me. His eyes never left mine as the other men silently left the room. I didn't look at them.

I had eyes only for him.

He was looking at me like Luca had the night before when I'd first spied him on the porch...

Predatory.

That was the word.

But unlike with Luca, I wasn't scared.

I was... ready.

"James," I repeated, my voice low.

His strides were long and sure as he approached me. His hands came up to encircle my neck. I raised my hands to hold onto his wrists.

But not to try and stop him.

No, because I instinctively knew I'd need something to hang onto.

"You came for me," I said as I met his eyes.

"Always," Vaughn said, his voice still sounding harsh, but not because he was angry. He held my eyes for a moment, then his mouth was on mine.

Despite his anger or desperation or whatever it was that had driven him to let his fists fly with his brother and friends, his kiss was incredibly gentle. I'd expected him just to take what he wanted, and I'd prepared myself for the onslaught.

But his mouth was so soft and the kiss was short. A quick press of his mouth against mine.

Then another.

And another.

Over and over he kissed me and every time caused something inside of me to build, explode, then start to build again. His hands were firm on my neck, but it was his head that moved as he took my mouth at different angles. His beard tickled just the littlest bit, but there was nothing funny about it. If anything, it just made the sensation more vibrant.

It was an assault on my senses but in the best way ever.

Vaughn pulled his mouth from mine and kissed the corner, then began peppering my cheek, jaw, and chin with little kisses. I was sure my nails would leave half-moon marks on his skin because I was holding onto his wrists so hard.

"James," I breathed when he kissed me softly again.

He pressed his forehead against mine. "I was so fucking scared, Aleks."

"I'm sorr—"

"Don't be sorry," he said before I could get the entire word out. "Just swear to me that you won't ever walk out on me like that again."

I nodded frantically. "I swear I won't, James... I just..."

"What?" he murmured.

I opened my eyes. I could see that his were closed. He was still clinging to me, but I knew if I'd wanted him to release me, I would have just had to pull back a little.

"It had to be my choice to come here and I knew it was one of the few you wouldn't let me make."

He nodded against me. "Not safe," he muttered.

"You'll keep me safe," I whispered, then I took a chance and pressed my mouth to his. He moaned, and I felt a thrill go through me that I'd done that to him. But when his tongue suddenly licked along the seam of my mouth, I jumped in surprise and broke the contact.

Vaughn kissed me again gently, then whispered, "Just trust me, Aleks."

I stilled and let him kiss me again like he had before. It took just seconds for me to get lost in his touch again. This time when his tongue traced over that same spot, I managed to hold still.

"God, so sweet," Vaughn groaned against my mouth. "Open up for me, baby."

I didn't understand what he wanted and went to ask him just that at the same time that his tongue did the move again. I jumped when his tongue came into contact with mine. I'd barely processed that he tasted like butterscotch because he immediately drew his tongue back and kissed just my lips. When he repeated the move with his tongue, I found myself trying to figure out what it felt like.

It was weird and awkward and amazing all at the same time. I'd seen people kissing before, but I'd never realized *this* was what they were doing when their mouths were so passionately melded together.

"Okay?" Vaughn asked, sounding out of breath. He put enough space between us so he could look me in the eye.

I nodded because my throat felt so thick with emotion.

"Do you want me to stop?"

I didn't even have to think about *that* for a second. I violently shook my head. His smile was the sweetest thing I'd ever seen. This time when his mouth closed over mine, I was ready.

And what was weird and awkward and amazing became *just* amazing.

Then it became something else entirely.

"James," I managed to get out when he gave me a second to catch my breath.

"I know," was all he said, then his mouth was back on mine and my instincts kicked in. I didn't care if I wasn't doing it right or it wasn't pretty or what it would lead to... I just kissed him back. My arms went around his neck of their own volition and I was pressing into him so I could get more of whatever was causing all the little sparks of delight to go off in my belly like firecrackers. Since moving in with Dante and Magnus, I'd watched the annual fireworks on television every summer and always marveled at the end of the show when it seemed like hundreds of the things were going off all at once and lighting up the sky.

Those fireworks had nothing on the lightshow that was going on inside of me. My groin hurt from how hard my penis had gotten, but I didn't want to take away even one brain cell from enjoying what Vaughn was doing to me to consider what any of that meant.

Vaughn's hands ended up on my back, then drifted lower. When they drifted over my backside, I couldn't help but tense up.

And he noticed. He eased his hands up to my waist but I knew I'd ruined the moment.

"I'm—"

"Perfect," Vaughn said. "That's the only word I want to hear from your mouth right now because that's what that was, do you hear me?"

My body sagged in relief. I certainly didn't believe I was perfect, but whatever the heck had just happened between us couldn't have gotten any closer to perfect than if God Himself had created it with His own hand.

"Perfect," I whispered as I dropped my head so it was tucked beneath his chin. I wrapped my arms around his waist and curled the fingers of one hand around the forearm of the other to lock my arms in place in case he got the foolish idea into his head that he should let me go.

It was a long time before he spoke, but I liked that he held onto me when he did.

"Why, Aleks?"

I knew he wasn't asking why I'd left without telling him. He already knew the answer to that. No, he wanted more than that… needed more, probably.

"I spent all those years surviving because I knew Dante would come for me," I said softly. "There were so many days I wanted to just go into my head and never come out again. I… I once had the chance to end it all when I found a piece of broken glass, but I didn't want to die. I just wanted to go home. Wherever Gio is at this very second, all he's thinking about is surviving so he can see his father again… so he can see his uncle and his mom and all the people he loves." I shook my head and pulled back so I could look Vaughn in the eye. "I had Remy and Dante and you to save me, but what if Gio doesn't have anyone? What if I'm the only one who can make sure he gets to come home? God gave me so many people to look out for me. What if He's given me to Gio? I… I couldn't live with myself if I did nothing."

"It's too dangerous—"

"You saved me and Dante and Magnus when it was just you, James. No one will be able to touch me with you and your family watching out for me," I said.

Vaughn sighed and dropped his forehead to mine. "I don't want you to do this," he whispered. "I just want you to be safe. But I want Gio back so fucking bad."

I put my hand to his cheek and he immediately pressed into it. "You're going to have both, James."

"Promise me," he demanded. "Promise me I won't lose you."

But he didn't let me answer.

Maybe because he knew it was a promise I couldn't make.

He kissed me instead and I let him because it was easier.

And for once, I wasn't ashamed for taking the easier path.

Chapter 15

VAUGHN

"I will, Dante, I promise," Aleks said softly into the phone. "Tell Magnus I love him. Matty too. And Leo and Jamie and Connor and Miss Savannah..." Aleks fell silent and then smiled and nodded. Whatever Dante had said to him in response to the long list seemed to lift some of the sadness from his expression.

I'd somehow managed to release him after what had to be the most incredible kiss... or series of kisses, rather... that I'd ever known. I'd held onto him for a long time and neither of us had seemed eager to speak. When I'd finally pulled back, he'd asked me if he could call his brother to reassure him he was okay.

That had been a few minutes ago. Aleks hadn't put the phone on speaker and I hadn't asked him to. I hadn't really needed him to, either. Aleks was like an open book when talking to his brother, and it hadn't been hard to figure out that the first minute of the call had been Dante trying to convince his little brother to tell him where he was.

But Aleks had held firm and he'd also kept it together surprisingly well.

There was no doubt he was scared shitless about what was happening, but he wasn't regretting his decision. I also knew if he'd been given the choice to do what he'd done over again, he would have in a heartbeat.

Including leaving me without telling me.

It'd been a smart move on his part, because there was no way in hell I would have let him make that choice.

At least he didn't hold that fact against me.

I was all for Aleks making his own decisions, but if there was one I would have fought him on, it was this one.

As it was, I was trying to figure out if I should still try and talk him out of it. But a little part of me was so fucking grateful for this chance to find Gio that it was keeping me from voicing all the objections in my head. It helped to know that Aleks seemed so certain. Because if there was anything that would have made him second-guess himself, it would have been his brother.

"I love you too, meu melhor," Aleks said softly, waited a beat and then hung up the phone.

Thank fuck Dante hadn't wanted to talk to me. I might have been tempted to tell him where we were so he'd come get Aleks and we'd be forced to give up on this insane plan to use him to draw Stylianos out.

Aleks wiped at his eyes, but he managed not to cry. "They're safe," he said. "They took Matty to a house that belongs to some friends… lots of the family is there so they're all keeping an eye out for each other."

"That's good," I said as I reached for his hand. I linked our fingers and then Aleks leaned into me.

"He's still upset," he said quietly.

"Not at you," I reminded him.

"He doesn't understand why I don't just come home so he can watch out for me."

Aleks hadn't told Dante anything about what we were planning and he'd never brought up Luca or Gio, so as far as Dante knew, Aleks was choosing to stay with me until the danger had passed. If the man found out how close Aleks would actually be to those who were hunting him, Dante would lose his shit for sure. Not to mention Luca's role in Aleks's abduction…

"He does, Aleks. He knows you're trying to protect your family."

"He also knows I'm not strong enough for this... I'm too broken."

I'd been in the process of rubbing my thumb over his skin in the hopes of soothing him but stopped at his words.

I shifted so I could look at him. "Aleks, do you really believe that?" I asked gently. "That you're broken?"

He looked at me like I'd grown two heads. Then his face fell. "Please don't play with me," he said, then he dropped my hand and stood. He stepped away from me and toward the window, bypassing the one that he'd shattered to break up the fight between me and my brother.

"Aleks, I'm not—" I began as I got up to follow him.

"Then don't say that I'm okay... that I'm perfect or normal or whatever."

He actually seemed angry. He crossed his arms as he stood in front of the window and stared at the ocean, which was just a few dozen yards from the back of the house.

"I wasn't going to say that," I said. "But you're not broken, Aleks. I've never met anyone more unbroken."

He shook his head and hardened his jaw. As much as I hated seeing him upset, it was also weirdly comforting.

"Aleks, look at what you're doing," I said softly.

He looked at me, his mouth pulled into a mutinous frown. "What?" he asked. "What am I doing?"

"You're arguing with me. You're letting me know you're angry with me."

"I'm not angry—" he began but fell silent when he looked down and saw his own folded arms. He dropped them and flexed his hands like he was trying to figure out what to do with them.

"Two days ago, you wouldn't speak to me unless I spoke first. You wouldn't ask questions, you called me sir..."

"I called King sir," he admitted.

"Since you left this morning, have you spoken to my brother and friends without being given permission to do so first?"

"No," he began automatically, then snapped his mouth shut. Then he nodded. "Yes, but…"

"But what?"

"I trust you. I know I can say things to you and you won't punish me. I don't… I don't trust your brother or your friends like I trust you."

"Did you think about what Luca would do to you when you broke the window?"

He nodded.

"Did you *care*?" I asked.

He hesitated, then shook his head.

"Two days ago, you couldn't choose what you wanted to eat from a menu… you didn't *want* to choose. But everything you've done since then has been your choice, Aleks. That's not a sign of someone who's broken."

"But I'm so scared," he admitted.

"You're not alone in that. I'm scared shitless." He seemed confused, so I moved closer to him and stroked my fingers down his temple, more to touch him than anything else. "Do you know how many people never have to deal with even an ounce of what you've had to since you were a little boy?"

"But I let those men hurt me. I didn't try to stop them. I never said no, I never fought back. I never even tried to run," he whispered.

"You did fight, Aleks… in the only way you could… by surviving. Those men tried to break you. They probably think they succeeded. But look where you are. Not only did you get out and start living your life, you're about to go back into that world to bring some of those same men down. If that isn't a big 'fuck you,' I don't know what is."

He dropped his eyes and crossed his arms again. But he wasn't angry, just lost in thought. "Fuck them," he suddenly said so quietly, I almost didn't hear him. The swear word sounded so strange coming from him, but I couldn't help but smile when he nodded his head just a little after saying it.

Like he was just now realizing it was his choice, his *right* to say the word.

"Fuck them," he repeated, a little more loudly this time. His eyes lifted to meet mine.

"Fuck 'em," I confirmed.

"Fuck them," he said firmly and with a nod. "Fuck them." He shifted his gaze so he was looking out at the ocean. "Fuck you!" he suddenly screamed. When he shouted it again, I stood behind him and wrapped my arms around his upper chest and dropped my head so it was resting on top of his. His fingers dug into my arm as he yelled the swear word over and over again. He was hoarse when he finally stopped, then he slumped against me.

"Better?" I asked as I pressed a kiss against his temple.

He nodded. "I hate that word, by the way."

"My mother did too," I said. "She used to say things like fudgesicles or fiddlesticks when she was upset… she had a whole catalog of non-swear swear words."

I could see enough of Aleks's face to see him smile. "I think I would have liked your mother a lot."

I felt a pang of sadness that he'd never get to meet her. "She would have loved *you*," I said.

"Will you tell me more about her someday?"

I wanted to ask him if we had a someday, but then remembered I already knew the answer to that. I was saved from having to answer him when motion to my right caught my attention. Aleks and I both watched as Con walked along the small walkway that led to the back patio that bordered the room we were in. He reached down and pulled something out of the bushes.

It was the sculpture Aleks had thrown through the window.

Con stepped through the shattered window, his boots crunching on the broken glass. He was rubbing the green rock as if to get some scuffs off it. Somehow the ugly decoration had survived Aleks's rare show of force. Con glanced at us and shook his head like he was disappointed. But I could tell he was just fooling around.

Aleks, on the other hand…

"This thing cost me a fortune," Con said, feigning anger as he went to open the main door to the room. King and Luca were both standing outside it. "Look, Luca, it's okay," he said with a big smile. "No reason to worry."

Concerned Aleks would take Con's pretend irritation to heart, I said, "Stop fucking around with him, Con."

Aleks was tense in my hold but relaxed when Con winked at him.

Luca grabbed the sculpture. "Oh good," he muttered. He looked at me and Aleks. "Everything okay in here?" he asked. His face was a mess. He'd cleaned the blood off the worst of the wounds I'd inflicted on him. I was still every bit just as angry as I'd been when I'd stormed through the door, but my fury was tempered by the fact that Aleks was safe.

"Yeah, we thought we heard yelling," Con said. He looked pointedly at Luca and King. "Told you fighting isn't what they were doing in here. Pay up," he said as he held out his hand.

"You need to grow the fuck up, brother," King said with a shake of his head, then he went to sit down on the sofa.

"What?" Con asked innocently.

Luca warily approached us. His eyes met mine briefly, then surprisingly, they shifted to Aleks. I was stunned to see what looked like protectiveness in my brother's gaze as he looked at the man in my arms. "You good?" he asked.

Aleks nodded. "I'm sorry about your window… and your rock," he said as he motioned to the sculpture. He was still a little stiff in my hold, but he wasn't pressing into me like he was afraid. And I loved the fact that he was still in my embrace and the fingers of his left hand were running up and down the forearm I had pressed against his chest… like he was trying to soothe me as if I were a wild animal or something.

"The window can be fixed," Luca said. "As for this thing," – he held up the sculpture – "we just need to work on your aim a bit." With that, Luca drew back his arm and threw the sculpture through the broken window. It landed in the huge pool that was a good deal away.

"Hey!" Con called indignantly. "Do you know how long it took me to find something pretentious enough for this room?" he asked. "See if I bother to get you something for your next birthday."

I couldn't help but smile. But it was Aleks who surprised us all because he looked pointedly at Con and said, "Con, I'm sorry, but that rock was ugly as fiddlesticks."

We were all silent for a beat before bursting into laughter.

Even Con.

And Luca.

"Good one, baby," I said as I hugged Aleks from behind.

"It wasn't quite right, I think," he said.

I tipped his head back enough so I could brush my mouth over his. "Actually, I think it was fudging perfect," I said with a smile.

He laughed and turned into my arms. I held him as I met my brother's gaze. Seeing Luca laugh for even that brief moment made him seem twenty years younger. My brother had never exactly been an easygoing guy, but he'd been a different man around his son… a side of him our father had tried really hard to snuff out. But Gio had allowed my brother to be who he really was and that light had been stolen just as surely as his son had been. I was certain I'd never see it again.

But just those few seconds was enough to temper some of the rage I was still feeling toward him.

If Aleks could put aside his fear to help us find Gio, then I could put the shit with Luca aside for a while too.

Everything from here on out would need to be about finding Gio and protecting Aleks.

I held Luca's gaze and saw him nod slightly.

So he was on the same page as me.

It was a truce.

For now.

Chapter 16

ALEKS

Despite Vaughn's reassurance that I wasn't broken, I was a far cry from being fixed. Not that I'd expected some miracle cure with his words or because I'd given myself permission to shout a swear word a few times. Even now as the men around me began strategizing, it was all I could do not to call out for the darkness that had been my comfort for so long. Since I needed something to ground me, I began twisting my hands together as I tried to listen.

But it wasn't enough.

Vaughn and I were sitting on the couch and our legs were touching, but I found that wasn't enough either. Since he'd seemed okay with his brother and friends seeing him holding me earlier, I had to hope what I was about to do wouldn't upset or embarrass him. I kept my eyes on whoever was speaking as I let the fingers of my left hand slide over my own leg and then brush against Vaughn's. My goal was to just have the little bit of contact with him, but he surprised me when he calmly slipped his hand down to cover mine. Then he was linking our fingers.

And he kept right on talking without missing a beat.

Like holding my hand was the most natural thing in the world.

I pulled in a breath, then another and felt my body relax a bit. My mind cleared and I zeroed in on Vaughn's voice as he spoke.

"We need to let Stylianos seek us out," he said to Luca. "If you just start parading around the fact that you have Aleks, he'll get suspicious... most people will. He's already going to be looking at you for killing his men."

"I had my team plant evidence that points to a few other potential parties," King said. "Hopefully that will throw Stylianos off... he'll just think you were one of a few guys going after Aleks."

Although I knew none of them considered me property, I knew it had to look that way if any of this was going to work. But it still made me sick to think about how that's what I'd once been... and that there were people out there who wanted to make me that again.

"I think we need to throw Stylianos off even more," Vaughn said. "We need to make it look like an independent party took Aleks for the cash payout and Luca just happened to find out about it before anyone else... it'll legitimize Luca too." Vaughn looked at King. "Do you have any guys who can play the role?"

"Yeah," King said, his face pulled into a mask of seriousness.

"We'll need to get Lex and his team on creating Luca's posts saying he has Aleks—" Vaughn said.

"No," King interrupted. "Lex isn't available. I'll take care of the posts."

All three men looked at King in surprise. Con said, "King, he'd want to be involved in the search for Gio—"

"No," King repeated, his expression unwavering as he pinned Con with frosty eyes. "He's not available."

I could see that Con wasn't satisfied with the response, but when he went to say something else, Luca called his name and then shook his head. Con frowned and there was a moment of awkward silence as he seemed to decide if he was going to confront King further. He finally shook his head, then looked at Vaughn. "We'll need a picture of Aleks to show online," Con said. "It's going to need to be convincing," he said softly as he looked at me.

I swallowed hard. I looked to Vaughn because I couldn't find my voice to ask what Con meant.

"We've been using photoshop to make up fake pictures for Luca to post online as he tries to get deeper in the ring. People are suspicious of him because of who he is… so we've spent the last two years making it look like he's one of them with the fake pictures and posts in forums. It's been a painstaking process because we also have to cover everything we do so it can't actually be linked back to him, or he'd end up being prosecuted for all those things, even though he didn't actually do them," Vaughn explained.

I nodded. "The proof has to be so good that it fools even the police," I said.

"Exactly," Vaughn said. "While Luca hasn't actually committed a crime, if the stuff we've put out there ever gets linked back to him by someone other than the people we're trying to convince, it would all be over for him."

"So you need to take a picture of me?" I asked.

"Not just any picture, Aleks," Luca said gently. "It has to be of me and you and it has to show what our relationship is."

I felt bile rise in my throat. I looked at Vaughn. "Father took pictures like that." I began shaking my head. "No, I can't. No, I'm sorry, I can't." I couldn't stop from repeating the words over and over.

"Aleks," Vaughn said as he grabbed my face and forced me to look at him. "They don't need to be like those pictures," he said quickly.

I closed my eyes. "You saw them?"

He caressed my face. "It doesn't matter, do you hear me? It doesn't change anything for me."

I knew I was being ridiculous. He'd seen me do far worse things than those pictures, but the pictures had been a permanent tribute to what I'd been to Father and they were probably still out there for any manner of men to use however they wanted.

"Aleks," Con said, and I made myself look at him. "The picture with Luca just has to have a certain essence to it… you guys will be acting and nothing more. He won't be touching you in it and you can be fully dressed… it's about portraying a certain dynamic."

I didn't really understand the last word, but I got the gist of what he was saying. I looked at Vaughn. He was still holding my face. "So it can be like when Father had me sit on the floor next to him?"

Vaughn swallowed hard and nodded. "Yes," he said, though it sounded like the word was hard for him to get out.

"Okay," I said. A picture like that wouldn't be so bad. Father hadn't always made me undress when I'd knelt next to him after I'd pleasured him. I'd just have to pretend Luca was like Father.

I glanced at Luca and felt a little better when he dropped his eyes. He clearly wasn't happy about needing to do this either.

"Okay," I repeated and Vaughn released his hold on me but picked up my hand again.

"Do we stay here or in Chicago?" King asked. "I need to plan for logistical support."

"Here," Vaughn said.

"Isn't Chicago where that man is?" I asked. For the life of me, I couldn't figure out how to make my tongue pronounce his name. "I heard his men say that was where they were taking me in the van the night they took me," I added.

"In all likelihood, yes, Stylianos is in Chicago. But Luca going there with you so soon after acquiring you would set off red flags."

"If we're lucky, we can draw him here on our turf," Luca said to me. "The goal is to play it like Marcus did… that I have no interest in selling you but if the price were right…"

This time I actually had to swallow the bile down and the burn made my throat hurt.

King cleared his throat. Everybody looked at him but me. I was still trying to keep from throwing up.

"My people found chatter online about a viewing party that's happening weekend after next. If Luca takes Aleks to that, it'll get back to Stylianos faster. He may even show up there if we mention the party in a post. He'll be worried about losing out to another potential buyer, especially if we hint that Luca's not entirely satisfied with his new acquisition… that he was hoping for someone a few years younger and with lighter features."

"No, absolutely not," Vaughn said, shaking his head. "We don't have enough control in that kind of environment."

King put his hands up in supplication as Vaughn's anger grew with every word. The idea of going to one of the very events I'd so often been forced to attend, sometimes as someone's property and sometimes as merchandise, made my stomach turn violently and part of me was glad Vaughn was so adamant about the whole thing.

But then I remembered none of this was about me.

"Will it work better if we do that?" I asked. "Will it help us find Gio faster?"

"Aleks—" Vaughn began, but he quieted when I squeezed his hand and then did to him what he was always doing to me to comfort me – I began running my thumb back and forth over his.

"There's no guarantee," King began.

I sighed and looked at Vaughn briefly, then back at King. "But you wouldn't have mentioned it if you didn't think it would help."

King didn't respond.

It was answer enough.

"I think we should do it," I said, even as my mind screamed at me to keep my mouth shut, or to at least say no.

"No," Vaughn said. "Out of the question." He released my hand and jumped to his feet.

"Vaughn—" Con began, but Vaughn cut him off.

"No! We're not risking it. It's not up for discussion!"

With that, Vaughn suddenly left the room. I watched him go. No one in the room moved or spoke. I knew there was a lot left to discuss, but it would have to wait. But there was one thing I could take care of before I went to find Vaughn.

"King," I murmured.

"Yeah, Aleks," King said. I could hear in his voice that he knew what I was going to say. It appeared that Vaughn was the only one trying to deny the inevitable.

"Get us into that party," I said softly, then climbed unsteadily to my feet.

It was Luca who said, "He'll be by the water… east side of the house." He pointed in the direction for me.

I nodded my thanks and then left the room. It wasn't hard to find him. He *was* by the water, but when I got closer and saw the white wooden bench he was sitting on, I knew it might not have been the beautiful view that he'd been seeking out.

The back of the bench had the words, *For My Theodora* carved into the top slat.

I went around the bench and sat down next to Vaughn. I leaned into him so my head was resting on his chest. He put his arm around me.

"Was this her spot?" I asked.

Vaughn began playing with my hair as the slight ocean breeze blew it around. I could feel a slight tremor in his hand.

"She'd come out here and walk every day, even when the weather was bad."

"Will you tell me what happened to her?"

"It was a few days before Christmas. Luca and I were in the living room in the townhouse our parents owned in the city. Our mother had wanted to do some shopping, so we'd gone there for a few days. The plan was to spend Christmas out here."

"You said your mother spent more time at this house, right?"

"Right," Vaughn murmured. "Luca and I went to public school, she did all the cooking and cleaning and grocery shopping herself, even though our father had hired people to do all that… she just wanted to live a quiet life. It wasn't even really this house that she loved – but the water, it called to her."

"Like trees called to you," I said.

He chuckled, the sound of it rumbling beneath my ear. "Yeah, like that."

"What about your father?"

"My father," Vaughn murmured. "He liked winning. He liked knowing people were afraid of him. Power was his drug and he was a full-blown junkie."

I sighed because I'd heard Remy use that term to describe himself when he'd been hooked on drugs before moving to Seattle. He'd been clean for two years, but I knew it was something he still struggled with on a daily basis. I didn't understand addiction, but I understood power. Vaughn's father may not have hurt kids the way Father and Brian had, but he'd gotten off on having that power over someone or lots of someones.

I had a pretty good idea of who was included in that list of someones.

"Did your father live here with you?" I asked.

"He'd make the commute sometimes, but it wasn't unheard of for him to spend several days in the city. Every once in a while our mother would go to him and leave us with a sitter, but it wasn't very often. If it hadn't been Christmas, I doubt we'd have been in the city that day."

"What happened?"

"She was getting some shopping bags out of her trunk. Luca and I were in the house... I was old enough to watch him. She called us to come help her. We were in the process of getting our coats on when we heard this loud bang. Then another." Vaughn let out a harsh laugh. "Luca and I thought it was a car backfiring... we actually told each other it sounded really cool because it'd been so loud."

I reached up my hand to search out Vaughn's where it was resting on my shoulder.

"I saw her first, but I wasn't fast enough to stop Luca from coming around the car. Her eyes were open and there was just the smallest amount of blood coming from this tiny hole on her forehead. But there was so much of it beneath her head and back. I started screaming for help and tried to shake her awake, but Luca, he just... he just stood there like he didn't understand what he was looking at."

Vaughn was silent for several seconds before saying, "It was one of our father's business rivals. Our father had stolen from him and the man had lost everything. So he took our mother's life, his wife and child's, then his own."

"I'm sorry, James," I said as I sat up so I could look at him. But he was staring at the ocean.

"My father had never been a particularly soft man," Vaughn said. "But he buried what little kindness he'd had with her."

"You said he promised your mother he'd always look out for you."

"No, I said he promised he wouldn't get rid of me."

I felt my throat close up. "What does that mean?"

He shook his head. "Doesn't matter."

"It matters to me," I said.

He looked at me and then reached out to touch my face like he had to be sure I was really there. He smiled, but it didn't reach his eyes.

"He used to tell me and Luca that no one could ever take anything from him again. It was bad for business. That pretty much became the family motto after that." Vaughn's eyes drifted to the ocean again. "He had two sons so he figured he'd make use of that. Luca learned the business side of things because he was the 'real' kid and my job was to make sure no one stole from him or our father ever again."

My eyes drifted to the gun tucked in Vaughn's waistband.

The gun he rarely had out of his sight.

"He made you do bad things?" I asked.

"He didn't make me," Vaughn said. "I wanted to make my dad proud so I did it all without question. He wanted me to learn how to fight – I learned how to throw a punch with the best of them. He wanted me to carry a gun – I made sure I always hit my target. He wanted me to rough a guy up – I didn't even ask why I was doing it."

I felt sick to my stomach because I couldn't envision Vaughn hurting people for no reason.

"Fortunately, the old man still had a conscience. My job was mostly just to push people around until they saw my father's side of things," Vaughn murmured. "Only fuckers I've ever put in the ground were the ones I met after Gio was taken."

"That's why Con said you were the best equipped to go after Gio from the inside."

Vaughn nodded. "King's good, but he and subtlety aren't the best of friends. After I move on to the next 'client,' King and his team get the kids out and eliminate the fuckers. Con gets the kids to safety and Lex helps them either go home or start over. Luca finances all of it and uses his contacts to take down any network he can, usually by leaking evidence to the cops or task forces around the country. He also chases down every lead on Gio while still maintaining the outward appearance that he's just another super-successful businessman."

I leaned against the bench and let my fingers roam over the inscription on the back of it.

"You've all paid too high of a price," I said softly.

Vaughn shook his head. "Luca's suffering is far worse. That kid was… is his entire life. Luca was on the same path as our father until Gio came into his life. Then it was like he just woke up." Vaughn smiled. "You should have seen our father's face when Luca told him he was taking all the businesses legit. Fucker nearly had a coronary on the spot. Finally did six months later."

"What did you do?" I asked. "After Luca told your father that."

"You'll just laugh," Vaughn said with a smile.

"No, I won't," I responded. I nudged his knee with mine. "Tell me."

"I finished high school first. Got my GED."

"Your father hadn't let you finish school?"

"No reason to. You don't need to understand algebra or biology to know how to shoot a gun or beat the shit out of someone," he said.

The lightness I'd been feeling dissipated. "How old were you when you got it?" I asked.

"Twenty-seven."

"What did you do afterwards?"

"I'd always dreamed of being a pilot but to fly for a commercial airline, it meant going to college and I wasn't so sure I wanted to do that at that age. Luca surprised me with flying lessons. I knew after the first one that it was what I wanted. I enrolled in college the very next day – full-time. Luca paid for everything. I tried to argue with him that I should be working while I was going to school so I could pay my own way, but to Luca everything was ours, not just his. The profits from the business, this house and the other properties he owned, the planes, the cars… all of it. It was just one of those things we never really agreed on, but I wanted to be a pilot and the sooner I could have that, the better. So I accepted the money." Vaughn dropped his gaze and stared at the gun tucked in his waistband. "Gio was taken three days after I started school."

"You were close to him?" I asked. I'd already guessed as much, but I wanted to hear about his relationship with his nephew.

Vaughn nodded. "I guess he woke me up too." He looked at me. "I love that kid so fucking much, Aleks."

"I know you do, James." I reached out to brush some hair off his forehead. "We'll get him back."

He shook his head. "I don't want you at that party."

I sidled up to him and put my arms around his waist and made him the promise I hadn't been willing to a mere hour earlier. "You won't lose me, James. I promise."

He sighed but didn't relax.

And I couldn't really blame him.

Because we both knew there was a good chance it was a promise I couldn't keep.

Chapter 17

VAUGHN

Can I go flying with you today, Uncle Vaughn?
Not today, buddy. But soon, I promise.
I'm gonna be a pilot just like you.
I thought you wanted to be a businessman like your daddy.
I'm gonna be that too. You can fly me and Daddy around on our business trips and when you're too old, I can fly us. And I can fly Uncle Con to his fights and Uncle Lex to his con…con…
Conventions.
Right. And Uncle King… I can fly Uncle King wherever he wants to go when he needs a time-out. But I'll go with him because no one should be in so many time-outs… it means he's being too naughty.
Sounds like a good plan, Gio.
It is, Uncle Vaughn… because I'm smart like Daddy.
"James, open your eyes."

I did as I was told because it was Aleks speaking and I would always do what Aleks asked. I pulled in a breath as I opened my eyes and saw him leaning over me. At some point, he'd turned on the light on the nightstand next to me, which meant he'd leaned across me to do it and I hadn't even noticed.

God, why was I suddenly sleeping through so much?

"Sorry," I muttered. "Guess we shouldn't have slept in the same bed. You need your sleep."

Aleks had his left arm bent at the elbow so he could rest his cheek on his hand. His right hand was on my face. My body reacted to the sensation of his lithe body pressed up against mine beneath the blanket.

"I sleep better with you," he said. "I like how big and warm you are and how you wrap yourself around me when you sleep… like you're afraid to let me go."

His bluntness had me looking at him in surprise. I could see that there was a hint of color in his cheeks. It was then that I realized my right arm was indeed beneath his body. We hadn't fallen asleep like that because I hadn't wanted to crowd him.

Aleks's fingers played with my beard as he held my gaze. His thumb skimmed my mouth and I couldn't help but press a kiss against it. I knew I needed to put a stop to whatever was happening between us because it would only hurt all the more when I had to let him go once all this shit was settled, but when Luca had asked tonight if we needed one room or two, I'd blurted one before even giving Aleks a chance to answer. Con had bought Aleks some clothes, including a T-shirt and shorts he could wear as pajamas. While Aleks had been in the middle of changing in the attached bathroom, I'd offered to talk to Luca about sleeping in the room across the hall so Aleks could have some space.

Then he'd come out of the bathroom and I'd nearly swallowed my tongue.

Not only because of how great he looked in the shorts, especially since they were snug along his slim thighs and shapely ass, but because he'd chosen to wear my T-shirt instead of the new one Con had gotten him. He'd been nervous and hadn't been able to stop rubbing one of his arms with the opposite hand, but as he'd gone around to the other side of the bed, he'd murmured that we could share the bed.

We hadn't talked after that and there'd been a gap between us when I'd turned off the light, but apparently my body hadn't been satisfied with the lack of contact.

"I don't usually dream," I said as I tried to get control of my lust. The last thing Aleks needed was to know what the proximity was doing to me.

"We're the same," Aleks said as he continued to touch me. "Our minds have been hiding from the past but the memories don't want to be forgotten."

I nodded because that was exactly it.

"Sometimes I wish I could forget..."

"Me too," I admitted as I used my free hand to brush the hair that was dipping down on his forehead just a bit.

Aleks seemed to hesitate for a moment before he added, "But not you... I wouldn't want to forget you."

I felt my throat threaten to close up and all I managed to do was shake my head. I hoped he understood what I was trying to say. I had no idea why this one man had the power to leave me speechless with the simplest of words, but I was tired of trying to fight it or pretend he didn't completely own me. He'd done something from the moment I'd first seen him and there was no going back.

Aleks smiled as he took in my nonverbal response.

Yeah, he knows, I thought to myself.

"You said I never had to ask to touch you," Aleks murmured as his eyes fell to my mouth for a moment. "Does that mean... *anywhere?*"

"Yes, it fudging does," I managed to say.

He smiled wide as his finger continued to stroke back and forth over my lower lip. Then he leaned down and tentatively brushed his mouth over mine.

I kissed him back but let him set the pace. Much like our first kiss, it took a little while to find that perfect rhythm, but he was a quick study.

He also had this thing with touching my face as he kissed me. Like he wanted to make sure I didn't try to pull my mouth away.

Like that would ever happen.

I let my lips part in invitation, which caused Aleks to pull back just a little. "I'm not good at this," he said with a shake of his head.

"Aleks," I said with what was supposed to have looked like a grin but probably came off looking like a grimace instead, because my body was lighting up like a brushfire. "If you were any better at this, I'd end up stroking out."

I could see that last part confused him, but before I could explain, his mouth was back on mine. He still hadn't tried to deepen the kiss when he pulled back again, but his entire upper body had shifted so he was lying on my chest.

"I... I like kissing you," he began hesitantly. "But..."

"It can be as much or as little as you want, Aleks. You're in control."

His eyes widened at that.

I used my free hand to run my fingers along the back of his arm, which he had pressed next to my body so he could support some of his upper body weight.

"Anything we do together is about choice, Aleks. Yours and mine. Together. If there was something I didn't want you to do, I'd tell you and I'd expect you to stop just like I will always stop when you ask me to."

My words seemed to stun him into silence and he actually pulled back a little more as if he needed the distance to process what I'd said. I kept toying with the skin behind his elbow because I wanted to maintain as much contact with him as I could.

"I won't ever hurt you, James," he finally said, then he dropped his weight down on top of me again.

"I know you won't."

"But I may do things wrong... you'll tell me if I do, right? I want to make you happy."

I shook my head in disbelief at him. "Jesus, Aleks, what you do to me," I murmured, then I brushed my mouth over his. He kissed me back and this time his tongue ventured into my mouth. I groaned at how sweet he tasted and my entire body tensed in anticipation with every pass of his tongue over mine. I fought the natural instinct to kiss him back and just let him explore my mouth instead. It was a good minute before he suddenly whimpered and grabbed my face more firmly.

Then his kiss turned possessive and needy.

"James," he breathed against my mouth and I knew what he wanted. When he kissed me again, I kissed him back.

Hard.

Deep.

Desperately.

I closed my fingers around his upper arms as he lay more of his body on top of me. I barely noticed his weight, but I didn't miss the hardness that was brushing my stomach as Aleks started to squirm.

I knew what he was trying to do, but I doubted he did.

I used one of my hands to pull the hem of my T-shirt up so my abdomen was exposed. The move had Aleks freezing and then looking down between our bodies. His skin was flushed and I could feel a tremor running through his body.

"Aleks," I called. He looked up at me, his pretty brown eyes wide with confusion… and desire. "Take what you need," I said. "I'll like anything you do."

He looked like he wanted to say something, but then his mouth was back on mine.

Ravenous.

He began grinding his dick against my abdomen. Slow at first, then a little faster. He began twisting his hips. Suddenly he grabbed my face. "James?" he asked, his voice full of so much question and lust that my heart broke for him.

Had he never felt pleasure before? Was the torrent of need his body was putting him through *that* new for him? I'd known him to be innocent despite all that had been done to him, but clearly I hadn't understood how much.

"Do you trust me, Aleks?" I asked as I cupped his cheek. He was breathing so hard he couldn't actually answer me, but he vigorously nodded.

And he was still grinding against me.

I reached down and slowly slid my hand over his lower back. I carefully worked his T-shirt up and since it was actually my shirt, it took a little bit of effort to get the folds of the shirt clear of our bodies. I left it on him but made sure our skin was touching. We both gasped at the sensation. Aleks's humping increased, so I took a chance and moved my hand to his ass. When he didn't panic, I slipped my fingers up to the waistband of his shorts and started drawing it down.

He froze.

"Just trust me, baby," I reminded him.

I waited until he nodded, then said, "Lift up a little."

He seemed to finally understand what I was trying to do. He lifted his hips.

"Free yourself," I urged.

Aleks swallowed hard, then his hand was reaching down to pull his dick free from the confines of the shorts. I slipped them down enough to expose his entire shaft, as well as his ass. I used my hand on his slim backside to urge him back down. My own dick was like a spike in my shorts, and there was no doubt he could feel it against his body, but I kept one hand on his ass and the other on his back to steady him.

"Just feel, Aleks," I said, then I lifted my hand to the back of his head and pulled him down for another kiss. He moaned and began kissing me like a starved man. His cock was hard and hot against my abdomen and I could feel pre-cum leaking from the head. I would have given anything to touch him there, or better yet, taste him, but I knew he wasn't ready for that.

Aleks's instincts took over as he fervently kissed me. He humped my stomach as hard and heavy as if he'd been inside of me and I nearly came at the thought of it. I'd let a few guys fuck me early on when I'd realized I was interested in men and not women, but it'd been a long time since I'd allowed anyone that level of intimacy.

But I knew I'd give it to Aleks in a heartbeat.

"That's it," I groaned as I squeezed Aleks's ass just a bit, then urged him to grind into me even harder. He dragged his mouth from mine and buried his face in my neck. He was panting hard, his hot breath further dampening my already sweaty skin. His whole body twisted and writhed on top of me and I lifted my legs so I could pump my own hips upward. I had nothing to actually fuck besides the material of my shorts, but that was more than enough.

The fingers of Aleks's right hand twisted into my hair as he began to cry against my throat.

But I knew he wasn't scared or upset.

He was just completely overwhelmed.

"That's it, baby, just let go," I said as I kissed his cheek.

His left hand sought out mine. He linked our fingers and then he pressed our hands onto the bed. His hold on my hair tightened as his entire body drew taut.

"James," he groaned.

My own orgasm was right there, but I managed to hold it off. I slid my finger along Aleks's crease but didn't apply enough pressure to let it slip between his cheeks. I eased it beneath the shorts and gently touched his balls before giving them a little squeeze.

"James!" he cried. I sought out the shell of his ear with my tongue, then bit down on the lobe as I massaged the sensitive skin between his balls and his hole. He came apart at the contact. Hot liquid spewed all over my abdomen as he desperately fucked me. I kept massaging him through the orgasm as my own climax raced up my spine. I moved my hand up to grab his ass as I fucked upward, imagining it was his tight body I was about to empty myself into.

Aleks clung to me as I came. I shouted into his ear as my cum shot from my dick and soaked through my shorts and began dripping down the inside of my thigh. My brain turned to mush as the pleasure quaked throughout my body and caused my limbs to tingle with sensation. When I finally relaxed, Aleks's body was still on top of mine and his mouth was pressed against my ear. He'd unlinked our hands at some point and was holding my face. My hands had somehow both ended up on his ass, one closer to the dip in his back, the other lower down where the fabric was bunched up. I could feel his cum sliding down the sides of my abdomen as well as pooling in my belly button.

What I wouldn't have given to have been naked beneath him and felt the hot liquid mixing with my own juices and drenching my spent dick.

I felt the moment Aleks came back to himself and realized what we'd done. He tensed up and then he was lowering his hands.

I expected him to panic and climb off me, but he didn't. Instead he whispered, "I don't know what I'm supposed to say now."

I kissed his neck.

"Anything you want."

"You'll think I'm being foolish," he said.

"I can guarantee you that's not going to happen."

I felt him smile against me. "I think I messed up your shirt."

"Good," I said with a laugh.

"Not good," he said. His fingers began stroking my beard. "I love wearing your shirt."

"Then we'll wash it."

"Now?"

"Now," I agreed.

He finally leaned up so he could look at me. His smile was languid and wistful. He ran his thumb over my mouth. "Will you feed me?" he asked. "I'm very hungry."

"Absolutely," I said.

"Grits?"

"If Luca doesn't have the ingredients, I'll go find a cornfield and cut some of that shit down and figure out how to make it... with jalapeños," I said in complete and total seriousness.

His mouth went still for a moment and I knew it was because he could tell I meant every word I said. He smiled again. "Or maybe just cereal with rabbits on the box?"

"One trickster rabbit coming up," I said.

Aleks leaned down and kissed me. "Did I do it right?" he asked, his voice taking on a desperate quality. I remembered his fear of not being able to please me. I took his hand and first put it on my heart, which was still pounding.

"If that doesn't convince you, this will," I said as I moved his hand down to my damp groin. I made sure I wasn't inadvertently making him touch my still half-hard dick in the process. But to my surprise, when I released Aleks's hand, he let it linger and then he was brushing me through the shorts.

"I guess you have to do laundry too," he said with a sheepish smile.

"I guess so."

"Maybe next time we take our clothes off first," he said, his voice holding a hint of uncertainty.

I was just thrilled there'd be a next time. I sat up, grabbing his waist as I did so that he wouldn't topple off me. "That sounds like an excellent plan," I assured him. I kissed him softly and said, "You can use this shower and I'll use the one in the guest bathroom. Do you know where the kitchen is?"

Aleks nodded as he wound his arms around my neck. "Or you could just show me where it is… after we take a shower… together?"

I kissed him again. I loved his shyness but I loved even more that it wasn't silencing him.

"Now, that sounds like an even better plan."

Chapter 18

ALEKS

As usual, dinner was a quiet affair, which was so very different from the dinners I had with my own family back home. But it made sense because even though some of the tension between Luca and Vaughn had eased a little, the reason we were all there wasn't lost on any of us. If I hadn't had the nights to look forward to, I'd probably be going crazy. But knowing what I had to look forward to every night with Vaughn made it easier to get through the days.

I supposed when it came to what people normally did in regard to sexual activity in bed, we were still keeping it pretty tame.

And that was on me.

But everything was so new to me that I didn't want to mess it up with trying anything else. And Vaughn didn't seem to be in any hurry to do more, either. It seemed like he was perfectly content to just kiss me for as long as I wanted and then let me grind against him until my body exploded with pleasure. He always came too, but despite my comment that first night about taking our clothes off the next time, when it'd come time for bed, I hadn't had the guts. The only thing I had managed to do was wear the shirt Con had bought me so I wouldn't mess up Vaughn's shirt.

After all, why spend nights doing laundry when there was so much other pleasure to be had when darkness fell?

Once usually wasn't enough for me anymore... I finally understood a little bit about what the word "addict" meant now.

Because Vaughn had surely turned me into one, though he hadn't actually had to do anything other than let me use his body night after night.

I couldn't get enough of that feeling of being free and floating. And when Vaughn closed that bedroom door behind us and locked it every night, the outside world fell away. After that, things played out much like they had the first night. I wasn't comfortable having Vaughn's weight on top of me, even just for kissing, so it was always me lying on top of him. And while I was okay with being naked when we showered together afterwards, my mind was convinced that things would go terribly wrong if we were naked beforehand.

Which wasn't really fair to Vaughn, since he was forced to find his pleasure while still wearing his pajama bottoms.

But he never once complained, and when I once tried to apologize that I couldn't get over my fears more quickly, he'd silenced me with a passionate kiss and had told me what was happening between us was perfect just the way it was.

As slow as things were progressing in the bedroom, they were moving at a snail's pace when it came to finding Gio. Vaughn and the guys spent most days strategizing and going through all the chatter that my "return" had generated. I'd asked Vaughn to let me read some of the comments on one of the fake posts King had created, but it'd been a mistake because all it had done was set me back. Technically, the posts Vaughn had let me see were probably pretty tame, but it hadn't mattered... my mind had sought to defend itself. I hadn't blacked out, but I'd retreated to our room, thrown up the full lunch I'd eaten, and cried in Vaughn's arms as he'd gotten me in the shower to clean me off. Despite the fact that he'd seen me naked a dozen times in the shower at that point, I'd been so upset I'd freaked when he'd tried to take his clothes and mine off. We'd ended up showering in our clothes and only when I'd calmed down had I let him undress me.

I'd tried to apologize to him, but he'd reminded me that the old me either would have escaped the whole thing by blacking out or shutting down to the point that Vaughn would have been able to do anything he wanted to me. He'd said my behavior was more in line with what he would have expected to see.

It'd been a compliment of sorts, though I knew he hadn't exactly meant it that way. But I'd seen it as me reacting to an extraordinary situation like a normal person instead of a freak who wasn't in control of his own mind or body.

I hadn't looked at any of the comments on the posts after that, and Vaughn had made sure none of the guys talked about specific posters and whether or not they were Stylianos if I was around.

The picture I'd had to take with Luca had been another really rough time. The mere act of kneeling at the man's feet while he'd put his big hand on my head like I was a prized pet had made it really easy to not need to act for the camera. We'd gotten the image in one take and as soon as King had said it would work, Vaughn had told everyone to leave. Luca had already been on his feet, stopping only long enough to help me up. Then he'd been out the door like a shot. I'd stood numbly in Vaughn's embrace for a while and then we'd gone for a long walk on the beach and he'd held my hand the entire time.

I'd never looked at the picture.

During the week, King and Con had come and gone and Luca had spent most of his time holed up in his office. Dinners were the only times they came together unless they needed to have a strategy meeting.

And while the lack of leads seemed to cause Luca to withdraw into himself more and more, he'd done something very unexpected on my third day at the house.

He'd had flowers delivered.

And not flower arrangements.

Actual flowers.

For *me* to arrange.

There'd been dozens of types and they'd kept coming each day, along with a slew of different kinds of vases and bases. I'd been shocked, but when I'd tried to thank him, he'd waved me off and told me to put the arrangements where I wanted to in the house. Vaughn had seemed stunned by the gesture as well but hadn't said anything to Luca.

Most of my days were spent coming up with creative arrangements that incorporated things I found on the beach during my daily walks with Vaughn. And the nights found me wrapped in Vaughn's arms. When I wasn't with Vaughn, I was thinking about him.

Yeah, I was definitely addicted to him.

But I didn't know what that meant when all of this was over.

"Don't you agree, Aleks?"

The sound of my name drew me from my thoughts.

"What?" I asked. I looked down at the food on my plate and noticed I'd managed to eat quite a bit of it while I'd been lost in thoughts of Vaughn.

That was new too... my body was finally starting to look forward to eating.

Maybe it was all the exercise I was getting by walking on the beach every day?

And grinding against Vaughn's hard body at night...

"Aleks..."

"What?"

I looked up and realized I'd zoned out again.

Con was the one trying to get my attention.

Jesus, I really needed to focus.

"Sorry, what?" I asked as I put a piece of meat into my mouth. It was some kind of lamb dish that Vaughn and Luca's mother had made often and that Con had learned how to make. I'd learned recently that although Vidone Covello had been Italian, Theodora had been Greek.

"I said, don't you think that if Vaughn's going to wash his pajamas every night, he should invest in more than one pair? How dirty could he possibly be getting them that he's gotta run to the laundry room every night?"

I began choking on the food at the question. Vaughn's hand

came up to slap me gently on the back. He had a big grin on his face. Con, for his part, seemed to be completely clueless about the loaded question he'd asked.

"Um..."

"Yeah, Aleks, why do you suppose I can't keep my shorts clean?" Vaughn asked.

"Must be his newfound love of grits," Luca suddenly said out of the blue.

"Since when do you like grits?" Con asked, still totally oblivious. "Isn't Aleks the one who likes grits?"

I was still struggling to chew the piece of lamb well enough so I could get it down. Vaughn's hand was on my back rubbing circles into it. "Yes, he is," Vaughn murmured.

"Hmmm, guess I'll need to make another go at making him grits," Con said absently. "I'm a way better cook than you, Vaughn."

"Keep your hands off his grits, Con," Vaughn said as he shot his friend a dark look.

"My brother's fiancé makes me grits!" I blurted. "But Vaughn's are better."

All eyes turned to me.

"They are?" Vaughn asked me, his eyes going all soft.

"Um, yeah," I stuttered. "I like how you, um, added shrimp... Magnus's are really good but yours... I really, really like yours. They're the best," I added lamely.

Vaughn's smile of pleasure did gooey things to my insides.

"I still don't get what grits have to do with Vaughn's shorts," Con announced.

"Jesus, brother," King muttered as he stood and grabbed his plate to take it to the kitchen. He smacked Con on the back of his head and snatched his plate too.

"Hey, I'm not done."

"Yeah, you are," King said. "Let's go, Mr. Oblivious."

Con's gaze shifted to me, then Vaughn. He suddenly grinned and said, "Oh, gotcha... *grits*. Aleks, you sure you want to settle for his grits—"

"Okay, you're doing the dishes," Luca said as he stood and grabbed his own plate, then Con's arm.

"I cooked," Con protested as Luca practically dragged him from the dining room.

"Sorry," Vaughn said. "They can be a bit much."

I wanted to laugh at that. I *did* laugh at that.

"You haven't seen anything yet."

Vaughn's fingers moved up to my neck and I found myself leaning into his sensual touch.

"What do you mean?"

"My family... they're..." I shook my head. "Huge, for starters. I mean, I don't go to many of their get-togethers... okay, none, really," I began. "But some of them come over to our house and the way they all joke... it's like nothing I've seen before. And Dante, he just... he loves it," I said with a smile. "He *deserves* it."

I felt Vaughn's eyes on me and felt my body go all warm. "You'll see what I mean when you meet them someday."

I caught myself the second the words were out.

Did we have a someday?

We hadn't actually talked about that.

Even if I made it through this and got to go home, Vaughn wouldn't be coming with me. He'd said as much when he'd admitted that he'd keep helping kids even after he got Gio out. He couldn't live that kind of life and still be with me, could he?

Could I?

Could I spend every day for God only knew how long, worried about the day he wouldn't come home to me?

I dropped my eyes and fought back the nausea threatening to ruin the delicious meal I'd just eaten. I waited for him to say something, anything that would confirm he *would* meet my family, but he remained silent.

I began picking at my food again, though my appetite was gone.

"Can I ask where Gio's mom is? You guys don't mention her," I asked, hoping to get past the awkward moment.

Mission definitely *not* accomplished because when I looked up at Vaughn, he looked stiff and tense.

"Sorry," I whispered.

"No," he said as he put his hand on my thigh when I started to get up. "No, it's just... it's not something we talk about... ever."

"How come?"

"She's gone... she was killed when Gio was taken. She tried to stop the guys and they shot her... in the head."

"Oh God, James, I'm sorry..."

He shook his head. "She and Luca weren't in a relationship, but he really did love her and she was such an incredible mother to Gio. He pretty much lost his best friend and his son all in one day. He's never really recovered from that... he kind of went off the rails for a while afterwards. Wouldn't eat or sleep or even talk to anyone, really."

"You guys said he went in on his own in the beginning to look for Gio."

Vaughn nodded. "He didn't tell any of us. Could've gotten himself killed. Luckily, he never told people who he really was and no one seemed to make the connection. He looked different back then, too... younger, less..."

He fell silent and this time I was the one to put my hand on *his* leg.

Vaughn didn't need to finish the description... I'd seen what that other world did to its victims, and even if Luca hadn't suffered the same kind of pain, he'd suffered. The whole family had.

I pushed my plate away because my appetite was completely gone.

"You should finish," Vaughn said gently.

"No, I just want to go to our room... with you."

He seemed to understand my need to be with him in that way because he kissed me softly and then said, "Let's go."

We took our plates to the kitchen, which was empty, and left them in the sink. Vaughn held my hand as we made our way down the hallway to the room we were sharing. Once we reached the door, he turned to me as he was reaching for the knob. "Do you want to call Dante?" he asked.

I did, but my mind was somewhere else at the moment and I

wanted to go with the feeling before I chickened out. I shook my head and then pulled him down for a kiss. I let my tongue slide into his mouth before inviting him to take over the kiss. I'd become a self-proclaimed expert at kissing in the past week, and I knew what to do to get him to take control, at least of my mouth.

Vaughn groaned and leaned into me. His hands moved down my back to my behind. He pulled me against his erection and then he was leaning back against the door, taking me with him.

"We should go inside," I said against his mouth. "I don't want Con to offer me his grits while we're getting naked."

Vaughn stilled, but I wasn't sure if it was the grits comment or the fact that I'd just changed the game on him by announcing we should get naked. When he moaned and then suddenly used his hands to lift me and spin me so my back hit the door, I knew it was the latter.

"Door," he ground against my mouth between kisses. "Open the fucking door."

I fumbled for the doorknob and managed to turn it. Luckily, Vaughn managed to catch my weight before we both stumbled through it. He kicked the door shut behind him and then he was carrying me to the bed. I felt a moment of fear when his weight came down on top of me when we hit the mattress, but then he rolled us so he was the one on his back. I put my hands on his shoulders and urged him to stay where he was as I broke the kiss. "I want to try it the other way," I said. "Can we do that, but if I get scared—"

"Anything, Aleks," Vaughn said as he sat up, taking me with him. His feet were still on the floor so I ended up straddling his lap, my knees on each side of his hips. "Can I take this off?" he asked as he tugged at my shirt.

It *was* actually *my* shirt, since I'd taken to only wearing his at night while I slept.

I nodded and lifted my arms. I forced some oxygen into my lungs and reminded myself he'd seen me naked many times. He'd touched me while I was naked many times. The only difference was that he would be doing it while he was aroused.

God help me, but in my mind, that was a pretty big difference.

But this was Vaughn.

My Vaughn.

My *James*.

Vaughn's big hands lifted my shirt as he slid his rough palms up my sides. I shivered at how good it felt. His eyes held mine as he worked the shirt off over my head. Once it was gone, he just held there, studying me, his eyes open and soft.

The way he was looking at me made me feel like the most beautiful, most cherished thing ever.

But not a possession.

Never that.

I put my hands on his face and relished in the softness of his beard. I kissed him, but he kept it quick and simple. I was expecting him to shift us so I was beneath him, so I wasn't prepared for him to dip his head.

And close his mouth around my nipple.

Air rushed out of me as electricity fired through my entire body.

"Oh, God," I whispered as he sucked on me, then licked over the sensitive flesh. His hands roamed over my back slowly, lingering on all the lines of raised flesh. We'd never talked about my scars, but he'd always touched them reverently in the shower... like he'd understood what I'd had to go through to survive them.

"James, please," I whispered when he started teasing my other nipple. One hand slid down to my waist, then beneath the waistband of my jeans. I wanted to actually thank Con for buying me pants that were just a bit too big because it meant Vaughn could easily slide his fingers past the material. My underwear was another matter, though. It was too snug for him to easily get his hand beneath and he didn't seem to be in any hurry to do so.

I, on the other hand, *had* felt his hand on my bare skin there several times and I *was* very much in a hurry to feel it again.

I grabbed him by the ears to get him to release my nipple. He lifted his head and then my mouth was on his again. Our positions meant I was a little higher than him and I took complete advantage of that fact.

But it didn't last.

I let out a little gasp when he lifted and moved me beneath him with next to no effort. My heart was in my throat when he pressed me into the mattress, but I managed to quell the immediate need to tell him to stop.

But he'd already stopped.

No, he hadn't moved off me, but he wasn't kissing me anymore.

"James," I began, but he shook his head.

"I'm not going anywhere, Aleks. We're just going to take as much time with this as you need. Remember, our pleasure is about both of us. And trust me, I won't get even an ounce of pleasure out of any of this if you aren't with me one hundred percent."

I felt both relieved and foolish at the same time. I doubted there were any other men on the planet who had to work as hard as Vaughn did… and who were even half as understanding.

"Okay," I said. I let my hands roam over his shoulders and down his back. "Will you take this off?" I asked as I tugged at his shirt.

He nodded and reached behind him with one hand to pull the shirt off over his head. He tossed it aside. I made a mental note to wear that one to sleep in tonight because it would smell like him.

It was silly, I knew, because he'd be right next to me and if all this worked out like it should, I'd want to be naked next to him all night, but I did have a weird fascination with his shirts. Maybe because it felt like he was a part of me when I was wearing his shirt.

Maybe that would change tonight.

Though I knew in my head I wasn't ready to go that far. In my heart, I really wanted to give him all of me, but my brain was already screaming at me not to let it happen. It was warning me that he'd change once he was inside me. My gut was telling me he wouldn't, but I couldn't get past that wall in my brain that was meant to protect me from reality.

Because it would destroy me if he turned out to even be a tiny bit like the men who'd hurt me.

It wasn't fair to him, but it also wasn't fair to pretend it was something that it wasn't.

I just wasn't ready.

Vaughn braced his weight on his elbow so he could caress my face as I ran my hands over his back. He was so well muscled that I couldn't get enough of testing how different his body felt than mine.

"You're so beautiful, Aleks," he murmured.

"You too," I said. "Handsome, I mean."

He laughed. "I'll take beautiful."

He kissed me gently over and over until I was the one deepening the kiss. My legs were still hanging off the bed so I spread them to ease the awkward position and his body notched between them. I tensed when his groin pressed against mine.

He didn't tell me to relax or settle down or to not be afraid. He just held really still and watched my eyes.

I took several deep breaths and then began rubbing his back again. Somehow touching him actually calmed *me*.

We began kissing again and I was just starting to relax and get into it when he practically ripped his mouth from mine. He was panting like crazy and I could feel his hardness grinding against me. I was hard too, but he seemed worse off.

This is it. He's going to do it now. He's going to fuck me. He won't be able to control himself.

"Aleks," Vaughn breathed.

I needed to tell him no. I needed to tell him I couldn't do it, but my fear of upsetting him took over. What if he didn't want to be with me anymore because I wasn't normal? Was it really worth losing him?

I opened my mouth to tell him I was ready but he suddenly kissed me softly. "Aleks, I want you inside of me… do you want that too?"

Wait.

What?

Chapter 19

VAUGHN

"What?"

I cursed myself for just blurting the words like I had, but I was so turned on and my body was craving the feel of him inside of me so badly that I hadn't been able to find a better way to ask him. Ever since the first night when he'd come all over my stomach, the obsession to know what it would feel like to have his cock buried deep within me had become like a living thing beneath my skin. I'd meant to bring it up in a more casual way and during a time when I wasn't completely lost in lust, but my brain had short-circuited a little bit when my dick had met his the second he'd opened his legs for me.

I started to pull off him, thinking I'd ruined the moment, but he held on to the backs of my arms.

"I don't understand," he said softly, and I could see a little bit of shame in his eyes. Aleks was one of the smartest men I knew, but he struggled with how to process things he didn't understand. In the past, he hadn't had to… in fact, he'd gone out of his way to avoid such thoughts. Instead, he'd hidden in his head until the thing he'd been forced to deal with had passed. So now, many of the things men his age knew and took for granted were an entirely new experience for Aleks and it didn't surprise me in the least that it was so incredibly overwhelming for him. "You want me to... to..." – his voice dropped to a barely there whisper – "*fuck* you?"

I used my fingers to lift his chin. "I want you to make love to me," I clarified.

This time he did release me and he scrambled upright. But when I got up to give him some distance, he held out his hand. I took it and sat back down on the bed so I was facing him. I shifted my body so I could put my legs on either side of him because he was on his knees.

"It doesn't need to be tonight, Aleks... or ever," I said. "It's just something I've been thinking about—"

"Is it because I'm not ready?" he asked sullenly.

"What?" I asked.

"Do you pity me and want to show me it isn't so bad or something? So I'll let you do it to me?"

I forced myself to ignore the little sting of pain that came with his show of doubt.

"First off, I don't pity you, Aleks... I've never pitied you. You're a survivor, not a victim, and surviving takes strength. I don't pity strong people."

Aleks lifted his eyes a little. "Then why?" he asked.

"Because I want to be that close to you. I want to know what you feel like inside of me. I want to know that you're part of me in a way that no one else can claim."

The statement made him more tense. "You've never..."

"I have," I interjected. For some guys, it would have been a turn-on to learn their partner had never had certain types of sex. But the added pressure of taking someone's virginity would have just heightened Aleks's anxiety.

I could tell he was both relieved... and something else... he actually looked a little jealous.

I let myself touch his cheek. "But when it's you inside of me, it's going to be so different, Aleks." He shifted his eyes to me, clearly curious. "I've fucked plenty of guys and I've been fucked by a few," I said. Aleks flinched at the word, but I knew it wasn't just because he himself didn't like to swear.

No doubt his perpetrators had used that word to describe what they were going to do to him.

The jealousy in his expression had also increased so I quickly added, "But it's never been about more than just pleasure. Does that make sense?"

Aleks nodded. "I didn't think…you're big and strong and experienced… I didn't think you'd ever let anyone do that to you."

And there it was, the crux of the discussion.

I took in a breath because I didn't want to risk saying anything that could even chance screwing this up.

"It was a choice like any other. What those men did to you wasn't about choice, or even sex. It was about power and control. Look at your brother and his fiancé… does anything about their relationship seem to be like any of those things?"

"No," Aleks said quickly. "They kiss all the time and sometimes…"

He blushed prettily. "Sometimes I can hear them at night or even in the bathroom every once in a while—"

Aleks slapped his hand over his mouth for a second. "Oh God, Dante would die of embarrassment if he knew I knew that." A small smile graced his lips and I used the opportunity to move even closer to him.

"It sounds like your brother and Magnus can't keep their hands off each other," I said as I began running my fingers over the back of the hand Aleks had clenched in his lap.

"They can't," he agreed.

"If you're going to compare what you and I do to anything, compare us to them, not those assholes who used sex to hurt and humiliate you."

Aleks opened his hands so I could play with his individual fingers. He dropped his eyes to watch me touch him.

"You really want that with me?" Aleks asked.

I wasn't sure if he was talking about him fucking me or the

actual relationship stuff like his brother had. Didn't matter because the answer was and always would be the same.

"Yes."

He looked up at me. "What if I'm never ready for you to—"

"Then that won't be a part of our relationship. Would it surprise you if I told you plenty of gay and bisexual men just don't like anal sex, period? It isn't because they were hurt by someone or because they don't trust their partner… they just simply don't find the act pleasurable. Couples, whether they're straight or gay, figure out what works for them."

"So if what you and I have been doing this week were all it could ever be—"

"Then I'd consider myself a lucky man, because despite what brought us here, this has been one of the best weeks of my entire life, Aleks," I told him.

He flushed with color and then nodded. "Me too."

I hadn't realized how badly I'd needed to hear that from him. Between his comments earlier in the evening about liking my grits better (which I'd known had absolutely nothing to do with my actual cooking of grits since I kind of sucked at it) and his affirmation that he was glad to be with me right now, here in this moment, I was reeling from the onslaught of emotion.

"Aleks, what I said earlier about wanting you inside of me… it doesn't need to be tonight and if it's something you don't want at all—"

That was as much as I got out because he raised himself up and kissed me. His arms went around my neck so I wrapped mine around his waist.

His kiss rocked my world. When he pulled back to let me catch my breath he said, "James, I love when you explain things to me and let me choose, but you can stop talking now. I've chosen."

I smiled when he kissed me again, his tongue dominantly controlling mine. We were both breathless by the time we separated again. In true Aleks fashion, insecurity swamped him as he blurted, "You have to tell me what to do so I don't hurt you even a little, James. And if I'm doing it wrong or you want me to stop, you have to promise you'll tell me. I couldn't... I couldn't live with myself if I hurt you—"

"Promise," I interjected before kissing him. I shifted on the bed so I could reach the nightstand drawer. I grabbed a condom and lube and set them on top of the nightstand. The sight of them rendered Aleks mute.

"We can get tested tomorrow when we go into the city," I said, since the idea of Aleks bare inside of me was already taking on a life of its own. "But until then, we need to use condoms because I haven't been tested in a while."

Aleks nodded. "I got tested after I went to live with Dante and he explained all that to me. All the tests came back okay."

I nodded and said, "Okay, then you don't need to get tested again unless you've been with someone since then."

Aleks shook his head violently. "No... no. Just you, James."

I grinned at how worried he looked. "I'll get tested tomorrow and then we can decide together what happens next... if we use condoms, if we do this again, if I can get my mouth on that beautiful dick of yours..."

He'd pretty much turned a shade of red by the time I pulled him so he was lying on top of me. It took only seconds for him to get back into the act of kissing me and then his mouth was exploring my chest as his hands trailed down my sides. I lifted my hands above my head when Aleks's mouth sought out the sensitive skin of my armpit. He nuzzled the hair there, then inhaled deeply.

"God, you smell so good," he said unabashedly as he sealed his mouth over mine. For all the trauma Aleks had experienced, he was such an open and honest lover. His eyes were, more often than not, gateways to his soul, and they were what I used to gauge how he was feeling about something.

Aleks let his sinful mouth slide down my neck, then my chest. But he hesitated when he got to the buckle on my pants. I was about to tell him I could take the jeans off myself, but then his nimble fingers were working the belt free, then the button and zipper. I held my tongue when he paused, his gaze staring at my erection, which was pressing against the material. His tongue darted out to wet his lips and it was all I could do not to groan at the sight.

I wouldn't lie and say I hadn't thought about how his mouth would feel on my dick, but it wasn't a game changer. In fact, there really wasn't anything that would change anything for me. If all Aleks wanted to do for the time we had left together was hold my hand, I'd give him exactly that.

Aleks's hand tentatively reached out to stroke the outline of my cock.

"You really want this," he said bluntly when he looked up at me.

His surprise didn't bother me at all. I knew it wasn't about him not believing what I'd said earlier... it was just taking his brain a little longer to catch up. His heart hadn't needed proof when I'd told him how much I wanted him inside of me, but his brain clearly hadn't been able to conceive the idea. But seeing how my body couldn't deny my words seemed to cause that final wall between me and Aleks to come crashing down. He crawled up my body and kissed me. "I'm sorry."

I knew what he was apologizing for.

He saw it as a lack of trust on his part.

I didn't.

"Don't be," I said with a shake of my head. "Just make love to me, Aleks."

He nodded and kissed me softly, then moved down my body again. His moves were a little more confident as he pulled my pants and underwear off. His eyes strayed to my cock as he worked, and I could see the occasional flicker of fear in his eyes, but I didn't try to reassure him that I wasn't going to throw him down and fuck him.

His brain was in control for the moment, so it needed validation that everything I'd said was true.

His body... and hopefully his heart... would take over soon enough.

Once I was naked on the bed, Aleks seemed unsure. His eyes met mine, then he started pulling the rest of his own clothes off. He did it quickly so I didn't really get to see the show, but when I saw his dick, which was damp with moisture, I knew he was with me. He might not have understood his body's needs, but he wasn't trying to fight them... he just needed time for his head to catch up.

"Come here," I murmured when he stood next to the bed stiffly and looked at my cock.

I held out my hand to him. He straddled me, then lay down on top of me, but was careful to keep our dicks from touching. "I don't know what to do next," he admitted. "I should touch you there, right? With my mouth?"

I shook my head. "Only if you want to. But I'm so turned on, I'd probably come the second those beautiful lips of yours even got near me," I said with a grin.

That seemed to relax him a bit.

I rubbed his back to try and soothe him but didn't force him to drop any more of his weight onto me. I let him take the initiative.

Which he did, about fifteen seconds later.

After letting out a deep breath, he kissed me. It was sweet and soft at first, then our desire took over and we were ravishing one another. When Aleks's body sank onto mine, we both gasped because our leaking, bare cocks came into direct contact for the first time.

"Fuck," I whispered as sensation rocketed through me. I had a hold of each side of Aleks's face as I spoke. His eyes were closed, like he was in pain.

But I knew he wasn't.

"Yeah, that," he breathed.

I shifted my legs so I could open them. More of Aleks's body rested on mine. Since he was shorter than me, the tip of my cock was closer to the base of his and I could feel the weight of his balls on my skin.

Aleks began humping me like he always had the past several nights, but this time the sensation was a thousand times better because there was nothing separating us. I dropped my hand to his ass to help him grind against me. He tensed up and I immediately removed my hand. But then he was reaching down with his right hand to search out mine and put it back on his ass. I dropped my other hand and gripped both of his cheeks as I planted my feet on the bed and began to lift my hips. Aleks let out a little whimper as he pressed his head to my chest and began pumping his dick against my stomach. He was grinding so much that my dick slipped between our bodies and ended up behind him… against his ass. I thrust against him before I could stop myself, but to my amazement, he didn't ask me to stop or try to pull away.

His hand came up to find my cheek and then he was turning his head so he could kiss me. "Again," he groaned.

We began grinding against each other like crazy men. I could feel pre-cum from Aleks's cock streaking over my stomach.

"What's next?" Aleks ground out when he ripped his lips from mine. "I'm really close."

I nodded and slowed my own gyrating hips, then forced his to stop by grabbing his waist.

"You need to get me ready," I said.

"Show me how?"

I loved the confidence in his voice. Yes, there was a hint of fear there too, but it was obvious that he still wanted this and that he wasn't doing it just because he needed to get off.

I reached for the bottle of lube and pulled in a breath. I'd gotten so caught up in the fact that I was going to be with Aleks in a new way that, up until now, I'd forgotten to be nervous.

But those nerves all came racing back with the snicking sound as I flipped open the cap on the lube. I told myself not to let Aleks see my apprehension, but the second my eyes met his, I knew he knew.

Apparently, he wasn't the only one who had eyes that were gateways to their souls.

Chapter 20

ALEKS

He's nervous.

That fact should have made me want to call off this whole thing, but it actually made me feel a little better. It was hard to always be the one who was lacking in knowledge and confidence. I knew Vaughn had some vulnerabilities, like his family and how hard his work was on him mentally, but this was the first one that *I* could do something about.

He was trusting me to take care of him.

I could do that.

I *would* do that.

No matter what.

Even if I hated what I was about to do, which my gut was telling me I probably wouldn't, I'd still make sure Vaughn felt only pleasure.

My lust had eased a little bit in the minute it had taken for Vaughn to get the lube and open it. I knew what the slick liquid was for because one of the men I'd been with had used it most of the time.

I'd actually considered myself lucky after the fact because Brian, then later Father, had only used spit. *That* was something I never would have been okay with doing to Vaughn, even if he'd asked.

I shifted off Vaughn enough so he could turn over, but to my surprise, he didn't move.

"Put out your fingers," he said.

Maybe he wanted me to prep him from the front, then he'd turn over?

I held out my fingers.

They were shaking.

Despite some of the confidence that I was feeling that I could still do this, I *was* scared. My mind still couldn't make sense of the fact that some men liked this part.

The liquid felt cold on my fingers, so I began rubbing them together to try and warm it up. Vaughn tossed the lube on the bed next to him, then settled one muscled arm beneath his head and watched me through hooded eyes. His legs were on either side of me and his penis was lying against his groin like a stiff piece of pipe. There was clear fluid collecting on his skin. To my amazement, my mouth actually filled with saliva at the sight.

What the heck was that about?

I didn't like the taste of a man's release or the stuff that came before it… the guys I'd been with had had all sorts of names for it but they'd all been vile, dirty terms I'd never repeat.

"I never really liked the taste, either," Vaughn suddenly said and I looked up at him in surprise. "Till yours," he added.

"What?" I asked stupidly. "But you've never…"

"I've been covered in your juices nearly every night, Aleks."

I froze.

He'd tasted it.

Vaughn chuckled and sat up, putting an arm around my waist as he did so. "The before *and* the after," he said softly. He looked down at his own stomach and then quickly swiped a finger through the liquid clinging to his skin. "I'm betting yours and mine together is the sweetest," he murmured.

I had no clue what possessed me to do it, but before he could lick the juices off his finger, I leaned down and closed my mouth around his digit.

He sucked in a breath as I slowly drew my lips up, collecting the fluid as I did so. It had a weird, earthy taste that was also a little sweet. I let my eyes meet his. "You're right," I declared quietly. "Definitely the sweetest."

Vaughn let out a groan and then he kissed me hard and fast. His tongue stole what little of the taste lingered in my mouth.

It turned me on like nobody's business.

"Get me ready, Aleks," Vaughn said as his hand closed around the back of my neck and he pressed his forehead to mine. "It's not going to take much at this point," he admitted.

He lay back down and then he was shifting his position so more of his backside was exposed. I let out an audible gasp when he lifted his legs up and back just a little and used his own hands to open his body for me.

I was on sensory overload as I stared at his opening.

It was so small.

There was no way I was going to be able to do this and *not* hurt him. But I also couldn't deny the fact that my penis had gotten even harder.

Oh God, what did that make me? Was I like Father and the rest of them now? Were my body's needs more important than the person in front of me? Would I end up hurting Vaughn and not knowing… or caring? What if he told me to stop and I couldn't? What if I became a monster like *them*…

"Aleks," Vaughn called, but it was hard to hear him because I was so caught up in my body and my mind warring with one another. Then Vaughn's hand was on my face. "Aleks, baby, look at me," he implored.

I did.

"What those men did to you wasn't about them going crazy with lust or not being able to control themselves around you or any one of the kids they hurt. Everybody, man or woman, has enough control over themselves to be able to keep from hurting someone else. And anyone who tries to say any different is a fucking coward who is afraid to admit they chose their own satisfaction over another person's pain. You are not like any of those men and you couldn't be, even if you tried."

"I want you so bad, James, I hurt with it... what if that's all I can feel? What if I don't see you during—"

He kissed me. "Not possible, Aleks. Your mind is playing tricks on you."

"But the blackouts—"

"Those were driven by you needing to protect yourself. I promise you, it won't happen while you're making love to me. Your focus is going to be on me and only me. And my focus is going to be on you... because that's what making love is... finding pleasure in just being together."

I nodded. "I'm sorry," I said.

He chuckled. "What have I told you about being sorry?"

I laughed and managed to repeat the words he'd repeatedly said to me. "Don't be..."

Vaughn kissed me until I was breathless. But instead of lying back on the bed, he reached for my hand, the one with the lubed fingers, and gently took it by the wrist. I watched in stunned silence as he got to his knees. It made him a bit taller than me, but for some reason that just turned me on.

Vaughn maneuvered my hand around his side, then over his backside. He guided my slick fingers between his cheeks. I raised myself up so I was as tall as I could be on my knees. I was still a bit shorter than him, but it didn't matter because I just wanted to be as close to his mouth and his eyes as I could get.

"One finger at first," Vaughn said as he nuzzled my neck.

I sucked in a breath and nodded, then waited until he let my hand go. I brushed his hole lightly to test what it felt like. Vaughn let out a rush of air, so I did it again. My groin tightened more when he began pumping his backside against my hand a moment later.

Seeking more.

God, he really did want this.

I moved my finger so that I could ease a little bit of the tip inside him. Vaughn stilled, which caused *me* to still. "Keep going, baby," Vaughn said with a rush. "You'll know when to stop."

I took his word for it and began pushing farther into him. The pressure was intense and my brain was telling me to stop because I knew how badly this first part always hurt. It was the body's way of trying to keep something out that didn't belong. But instead of trying to escape my touch, Vaughn was pressing into it, urging my finger deeper inside of him. When something finally gave and the first half of my finger slipped into his body, Vaughn gasped and my instincts had me stopping.

So he could adjust.

Vaughn's mouth was pressed against my neck, his hot breath coming in pants against my skin.

"More," he finally breathed against me.

I wasn't sure why I did it, but I actually pulled my finger out a little before pushing it farther into him. His muscles were so tight around me that my penis was bouncing against my abdomen in anticipation. I had no experience to base it on, but I just knew he'd feel amazing around me when the time came.

I just hoped *I* felt amazing to *him*.

"So good," Vaughn growled in my ear as his right hand closed around the back of my head. He began kissing the shell of my ear.

"Fuck me with it, baby," he said.

His use of the word "fuck" should have had me wanting to end this whole thing, but the word just didn't mean the same thing.

Especially not how he'd said it.

And especially since I was the one doing the fucking.

I began pulling my finger out and pushing it back into him in what I hoped was a smooth, rhythmic glide. His body seemed to loosen a little around the digit and soon Vaughn was the one doing the fucking... of my finger.

"Add the other one," Vaughn ordered.

I gladly followed the demand because I could hear the need in Vaughn's voice.

And he was right.

I was totally focused on his pleasure.

I took my time pushing my second finger into him. Like the first one, there was a point where I could tell he needed me to stop, then move slowly before speeding up. I was so in tune with his needs that it was both frightening and freeing at the same time.

Within a couple of minutes, I was pumping my fingers into him without any kind of finesse.

"Aleks, can I touch you?"

I knew what kind of touching he meant.

…that's what making love is… finding pleasure in just being together.

He was right. I was getting just as much pleasure out of touching him like this as when I'd been grinding my penis against his belly all these past nights. Why wouldn't it be the same for him? That touching me was about him both giving and receiving pleasure?

"Yes," I whispered harshly, because I wanted to make sure there was no question about my answer.

A big, hot hand closed around my dick and I let out a gasp and then pressed my mouth against his chest. I kept my fingers inside of him but had to stop moving them because it felt like my head was going to blow off when Vaughn began stroking me.

His palm was just a little calloused so his skin felt kind of rough against mine, but that only made it feel that much better. I began pumping into his hand, much like he'd pumped against the fingers I had inside of him. As badly as I wanted to experience all this new sensation, I knew I wasn't going to last.

"It's too much," I cried out desperately.

Vaughn's hand stopped, then slowed. "Make love to me, Aleks," Vaughn said.

"Yes… yes," I said raggedly as I nodded my head. I knew he was talking about the next step. I carefully removed my fingers from his body and instantly missed the heat and tightness. Vaughn shifted away from me briefly, then he was back with the condom in his hand. I watched as he removed it from the packaging. He worked it down my penis and I had to hold my breath from exploding then and there. He worked quickly to add some lube, then his mouth was on mine.

"Just go slow and you'll know when I need you to let me adjust and when I'm ready for more," Vaughn assured me. He moved so that he was lying flat on his back.

I was confused by the position. When he lifted his legs and separated them, understanding registered.

He wanted me to take him that way.

I hadn't even known such a thing was possible.

But it meant I'd get to look at him while I was inside him. I'd be able to tell more easily if I was hurting him or pleasuring him.

I leaned over Vaughn and used my hand to guide myself to his opening. The condom felt weird on my dick, but that actually helped cool my passion a tiny bit. Enough that I'd hopefully at least be able to get inside him and do whatever it was he needed me to do to make him come. I could only pray that I was better at it than the men I'd been with.

That wasn't about making love, Aleks... they weren't interested in your pleasure or comfort, I reminded myself.

I took a breath and just like with my fingers, I slid forward slowly. I latched my eyes onto Vaughn's. He kept his open and on mine until the head of my penis pushed past that really strong muscle. Then he closed them.

"James, please, open your eyes," I begged as a moment of insecurity overcame me. "I need to see them."

He instantly did as I asked. He reached out to touch my face.

"It just burns a little, Aleks. But I can already feel it changing over... I'm good, I swear it."

I didn't know what it could possibly be changing over to, because all I'd ever felt at this point was like I was being torn in two, but the wonder I saw in Vaughn's eyes as he seemed to experience a range of sensations and emotions made me relax. I held where I was until I saw the silent signal in his beautiful, dark eyes that said he was ready for more.

So I gave it to him.

Chapter 21

VAUGHN

ALEKS WAS SO FOCUSED ON NOT HURTING ME THAT HE DIDN'T KISS me again until he was fully seated inside of me.

And I'd actually missed his mouth for the minutes it had taken for him to bottom out. I hadn't expected for so many emotions to pile up inside of me as Aleks made me his, but they were there just beneath the surface and when he kissed me and asked me if I was okay, it was all I could do to keep the tears stinging the backs of my eyes from falling.

"I'm perfect," I whispered. "Absolutely perfect."

"I never knew, James," he said as he kissed me over and over. He had yet to move inside of me, but I was grateful for it because my body was still adjusting to the feel of him while my heart was adjusting to all the emotions.

How the hell was I ever going to let him go after all this?

"Knew what?" I asked.

But Aleks shook his head. "I just never knew," he murmured again and I took that to mean that, like me, he was dealing with some heavy shit on the inside he hadn't been anticipating either.

Aleks began kissing me more heartily and I could feel his dick thickening inside of me.

"Are you okay?" he asked.

I knew he was asking the same question for a different reason. I slid my hand down to his ass, which flexed beneath my hand, but didn't tense up in any kind of way. My nonverbal answer seemed to be answer enough, because Aleks kissed me again and pulled slowly out of me, then slid gently home.

He did it over and over, his face pulled into a mask of pleasure as he adjusted to how good the friction and pressure felt on his cock. My own body was screaming with the need for release. My ass burned as Aleks's dick continued to stretch and fill it but the burn quickly changed over into something more… something that was so very different from the sensations I usually dealt with as the guy doing the fucking.

Aleks began slinging into me as his body's instincts to find his release kicked in, but as I'd predicted, he never once lost track of me in the process. His eyes kept coming back to search out mine and his hands were touching me everywhere they could reach. I lifted my legs so I could get him deeper inside of me and the move caused more of his lower body to press against my dick. The added friction on my shaft had me groaning and seeing stars. This time when I closed my eyes, Aleks didn't ask me to open them again.

We didn't speak or even look at one another as we raced for the finish line together. It was like our bodies had become one and I could hear, see, and feel everything without having to actually do any of those things.

They were just there.

Beneath the surface of my skin, along with the epic orgasm that was building and building.

I closed both my hands around Aleks's ass so I could get him to shove into me deeper with every thrust, though he was already as deep as he could go. But he seemed to understand what I wanted because he dug his knees into the bed and began fucking me hard and fast and deep. His fingers threaded through my hair in a painful hold that just intensified everything else. He grunted as he fucked into me and his hot breath blew first over my neck, then my ear, then my mouth. I was gripping his ass hard enough to leave bruises, but it had the desired effect.

He ground his groin against mine enough that I didn't need to go for my own dick.

A first for sure.

"I need to come," Aleks said as he began kissing me. "But I need you to come with me."

Sweat was pouring off us and my heart was racing in my chest. I'd never had someone say something to me one way but have it mean something entirely different.

Aleks wasn't just worried about leaving me behind. He wanted me with him when he finally found that elusive pleasure that had been denied to him for so very long.

He began peppering my face with kisses even as his cock slid in and out of me with hard, heavy thrusts. His balls slapped against my ass.

"I'm there," I acknowledged. "Just a few more," I insisted.

Aleks shifted just slightly and the move suddenly had him nailing my prostate. I let out a shout of pleasure that startled him, but fortunately, he seemed to understand he wasn't hurting me.

"Right there," I gasped.

He hit me there again.

And again.

And I lost the ability to speak.

I came suddenly and without warning. I cried out and closed my teeth over Aleks's shoulder. Blunt fingernails dug into my scalp as Aleks slammed his hips forward over and over, still getting my prostate each time.

Which only caused me to spew more and more cum between our bodies as the orgasm went on and on. My inner muscles reflexively tightened on Aleks's dick. He screamed and then clung to me as his body began to spasm. He continued to thrust into me hard as he shot into the condom, and despite my own blissed-out state, I could feel the heat of him through the latex.

Aleks's body quaked as his climax continued. My own had finally started to ease so I got to enjoy Aleks experiencing his own pleasure. I wrapped my arms around his back as aftershocks ripped through him with violent force. My ass stung from how hard and well he'd fucked me, but I balked at the idea of him pulling out of me, because I knew how I'd feel when he did.

Empty.

There'd be no trace of him left inside of me.

Yeah, first thing I'd do when we got to the city was make sure I got tested because I wanted to feel Aleks's essence burning my insides almost more than I wanted my next breath.

I kissed the shell of Aleks's ear as he came down from his high. He'd collapsed on top of me, not caring that I was holding all of his weight.

A fact I was very happy about.

We were practically glued together because he was lying in the huge pool of cum I'd spewed all over myself, but neither of us were in any hurry to move. I knew I'd need him to pull out soon because of the condom, but we could spare a few minutes.

Aleks seemed to rouse from his stupor after about a minute. He turned so he could rest his chin on his hands, which were folded on my chest. There was a soft smile on his face.

"What?" I asked as I toyed with his hair. The sweat had caused some of his curls to dampen and cling to his forehead.

"Now I know why naked sex is so much better," he said.

I laughed and said, "Right?"

He carefully eased out of me and then slid up my body enough so he could kiss me on the mouth. "Yeah, naked sex means less laundry."

I pinched his ass and he jumped and then rubbed his hand over his butt.

"And?" I said, pretending to be offended. "Is that the only reason naked sex is better?"

He thought about it for a moment. "Less laundry means using less water and water conservation is very important." He grinned mischievously, then started to climb off me. I grabbed him and rolled him beneath me. I reached between us and quickly removed the condom from him and tossed it on the floor, knowing the chances I'd hit the wastebasket next to the bed were slim to none.

"Try again," I said. I was glad that instead of tensing because I was lying on top of him, he seemed to sink into the mattress. He wound his arms around my neck.

"Luca will save a fortune on laundry detergent."

I kissed him hard and fast. "Not even close."

I almost forgot what we were talking about when he began kissing me back.

"I've got it," he finally said and nodded his head like he'd had some big revelation. He kissed me victoriously. "You won't need to buy more pajamas!"

I shook my head at him, but inside I was doing cartwheels at the mirth I saw on his face. It was just so goddamn natural. It was as much a part of him as a limb or organ. The men who'd hurt him had tried to wipe it out, but they'd failed.

"I guess we're just going to need to have a lot more naked sex until the answer comes to you," I declared.

He let out a rough sigh. "Fine, if we must." We watched each other in amusement for a moment, then his expression turned serious and he was pulling me down for a kiss. "Naked making love," he murmured. "Okay?"

The change in terminology did crazy things to my heart. It spoke volumes about what we'd just done and what each time we came together would be like. Whether it was hard and fast or dirty and rough or soft and slow, it would always be lovemaking.

"Yeah," I agreed.

He stroked my beard as he stared at me. An overwhelming need to give him even more of myself became like this pervasive thing in my blood. But I knew I couldn't tell him the words that were stuck in my throat, so I swapped them out for a question that would hopefully accomplish the same thing.

"Will you come flying with me tomorrow, Aleks?"

He didn't even ask how or when or where. He just held my gaze and gave me the simplest of answers that still managed to blow my entire world apart… in the best way.

"Yes."

I WENT LOOKING FOR HIM IN HIS OFFICE BECAUSE THAT'S WHERE THE man always was, but when I found it empty, I had to ask one of the handful of private bodyguards he employed where he was.

I found him by our mother's bench on the beach.

By it.

Not on it.

Because Luca never sat on it.

I didn't really know why.

Maybe because sitting on it would have meant he'd have to actually be still for more than a few minutes.

Or maybe it was about the cigarette in his hand. Maybe he was worried that smoking on our mother's bench would somehow be disrespectful to her.

Luca didn't even try to hide the cigarette from me when I reached his side.

It said a lot about where his mind was.

"You remember what Mom did when she caught us trying that cigarette that one of the construction workers who were putting in the pool left behind?" I asked as I motioned over my shoulder toward the house.

Luca took a drag on his cigarette and inhaled deeply. He didn't respond at first, then nodded. "She probably thought making us smoke the rest of the pack would be a hardship."

"It was… for me," I reminded him.

"She probably should have checked the pack first," Luca murmured. "Two cigarettes besides the one we'd started was nothing."

"You were ten," I said. "She probably figured you'd get so sick you'd never do it again."

He finally chuckled. "The look on her face when I finished mine, yours, and then asked for another…"

"I don't think I ever saw her get that angry before."

I was about to add the words "and after" when I realized there hadn't been much of an after. She'd died less than two months later. Luca hadn't smoked again until he'd been well into his twenties, because he'd been too afraid of pissing off our father. No cigarette was worth a smack to the face... or worse.

As hard as I'd had it with the old man, Luca had had it worse because he'd had the added pressure of needing to succeed at so many things. As basically just hired muscle, all I'd had to do was throw a good punch or instill just the right amount of fear into someone and not get caught. Luca had had to wear multiple hats when he'd started learning the business and ultimately taken it over. My brother had always been the more sensitive of us, but he'd been forced to snuff that out after our mother had died.

Because sensitivity was a weakness.

Softness was a weakness.

He'd been well on his way to being the ruthless tyrant our father had been grooming him to be when he'd gotten the surprise of his life during his first year of college.

His best friend, a girl named Genevieve, who he'd had one drunken sexual encounter with to prove to himself he wasn't a fag, had stunned him with the news that they were going to be parents.

The night Genevieve, or V as we'd come to call her, had told Luca, he'd come to me and in a rare show of self-doubt had cried in my arms as he'd tried to deal with a myriad of things all at once.

That he was, indeed, only interested in men.

That our father was going to disown him if he didn't kill him outright.

And that he was going to be a father.

That last part had been the hardest thing for him to accept because he'd been convinced he'd turn out to be just like Vidone Covello.

When he'd gone back to V, he'd intended to tell her that he just couldn't do it... that he couldn't be a father to any child.

Then he'd seen the tiny outline of his baby on a sonogram and everything had changed.

Well, not quite everything.

Luca had waited until little Gio was almost five to tell our father about his grandson. I'd suspected it had been some kind of final hope on Luca's part that we could go back to being the family our mother had always wanted us to be.

Vidone had been in a rage at first, because he hadn't wanted another bastard in the family. He'd barely even looked at me when he'd said those words to Luca and I'd hardly even flinched because I'd gotten used to that title. But when the old man had actually met the little boy who'd come running into the room in the middle of the argument, Vidone had paused and considered the child. He'd grumbled about it quite a bit as he'd eyed his son holding his grandson in his arms and whispering words of comfort to him. He'd called Gio over to him and looked him up and down and then, just like that, he'd suddenly declared that the boy was a Covello and that Luca and V would make it official that weekend. My poor brother hadn't even had a chance to respond to the declaration because our father had started talking about how little Giovanni Covello was the future of the business and he'd one day rule an empire that would make Covello a household name.

That was what had changed things for my brother.

While Gio's birth was what had woken Luca up, it was that moment with our father that had set him free.

Because Luca had calmly walked up to our father and taken his son from him and carefully led the little boy back to V and had asked her to go wait outside. He'd asked me to go with her and though I had technically answered to our father at the time, I hadn't even hesitated to turn on my heel and follow V and little Gio.

Luca had emerged from the house less than five minutes later, our raging father on his heels.

I still had no idea what exactly had been said between the pair, but I'd gotten the gist.

Luca had chosen his son over his father.

And he'd chosen me too.

Because when Luca had gotten V and Gio settled in the car, he'd turned to me and softly told me to get in the car as well.

It hadn't been an order.

Our father had been shouting orders.

At me.

First to tell me to stop Luca from leaving, then to get my ass up the stairs so I could take my place at his side, which really meant behind him.

I still hated the fact that I'd hesitated even for a second. When Luca had quietly whispered in my ear to trust him, it was like he'd given me what I'd needed to break the collar *I'd* been wearing around my neck for most of my life.

My collar may not have been a physical one like Aleks's had been, but I'd been owned just the same.

And I'd been released from my prison by someone who'd always vowed to watch out for me.

Which he had.

I'd learned only after we'd left our father's overpriced, oversized mansion that just about everything was already in Luca's name. Our father had been so confident in being able to keep the noose around Luca's neck for his entire life that he'd started transferring assets to either Luca's name or the business in order to stay under the IRS's radar.

But Luca had slipped the noose and it had cost our father everything.

By the time he'd died six months later, Luca had been giving him just enough money to survive on… and he'd only done that out of respect for our mother. For whatever reason, she'd loved Vidone Covello and Luca hadn't been willing to shit on that.

But despite Luca being able to break free of our father's control, he'd known from the day Gio had been born that in addition to inheriting Vidone's business and assets, Luca had also inherited the man's enemies.

The solution had taken its toll on Luca, but he'd been adamant that he wouldn't lose his son the way we'd both lost our mother, and I'd wholeheartedly agreed with him. To protect Gio, Luca had never publicly acknowledged the boy was his child, even after he'd told our father about him. He'd still showered his son with all the love he could and he'd given him everything money could buy and had made sure V had never wanted for anything, but the lengths we'd had to go to while Luca had spent time with his son had been extreme. There hadn't been days where he could just go pick his kid up from school and walk him home. There'd been no career days or going to school carnivals or any of the little plays that Gio's class would put on.

Any activity where Luca's real name could come out had had to be nixed, but that hadn't meant there hadn't been lots of family dinners both at V's house and at the house in the Hamptons. Our entire little extended family had bonded with Gio and had made sure he never felt like he just had a mother and nothing else. But we'd had to work harder than most families to make it happen.

But it had worked because Gio had been safe from Luca's enemies.

Until an enemy we hadn't seen coming had snuck under our radar and stolen both Gio and V from us.

And changed Luca's – and all our lives – forever.

"You took him flying, huh?" Luca asked after a few minutes of silence. Some of my anger at Luca for his role in trying to abduct Aleks was still there, but I'd had time to accept that desperation and a sense of betrayal had driven my brother to do what he'd done. He'd treated Aleks with kid gloves since then, so I did believe that if he'd been successful in taking him in Seattle, he wouldn't have allowed any harm to come to him.

"Yeah," I said as I glanced at my brother. The fact that I'd taken Aleks up in the little Piper single-engine plane was pretty telling. Even back before Gio had gone missing and I'd bought the plane, or rather, Luca had bought it for me and surprised me with it one day, I hadn't taken anyone up in it with me. I'd paid a guy at the private airport nearby a small fortune to store the plane for me and to keep up the maintenance on it, but I wasn't sure if Luca had known that.

Clearly, he knew pretty much everything.

He probably also knew I'd kept my pilot's license up to date, despite the fact that I hadn't flown much in the past several years. Only on the rarest of occasions had I left the dark world I lived in to escape to the skies for an hour or two.

But being in the air with Aleks by my side had brought a host of emotions to the surface that I hadn't been expecting.

Like how much flying really was in my blood. It was a high that was second only to being with Aleks.

So Aleks and flying at the same time… utter heaven.

And as soon as we'd landed I'd felt so fucking guilty for having those few hours of pleasure.

Hours where I hadn't allowed myself to remember that Gio was out there waiting for us to come and get him. Hours where I didn't fucking drive myself crazy wondering what was happening to him while I was letting myself feel the freedom he might never know again.

"I'm sorry," I said.

Luca looked at me. "Why are you sorry?"

I opened my mouth to answer, then found I couldn't give voice to my shame. He sighed and looked away.

"I never should have done it," he said quietly as he flicked his cigarette away and then started looking for another.

"Done what?" I asked.

"Take Aleks. It was a mistake. Just like asking you to…"

"To what?"

When he didn't answer, I got in between him and the bench and snatched the new cigarette he was about to light.

"What?" I bit out. "To help you find your son?"

He didn't answer but he dropped his eyes.

Something Luca rarely did.

"You didn't ask me or our family to do that, Luca," I said. "We all love that boy and we all want him back. That shit I said the other day about never asking you for anything… that was my fear talking… I would have spent the rest of my days in that life to find Gio."

Luca turned his head away but fortunately, he didn't turn away from me.

"I *will* spend every day looking for him until we bring him home. Every. Fucking. Day," I vowed.

He still wouldn't look at me and I knew it was because there was something he wasn't telling me.

"What?" I whispered. "What is it?"

He shook his head.

"Tell me," I almost pleaded.

"There was a boy, Vaughn," he began as his dark eyes lifted to meet mine. The agony and shame I saw swimming in them was a punch to the gut.

"When I first went in after Gio without you guys. He was only thirteen or fourteen. I had to… to prove I was who I said I was."

I swallowed hard because I knew what he was trying to say. The people who'd stolen Gio would have wanted to make sure Luca wasn't a cop or someone trying to expose them.

"I didn't touch him," Luca quickly said. "I knew there were video cameras in the room, so I couldn't just *say* I'd fucked him… They wanted me to prove I wanted a little boy. I'd told them I wanted a younger kid… someone with light hair and fair features, but they put me in with him and told me to have fun while they checked their 'inventory' for someone who matched what I wanted and was closer to the age I was looking for. That's the fucking word they used, Vaughn. I knew it was a test and I knew what would happen if I failed it."

I knew too.

He never would have been shown any other boys.

And they likely would have killed him even for just suspecting he was a fraud.

"What happened?" I asked.

"He was terrified… he was crying in the corner and begging me not to touch him. Kept saying he wanted to go home."

I watched in horror as my brother actually wiped at his eyes.

"I grabbed him by the arm and pulled him to his feet… we were in full view of the camera so it had to look real. But I swear to God, Vaughn, I didn't hurt him."

My brother was so distraught that I put my hands on his upper arms. "I know you didn't, Luca. Tell me what happened."

He sucked in a breath to collect himself. "I turned him around and made him face the wall. I knew they'd only be able to see my body from behind. I leaned down and whispered in his ear that I wouldn't hurt him and that I'd find a way to help him go home. I told him I needed to make it look real and to not be scared. He... he nodded and asked me to promise him I'd take him home."

Luca covered his eyes with his hand. "I did. I promised him. While I was pretending to... to hurt him I just kept whispering in his ear. I told him about this beach. How you and me used to play out here every day and how Mom used to collect shells and how we'd see dolphins while we were swimming and that one came up to you the one time and you touched it. I promised I'd show it to him someday. When I was done, I told him he needed to sit on the floor and cry so it looked like I'd really done that to him. He said he would and then he made me promise I wouldn't forget about him."

I began rubbing Luca's arms because he was shaking, though I knew it had nothing to do with the slight breeze.

"What happened to him, Luca?"

"I left him there, Vaughn. There weren't any other kids there – it had all been part of the test. I was told to go to a different address to look at the merchandise they had for purchase that met my needs. That address led to another and another. But none of the places had Gio so I had to keep pretending they didn't have what I wanted so they'd show me more boys. Then I got a lead on a boy that sounded exactly like Gio and I just couldn't risk losing it... it took me three days to get back to that house but it was empty. The boy was gone... the whole place was abandoned, like none of them had ever been there. All the other places were empty too."

"You couldn't have known they'd be gone," I said, but Luca shook his head.

"You and I both know that's how they operate... they never stay in the same place for long. I knew there was a good chance they'd move that boy that very day. But I thought I'd have at least twenty-four hours." Luca shook his head and wiped at the tears he hadn't managed to hold back.

"But you couldn't have known that back then. You had to make it about your son, Luca. And I know if you could have, you would have done all you could have to get that boy out. But you didn't have the resources back then."

I realized then that that boy was probably the reason Luca had set up such a vast network of resources to not only get kids out, but to get them back to their families whenever possible.

"He was somebody's son, Vaughn. And I promised him I wouldn't forget him. But I left him there."

Luca tugged free of my hold and turned away. I was about to reach for him again when I heard my name being called.

I turned to see King flagging me down from the back of the house. Fear skirted through me as he began trotting toward us.

Aleks.

I hurried past Luca. King met us right where the back deck hit the sand.

"What? What is it?" I asked, hoping like hell it wasn't about Aleks, but I knew it was.

"Hurry up," was all King said as he grabbed my arm. "He needs you."

I threw King off and sprinted toward the house. "Luca's office!" King shouted.

It took me less than a minute to reach that part of the house. I could hear Con's voice coming from inside the room, but it wasn't until I stepped inside it that I heard what he was saying.

"Hang on, Aleks, Vaughn is coming."

I could hear Aleks's sobs before my eyes searched him out. He was sitting in the corner on the floor, his hands wrapped around the back of his neck as he hung onto his head and rocked back and forth.

"Aleks," I called as I rushed to him and knelt in front of him.

Aleks shook his head violently. "No, no, no…"

He kept repeating the word over and over. I eased his chin up because I needed to see his eyes.

To know if he was still there or if he'd been swallowed by a blackout.

"I can't, James. Please don't make me!"

I wrapped my arms around him. "I won't, Aleks. You're safe, baby."

He sobbed against me and put his arms around my neck.

"I'm sorry, Vaughn," Con sputtered behind me. I could hear the distress in his voice.

I still had no clue what was going on, but I didn't care. I pulled Aleks forward so he was practically straddling my lap. It allowed him to curl into me as far as he could. It was like he was trying to burrow under my skin.

"It's okay, Aleks, everything's okay," I repeated over and over until Aleks's sobs slowed, then finally stopped. My neck and my shirt were soaking wet, but I didn't give a shit. Aleks's breaths were harsh and choppy, but the more I rubbed his back and just held onto him, the quieter he fell. We'd been left alone in the room at some point.

"I'm sorry," Aleks murmured against my neck after about twenty minutes. I could hear the exhaustion in his voice.

"It's okay," I responded. I'd have plenty of time to ask him what had happened, but for now, I just wanted him to rest. "Let's go to our room, okay?"

He nodded against me.

I got to my feet and pulled him up with me. He leaned heavily against me so I swept an arm beneath his legs and put the other at his back, lifting him. "No, James, I'm too heavy," he whispered, even as he pressed his face against my chest. His arms went around my neck again.

"No, you're not," I said. "And I don't think I've ever told how much I love carrying you. It makes me feel all caveman-like."

I felt him smile against my neck. "There's nothing caveman-like about you, James," he said softly. "Besides, I think cavemen drag people back to their caves by the hair."

"Your hair isn't long enough for that, so you're just going to have to settle for me carrying you around when I'm feeling all possessive and dominant."

Another smile.

"Okay," he said on a sigh.

The door leading to the office wasn't completely closed, but it didn't matter because as soon as I reached it, it opened. Luca's worried eyes skimmed over Aleks, then me. I nodded my head to indicate the younger man was okay, but not surprisingly, it didn't diminish much of the concern in Luca's gaze. Just beyond the door were King and Con. Con still looked devastated and King looked pissed – at Con.

I couldn't imagine what the hell had happened to cause the brothers to be at odds, but I couldn't deal with any of it right now.

I got Aleks to our room. Con ran ahead of us to open the door. As we passed him, Aleks said, "I'm sorry, Con. I didn't mean to yell at you."

"No worries, Aleks," Con said, completely flustered. For once, he looked at a loss for words.

I kicked the door shut behind me and then carried Aleks to the bed. I settled him on top of it, then crawled in behind him. He turned over and pushed into my arms and I gladly wrapped them around him.

"I didn't go away, James," he said softly against my neck. "That's good, right?"

I knew he was talking about the fact that he hadn't blacked out.

"That's amazing," I said. "I'm so proud of you, baby."

"It means I'm fighting back," Aleks murmured. I could feel him trying to ward off the sleep that was threatening to take him.

"Yes, it does," I said. I rubbed my hand up and down his back. "Just sleep, Aleks. I'll be here when you wake up."

He nodded and snuggled deeper into me. "Tell Con I'm sorry I got upset. And tell him I'll do it, okay?"

"Do what, baby?"

Aleks was so quiet that I thought he'd actually fallen asleep. But when I heard the words he whispered right before he drifted off, I felt a chill go through my bones.

"Wear the collar."

Chapter 22

ALEKS

It was interesting to watch the men fight, even when they were all in agreement about an issue.

It was also really exhausting.

And loud.

The issue in question was the dreaded collar that was currently sitting about twenty feet from me on Luca's desk. I couldn't actually see the collar, but I recognized the box from the previous week when it had been sitting on his desk in the other house... the one in the Hamptons.

Because of my freak-out when Con had shown me the collar, we'd ended up spending another night in the ocean-front house and it hadn't been until the following afternoon that we'd made our way to the city. I'd slept through the entire night after my meltdown, so Vaughn and I hadn't made love. I'd woken up in his arms with him watching me with a solemn expression on his face. I'd kissed him and told him I was okay, but it hadn't been hard to figure out that he was upset. He hadn't asked me about what had happened, so I'd figured he'd talked to Con about it at some point while I'd been asleep.

But it wasn't until Vaughn and I had entered the kitchen that morning for breakfast that I'd realized Con hadn't had a clue about the collar I'd been forced to wear for so many years.

And how hard it had been to give it up, both figuratively and literally.

Poor Con had been an absolute mess when Vaughn and I had shown up for breakfast.

The first thing we'd both noticed were grits.

Everywhere.

They'd been in containers all over the counter and Con's clothes had been covered in flour and all manner of ingredients. When he'd caught sight of me and Vaughn, he hadn't stopped moving for even a moment.

He'd just kept right on cooking.

And talking.

Dig in, guys. There's all kinds… sausage and cheese, bacon and cheese, ham and cheese, just cheese… this one's got cinnamon and that one's got fruit on it but maybe don't try that one because it was more of an experiment. I didn't make shrimp ones because that's Vaughn's thing but if there's another kind you like, I can make them for you…

As he'd spoken, Con had pointed to the different containers full of grits. And he hadn't stayed still for a moment. I'd never seen one of his fights, but I could picture him in the ring… always on the move and always waiting for that next strike to come his way.

My heart had broken for him and when I'd tugged my hand from Vaughn's, he'd instantly let me go. I'd walked around the large kitchen island. Con's verbal diarrhea had only gotten worse as I'd approached him but when I'd walked into his body, he'd shut up and then he'd put his arms awkwardly around me.

Then he'd hugged me hard. *I'm sorry, Aleks. I didn't know.*

It hadn't really bothered me that Vaughn had told him about the collar I'd been forced to wear because I'd known Vaughn wouldn't have shared anything beyond the facts.

I'd squeezed Con in response and it had been enough. When he'd released me, he'd handed me a spoon, and I'd started trying all the different versions of grits he'd made. I'd liked them all, but I'd ended up grabbing the cinnamon ones. I'd never seen Con looking happier than when I'd pushed my bowl away and let out a loud belch that I hadn't managed to quell.

That had been a week ago and things had been chaotic ever since.

The move to the city had been like a smoothly choreographed dance and I'd had so many of Luca's bodyguards surrounding me that it had almost reminded me of when I'd lived with Father.

Almost.

But not quite.

Because besides the bodyguards, Vaughn was nearly always with me. And despite him worrying about my safety, when I'd started to feel stir-crazy in Luca's fancy apartment, Vaughn had taken me to Central Park and he'd shown me all the trees he'd climbed as a kid and the place he and Luca had met Con, King, and the third brother I had yet to meet, Lex.

We'd still had bodyguards on those outings, but I'd been glad because it had helped Vaughn to relax a bit. He hadn't shown me any affection in public but he'd explained why beforehand. Because on the remote chance there were people from my past watching, it had to look like I was just another pet being taken out for some air.

Similar to when Father had allowed me to go to the flower shop every week.

But I hadn't felt any of the same emotions beyond the natural fear that came with knowing that there was a possibility someone was watching me. I hadn't actually felt that sensation myself, but at one point, Vaughn had thought he'd spied a man following us. He'd actually pursued him after leaving me with the bodyguards in front of Luca's building and I'd been hustled inside and had had to wait for nearly fifteen minutes before Vaughn had returned to declare he'd lost the guy. He'd set about to reassure me he wasn't even sure there'd *been* a guy, but we hadn't ventured out again after that.

That had been a couple days ago.

While Luca had stayed at the apartment with us, we hadn't seen much of him. Con and King had come and gone but hadn't slept in the penthouse like they had at the house in the Hamptons. I'd found myself missing the comradery between the men. Even when they were at each other's throats, like they were now, there was no missing the affection they had for one another.

The only real anger I'd seen between them in the past week had been when an argument had erupted between Con and King about their younger brother, Lex. Con had once again pressed King to explain why Lex hadn't joined them in New York or why he wasn't answering Con's phone calls, but King had refused to respond. They'd nearly come to blows and Vaughn and Luca had had to intervene and tell them both to walk it off.

I'd asked Vaughn about Lex but he wasn't sure what was happening with the man, either. He'd told me that as the youngest of their group, Lex had always been on the receiving end of some overprotectiveness, especially when it came to his older brothers, because he'd had both a hard childhood and some health issues, but he hadn't gone into details and I hadn't asked. I definitely understood what it was like to be younger and protected, and while I'd always welcomed it with Dante, I wasn't sure how it would have felt to be treated the same way once I'd been older and more independent.

And had had a normal childhood.

I'd only spoken to Dante a few times in the past couple of weeks. Each time, he'd practically begged me to let him come get me, but, of course, I'd always refused and had spent much of the time trying to convince him I was safe and that it would all be over soon. I'd only spoken to Dante for a few minutes on each call because it was really hard not to break down and just tell him where I was. Despite keeping the calls short, I'd gotten to talk to Magnus and Matty too. They were all still staying away from home, but Matty had turned it into an adventure and Magnus had said he was using the time to try and get Dante to commit to some wedding plans.

But when I'd questioned my brother about the wedding, he'd stubbornly had the same response.

We'll talk about it when you get home.

I'd taken that to mean he hadn't agreed to a date yet. I'd wanted to kick my brother through the phone for his stubbornness and blatant refusal to see how much Magnus loved him and that Dante was worth every single ounce of that love, but there were some things that would just need to wait until I was home.

Dante wouldn't know what hit him because the old me wouldn't have dared to confront him about something like that.

Well, the old me had changed.

A lot.

And I had Vaughn and his crazy brothers, both of the blood and of the heart, to thank.

"I agree, damn it!" Con snapped as he threw up his hands. "But we need to find a way to send some other message that he's taken."

"He's not leaving our sides, so it doesn't fucking matter!" Vaughn shouted back. "Those assholes won't approach him if he stays with Luca!"

I sighed as the back and forth continued. Not one of the men wanted me to wear the collar, but I knew what it would mean if I did.

It would mean I was Luca's property.

The picture had been the start.

But the collar would cement it.

It would make the whole scenario more convincing, and since I'd overheard the men talking about how rumors were swirling online that Luca wasn't a true "believer," we were already at a disadvantage going into the party. As it were, Luca, and me by proxy, would probably be carefully watched for any signs that our relationship wasn't what it was supposed to be.

There'd still been no contact from the Stylianos character who'd supposedly had the lead on Gio at one point, but there had been multiple offers from other men to purchase me. Vaughn had warned me that they'd made it look like Luca was open to selling me for the right price, but it was only in the hopes of forcing Stylianos's hand. If the sick man thought he was going to lose me to someone else, he might be more inclined to make himself known.

I glanced at the box again.

It's not real, I reminded myself. *And it could be what brings Gio home.*

I climbed unsteadily to my feet and went to Luca's desk. None of the men seemed to notice me, so I tuned them out. For all the determination I'd felt just seconds ago, the moment I flipped the lid up on the jewelry box, my resolve fled.

In a big way.

Close it.

Close it!

My brain kept screaming the order at me and I knew I could.

It was a choice like any other. And it wouldn't make me a coward. None of these men would look at me that way.

I left the box open and wrapped my arms around myself as I studied the piece of gold jewelry. It wasn't exactly a necklace, but it looked nothing like the dog-style chain Father had put around me so many years ago and had one of his men weld together with a blowtorch while another had held me still, not caring about the screams of pain I'd let out.

Or the tears I'd shed.

Or the pleas to stop that I'd repeated over and over.

I'd thought the worst of it over when the blowtorch had been turned off.

But my humiliation and pain had only begun.

"Aleks."

My brain tried to shut out the memory as the familiar and oh-so-perfect voice filtered through me. I felt rather than saw Vaughn's hands on my arms as he came up behind me. He reached past me to close the box, but I stayed his hand.

"It doesn't look anything like the other one," I murmured. It was actually quite beautiful, and I guessed whichever of the men had purchased it had spent a small fortune on it. The links were very delicate and I suspected the whole thing could be ripped off one's neck with little force.

It was almost ironic.

Father had welded a collar on me so I couldn't remove it.

But this collar was meant to show that the pet who was wearing it could have removed it themself but was too well-trained to do so. And while I knew there was a whole other lifestyle where men and women chose to submit to another person, nothing about the world we were going into was about submission by choice.

"I made too much noise when Father put the collar on me," I said softly. "And I cried and said no… he didn't like when I did that. He said I was supposed to know better – that he'd paid a lot of money for me to know better than that. I tried to apologize, but he didn't like that either."

Vaughn's arm went around my collarbone and I felt his lips brush my temple. "It's okay, Aleks, you don't need to talk about it."

I nodded. "Yes," I whispered. "I'm fighting back," I reminded him.

He kissed me again and I felt him nod against me.

I knew the other men were still in the room and I figured they hadn't left because they would have had to move past me to get out. Maybe they'd been afraid they'd frighten me into another blackout.

I wasn't sure.

But I didn't want or need them to leave.

Because I wasn't embarrassed about what had happened to me.

I hadn't done anything wrong and I hadn't deserved it.

I understood that now.

I wasn't sure I would have if Vaughn hadn't given me my own chance to "wake up" like Gio had woken him and Luca up.

"When I apologized, I grabbed his arm," I said. "I wasn't ever allowed to touch any of the men unless they told me to or gave me some sign. I *knew* that, but I was scared and in pain and I wasn't thinking." I reached up to touch the burn scar on my neck. "He hit me and I fell. Then he grabbed my hair and forced me to my knees. He nodded to one of his men and the guy, he just *knew* what Father wanted. It made me wonder how, you know?"

Vaughn's arm tightened around me, but he didn't say anything.

"The man left the room. He was back within a minute. He had something black in his hand, but I didn't know what it was until he handed it to Father." I drew in a breath as a huge shudder ran throughout my entire body. I could still remember the terror that had gone through me when I'd identified the object.

"Fire poker," I breathed.

I heard someone gasp, but I wasn't sure who it was. "I wasn't wearing a shirt because they'd taken it off when they'd put the collar on. I again made the mistake of begging Father not to hurt me. I told him I'd be good and I'd never defy him again. He didn't even let me finish before he hit me on the back with the poker."

"Aleks," Vaughn whispered into my ear. I could hear the emotion in his voice. It sounded really thick.

But I couldn't stop now.

Not even for him.

"I thought each blow would be the one that killed me. I couldn't even go into my head because it hurt so bad. I almost passed out after the first few hits, but one of the men kept throwing cold water in my face to make sure I didn't. I could feel the blood running down my back but then after a while I didn't feel anything. I remember the fire poker hitting the ground and then I was pulled to my feet and bent over the desk. I was afraid Father would let his men take turns with me after he was done, but they didn't. Father just left me there, my pants around my ankles, and told his men to clean me up and put me in my room. I think… I think he was sorry he scarred his pet because he used to tell his friends that he regretted not using something lighter to teach me that first lesson."

I reached for the jewelry box and pulled it closer. "I never defied him after that. Not once… not until the night Dante showed up and Father bent me over that same desk and showed Dante what I'd been turned into."

"You're so fucking strong, Aleks," Vaughn said into my ear. "That's who you are and who you've always been."

"Unbroken," I murmured.

Vaughn kissed the back of my neck. "Yes," he said in a barely there whisper.

I nodded because I was finally starting to believe it for myself. But every step forward would be about that… about reminding myself that none of those men had done what they'd set out to do.

Break me.

So I reached for the small gold collar.

"No," a voice said, then a large hand was moving the box out of my reach.

Not Vaughn's hand, though.

Luca's.

I hadn't even noticed how close he'd moved to the desk. It was a testament to the fact that I really was coming to trust all the men as much as I trusted Vaughn.

"No," Luca said. "You're not doing this."

I knew it wasn't really an order because I could hear his voice breaking.

He was upset.

And I knew why.

"What was his name, Luca?" I asked.

Luca actually paled. "What?"

"The boy... the one you met when you were looking for Gio. The one you had to forget."

Luca looked at Vaughn briefly. "He told you?" he asked me. There was a little bit of hurt in his voice.

"No," I quickly said. "He didn't tell me anything. You did. That night on the porch at the house in Nevada... you said you had to forget a boy to find your son. You've never really forgotten him though, have you?"

The man hesitated, then shook his head. "No," he said. "They called him Billy, but I don't know if that was his real name or not."

"Probably not," I said. "They changed any names that sounded too unique. They let me keep my name but they always spelled it wrong. They said the name Alex was really common here in the U.S. But my name is spelled with an 's' – I was named after my father's father who was Polish."

I didn't say it out loud but my guess was that Gio likely had been given a new name as well.

"We'll find another way, Aleks," Luca said as he snapped the jewelry box shut. He kept his big hand on it, but when I leaned across the desk and reached for it, he released it.

"It's my choice," I said. I flipped the box back open. "Everything has been my choice from the moment Vaughn told me why he'd taken me. I don't want that to change... I won't let it," I said firmly. I forced myself to pick up the collar. It barely weighed anything, but it might as well have weighed a hundred pounds.

I felt sick as I found the clasp and worked it loose. The party wasn't for hours yet, but I needed to do this now so I could be one hundred percent focused on everything that was happening around me when the time came.

I swallowed back the bile that was trying to creep up my throat as I reached up to put the collar around my throat. I dropped my eyes and stared at the desk as I fumbled with the clasp.

But I couldn't get it to snap together and all my effort to be strong felt like it was slipping out of my grip just like the frustrating clasp.

"James," I whispered.

"I've got it, Aleks," Vaughn said as his hands took over the task for me. When his fingers drifted down my neck and rested on my shoulders, I knew it was done. I could barely feel the collar, it was so light. But I *could* feel it.

And I was still okay.

I pulled in a breath, then another.

It wasn't until Luca handed me a tissue that I realized I'd been crying the whole time.

I was tempted to lighten the mood by coyly asking how it looked, but I knew I couldn't pull it off. And from the looks on the faces of the men around me, I doubted any of them could find even a scrap of humor in the situation.

I reached up to touch the collar... no, the necklace, because that was all it really was. I'd take it off in a few minutes, but I wanted to prove to myself I could forget about it, so I stepped back into Vaughn's body and reached up to link my fingers with the ones that were resting on my collarbone. His touch did what it always did and calmed me.

I looked around at each of them. They all had different emotions on their face.

Luca looked torn, Con looked like he was feeling completely powerless, and King... King just looked pissed.

I didn't need to look at Vaughn to know what I'd see.

Because I saw a little bit of that emotion in everyone else's gaze too.

Pride.

Chapter 23

VAUGHN

That moment had been one of the hardest in my life.

Not the one where Aleks had put that collar around his neck, but that had been pretty bad. No, it'd been when I'd had to help him with the clasp. Logically, I'd known it hadn't been me putting the hated piece of jewelry on him, but now as I watched him obediently follow Luca into the darkened room, I felt like I'd forced that noose around his neck and I was terrified he wouldn't figuratively be able to take it back off when he physically took the thing off. He'd made so much progress in the past couple of weeks that I just wanted to take him some place where I could nourish that growth.

Protect it.

Cherish it.

But I didn't get to decide which choices Aleks made for himself, and he'd made this one and stuck to it. The most I could do was make sure that his stay in this world was as short as possible.

I let my eyes scan the room as we made our way to the lounge area. I felt sick as I watched all the men having a good time as their "pets" obediently stood at their sides or knelt at their feet. Most of the kids were in their teens, but I knew it wouldn't be long before I saw younger boys and girls too. Some, like Aleks, were wearing collars, which was a clear signal to the other owners to keep their hands to themselves. But the ones who weren't had to suffer through being passed around and pawed by other guests. Thankfully, the party wasn't the kind where the guests would just start fucking their property right there in the open.

There would be private rooms for that.

The party was actually an auction that was scheduled to start within the hour. There was a stage set up on the far side of the room, which was heavily decorated in varying shades of red velvet and gold trim. The furniture looked like what you'd find in any fancy living room and was spread throughout most of the room. Once the auction began, most of the chairs would be moved closer to the stage so the men could get a better view of what they were bidding on. While they waited, they had access to tablets that had information on it about each kid. Luca had handed the tablet he'd been given to me upon entering the party. I already knew it wouldn't have any kind of cellular or wireless connection, so there'd be no way to link to the outside world. The tablet was solely used to let guests look through the pictures and stats of the kids being sold. And anyone who'd ignored the rules about bringing any kind of phone, laptop, or camera had been turned away at the door. Extensive background checks had been done prior to the party and had included both the kids and any bodyguards the wealthier guests had brought with them. There'd also been a limit of one bodyguard per guest.

Which meant it was just me, Luca, and Aleks.

And we had no way to communicate with Con or King or any of the personal bodyguards Luca employed. They were all outside the building. The only way they'd know we were in trouble was by the one-way communication device Luca had on him. It was a small video camera with a microphone that looked like an ordinary button on his suit jacket. So Con and King could see and hear everything, but we wouldn't be able to hear them.

But it was the best we could do under the circumstances.

Our only goal was to see if Stylianos made contact. We'd agreed that if the man didn't reach out within sixty minutes, we'd end things and blow the whistle on the party. King already had a dozen of his men stationed in cars within blocks of the party. The second the sixty minutes were up, King would call his contact at the police department. Any guests who managed to get past the cops would be followed home by King's men.

But the snag was that Luca, Aleks, and I would be stuck in the building when King made that call, since guests weren't allowed to leave the party once they entered it. Everyone was required to wait until it was over so that no one could call the authorities during the party. That meant that Luca, Aleks, and I would have just minutes to find a way out before the cops showed up. In addition to making sure no one tried to get to Aleks during the event, I also had to find a workable escape route for the three of us. We hadn't received the address for the party until minutes before we'd arrived, so there'd been no time to scope the place out ahead of time.

We were basically flying blind for the next hour.

And it could all be for nothing, because there still hadn't been any kind of communication indicating Stylianos was attending or still even interested in acquiring Aleks.

I escorted Luca and Aleks to a set of lounge chairs in an area that was relatively empty. Luca looked the part of a ruthless business tycoon who didn't have a care in the world as he dabbled in a world where selling kids for sex was nothing more than a normal transaction. From his bored expression to the ease with which he sat, he looked like a guy who was being forced to endure an overpriced play or garish opera.

As planned, Luca sat in a chair that was closer to the back wall and had a view of the entire room. There were only a few guests milling nearby, but Luca played the part to the hilt as he said to Aleks, "Sit, my pet."

Even though I knew it was all an act, I wanted so badly to grab Aleks and get him out of there because he'd too easily fallen into the role. Part of me was afraid he'd escaped into his head but part of me was afraid he *hadn't*. Either way, he wasn't allowed to look at me, so I couldn't see what was happening in his eyes.

God, this was so fucked up.

Aleks didn't actually sit because, despite the words Luca had spoken, he hadn't really invited Aleks to take a seat. With downcast eyes, Aleks obediently dropped to his knees next to Luca's chair. He'd knelt close enough so that Luca could reach out and touch him if he wanted.

Con was the one who'd picked out the clothes Aleks was wearing, but only because I hadn't been able to bring myself to buy them. But I'd been the one who'd had to tell him what to get because I'd been to enough of these events to know what the kids were forced to wear. I'd settled on a snug black shirt that was made of fishnet material, since an owner like Luca would have wanted to show off what was his, but not actually share it. I'd told Con to find Aleks some pants that accomplished the same feat… showed off his body but left enough to the imagination. The thin black leather pants Con had selected did the job. But it was the fucking collar that pulled the whole outfit together.

Aleks looked well and truly owned.

And his behavior was proof of that.

God, please let him be acting.

I'd never forgive myself if all of this set him back to where he'd been two years ago… or even just two weeks ago.

After the incident with the collar out in the Hamptons, Aleks had managed to mentally recover from the trauma within a day and we'd made the trip to the city. But I suspected he'd only managed to function as well as he had because he'd put the collar and the upcoming party behind a wall in his mind. We'd spent most of our days cooped up in Luca's penthouse apartment in Manhattan, but we'd made the most of it by watching movies and playing video games. I'd ended up turning Aleks into somewhat of a video game addict because he'd become fascinated with some of the older-style arcade and strategy games. Not surprisingly, he hated the games with violence and bloodshed. I wasn't particularly fond of those either – I saw enough of that shit in real life, thank you very much. I'd been more than happy to join Aleks for Minecraft marathons and he'd actually managed to get me to participate in dance-party games.

In those moments as we'd been dancing our asses off or watching or talking smack to each other about who was going to win, we'd been just a normal couple living a normal life. And we'd used the nights and the privacy of our bedroom to explore each other's bodies and learn all we could about what brought the other the most pleasure. Aleks had made love to me every single night and I'd finally gotten to taste his cock a few nights earlier. He'd been horrified when he'd come inside of my mouth and we'd had a long talk about it being something I wanted. Aleks had admitted that he hated needing so much reassurance from me, but I'd made it clear that I'd gladly spend the rest of my days both telling and showing him that the things we did together were natural and normal and nothing like what he'd known in the past.

The only problem was, we didn't have that many days left. As much as I loved these weeks I'd spent with Aleks, he wasn't mine to keep. I'd already talked to Luca, King, and Con about the fact that Stylianos hadn't made contact in the two weeks since we'd made it known that Luca had Aleks. We were coming to accept that either the man had lost interest in Aleks, which seemed unlikely, or something had happened to him where he *couldn't* communicate. He could have been hospitalized, put in jail, killed, or he'd just needed to keep low and out of sight for some reason… there was just no way to know. There was also the possibility that we'd gotten things wrong and the men who'd taken Aleks from his shop hadn't worked for Stylianos.

Either way, I couldn't keep Aleks with me indefinitely. As much as he seemed to enjoy being with me, he had a family that he wanted to get back to and who were eagerly waiting for him to come home. And Dante and Magnus now understood the danger Aleks faced so they'd take steps to make sure no one could ever get to him again. They'd do all the same things to protect him that I was.

And I still needed to find Gio.

Even if Stylianos was out of the picture, Gio was still out there.

I couldn't have the life with Aleks I wanted, even if by some miracle we found Gio. There were too many kids like Gio and Aleks and the boy Luca had been forced to leave behind who needed to go home.

I forced myself to let go of thoughts of a future without Aleks as a couple of men approached the seating area we were in. "Mr. Black?" an older man with carefully groomed gray hair said as he used Luca's online alias. Chances were good he knew who Luca really was, but the guests usually referred to each other by their online monikers. The man reached out his hand toward Luca.

Luca didn't react to him at first. Instead, he glanced at me and then waved his hand. "Get me a drink," he ordered.

"Yes, sir," I said.

It was all part of the plan... getting Luca a drink would give me the freedom to check out the initial layout of the building. Since no one would dare touch Aleks while he was with Luca, I didn't hesitate to walk away from the pair. I overheard the man whose hand Luca finally deigned to take mention how lucky Luca was to have found such a prize, and I knew the fucker was talking about Aleks. I glanced over my shoulder to see my brother looking at the man like he was nothing more than a bug he'd inadvertently stepped on and messed up his fancy shoes with.

I had to give our father credit for making Luca such a stunningly convincing actor.

Aleks, for his part, didn't even flinch or respond to the comment. I wished there was a way I could show him how proud I was of him and that I was there and always watching out for him, but I couldn't interact with him in any kind of meaningful way in public or it would all be over.

I scanned the room as I made my way to the bar. There was only one marked exit besides the front entrance and both were heavily guarded by several men. There was another doorway that wasn't marked. There was one guard there along with a smaller man dressed in a tux. I watched as two men and a young girl stopped in front of Tuxedo Man. He said something to one of the men and pointed behind him, then gave the man a slip of paper. I felt my stomach drop out because I knew where the men were taking the girl. I confirmed it when I reached the bartender and ordered Luca's drink. As I waited I asked, "Are there private rooms?"

"Yes, sir," the bartender said as he motioned toward where Tuxedo Man was standing. "Douglas will get you all set up with one."

I nodded and mentally told the girl to hang on just a little longer.

I took the drink he slid me. "Restrooms back there too?" I asked.

The man nodded. "Don't let your boss fuck his pet in there, though," the guy said crudely. "Management frowns on that."

I wanted to punch him but managed to force out a chuckle. "Good to know. Thanks." I nodded at him and grabbed the drink. By the time I reached Luca, all the other chairs around him and Aleks were taken. Most of the men were alone, but one had a young boy with him. The boy was in his early teens and very petite with feminine features and long black hair. In reality, I couldn't be completely sure the child was a boy. He or she was sitting on the man's lap and was fondling the man discreetly through his pants.

The kid had dead eyes.

Just like Aleks's had always been.

I schooled my features into a mask of indifference as I went around the chairs and set Luca's drink down on the table next to him. When I went to stand behind his chair, one of the men said, "Vaughn, it's good to see you."

"Mr. Stark," I said with a nod. It wasn't the fucker's real name… he was just an avid fan of superheroes. I'd never worked for him, but he'd tried to lure me away from Marcus at one point. The man was extremely wealthy, but he wasn't a big player. He bought and sold kids like they were a new pair of shoes, and he preferred girls.

"A shame what happened to Marcus," Mr. Stark said. After Marcus's death, people hadn't bothered with his alias anymore. "I was so happy to learn you weren't at the home when tragedy struck," the man said to me. "You were always such a valuable asset to our community," he added.

If I hadn't wanted to slit the guy's throat, I would have found the situation humorous. He was clearly still looking to add to his security team. "And of course, the news that Aleks had survived as well was like we'd won the lottery or something," he said with a chuckle. "Mr. Oak here" – he used the hand he was holding his drink with to point at the man who had the child on his lap – "was actually disappointed he'd already made a purchase... said he'd have made an exception on his age preference for Aleks."

The man laughed heartily and took a drink. Mr. Oak shot him a glare but it was clear the man was correct because the fucker then leered at Aleks.

"Yes, I believe you reached out to me about an exchange," Luca said in a bored voice as he reached for his drink but didn't take a sip. "Your... 'acquisition' is quite lovely, but Aleks and I are still getting to know each other, aren't we, my sweet?" Luca dropped his hand to Aleks's head and Aleks obediently looked up and nodded.

My gut wrenched painfully because I could see Aleks was one hundred percent there... no escaping into his head, no blackout.

He was hearing, seeing and feeling everything.

"Yes, Sir," Aleks said softly, reverently.

I wanted to throw up.

Luca touched his chin briefly in what one could have almost called an affectionate way. But then his expression hardened, and he motioned to the floor and Aleks immediately dropped his eyes and went silent. "Of course, if the price were right and I found something that was more in line with my tastes..."

Luca let the words drop off and took a sip of his drink. We'd made it clear online what Luca was actually looking for.

A teenager with fair hair and light eyes.

I forced myself to listen to the conversation as the men talked about different pets they'd had and had either lost or gotten rid of for one reason or another... they could have been talking about cars for all the emotion they showed. Almost forty minutes had passed before Luca reached his hand up to motion to me.

"Yes, sir?" I asked as I stepped around the chair.

"Take him to the bathroom. I don't want to be interrupted during the auction."

"Of course, sir," I said.

Aleks didn't move until Luca told him to go with me. Then he carefully got to his feet, keeping his hands folded demurely in front of him. Since I was allowed to touch Luca's property for this purpose, I took Aleks's arm and led him toward where Tuxedo Man was still standing by the back hallway. I discreetly rubbed my thumb into Aleks's upper arm, but he didn't react.

He couldn't.

I shouldn't have even done that much, but I wasn't as strong as him.

When we reached Tuxedo Man he asked, "Private room for how many, sir?"

"Just the restroom," I said.

"Of course. Down this hall and to the right."

I led Aleks down the hallway. All the private rooms had letters on them and there were keypads on the doors.

Which meant the little slips of paper that Tuxedo Man had been handing out were the codes for the doors.

I tuned out the sounds I could hear coming from the other side of some of the doors and hoped Aleks was doing the same. The bathroom was clearly marked and empty. I ushered Aleks inside and closed and locked the door. I quickly scanned the room for any video cameras. There usually weren't cameras at these things, because not only did they take too long to set up, but it wasn't like these people wanted their activities recorded on film in any way, shape, or form.

"It's safe, Aleks," I said after a moment. "There aren't any cameras or recording devices."

I began to reach for him, but he put out his hand to stop me. "No," he whispered. "Don't touch me."

Shock reverberated through me.

And hurt.

So much fucking hurt.

"Aleks—" I began in disbelief, but he shook his head and lifted his eyes to meet mine. They were swimming with tears but somehow, he managed to keep them from falling.

"I'm okay, James. But if you touch me, I'm going to lose it and I won't be able to go back out there."

His words made me feel both better and worse at the same time.

"It's almost over, baby. Just hang in there a little longer."

Aleks stiffened his spine and nodded, then wiped at his eyes. He went to the bathroom mirror and checked his face to make sure there wasn't any proof of his tears. He was careful not to look at the collar or his outfit. He returned to me and sucked in a few breaths. "I'm ready," he murmured.

"When we go out there, I'm going to look around a bit to see if there are any doors leading outside back here. If someone stops us, I'm just going to play it like we got turned around while trying to head back to the main room, okay? We won't have long to look around so just stay with me and move quickly."

Aleks nodded. "I will."

I wanted to hug him and tell him how amazing I thought he was, but I knew he was right... if he showed even any of the emotion he was feeling, he'd break down completely.

I probably would too.

Or, at the very least, it would show on my face when we returned to Luca.

And like Aleks, I was just another piece of property out there. The hired help. I had a role to play just like everyone else.

Since I didn't have to worry about anyone ignoring the collar and trying to reach out and touch Aleks back here like I had in the front room, I had him walk behind me as I began figuring out the layout of the back part of the building. There was another exit, but it too was heavily guarded by armed men and I had to use my excuse about being lost to explain our presence.

"Okay, let's head back," I said to Aleks as we passed the bathroom we'd used.

We were just rounding the corner and heading for the main hallway when two men came out of a private room, along with a little boy who was crying. The boy couldn't have been more than nine or so.

I forced myself to keep moving, but when I heard the man say, "Aleks?" in surprise, both Aleks and I came to a stuttering stop.

I'd put Aleks in front of me and he'd kept his eyes down when we'd passed the men, but when he saw the guy who'd called his name, he let out a gasp and then went frighteningly pale. He stepped back so fast that his back hit the wall behind him. He began shaking his head violently.

"No," he breathed. "No."

The word just kept falling from his lips.

The man who'd called to him actually smiled. "Take him backstage and get him cleaned up," the man told the other one who had his fingers around the little boy's thin arm. The man and boy went the way Aleks and I had come and I realized there was probably a door that led to the other side of the building where the stage was.

Which meant the little boy was one of the kids up for sale tonight.

"The little one had a bit of stage fright," the fucker said to me as he motioned in the direction the man and boy had gone. "He needed a little refresher on his training," he added before turning his eyes to Aleks. "This one never needed any refresher lessons," he said with an obscene amount of pride.

I saw red in my vision and when the man reached a hand toward Aleks, I grabbed him by the wrist. The man gasped at my painful hold and pulled his hand free. He was a beefy guy, but not muscular... most of the weight was centered in his belly and chest. His suit, while expensive, couldn't hide the extra flab, and all it did was make him look like he was trying too hard. He had closely cropped dark hair and a pudgy face, and he looked like your average guy; there was nothing standout about him. Except his eyes...

There was no mistaking the evil in those eyes.

"He's taken," I growled as I tried to stick to the role I was supposed to be playing. But I couldn't have, even if I'd wanted to.

Because Aleks was still whispering the word "no" over and over again.

"Ah, yes," the man said as he eyed the collar. "I heard about Mr.

Black being lucky enough to stumble across our little Aleks here," he said. "Though it looks like the time away from us has caused a few unacceptable habits," he added distastefully at Aleks's continued display of emotion. "What did I always tell you about being good, Aleks?" the man drawled in a voice that had shivers running up *my* spine.

Aleks began to cry as he slid down the wall and dropped to his ass. I started to kneel down in front of him, but when the man tried to reach for Aleks again, I straightened and shoved him back.

"Hey," the man snapped as he smoothed out his coat. He seemed to catch himself, like the outburst wasn't the right reaction. He smiled and said, "Tell your boss that if he needs a hand in retraining this one" – he motioned to Aleks – "I'm happy to help. I prefer younger charges myself, but to each his own, right?" He let his eyes roam over Aleks. "I'm always up for new challenges," he murmured, his tone positively sickening now. "Tell your boss to come see me after the auction if he wants to take me up on my offer or trade this one in for something a little less... used. A couple of my students are expected to sell for top dollar tonight, though I doubt they'll go as high as little Aleks did." He paused and then said, "Tell him to ask for Brian."

Brian.

As in the Brian who'd been the first man to rape Aleks. Brian, who'd tortured Aleks by making him believe that if he didn't behave, his brother wouldn't come for him. Brian, who'd had an innocent woman brutalized and murdered in front of a little boy to teach him a lesson...

It wasn't something I needed to think about any further. I hit Brian hard enough to knock him out cold. His head hit the wall behind him before he crashed onto the floor. I was on him despite the fact that he was unconscious. It was only Aleks calling my name that eventually got through my muddled brain, and I somehow managed to tell my fists to stop their downward trajectory.

"James, stop," Aleks said as he frantically grabbed at my sleeve. My knuckles were covered in blood.

As was Brian's face.

What was left of his face, anyway.

I saw his chest rising and falling, so I knew I hadn't killed him.

I was glad for that because he wouldn't have felt even a single one of my punches after the first one.

"James," Aleks cried. All my faculties returned at once and I remembered where we were and what would happen if we were discovered. My eyes fell on a little piece of white paper on the floor next to Brian.

I snatched it up and breathed a sigh of relief.

It was the door code for the room he'd just been in.

The door right behind us.

I punched the code in and sent my thanks heavenward when the door clicked. I pushed it open, then reached down to grab Brian beneath his armpits. I dragged him into the room and threw him on the floor, then took Aleks's hand and pulled him inside with me.

"Are you all right?" I asked.

Aleks was staring at Brian's body. I'd put Brian down face first, so he couldn't see his front, but it didn't matter. He was clearly in shock and probably not because of what I'd done. I knew there was no way Aleks would be able to recover enough from this to get through the next fifteen minutes. Not to mention both my hands and probably other parts of me had blood on them. And someone was bound to come looking for Brian at some point, especially once the auction started.

"Aleks, we need to go," I said. I searched the room. It was simply furnished with a bed, dresser, and nightstand. The bed had clearly been used and I could see a condom discarded on the floor. I felt sick as I went to the bed and snatched the pillow off it. I mentally thanked Con for having had the foresight to make me wear a tie. I ripped the tie off my neck and pulled the pillowcase off the pillow. There were some towels on the nightstand, but the drawers proved to only have condoms, lube, and a handful of sex toys in them. I felt sick to my stomach at the sight and slammed the drawers shut before Aleks could see what was in them.

I wiped at my hands with one of the towels, then went to Brian and tied his feet up with my tie. I quickly worked my shoes off, removed my socks and used one to tie his hands behind his back. I ripped one of the smaller towels in half and stuffed the material into Brian's mouth, then used my other sock to gag him so he wouldn't be able to cry out when he woke up. I wanted to kill the man but I wouldn't do it in front of Aleks and I couldn't risk sending him in the hallway by himself to wait for me. But Brian sure as shit wouldn't be walking the earth long now that I knew who he was. The second I had Aleks safe, I'd find Brian and I'd make him feel everything he'd made Aleks feel and then some.

And I'd enjoy every moment.

I put the pillowcase over Brian's head and dragged his body to the other side of the bed so that if someone opened the door, they wouldn't see him right away. My hope was that since I had the code for the door, Tuxedo Man would just assume the room was still in use. And hopefully Aleks, Luca, and I would be long gone before the man who'd been with Brian realized he was missing.

"Do I have any blood on my face?" I asked Aleks.

Aleks was standing frozen by the door, his eyes on the spot where I'd placed Brian's body.

"Aleks," I said gently as I went to stand in front of him. I stroked his face. He'd asked me not to touch him earlier, but I figured that request had flown out the window at this point.

"What?" he asked.

"Do I have any blood on my face?" I asked. I had the last towel in my hand to use to clean off whatever obvious blood remained. I was hoping the lighting was dim enough that no one would notice the blood on my suit jacket or the dots of it on my shirt while we went to get Luca.

Aleks finally seemed to snap out of his daze when he looked at me. He took the towel from me and carefully wiped at my forehead, then my nose. "Are you okay?" he asked.

I wanted to laugh at that.

On the one hand I wasn't okay... not even close.

But on the other, beating the shit out of Brian had felt really good.

I probably should have been bothered by that fact but I really wasn't.

"I'm good," I said. "When we get back out there, I need you to play along for just a little while longer, okay?"

Aleks nodded. He looked like he was going to throw up and I didn't blame him.

"Let's go," I said softly. I grabbed his hand only long enough to get him out of the room, then dropped it.

I breathed a sigh of relief when Tuxedo Man barely paid us any attention as we hurried past him. It took less than a minute to get back to Luca. When his eyes met mine as we reached him, I could tell he could see something was up. Aleks went to his side and resumed his position on his knees. The men with Luca were all chatting about something, but my brother ignored them as I leaned over and whispered into his ear, "We need to go. Tell them you and Aleks need some private time."

He barely reacted other than to nod. Luca stood up and motioned to Aleks, who climbed to his feet but kept his eyes down. He was about to speak to the men surrounding us when a dark-haired man suddenly appeared at Luca's side. Like me, he had "bodyguard" written all over him.

"Mr. Black, my employer has requested a private meeting with you and your… ward," the man said as he spared Aleks the briefest of glances.

"Actually, my *pet* and I were just going to go have some quality time together before the auction," Luca said.

I knew King and Con were watching everything that was happening through the button on Luca's jacket, but they wouldn't have had any idea about Brian. And they probably hadn't overheard me tell Luca we needed to go. The plan was to tell our brothers what was happening the second we got to the back rooms.

"It will be worth your while, Mr. Black," the man said. "My employer is of the understanding that you're considering letting go of your property if the circumstances are acceptable, and my employer has been extremely interested in this particular piece of property for a very, very long time."

I stiffened at that but managed not to react. God bless him, but Luca managed not to react either.

There was only one man we knew of who'd wanted Aleks for a long time.

Stylianos.

"Mr. Stylianos will compensate you quite well for your loss, Mr. Black," the man said.

I could sense Luca's hesitation and I knew why he wasn't jumping to respond.

Because I'd told him we needed to go and he was focused on that rather than finally meeting the man who might know where his son was.

Luca was putting Aleks's and my safety first. Part of me wanted to just get Aleks out of there, but the other part knew we might not have this chance again. I glanced at Tuxedo Man. Both he and the guard were still there and I didn't see any kind of commotion to indicate Brian had been found.

"The auction won't start for another fifteen minutes, sir," I said to Luca in the hopes he would understand my message.

Luca considered it for a moment, then looked at the man.

"Lead the way," he finally said.

Chapter 24

ALEKS

I COULD BARELY BREATHE BECAUSE MY HEART WAS POUNDING SO hard in my chest. I still couldn't process that Brian was lying tied up in a room with Vaughn's sock in his mouth and the evidence of Vaughn's fists on his face.

I wanted to laugh because the whole thing was just so unbelievable.

But it wouldn't have been a real laugh... it would have been one of those loud, inappropriate laughs like when someone saw something truly horrible and their brain couldn't believe it and the signals got all jumbled in their mind and the only sound that came out was a weird, all-wrong laugh.

I'd somehow managed to keep it together up until that point, even when Luca had touched me and that disgusting Mr. Oak had started saying terrible things about the boy he owned like the boy wasn't there and couldn't hear every word. The old me would have tuned the man out, but the new me had actually had to keep from getting up and slapping the man across his fat face. The fact that Mr. Oak had wanted me hadn't even really registered because I'd known I was perfectly safe. Between Vaughn and Luca, I might as well have been wrapped in a protective bubble.

Yes, I'd been scared when we'd entered the party.

I would have been a fool not to have been.

But I'd been more scared for Luca and Vaughn and what would happen if we were all discovered. I hadn't been worried that someone would somehow manage to steal me away from them.

Brian's presence had changed things, though.

Because I hadn't even considered the possibility that I'd ever see him again.

All the growth I'd experienced over the past two weeks had pretty much been obliterated when Brian had spoken those words to me... the ones that still haunted me in the worst of my nightmares.

What did I always tell you about being good, Aleks?

I felt a chill run up my spine as I heard his voice all over again, but I managed to keep it together as I followed Luca toward the back rooms.

Where Brian presumably was still out cold.

I'd been so out of it when Brian had said that phrase to me that it had taken me several long seconds to process what the sound I'd been hearing in my head had been.

The sound that *hadn't* been in my head.

It'd been coming from right in front of me and Vaughn had been the one making it... every time his fists had connected with Brian's face.

It'd been a gruesome sight, but a small part of me hadn't wanted to stop Vaughn. But the risk of discovery had been too great so I'd managed to snap out of my stupor long enough to make Vaughn stop. Everything had happened so fast after that.

I'd wanted to tell Vaughn I could see this whole thing through before we'd left that room to return to Luca to tell him we were getting out, but I'd also known that if someone found Brian, we'd all be at risk.

And I honestly couldn't have guaranteed that I could have continued to play my role.

But it looked like I was going to need to do just that, because we finally had our shot at Stylianos. I just hoped that King and Con would be able to get to us in time if things went wrong. I'd heard how concerned all of the men had been that communication would be so limited. Vaughn and Luca also hadn't been able to bring guns in, so neither of them was armed. The only ones who had guns were all the guards standing by the doors. I'd heard enough to know that King and Con's first job when they'd arrived at the same time as us had been to figure out where all the doors were and find ways in when the sixty minutes were up or if Luca or Vaughn said the code word.

The man we were following was about Vaughn's size with black hair. He had on an expensive-looking suit, but I'd heard enough to know he was a bodyguard.

And I'd heard who he worked for.

I'd also known what Luca had done by hesitating to respond to the man and agree to the meeting right away and I'd wanted to hug him for that.

In the end, it had been Vaughn who'd decided we'd take the risk.

And I was glad for that.

If seeing all the kids who the men had been parading around like they were nothing but accessories hadn't been enough, seeing that little boy coming out of the room with Brian and the other man, tears streaking down his face, would have been. The boy had been about my age when Brian had bought me, and he'd had light hair like Gio.

If Vaughn and Luca were able to get any kids out tonight, I'd make sure that that little boy was among them.

Even if I had to go back for him myself.

Because every single fucking man in that room was going to pay for all the kids they'd hurt and I didn't care how I'd make it happen, but they wouldn't get to hurt anymore if I had my way.

I straightened my spine and sent a silent apology to Vaughn and Luca's mother for swearing. I hadn't told Vaughn, but I'd started talking to his mother in my head and telling her how amazing both her boys were and how much I wished I could have met her. I'd also promised we'd find her grandson and had asked her and Gio's mom to watch over him just a bit longer until we could get to him. I knew it was probably pretty silly to talk to a dead woman I hadn't actually ever met, but I'd used to talk to my real father all the time after I'd first been taken. My mother had always been big on prayer so every night when I'd been little, I'd prayed at bedtime. I'd continued the habit after I'd been taken, but I hadn't waited until bedtime to do it.

I'd pretty much done it all the time.

I couldn't remember when I'd stopped exactly, but it had been around the same time as when I'd started to accept that Dante might never find me.

Even if prayer didn't really work and there was no heaven, it made me feel better to talk to Vaughn's mother, even if it was all just silently and in my head. I doubted Vaughn would mind, and maybe I'd even start talking to my father again.

I forced myself to focus when we walked past the man who was handing out the codes to the men who wanted to use the private rooms. I held my breath when we walked past the room Brian was in. There was a small spot of blood near the baseboards, but the walls were dark enough that no one else probably even noticed besides me.

It seemed like we walked forever, but I knew it had only been a minute or so. The room we entered wasn't near the other private rooms as far as I could tell. It seemed like we'd ended up on the other side of the building, closer to where the stage was. I hadn't seen any guards besides the ones by the exit, so I wasn't sure if that was a good thing or a bad one.

Stylianos's bodyguard opened the door and entered first. He held it open for us. Luca stopped and waited until the man stepped back into the room, and I realized it was so the man wouldn't be at our backs. Luca entered the room, which was considerably larger than the one we'd left Brian in. I bit back a sigh of relief when I saw there wasn't a bed in it. Hopefully, that meant that Stylianos and his bodyguard wouldn't try anything.

And if they did, I was sure Luca and Vaughn could take them on. I'd seen proof enough that both men could fight, even without weapons. And since each guest was only allowed to bring one bodyguard, it meant it would just be Stylianos and his man.

Not like the five he'd sent after me in Seattle.

My confidence lasted for about three seconds because when my eyes settled on Stylianos, I felt my heart stop.

He was huge and built.

I'd had this picture of a meek, older man, but this guy was young, and even in his suit, I could tell he was pretty much one big muscle. His dirty-blond hair was long and tied back in a ponytail, and I could see a little bit of a tattoo on his upper body where his dress shirt had been left open.

Luca must have sensed something was off because he stopped abruptly and I nearly slammed into him.

He put out his hand to push me back a little so I was closer to Vaughn just as Vaughn reached for my arm. I instinctively turned to Vaughn because I knew we needed to get out of there. There was just something about the way Stylianos and his man were looking at us that spoke volumes.

It was a trap.

My heart was in my throat as Vaughn disregarded the "rules" and grabbed my hand in his, then pulled me toward him as he turned to head for the door. But it slammed shut from the inside before we could reach it. I couldn't see the figure in the shadows, but there was no mistaking the gun that emerged from the darkness. I felt Luca at my back, but I knew I was no longer safe.

None of us were.

Between Luca and Vaughn, I couldn't make out much, but it didn't matter because everything changed the second the deadly voice from the shadows spoke.

"Get your fucking hands off my brother."

Dante.

Chapter 25

VAUGHN

"Dante," Aleks croaked from behind me. His fingers squeezed mine, but I refused to release him.

Not until I figured out what the fuck was going on.

But it looked like Dante wasn't even going to give me an opportunity to ask questions because he walked straight up to me and put his gun to my head.

"Dante, don't!" Aleks cried.

"Take him," Dante said softly. I heard rather than saw the other two men in the room approach us. Luca went after the long-haired one but my brother was outmatched… not something that happened often. Not to mention the big fucker was armed and after punching Luca, he put his gun to his forehead. When the black-haired man reached for Aleks, I ignored the gun aimed at me and hit the guy.

"Keep your fucking hands off him!" I snarled.

"Dante, stop this!" Aleks said as he tried to push past me to get to his brother. But I held him firm.

Dante's expression softened only the littlest bit when his eyes met Aleks's. "Confie em mim, irmãozinho," he murmured.

I had no clue what he'd said to Aleks, but he quieted.

"Let him go," Dante said to me. "He'll be safe with Cole and Mace." He motioned to the other men.

I had no clue what the fuck was going on, but I'd seen enough to know this man would never betray his brother. "Go with him," I told Aleks.

"No," Aleks whispered.

I turned and said, "It'll be all right, Aleks."

But Aleks ignored me and as soon as I released him, he squirmed away from the dark-haired man and hurried to his brother. "Dante, please don't do this. It was my choice to go with him. This... I can explain all this."

Before Dante could respond, the door opened and several men entered. I only recognized one of them.

Magnus.

Dante's fiancé.

"Magnus," Aleks said softly, then he walked into the other man's arms. "Tell him to stop. It's all a mistake."

All of the men with Magnus were armed but one, and they moved into a circle around us. I hoped like hell King and Con were on their way into the building because Luca and I were sorely outnumbered.

"It'll be okay, Aleks," Magnus said softly.

Aleks began to cry as frustration consumed him. But when he tried to come back to me, Magnus gently grabbed his arm. Dante lowered his gun long enough to approach his brother. He wiped at Aleks's tears, but when his eyes fell on the collar, I could practically feel the rage rolling off him.

"It's not what it looks like," Aleks sobbed. I could see he was completely overwhelmed. Dante leaned down and whispered something to him, then clasped his face as he kissed his temple. Then his hand was reaching behind Aleks's neck and with one flick of his finger, the collar's clasp clicked open. Dante gently pulled it from his brother's neck, then turned to me.

He put the gun back to my head and I heard Aleks whimper.

"Look at me, not him," Dante snapped when I looked at Aleks.

"Fuck you, Dante," I said. "You're scaring him."

Dante actually flinched at that, then his anger was back in full-force. He threw the collar at my feet. "You know why you're still breathing?" he asked. "Do you know why I didn't kill you the second you entered this room?"

"Dante," Aleks whispered.

"Because of him," he said as he pointed at Aleks. "Because I heard something in his fucking voice in his calls that I haven't heard since he was a little boy. And the only reason I had the sense to actually listen to my brother's voice and what he *wasn't* saying was that man right there," he said as he pointed at Magnus. "But that" – he pointed at the collar – "and this" – he took a photo from his pocket and tossed it next to the collar – "is making it really hard not to put a bullet in your head."

I looked at the picture and saw it was the fake one we'd taken of Luca and Aleks.

And if Dante had the picture, that meant he'd probably seen the posts we'd made up about Luca "owning" Aleks now.

"It's not real!" Luca snapped. "It was all a set-up!"

Most of the men with Dante had formed a circle around us, but there was one who'd stayed by the door. I could tell he was the leader of their little group because he had an air of authority about him.

"We know that, Mr. Covello," the man said as he stepped in front of Dante for a brief moment so he could see my brother as he spoke. He seemed unconcerned with the gun that he'd stepped into the line of fire of for that short moment. "I think we should wait for your brothers before we chat some more."

I stiffened at that because I knew we were royally fucked if he knew about King and Con waiting outside.

"Yeah, why don't we?" Luca bit out. "We'll see who's got more firepower then."

A couple of the men around us actually chuckled. The man watching my brother merely smiled. "Your brothers put up a good fight, Mr. Covello, but they were at a disadvantage," he said patiently. "You see, my men also know how to do their homework. And while your brother, King, has an impressive list of men on his employee roster, there is one thing that makes them different from my men."

Luca didn't respond to the comment and I knew it was probably because he was still struggling to accept what the man had said about our brothers putting up a good fight.

"They're not family," the man said softly, his voice holding a bit of an edge to it. "You stole something precious from that family, Luca." The man's gaze shifted to me. "Your intentions toward keeping Aleks safe were honorable, Vaughn. But you and your brothers should know better than anyone what it feels like to not know what's happening to someone who's so much a part of who you all are."

He couldn't be talking about Gio.

There was just no way he knew about him.

Before Luca or I could respond, the door opened and King and Con were escorted inside. I was relieved that they both looked unharmed. There were several men surrounding them and a couple of those men had bruises, but clearly King and Con had been caught unawares.

"My men will tear this place apart, Luca," King muttered.

"Mav," the man who'd been talking to Luca called. A man with long black hair stepped forward and held out a small device.

"Know what this is?" the man called Mav said. He didn't wait for an answer. "It's a nifty little device that jams all radio and video signals within a twenty-five-foot radius. That's why you" – he looked pointedly at Con and King – "didn't know your brothers were in trouble. Cole is carrying one. As are most of the men who surprised you in your car. But see, we figured that wasn't enough, so we had the lovely young woman who also works for Ronan here" – he pointed at the man who'd been talking to me and Luca – "intercept the signal your brother's camera was transmitting. She recorded a few seconds of the video of him sitting at the party and then muffled the sound with static so you would think it was just a problem with the sound. It was enough time to distract you both while you tried to figure out if it was a technical glitch or not." Mav smirked at King and Con. "Seems to have worked, huh?"

"Fuck you," King bit out.

The man called Ronan looked at me. "Daisy, that's the young woman Mav was talking about, is monitoring the police frequencies. So even if one of your brother's men gets wise and calls the cops, we'll know."

The asshole really did have us beat. I glanced at Aleks and saw how heartbroken he looked. His eyes met mine and I smiled at him. Then I looked pointedly at Dante and said, "I'd do it all again in a heartbeat. There's only one thing I'd change, and it has nothing the fuck to do with you. The only one I owe an apology to is Aleks for something that happened when I first took him."

I looked at Aleks again and he nodded.

Yeah, he knew what I was talking about.

That moment I'd chosen to leave him bound rather than take the time to tell him the truth after I'd gotten him out of that van. "I'm sorry, baby," I said, not caring that we were surrounded by Dante and all the other men. "If I could relive that moment, I'd do it differently. I'd have told you everything then and there, no matter what the risk."

Aleks wiped at his face. "Don't be sorry," he said. I laughed when he repeated the words back to me that I'd said to him so many times.

I looked at Ronan. "You talk a good game. But talking isn't going to help any of those kids out there," I said as I motioned to the door. "When you've spent as many years as I have watching kids suffer like Aleks did, then you can fucking preach to me about family and loyalty."

Ronan studied me for a moment, but he seemed unimpressed by my words. He looked at Aleks. "Aleks, is there something you want to tell your brother?"

Aleks looked both surprised and relieved at the same time. "Yes," he said with a nod.

Ronan motioned toward Dante. Magnus released his hold on Aleks and the second he did, Aleks hurried to stand in front of his brother. Dante lowered his weapon.

Aleks opened his mouth to speak, but nothing came out. He

looked at me in distress and I knew what was happening. His mind was struggling with the processing thing that happened when he was completely overwhelmed. With everything that had happened, it was no wonder he was having a hard time putting his thoughts into words.

Not to mention the huge audience he had…

"Just breathe, baby," I said. "Remember that story you told me… about the do… do…"

Aleks pulled in a breath. "Dobradinha," he said softly. The reminder of the funny story seemed to ground him for the moment he needed to get his thoughts in line. He looked relieved. I could feel Dante's and just about everyone else's gazes on me, but I didn't care. I couldn't take my eyes off Aleks because I was just so fucking proud of him. If there'd ever been a time for him to escape into his head or lose himself to a blackout, this was one of those moments.

But his voice was firm as he began speaking.

Firm, but quiet.

Soft.

So very much him.

"Dante, I've missed you so much," he whispered. "So very much."

Dante actually seemed to shudder as some unnamed emotion went through him. "Me too," he said with a nod. "I was so fucking scared, Aleks."

Aleks nodded and wiped at his face. I wished I could see his eyes, but he was facing away from me.

"Do you remember when you came to Fath… *Marcus's* house?" he asked. "I betrayed you at first."

"No," Dante said firmly. "No, you never betrayed me, irmãozinho," he said, his own voice thick with emotion.

Aleks managed a nod. "Vaughn knows why I told Marcus about you." Aleks's tongue seemed to trip over using Marcus's name, but I was so damn proud of him for not referring to the man by the title he'd forced Aleks to use. It was yet another step forward for Aleks.

"You had no choice," Dante said.

"I did, Dante. But it was the only choice I knew how to make. I knew if I fought when they took me, I'd die. I didn't want to die and I knew you were going to come for me so I did what they told me to do. This man… Brian… he said if I was good enough, if I behaved, you would come get me and take me home and Mama and Papa would want me again. So I was really good."

Aleks let out a harsh sob. "But you didn't come and I started to think that maybe it was true, but I knew in here it wasn't." Aleks pointed at his chest.

I heard Dante suck in a ragged breath, but I didn't look at him. I didn't need to. I knew what he was feeling. Luca and I and our brothers felt it every single damn day when we thought about Gio.

"I found ways to escape but only in here." Aleks pointed to his head. Dante reached out to clasp his cheek, but he didn't speak. Aleks reached up to cover his brother's hand with his own. "When you came and I saw that note, I thought it was a trick… it was someone trying to make me be bad so Fath—Marcus could punish me. And even when I saw you in that office, I was still afraid. It took so long for my head to catch up to my heart," Aleks whispered. "But in my heart I knew it was you and that you had come to take me home."

"Always," Dante breathed. "I will always come for you, Aleks."

Aleks nodded and pulled in several breaths. "My mind still plays tricks on me, Dante. I thought if I couldn't be normal, you might not want me anymore. So I pretended. I got a job and I made decisions and I told you I was okay all the time… I'm not okay, Dante."

Dante pulled Aleks to him and wrapped his arms around his brother. "You're perfect just as you are, Aleks. You don't need to change for anyone but yourself. I will always love you, no matter what."

Aleks nodded against his chest.

"Meu melhor," Aleks said softly.

Dante let out what sounded like a wet laugh and then responded in Portuguese. They only did their little back and forth a couple times before Aleks pulled back and wiped at his eyes. "I chose to help them." He looked at Ronan. "It was always my choice."

Ronan nodded gently at him. Aleks looked over his shoulder at me, then Luca. "They're like us, Dante. They argue and they fight and they love each other. Luca is the one who takes care of everyone but himself." Aleks looked at Con and King. "Con is the peacekeeper and he cooks when he's upset… he makes me grits and they're almost as good as Magnus's. And King yells when anyone scares me. Otherwise he's really quiet. And I haven't met Lex yet, but he's the baby of the family and they all watch out for him. And Vaughn, he…"

Aleks paused and then looked at me.

"Vaughn is *my James*… he showed me that I'm not broken, and that I'm strong enough to make choices and it's okay to make the wrong ones and… and he loves me like Magnus loves you and you love Magnus." I felt my heart slamming against my chest as Aleks's beautiful eyes held mine. As far as I was concerned, all the other people had disappeared, and it was just me and him. "And I love him too."

Aleks was in my arms a moment later, though I wasn't sure if he'd come to me or the other way around. I kissed him softly, since I couldn't discount the fact that his brother and the rest of his big-ass family were all watching us. "I do," I said softly as I pulled him against me and wrapped my arms around him. "So much, Aleks."

"Me too, James," he sighed. I held him for a moment and then he was carefully pulling free of my hold.

But only to turn around and face his brother.

He linked our fingers together, then said to his brother, "Don't make me choose between you and him, Dante. Please… that's one choice I don't want to ever make… but I will."

Chapter 26

ALEKS

I held my breath for what seemed like the longest time.

"No, irmãozinho," Dante said.

I felt my stomach drop out because I thought that was his answer, but relief shot through me when he quickly added, "I would never ask that of you." He glanced at Magnus and I saw the pair exchange a smile. But it wasn't until my brother tucked his gun into his waistband behind his back that I finally relaxed.

Until I remembered where we were.

And why.

I dropped Vaughn's hand and rushed to Dante. "They lost someone just like you did, Dante. I need to help them. *We* need to help them. And all those kids out there. Please—"

"We will, Aleks," Dante quickly assured me. He looked at Ronan. I still felt like a fool for not having recognized the man at first when he'd entered the room, but I'd been too scared to really process what was happening. The sight of Dante pointing a gun at Vaughn's head had pretty much caused my brain and my body to go to war as one tried to win out over the other.

"How did you know about Stylianos?" Luca asked. "We never posted his name online."

"You think you're the only ones who know how to track who hired a bunch of assholes to kidnap a person?" Dante asked.

"We also know they weren't the only men sent to take Aleks that day," Ronan said. "The part that wasn't clear was why the brother of the man who'd had his own men try to kidnap Aleks would stop them... and then let Aleks call home to tell his family he was okay. It took longer than we would have liked to figure out exactly who you were," Ronan said to Vaughn. "But once we did, the pieces started to fall into place. And led to you," the man continued as he stopped in front of Luca. "You all are pretty good with computers," he acknowledged. "But you don't have what we do."

"What's that?" Luca asked.

"Our wife," one of the men near Luca said. He was huge with short black hair. He was motioning to the man next to him.

"That's Cash and that's Sage," Ronan said as he pointed first at the bigger guy, then the one with the reddish-orange hair. "They're married to Daisy, who's currently expecting their first child. Daisy is the one who helped us put the brakes on your plans by messing with your tech." Ronan nodded toward Luca's suit jacket and I knew he was talking about the button that was also a video camera.

"Once we found out who you were, we had to find out why you'd taken Aleks. The picture nearly ended it all," Ronan admitted. "You have Magnus to thank both for stopping Dante from storming into your house and killing you all and for making us look harder for the truth." He looked at Vaughn. "He was convinced that something he saw between you and Aleks two years ago was the real deal."

I looked at Magnus. He sent me a reassuring smile and then his eyes met Vaughn's and he tipped his head.

I got the impression they were even now. Vaughn had saved all our lives two years ago and Magnus had returned the favor.

"So you know about Gio?" Luca asked, his voice losing some of the edge it'd had before. "And Stylianos." I knew it was just now hitting him that we weren't any closer to finding Gio.

"We do," Ronan said. "As I said, Daisy is the best. She hacked all of your computers and found the transcripts you'd saved where you tried to draw the man out two years ago. We made the connection as soon as we saw you were trying to locate a child with hair that was so light it was almost white and nearly clear eyes."

My heart broke for Luca as he dropped his eyes. I felt fresh tears stinging my own eyes as I realized we'd never really even gotten close to finding the now fifteen-year-old boy.

"We found Stylianos, Luca. We have him," Ronan said softly. The entire room went so incredibly quiet as Luca, Vaughn, and I, and presumably Con and King, looked at Ronan.

"What?" Luca whispered.

"He was in Chicago. He's now in a secure location trying to save his ass by naming names."

"And Gio?" Vaughn asked, his voice breaking. I suspected he and his brothers both couldn't wait to hear the answer and were afraid of it too.

"He told us about a boy who matched your son's description," Ronan said to Luca. "But he swore up and down he didn't know where he was."

"He was probably lying," King cut in as he stepped forward. "You have to question him the right way!"

"We did," Ronan assured him. "This is Vincent," he added as he motioned to one of the taller men in the group. He was older than most of the other men in the group, but just looking at him intimidated the heck out of me. "Vincent came out of retirement to help us with this," Ronan said.

King turned on Vincent and began asking him what techniques the man had used. He wouldn't even let Vincent respond before he turned back to Ronan and said, "Let me talk to him. I can get the truth out of him."

"We got what we needed," Ronan responded. "Vincent," – he nodded toward the older man – "got what we needed." Ronan looked at Luca again. "Stylianos didn't know where Gio was or who he was with, but he did eventually remember something."

"What?" Luca breathed. He seemed terrified to even ask the question.

"The online screen name the man who was talking about Gio

used." Ronan paused only for the briefest of moments before saying, "Daisy's motto is that you can't ever really delete things from the internet and she was absolutely right. She found the alias and that led us to the man who your son was sold to shortly after he was taken."

"And?" Con asked.

Ronan kept his eyes on Luca. "We found a boy that matches his description, Luca. Alive."

Luca let out a harsh sob and then covered his eyes with his hand. He reached out his other hand to Vaughn and his brother immediately took it.

"Where?" Luca asked. "Where is he? Please…"

"He's safe," Ronan said. "As I said, he fits the description and we had one of our guys who used to work for the FBI do an age progression photo using one of the last photos you'd taken of Gio… the one you use as wallpaper on your phone and computer. It seems to be him, Luca, but the only way to know for sure is to do a DNA test."

"I'll know," Luca said. "I'll know it's him," he cried, then he and Vaughn were hugging. "It has to be him, Vaughn. It has to be."

"It is, Luca," Vaughn said. "They wouldn't have told you if they didn't think it was."

I turned and walked into my brother's arms. He hugged me hard. "It's him, right, Dante?"

He kissed the top of my head as he hugged me back. "We're pretty sure it's him, Aleks."

I let out a sob and nodded. I knew Dante and Ronan were both reluctant to commit to saying it was Gio, but Vaughn was right. They wouldn't have gotten Luca's hopes up if they hadn't truly believed they'd found his son. No matter how angry my brother might have been with Luca and his family, he never would have used something like that to punish the men.

"Where is he?" Luca asked. Con and King had moved to his and Vaughn's side.

"He's in Seattle," Dante said.

"Luca," Ronan said softly when Luca and his brothers began talking excitedly amongst themselves. Luca turned to look at Ronan.

"The boy is physically okay, but he had to be hospitalized."

"What?" Luca asked. "I don't understand. If he's physically okay then why—"

"The man he was living with killed himself as my men were closing in. Gio witnessed the whole thing. He tried to kill himself with the same gun the man used, but my men were able to stop him."

Luca went ghostly white.

"Why?" King asked. "Why would he do that if he was being rescued?"

I saw Ronan and Dante share a look and I knew whatever Ronan was about to say was really bad. I went to stand by Vaughn and closed my hand over his.

"Gio told my men that the man was his husband… he said he loved him and he didn't want to live without him."

I felt like I was going to be sick, and I didn't need to look at Luca or the other men to know the shock they had to be feeling.

"My men brought Gio back to Seattle and took him to a house my husband and I own on Whidbey Island. We were hoping once we'd gotten him out of that environment that he'd feel safer. The second we turned our backs, Gio grabbed a knife and tried to slit his wrists. He didn't cut deep enough to do any permanent damage, but we knew he was mentally beyond our help. I had to have him admitted to keep him safe. It's a private institution. A man my men and I once helped many years ago faked the admission papers so no one would question who Gio really is. As far as the staff is concerned, he's just the mentally disturbed son of an anonymous but very wealthy family. The man we helped is the only one who's actively treating Gio. Your son has been there a little over a week now and he's shown no improvement. He continues to deny he was ever abducted and just keeps saying he wants to be with his husband."

"Oh God," Luca whispered.

"He's alive, Luca. That's what matters," Vaughn said firmly. "He'll be okay."

Luca looked at him, then me. He held my gaze for a long time before he nodded. "Yes, he will."

"Would you like to see a picture of him?" Ronan asked as he pulled out his phone. "It was taken during one of his calmer moments," the man added.

Luca nodded and dashed at his eyes. "Yes."

He steeled himself as he took the phone from Ronan. We all gave him a moment to himself to take in his son's image. "It's him," he whispered. "It's him." His voice cracked as he spoke. Vaughn, King, and Con looked over his shoulder at the phone. I managed to get a look but didn't want to crowd Luca, so I did so from a distance.

I didn't have a good enough view to see if the boy resembled the picture Luca had shown me weeks ago, but it wouldn't have mattered because I doubted I would have known one way or another. What mattered was that Luca seemed certain.

"Ronan," one of the men called from the opposite side of the room. "It's done. We need to go so Declan can make the call."

Ronan nodded and the men began heading for the door. "Wait, no!" I cried as I hurried to Dante. "No, we can't go, Dante. We have to help the kids. The boy Mr. Oak had on his lap and the one Brian hurt and—"

"It's okay, Aleks," Dante began.

"No," I said almost violently. "Please, Dante. You have to do something."

My brother grabbed my face. "It's already done, irmãozinho," he said gently.

"What?" I asked. I felt Vaughn at my back. His hands came to rest on my shoulders.

"It's done, Aleks. They're safe. Come see." Dante put his arm around my shoulders, but when Vaughn didn't move, it became a weird stand-off.

It was Magnus who intervened. He closed his fingers around

Dante's and said, "Come on, MawMaw. You and Vaughn can have a 'whose is bigger' match later."

I swore I heard my brother mumble that his was bigger, but he gave in and followed Magnus. There was also a comment about the hated nickname Matty had given Dante two years earlier. Since he called his grandfather Pop-pop, he'd taken to calling Dante MawMaw. It had started as a joke, but Matty and his little friends had gotten a kick out of how much it had annoyed Dante, so they'd all started calling him that.

And it had stuck.

Vaughn took my hand and we followed the men out of the room. As we made our way back toward the main room, I saw that all the doors to the private rooms were open and they all had damage to them.

Like they'd been kicked in...

I felt my blood run cold when I saw that the room Brian had been in was open too.

I came to a stop and stared at the empty room.

Vaughn wrapped his arm around me from behind. "We'll find him again, Aleks. I promise."

I nodded and then let him tug me away. My brother and Magnus had stopped at some point to watch the exchange between me and Vaughn, but Dante didn't ask me about it. I was still trying to deal with the fact that Brian had managed to elude punishment, so I didn't notice what was happening in the main room until I heard Con say, "Holy fuck."

I looked up and gasped when I took in the sight before me.

More than a dozen men with guns had formed a large circle around another group of men, all on their knees and bound and gagged.

Some of the bound men were sobbing, others looked sullen. But not one of them was making any kind of sound otherwise. I recognized Mr. Oak and Mr. Stark among the men on their knees... along with Brian and the rest of the party guests.

They were all bound and gagged.

Caught.

Helpless.

Afraid.

Like all the kids they'd hurt.

"What is this?" Vaughn asked in disbelief.

"*This*," Ronan said as he came up next to us, "is Aleks's family." He nodded at the men forming the circle. "Every single one has suffered at the hands of another or known someone who has. And like Aleks, they had to choose to let it break them or to survive it and then fight back when they could. This is them fighting back for themselves, for the people they love, and for those who aren't able to fight for themselves just yet."

My eyes scanned the faces of all the men. I didn't know any of them, but my heart swelled at knowing that they'd been willing to risk their lives to help me, Luca's son, and most importantly, the kids who'd spent every second of tonight wishing a miracle would happen and they'd get to go home.

"Where are the kids?" I asked.

Ronan motioned to the door. Several men were ushering a line of kids out the door. A couple of the smaller children were being carried by the men and a couple of the older kids. I saw the little boy that had been with Brian in one of the men's arms.

"Did your brother ever tell you how he and I met?" Ronan asked. "Or how he came to work for me?"

I shook my head.

"It was several years ago. We were both in Chicago looking for the same man. That man had hurt Mace and Cole's then-boyfriend, Jonas. They're now all married to one another," Ronan said with a smile.

I glanced at Vaughn, who looked positively confused at the mention of three people being married. I'd been in the same boat when I'd been introduced to one of the many threesomes in our family. Dante had explained to me that none of them were legally married, but they'd said vows in front of their family and friends to show that they were going to spend their lives together just like regular couples. I took Vaughn's hand in mine and waited until he looked at me. "I'll explain it to you later," I said with a wink. He laughed at that and I smiled.

It felt good to finally be the one who had more experience with something.

"The man who hurt Jonas tried again shortly after Mace, Cole, and Jonas fell for one another. I knew he'd always be a threat to Jonas, so I made sure he wouldn't be anymore," Ronan hedged. "Your brother and I sort of stumbled upon one another. He was not happy with me," Ronan said with a smile.

Dante appeared at my side. "I was looking for leads on you and Ronan had taken out the one lead I'd had in a long time. It wouldn't have panned out anyway, because the guy hadn't had any information on you, but Ronan offered to help me in my search. He had more resources than I even knew was possible."

Dante looked pointedly at Vaughn, who ignored him.

Oh God, they were just going to kill each other at this rate.

"We haven't been in this world for as long as you, Vaughn," Ronan said. "But we've seen the same things. Some of my men more than others. But like you and your family, we've discovered that if you cut the head off a snake—"

"Two more will grow in its place," Vaughn murmured.

"But we keep cutting and like you and Luca and your brothers, we try to get the kids out. Having more resources means we've learned some new tricks," Ronan said. "We did what you did – we got some men in– we just did it on a bigger scale."

Ronan motioned to a few of the men who were guarding the others.

I recognized a couple as men who'd worked the party or had been guests. One of the men had been one of the guards at the back exit near the bathroom. I also recognized the bartender. He actually waved at Vaughn.

So that was how Ronan and his men had gotten into the building. They'd had men already on the inside.

"What's the plan?" Vaughn asked.

"The cops will be here within minutes of us leaving. We have a friend in Seattle, the captain of the Seattle Police department actually, who is going to call his brethren out here and mention an anonymous tip he got from a suspect about a bunch of sick fucks who like to abuse kids getting together for a drink. We'll leave enough men here to make sure these assholes can't go anywhere, and they'll slip out before the cops surround the building." Ronan motioned to the men. "Behind every man's gag is a flash drive," Ronan said as he held up a little stick that was about the size of my thumb. "Daisy's been very busy collecting information on every single piece of shit here, and in the rare case she wasn't able to find enough to make sure a lengthy prison sentence is coming, we did a little bit of photoshopping. Those men who manage to get off because of technicalities will receive a death sentence," Ronan said easily.

Even I understood that.

And I couldn't be anything but happy about that.

"What if they swallow the drive?" Luca asked.

"Well, if they're lucky enough to get it past the rags in their mouths, the cops will just have to go in after it... the drives will survive that long. And if not, like I said, death sentence."

Ronan reached out to brush my arm. "We should get going. We need to get those kids home."

I managed a nod but nothing more.

The kids were safe.

Gio was safe.

We were *all* going home.

"You go with Ronan and Luca, okay?" Vaughn said to me. "Your brother and I need to have a little chat."

"What? No," I said.

"It's fine, Aleks," Dante said with what I could only classify as an evil-looking grin. "We'll be along shortly."

Magnus was the one who took my arm. "Come on, Aleks. Let's let them get it over with."

I wanted to say there was no time, but Magnus was leading me away. I looked over my shoulder but it was hard to see past the men guarding the guests. I saw Vaughn say something to Dante and my brother's face went from somewhat amused to downright deadly.

Then Vaughn pointed to Brian.

Dante looked at me, then back at Brian. I saw him stride forward and grab Brian by the arm and yank him to his feet. Brian looked terrified and I could hear him screaming through his gag as Dante dragged him from the group. I knew Vaughn couldn't have told Dante the things Brian had done to me in such a short amount of time, but it was enough time for him to have told Dante that Brian was the first man who'd bought me.

And I remembered that I'd said Brian's name when I'd told Dante that Brian had told me that my brother wouldn't come for me if I didn't behave.

So either way, Dante would have put things together as soon as Vaughn had pointed to Brian and told him the man's name.

It was another case where I couldn't find it in me to care what would happen to the monster.

I didn't care what that made me.

Dante was grim-faced as he pulled Brian past me, Luca, Ronan, and Magnus. "This one's coming with us," he said to Ronan. "I've been meaning to ask Vincent to show me some of his interrogation methods and now I can finally get some hands-on practice."

Brian let out a cry of distress at that, but Ronan merely nodded and stepped aside.

Vaughn came up to us and took my hand. "Let's go home," he said.

I nodded and gripped his fingers hard as he led me from the building.

I just had one question, but I was too afraid to ask it.

Where exactly was home now?

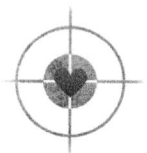

Chapter 27

VAUGHN

"The key is using stone-ground grits and if you have the time, put them in a slow cooker," Magnus said as he held up a bag of grits. I nodded in agreement.

"You writing this down, son?" the man asked as he looked pointedly at the piece of paper and pen in front of me.

The ones Magnus had put there as soon as I'd sat down at the kitchen island.

"Oh, um, yeah, sorry," I said as I rubbed at my eyes and grabbed the pen. I knew Magnus wasn't actually that much older than me, so calling me "son" probably wasn't an age thing, but it sure as shit was an indirect reminder that he loved Aleks like a son, not just a future brother-in-law.

I somehow managed to listen and take notes as Magnus got the grits in the slow cooker, but I was more than a little bit happy when he said the things needed to cook for several hours.

It was early Sunday morning and we'd been back in Seattle for just over thirty-six hours. Things had gone down exactly as Ronan had said they would after we'd left the party. I'd seen proof of that for myself on the morning news when we'd landed in Seattle.

Not only had the cops raided a building based on an "anonymous" tip and found nearly twenty men tied up with flash drives containing evidence of their crimes stuffed in their mouths, a whole passel of kids had been brought in by a couple of men who'd claimed to have found the children just outside the Emergency Room doors. Those same men had magically disappeared during the commotion of the kids being treated and the cops still hadn't been able to find them or whoever had left the gift of twenty perverts bound and gagged for the police to find.

Since learning Gio was alive, we'd all been eager to get to Seattle, and while Luca could have made arrangements for us to fly there on one of his private jets, we'd been too shell-shocked by the news of Gio to do anything but agree to fly to the Emerald City on one of Ronan's planes. Several of the men Ronan had introduced us to that night at the party had been on the plane with us, but two had been notably absent and that had made me very happy.

Vincent, the so-called interrogator.

And Dante.

And no, I hadn't been happy Dante hadn't been on the flight to annoy the ever-loving fuck out of me. I'd been happy he hadn't been on there because it meant he'd been dealing with Brian. And if Dante had had Vincent with him, it meant Brian had probably felt some pain before he'd died.

Well, a lot of pain.

And since Dante hadn't actually needed any information from him, the only end-game would have been to make Brian feel every one of the things Aleks had felt when Brian had hurt him. Oh, and of course, Dante's need for blood.

Aleks had been upset to learn his brother wouldn't be flying home with us, but he hadn't asked why, since he'd probably known himself why his brother had stayed behind. Magnus and Ronan had returned with us and while Aleks had slept against me, Ronan had used the time to talk to me and Luca more about Gio. King and Con had stayed behind in New York to monitor the fallout from the party and to make sure Luca's name didn't come up in the investigation, something Ronan had assured us wouldn't happen.

As grateful as I was to the guy, I was still struggling to accept the power and resources he seemed to have access to. Maybe once I saw Gio for myself, that would change. I just couldn't relate the little boy I'd known to the tormented young man Ronan had described.

But if what he was saying about Luca's son was true, bringing Gio back to us had gotten a lot more complicated. Because it didn't just sound like Gio had been sticking to certain behaviors like Aleks had when he'd been rescued... it sounded like Gio had been brainwashed into believing he really was married to the man who'd purchased him like he was some prize-winning steer. I'd already seen the damage a manipulator like Brian could do after just a couple of years. If this guy had had Gio the entire time, the damage to his mental health would be extreme.

"Here," Magnus said as he pulled my coffee cup toward him and filled it up again.

"Thanks," I murmured.

"Go get a few more hours of sleep," Magnus suggested. "They probably won't be up for a while yet... they were talking pretty late last night."

I nodded but didn't say anything and I didn't get up to go back to Aleks's room.

Magnus chuckled. "Yep, you've got it bad already if you can't sleep without him beside you." Magnus filled his own cup. "Been there, done that – last night, actually."

I smiled at that. I'd figured Magnus would be kicked out of his and Dante's bedroom while Aleks and Dante had "the talk" Aleks had insisted on the second Dante had gotten back home the previous day, but I hadn't realized the man hadn't been allowed to sleep in his own bed.

"Do you know if Aleks ate?" I asked. "He's just now starting to eat when he's hungry rather than waiting until his alarm reminds him to."

"I took them both some food before I went to bed... in the guest room," Magnus said. "They were under the covers just talking. The guest room is next to ours so I could hear them throughout the night... there was lots of laughter... some tears too," Magnus added solemnly. "But when I just looked in on them, they were both asleep."

I nodded and took a sip of my coffee.

"You and Luca going to check on Gio today?"

"The doctor thinks today might be a good day for Gio to see Luca. I guess the medication they've put him on is supposed to start kicking in and calming him down without knocking him out, you know?"

"Yeah," Magnus said with a sigh. "Just tell your brother… just tell him that no matter what he sees today, his kid's still in there."

The confirmation that the boy in the hospital was, in fact, Gio, had come in the night before. The second we'd landed in Seattle, Ronan had taken some blood from Luca for a DNA test. He'd already had a lab waiting to run the results, something I suspected the wealthy surgeon had paid quite a bit for. We'd had the results that the boy was Luca's son in less than twenty-four hours.

But Luca had known just by looking at his picture that the boy who now called himself Nick was his child. He hadn't doubted it for even a second. And he believed that as soon as Gio saw him, this nightmare would end.

I wasn't so certain.

I'd seen the results of long-term mental torture for myself. Yes, Gio was a fighter, but he'd been programmed to believe something and *that* was what he would probably fight for first. Like Aleks, at some point after he'd been taken, his brain had made the switch from needing to fight back and escape to needing to do whatever was necessary to survive.

I downed the rest of my coffee and pushed the cup away. Magnus took it, then said, "Can I fix you something while we wait for the grits?"

I shook my head.

"When was the last time you ate?"

The question came from Aleks and it actually felt like a balm on my soul. All the stuff with Gio was still there, but it ducked behind the shadows for now so that I could take pleasure in having the man I loved back in my arms.

Aleks's fingers slid up my back and along the nape of my neck as he sat down next to me. He turned my head so I was looking at him.

"Not sure," I admitted.

"Grits will be a while," Magnus said with a wink.

"Magnus, do we have any cereal with the tricky rabbit on it?" Aleks asked.

"No, but I know who does," Magnus returned. "Let me make a call."

Magnus stepped out of the kitchen and I used the opportunity to pull Aleks to me and kiss him deeply. He moaned under the onslaught and then tried to crawl into my lap. Someone clearing their throat had us separating.

Dante was standing in the kitchen, his hard eyes on us. "Aleks, I think we need to talk about some rules when it comes to having your... friend... over."

"Boyfriend," Aleks slowly corrected as he eyed his brother suspiciously. I was glad that there was nothing meek or nervous in his manner. I also liked that he was still touching me.

"Like maybe when you have a *friend* in your bedroom, you leave the door open."

"Do you mean all my friends, like Caleb and Remy, or my *naked sex* friends, like Vaughn?"

I had to give Aleks credit because his timing was stellar. Dante had just taken a sip of coffee when Aleks said the words "naked sex." Dante choked and then spit out the hot coffee. "Because I closed the door when Vaughn and I got home the first night. We were naked but we were too tired for sex."

I laughed as Dante glared at his brother. Whatever the pair had talked about the night before seemed to have given Aleks a newfound sense of freedom. He began trailing his fingers up and down my arm as he continued with, "So I should leave the door open when Vaughn and I want to have naked sex, but close it all the other times?"

"One trickster rabbit cereal coming up," Magnus announced as he returned to the kitchen. He patted Dante's back. "What's got you looking so surly this morning, MawMaw?" he asked.

Dante ignored the nickname and went to clean up the coffee he'd spit out. "I was just telling your future brother-in-law that we need to come up with a few ground rules if his fri—"

"*Boyfriend*," Aleks smoothly interjected.

"…if his boyfriend" – Dante swallowed as if the word left a bad taste in his mouth – "is going to be staying with us."

"What kind of rules?" Magnus asked. He winked at me and Aleks from behind Dante's back.

"Like no more closing his door when he and Vaughn are in there," Dante said, sounding proud of himself for how reasonable he'd made the request sound.

"I think that's actually a good idea," Magnus said.

"You do?" Dante asked in surprise as he watched his fiancé pull out a container of milk from the fridge, then go search for some bowls and spoons.

"Yeah," Magnus said, looking at Dante like he was crazy. "Aleks's bedroom door doesn't have a lock on it." He looked pointedly at me and Aleks. "Use the bathroom on the second floor. It's big and has a lock. It's also pretty soundproof."

"Um, no, it isn't," Aleks interjected as he eyed his brother briefly before shooting Magnus a grin. "And thanks, that's a great idea. Come on, Vaughn, let me show it to you."

"Nope, nope, nope," Dante said as he came around the island and stood in front of his brother. "Okay, okay, you win. You can close your door when Vaughn is in there with you. Just… just stay out of that bathroom. You'll just ruin it for us—" Dante said. "Me," he quickly corrected as he realized he'd pretty much just confirmed what he and Magnus really used that bathroom for.

Aleks laughed and hugged his brother. I returned to the island to sit down and watched as Aleks nudged Dante a few times, then motioned silently to Magnus with his eyes. I had no idea what was going on until Dante blurted, "I picked a date!"

Magnus stilled and looked up from where he'd been wiping down the counter.

"What?" The older man had a weird mix of surprise and hope in his expression.

Dante went around the island. "I know what day I want to marry you."

"Don't fuck with me, Dante," Magnus whispered in a rare show of distress.

Dante's eyes softened as he stepped up to Magnus and gently grabbed his face. "I'm not, baby. I swear, I'm not." Dante looked at Aleks briefly. "I'm sorry I've been so… so…"

"Stubborn," Aleks softly supplied as he moved back to my side and took my hand. Dante actually nodded, which led me to believe this topic had been one of probably many the brothers had discussed the night before.

"Yeah, stubborn. I'm sorry I've been so stubborn about committing to a date, but I just, I was trying to give you enough time to back out."

"Two years, Dante," Magnus growled as he closed his hands around Dante's wrists. But I could tell the man wasn't actually angry. "I've spent the last two years learning who you are, inside and out. And all it's done is make me love you even more. Whatever flaws you're waiting for me to see, I assure you, they don't exist."

"They're in my head," Dante acknowledged. "But here… here is where I know I'm enough for you." He pointed to his chest, much like Aleks had the night of the party. "I'm not sure my head will ever catch up," he said softly. His vulnerability was almost painful to watch, but it made him so much more human to me. And it was proof that Aleks's brother and I had a lot more in common than I ever would have guessed.

"It will, Dante," Magnus said with a sigh. "But even if it doesn't, I'm going to have the best time reminding you that you're not just dessert."

Dante let out a wet-sounding laugh at that. Aleks and I looked at one another because the statement made no sense to us.

But then again, it probably shouldn't.

Aleks and I had him liking my grits the best, these two men had a strange obsession with dessert…

"So when?" Magnus asked as he put space between his and Dante's bodies.

"Um, now?" Dante said. He glanced at his watch. "Well, in half an hour, anyway. The father or reverend or whatever he is is on his way. He's got to be back at his church by nine. It's Father O, remember? He runs that church that Levi and Phoenix volunteer for and Mav and Eli got married at."

"We're getting married today?" Magnus asked.

"I know it's crazy, Magnus. It's not that I want to get it over with or anything, but I want it to be just us and our immediate family for the ceremony. We can go to the courthouse tomorrow and make it official and then maybe have a party at some point—"

Magnus kissed Dante to shut him up. I put my arm around Aleks as he leaned into me. I could feel the happiness radiating off him in waves.

"We got it, Pop-pop," I heard someone call as the front door flew open behind us. Three little boys along with a big yellow dog ran into the kitchen, and I quickly tucked my gun into the waistband of my pants and covered it with my shirt so the kids wouldn't see the weapon. Magnus shot me a grateful smile.

One of the taller of the three boys was carrying a box of cereal and I smiled when I recognized what it was.

"Here, Aleks," the boy said as he shoved the cereal at him. "Pop-pop says you like Trix."

"Thanks, Matty," Aleks said as he leaned down to hug the little boy. I saw two men come through the door and I could see the tell-tale sign of a gun at the larger man's back when he shut the door behind him. I didn't recognize him, but I knew who he was just the same.

"Matty's fathers," Aleks whispered to me. "Hawke," he nodded at the bigger man with the gun. "And Tate."

"Hi," Tate said as he reached out to shake my hand. "You must be Vaughn."

"I am," I said. I shook his hand, then Hawke's, then looked at the three boys who were all watching me with curiosity.

"You've got lots of hair on your face," the boy in the middle said. He was as tall as Matty but had black hair, whereas Matty's was brown.

"And you have no pants," I said. "You must be Leo."

The kid looked down at his underwear that had some kind of superhero I didn't recognize on it. "We had to get here fast because Pop-pop said Aleks was hungry," Leo said as he eyed me like his comment should make perfect sense to me.

I chuckled and said, "Got it." I looked at Matty. "So, you're Matty. That must make you" – I looked at the smallest boy who looked like he was a couple years younger than the other boys – "Jamie."

Jamie nodded but remained silent.

"Guys, this is Vaughn," Aleks said.

"Is he your boyfriend?" Matty asked.

"No—" Dante said.

"Yes—" I responded at the same exact time, not bothering to look at Dante.

"Matty," Magnus called. "Guess what MawMaw and I are doing today."

Leo suddenly whispered something into Matty's ear. Matty nodded and spouted, "Cleaning the bathroom again?"

Aleks, Hawke, Tate, and I all burst into laughter as we looked at the two men on the other side of the kitchen island.

Magnus looked at a flushed-looking Dante. "I guess our secret's out, babe."

"Jesus," Dante muttered, then he went around the island and knelt down in front of Matty and his little friends. "No, your Pop-pop and I are getting married."

"Can we throw your flowers?" Leo asked excitedly.

"Oh, well, we don't actually have any flowers," Dante said as he looked around the room.

"We can use this, MawMaw," Matty said as he grabbed the box of cereal.

"Sounds like a plan," Magnus said. "But Leo, buddy, you're gonna need to wear pants for the wedding. Isn't that your dads' rule?"

Leo's face fell, but Matty grabbed his arm. "I've got my Captain

America pajamas here!" he exclaimed and then all three boys were off like a shot.

"Hey, this cereal doesn't have any fruit and flower shapes," Aleks said as he studied the bright red box of cereal.

"The company discontinued the shapes last fall," Hawke said as he went in search of coffee.

"I'm not going to ask how you know that," Dante murmured.

"Well, MawMaw, when you have your own kids, you'll get to deal with that day when your child discovers that his favorite cereal looks different and even though you try to explain that the taste is the same, you feel so damn bad that you decide to do something about it."

"What'd you do?" Dante asked. "Threaten the company or something?" he asked jokingly.

"We got a letter from the company's lawyer politely asking us to never contact them again," Tate said as he patted Aleks on the shoulder and then went around the island to get his own coffee. Then he was hugging Magnus. "Congrats, you two."

Then it was Hawke's turn. "I need a best man," Magnus told him.

Something warm passed between the two men that I didn't quite understand. But it had Hawke smiling and patting Magnus on the back.

"A lawyer?" Dante asked. "What exactly did you say, Hawke?"

"Nothing, MawMaw," Hawke drawled.

Dante shot him the bird at the nickname.

The behavior seemed par for the course for this group. It reminded me of my own family.

"Hmmm, *does* taste the same," Aleks said. "Wonder why the cereal Con gave me looked different?"

"We use that house as a safe house. Con keeps it stocked with nonperishable stuff. The cereal had probably been there for a little while. And you guys took that cereal with you to the beach house when you left—"

I had the sense to shut up when Aleks stiffened next to me. I thought it was because I'd brought up the reminder that he'd snuck out on me that morning, but when I went to reassure him I was no longer angry about that, he blurted, "Are you going back?"

The tremor in his voice had the entire room going silent.

"Back where? To the Hamptons?" I asked. "I don't actually live there," I began, but Aleks shook his head.

"No... are you going back *there*."

It hit me all at once what he was talking about. It was a topic we'd avoided since we'd left New York... well, in truth, we'd avoided it altogether from the moment I'd made it clear how much he meant to me. Mentioning the safe house had brought the reality of our situation crashing back in on him.

He was asking if I was going back into the dark world where kids were sold for sex.

"Shit, Aleks, I'm sorry," I whispered.

"No," Aleks said softly, the heartbreak in his voice clear. He pulled away from me and started heading for the door. I reached him before he could get it open. While Ronan had assured us the men who'd been arrested at the party had gotten the message that Aleks was off-limits, it still wasn't completely safe for him to be out and about by himself. To that end, several of Ronan's men were monitoring the outside of the house, but I was still reluctant to let Aleks out of my sight.

Not to mention I had a lot of explaining to do.

"Aleks, wait," I said as I pushed the door shut just as he tried to open it.

He turned around. Tears were streaking down his cheeks. "I want you to choose me," he whispered. "I know that's selfish and those kids need your help, but I still want you to choose me. Maybe... maybe you can still do that kind of work but come home to me whenever you can. I'll take that, James. It would be hard, but I could do it. And you'd know you had someone to come home to when things get really hard—"

"Aleks, I do."

"What?" he sputtered.

"I do choose you. I already have."

"*What?*" His voice cracked this time.

"I was apologizing to you because things have been going a million miles a minute since we landed in Seattle and that first day we just crashed and slept and last night I wanted you to focus on you and Dante talking so I was going to tell you today—"

"Tell me what?" he cut in.

"I talked to Ronan on the plane after everyone else fell asleep. He told me… he told me there were things I could do to help those kids without having to go back in. He said he's got men on the inside but what he really needs is someone who's lived that life… someone who can prepare the guys that go in."

I wiped at Aleks's tears. "He offered me a job, Aleks. And I accepted. I'll have to travel every now and then, but he says I can live anywhere… *we* can live anywhere."

"You're staying?" Aleks whispered in disbelief.

"I'm staying."

Aleks threw his arms around me. "I love you so much, James."

"I love you, Aleks," I said as I hugged him. Then I was kissing him and pushing him back against the door.

"Oh man, I don't need to see this," Dante muttered, reminding me we had an audience. "Magnus, can you send my best man to our room to help me find something to wear when Vaughn gets his tongue out of his mouth?"

I heard laughter behind us but ignored it and continued to kiss Aleks softly over and over. "We should go check out that bathroom," I muttered as my body responded to his.

"Yeah," Aleks said. "It's upstairs," he whispered.

Before we could head for the stairs, there was a knock on the door behind us.

"Sorry, guys, that's Father O," Magnus said as he held up his phone. I assumed he was showing us a text from Ronan's men notifying him the man of faith had arrived.

"Fudge," I said.

"Fiddlesticks," Aleks said at almost the same time. We both chuckled and then he released me. "I better go check on Dante." He gave me another quick kiss, then he was gone.

The wedding took place less than ten minutes later and

started with three little boys, one dressed in Captain America pajamas, throwing cereal all over the hallway floor as they made their way to the living room. Father O was standing in front of the fireplace. Tate and I were waiting off to the side as witnesses. Tate had managed to find the traditional wedding march on his phone and had figured out how to play it through the surround sound system that ran throughout most of the house.

Hawke entered the room after the boys, followed by Aleks. Magnus and Dante walked hand in hand to stand in front of Father O. There was little fanfare in the whole thing, but somehow that just fit for the two men.

Hawke and Aleks each stood off to the side of the grooms. I could see that the band Dante had been wearing on his left ring finger had been moved to his right hand, so I assumed that meant the couple had wedding bands to exchange.

Father O did the traditional introduction as he spoke to the rest of us about the couple in front of us wanting to commit themselves to one another. But when it came time for the vows, he seemed to catch Dante off guard when he asked, "Do either of you wish to speak your own vows?"

"What?" Dante blurted. "Oh shit, I didn't know that was a thing." He seemed oblivious that he'd just sworn in front of the reverend. He looked at Magnus and said, "Fuck, Magnus, I'm sorry, I just thought he'd ask us that love, honor, and obey shit and we'd say yes. But I should have thought of something special to tell you so you know how much I fucking love you."

Magnus and Dante had been holding hands as Father O had spoken, and as Dante's tirade continued, Magnus drew him closer and closer to himself. "How much, Dante?" he interrupted.

"What?" Dante asked, his entire attention switching to the man in front of him.

"How much do you love me, Dante?" Magnus repeated.

Dante seemed confused. I actually felt sorry for him. But the longer he looked at Magnus, the more he seemed to relax. He looked down at their hands and then took one of Magnus's in both of his. He turned his hand over and skimmed his fingers over the open palm.

It was Magnus's left hand.

I watched in curious silence as Dante took one of his fingers and began outlining shapes on the palm of Magnus's hand.

And then I realized they weren't shapes.

They were letters.

He was writing something on Magnus's hand.

But I had no clue what and Dante didn't say the letters out loud. When he was finished, he turned to look over his shoulder at his brother and held out his hand. Aleks placed a ring on Dante's palm. Dante and Aleks shared a smile that said volumes about what they were to one another, then Dante turned around and slid his ring onto Magnus's finger.

No one stirred or spoke as Magnus did the exact same thing to Dante's hand. Whatever message he wrote on Dante's skin had the man nodding and wiping at his eyes. When the ring was in place, the men joined both of their hands again.

Father O was a smart man, for sure, because the second the men joined hands, he said just a few words blessing their union, then he was announcing them as husbands. Dante and Magnus were in each other's arms before he even finished speaking and we all began clapping even as the kiss went on and on. The men kept it tame considering the children in the room, but the look they shared was proof that Aleks and I probably wouldn't have access to the upstairs bathroom anytime soon.

When the ceremony officially ended, Aleks came to me and I put my arm around him. Then I watched my new family start their celebration.

As happy as I was to be so warmly welcomed into the fold, I knew there was something I needed to do before I could really enjoy any of it.

I needed to tell my own family I wasn't coming home.

Epilogue

ALEKS

Two weeks later

"Are you sure, Aleks?"

I knew he wanted the actual word "yes" but my body was so crazy with need that it was hard to form the necessary sounds. Not to mention I could barely breathe.

Who would have thought Vaughn's fingers could make me so mindless?

Well, his fingers... and his tongue... and his hot breath against my neck... and his words...

Like how beautiful I was.

And responsive.

And tight.

And hot.

And *his*.

I probably could have orgasmed from that last word alone because the way he'd said it – growled it, actually – was like its very own sex act.

Oh, and of course, who could forget that spot inside me that

Vaughn knew just how to play to just completely rob me of the ability to speak or think?

In the *best* way.

"Please, James," I managed to get out, because I knew he liked hearing the words. When I felt his penis start to push into me, I closed my eyes and pressed my mouth against his shoulder to keep from crying out.

In pleasure.

It wasn't the first time Vaughn was penetrating me, but I swore, it seemed to get better each time and I had no clue how that was possible. The first time I'd asked him to put himself inside of me, I'd chickened out and then I'd freaked out. At that point, Vaughn had already introduced me to all the pleasures both his fingers and his tongue could bring my body, including that place where it had only ever hurt before. But my mind had started playing tricks on me as soon as his dick had touched me there. I'd started to cry and tell Vaughn I was sorry over and over again. He'd immediately stopped and then he'd just held me for what had seemed like hours until I'd fallen asleep. The next morning, we'd lain in our new bed and just talked and talked.

Well, I'd talked.

He'd listened.

I hadn't been telling him anything new, but he knew that talking things out helped my mind work through everything, so he'd patiently listened and then he'd reminded me that if that one aspect of making love wasn't something we ever did, he didn't care. Then he'd told me he loved me and we'd showered together where he'd proceeded to cherish my body and bring us both to a pleasurable end with his hands and mouth.

We'd tried again the next night, but only because *I'd* pushed so hard for it. If it wasn't something I could have with Vaughn, I'd wanted to know it. The whole process had been slow and awkward at first, but Vaughn had made every second of it about me and my pleasure. By the time he'd put himself inside of me, I'd been mentally prepared. I'd figured it was something I could tolerate.

Then he'd started moving.

And touching me.

And talking to me.

And I'd been a goner.

So had my body.

He'd made me come twice before he'd finally spilled deep inside of me.

And I'd once again become addicted.

This was our third time with him making love to me and while he was still being careful by going super slow, I was very, very over all that. "Fuck me, James," I practically demanded as I dragged him down for a kiss.

Vaughn smiled against my mouth. Then he pushed into me hard and deep. I dug my nails into his back and closed my legs around his hips. My body stung where his flesh was spreading me, but the burn that followed was like the sweetest drug. I threaded my fingers through Vaughn's hair as he thrust into me in a rhythmic glide that was both powerful and gentle at the same time.

But soon it wasn't enough anymore and he and I both knew it.

"Do you need more, baby?" Vaughn asked me as he wiped at my sweaty brow with his fingers.

I bit into my lower lip and nodded.

God, I needed so much more.

Of all of it.

And I needed it forever.

"Say it will be us one day, James," I said as I slid my hands to his shoulders. "Say it will be us standing in front of our family and friends saying words to each other that mean something just to us."

"It will be, Aleks," Vaughn said as he dropped his weight to his elbows and kissed me deeply before lifting his head again. "I'm going to tell you how one of the best days of my life was when you chose my grits."

I couldn't help but laugh. I caressed his cheek. He'd slowed his thrusts a little, enough so I could find my breath to speak, but it was just causing my orgasm to build on itself at frightening speed.

"And I'm going to tell you how much I love your butterscotch candy and that you're a terrible dancer."

Vaughn laughed. He'd gotten hooked on the dance video games I'd become obsessed with, but the man was as uncoordinated as a baby giraffe.

"You've got all the moves, baby," he said.

I slid my hand down to his butt and squeezed. "You've got some pretty good ones."

"Pretty good?" he asked. He suddenly pulled almost all the way out of me, shifted his hips and shoved into me hard, hitting my gland in the process. My entire body bowed off the bed, but I couldn't really go anywhere because his weight was holding me down.

"Acceptable?" I asked.

He nailed me again. I cried out at the sensation that rocketed throughout my entire body.

"Lots of potential," I gasped.

He chuckled against my mouth and then slammed into me again.

And again.

I clung to him as he drove me higher and higher. When I was right there, he suddenly stopped.

"No," I croaked.

"I like the word godlike." He kissed me softly but refused to move again until my body started to come down. Then he started all over again. When I was once again hanging on the edge of the cliff, he stopped.

"No, James, don't stop," I cried out in all seriousness.

"Aleks, look at me."

I forced my eyes open. His eyes were black with passion and his forehead was creased with tension. "There's only one word that's good enough to describe this... us."

I nodded because I knew what it was. I didn't know how I knew, but I did. "Perfect," I whispered.

His eyes widened just a little, then he slammed his mouth down on mine and began ramming into me hard, hitting my prostate every time. "Love you so fucking much, Aleks," he breathed against me.

I wanted to say the words, but he chose that exact moment to send me over and then he was flying with me.

And I reminded myself I'd have to tell him just as soon as we both landed.

If we ever did.

"Aleks!"

I turned to look over my shoulder at Caleb as he approached, his baby daughter in his arms. "Tell Remy he needs to stay," my friend said as he approached. My eyes shifted to the taller man behind Caleb.

"I should get back to work," Remy said, looking uncomfortable. Like me, he wasn't one for crowds and Dante's wedding reception was most definitely a crowd. I was doing okay with being around all the people, but if Vaughn wasn't by my side, I was constantly searching him out. He seemed to know how important it was for him to always be in my line of sight and so he went out of his way to make that happen.

"It's Sunday," I said to Remy.

He looked really tired and I was certain he'd lost some weight recently. I knew it probably had had something to do with my abduction. Dante had told me how frantic Remy had been, especially when he'd learned the original plan had been for me to be taken back to Chicago.

Chicago was where Remy had spent most of his life after he'd been taken as a child. He'd never told me the details of what had happened to him in captivity, just like I'd never told him about what I'd been through, but I knew from Dante that Remy had ended up working the streets of Chicago as a prostitute.

But not by choice.

I'd heard Marcus and his friends talking about how some kids who lost their "value" or were too much trouble to train were often sold to pimps. They were then turned into drug addicts to keep them dependent on their pimps.

Or they were threatened with death if they tried to walk away. With Remy, it had been both.

After helping to find me, Ronan and one of his men, Memphis, had helped get Remy set up in a methadone program. They'd also found him a job with a friend who owned a security firm. As far as I knew, Remy was doing well both with his recovery and working a desk job at Barretti Security, but his appearance had changed drastically in the month since I'd been kidnapped. I'd seen him only once in the past couple of weeks since I'd gotten back to Seattle. I'd invited him to come over to the house Vaughn and I were renting from Magnus. We'd moved in about a week after Dante and Magnus's wedding because as much as I loved my brother, trying to live with him and my boyfriend at the same time was a living hell. Dante was having a little bit of trouble accepting that I'd grown up in the past month and that while I'd always need him, I didn't *always* need him like I had before I'd been abducted.

"I just have a little bit of paperwork I want to get done before a meeting tomorrow," Remy said.

"At least wait until Magnus and Dante head out," I said. My brother and Magnus were finally leaving today for their honeymoon. No doubt they'd delayed the whole thing because they'd been reluctant to leave me.

But I was well protected with Vaughn, as well as Ronan's men, who were still shadowing me from afar. Ronan had promised me it wouldn't need to be for much longer... they just needed to be sure that the message I was off-limits had been received loud and clear. The fact that the very men who'd reveled in my return to their world were now facing substantial time behind bars seemed to have reinforced the fact that anyone who messed with me was messing with my family.

So between Vaughn and the men I was only now starting to meet and whose stories I was coming to learn, I was probably one of the most well-guarded people in the entire world.

"Hey, you got it back," Caleb said as he motioned to the bracelet on my left wrist.

I looked down at the little piece of braided leather and stamped metal. It looked exactly like the one Dante had had made for me before, but with one very big difference.

"It's just a bracelet this time," I said to Caleb. "I made Dante take the tracking part back out when he gave it to me."

Caleb smiled and I knew he got what a big step that had been for me.

He shifted Willa to one arm and then wrapped the other carefully around me. "Proud of you," he whispered. I nodded against his neck.

He pulled back, then handed me his daughter. "Will you hold her while I go find Jace? He was getting her bottle ready but probably got sidetracked."

"Absolutely," I said.

"I'm going to go find your brother and Magnus and say my goodbyes," Remy said when Caleb had left.

"Remy," I began, but he waved me off and gave me a sad smile.

"I'm okay, Aleks. Just really tired. Work's been busy."

I didn't believe him, but I was afraid to ask him the question that was lingering in the back of my mind.

Was he using again?

"He okay?" Vaughn asked as he came to my side.

"No," I said quietly. "I don't think he is."

"I'm sorry," Vaughn murmured. He kissed my temple.

"I'll call him tomorrow," I said. "Maybe I can convince him to come to lunch with me and talk. I don't start back at the shop until next week, so maybe he and I can hang out a bit before then." I hadn't told Remy I had decided to start seeing a therapist to deal with some of the issues from my past, but maybe I needed to do that. And maybe he and I needed to actually start talking to each other about the things that had happened. As far as I knew, Remy had sought help for his addiction, but he'd never gotten help for what had caused it in the first place.

Like me.

Vaughn rubbed my back. Then he was poking a finger at Willa's tummy. "How are you, sweetie?" he asked. His deep voice made the baby sit really quietly in my hold for a moment, then she was babbling and holding out her arms.

I chuckled. "Smart girl." I handed the baby to Vaughn, who easily took her. He began making all kinds of cooing sounds that clearly fascinated the child. Then she was grabbing his beard.

"Are we going to do this too, James?" I asked as I put my arm around him. I wasn't ashamed to admit to him that I wanted it all. We'd gotten the first part behind us already by moving in together, but I still wanted the vows and the kids and the white picket fence.

"Yeah, Aleks, we are," Vaughn said.

A moment later, Caleb and his boyfriend, Jace, appeared and Willa went crazy with happiness when she saw them.

And the bottle in Jace's hand.

"Hi, my girl," Jace said as he reached for her.

We were all admiring how quickly the baby got the nipple of the bottle in her mouth when Vaughn's phone beeped. He looked at it, then leaned down and said to me, "Luca's here. He's waiting in the driveway."

I nodded. "I'll come with you," I said as I took his hand. We said our goodbyes, then worked our way through the partygoers.

Things with Vaughn's family had gone well when he'd told them he was staying with me in Seattle and taking a job with Ronan. The men had figured as much and with the return of Gio, Luca's life was in limbo anyway, so Con and King were still trying to figure out things when it came to what role they played in continuing to get kids out of the sex trafficking world. I'd gotten the impression that Con was interested in working with Ronan and his men, but King wasn't as trusting. Lex had also become a bigger issue for the two brothers because the man was still MIA. He'd finally talked to Con on the phone, but he'd refused to tell him or anyone where he was. Con had actually gone to Los Angeles to look for Lex, but none of the people in Lex's life had known where he'd gone... he'd only told them he was taking some time for himself. The organization he ran that helped kids rebuild their lives was being run by his assistant and his video game business was being managed by his business partner.

He'd basically walked away from it all without any kind of explanation.

I could tell it frustrated the hell out of all the brothers, but Con was taking it especially hard. King seemed to know more than he was saying, but that didn't seem to be an unusual thing for King.

As for Gio and Luca, things were an absolute mess.

I hadn't been there when Luca had been reunited with his son, but Vaughn had.

It was as Ronan had predicted. The boy either hadn't recognized his father, or he'd pretended not to. When Luca had tried to touch him, Gio had lashed out at him. Then he'd gone silent.

Completely silent.

His doctor at the institute was calling it a complete break from reality and the result was that Gio didn't do anything more than lie in bed and stare at the ceiling. Luca had finally been able to touch his child, but he may as well have been touching a corpse for all the emotion Gio had shown.

The doctor was hopeful the boy would recover, but the whole thing was devastating for Luca and his family. The reunion they'd all envisioned wasn't to be.

Since Gio couldn't be moved, Luca had decided to stay in Seattle for the time being to be close to his son. His business apparently had a branch in the city that he could work out of, but Vaughn had made a comment about Luca having lost all his fire.

We found Luca about a hundred yards down the driveway. Dante and Magnus's reception was being held at Ronan and his husband, Seth's, house on Whidbey Island. The driveway was lined with cars. I could see that Luca's rental was double-parked next to another car, so I knew he wasn't planning on staying. And I suspected he hadn't come closer to the house because he hadn't wanted to intrude on the party.

When we reached Luca, Vaughn hugged him, but Luca didn't return it. Luca looked like I'd always felt when I was feeling too raw, so I didn't reach for him.

"How is he?" Vaughn asked.

Luca's expression remained stiff and there was just a little bit of a shake of his head.

Which meant there'd been no change with Gio.

"I'm just heading back into the city," Luca said after a moment. "But I wanted to drop this off for the grooms," he added as he handed Vaughn a bottle of wine.

"Come in and give it to them yourself," Vaughn said.

But the man shook his head. "No, I need to get back. Work," he said. There was no emotion in his voice. He'd turned back into the man who'd come with Con to the house in Nevada that first day.

"Hey, Aleks?"

I turned to see Remy heading toward us. I could see his car keys in his hand.

"Um, your brother wanted me to let you know they're leaving soon… something about just a quick bathroom break and then they were going to head out," Remy said in confusion when he reached us.

Vaughn laughed next to me and I shook my head. I was about to thank Remy when I saw how he was staring at Luca.

And Luca was staring at him.

But whereas Luca was looking at Remy with a mix of curiosity and something I could only classify as attraction, Remy looked… stunned.

"Remy, this is—" I began.

"Luca," Luca interjected as his eyes stayed on Remy. He reached out his hand. "Have we met before?" Luca asked.

It almost sounded like a come-on, but not quite. There was a genuine question there.

I was just in the process of turning to ask Remy if he was okay, because he hadn't moved or spoken, when he suddenly swung his fist and hit Luca square in the jaw.

Luca didn't fall, but the blow had him losing his balance and Vaughn grabbed his arm to steady him.

"Remy!" I cried in surprise.

But it was like Remy couldn't hear me. He cradled his hand against his chest. "Stay away from me, you asshole."

"Remy," Vaughn began, but my friend took another step back, like he was afraid Vaughn was going to try to grab him.

"You lied to me," Remy whispered as he stared at Luca. I could see tears swimming in his eyes. "Do you know how long I fucking waited for you to come back for me?"

Luca stiffened, then shook his head as understanding dawned. But it wasn't until he breathed "Billy?" that the pieces clicked into place for me.

Billy.

It was the name of the boy Luca had left behind so that he could find his son.

"Oh God," I whispered. "You're the boy Luca—"

"Forgot," Remy said softly. "He forgot about me… just like everyone else."

Remy turned to walk away.

"Remy, wait, please," Luca called, but then Remy was running down the driveway.

"Remy," I yelled, but he ignored me too and when I tried to go after him, Vaughn grabbed my arm.

"Let him go, Aleks. You won't be able to reach him in time."

Vaughn was right because Remy's little red sedan pulled out of its spot where it was parked farther down the driveway. The front of the car hit one of the cars on the other side of the driveway as Remy tried to turn around. The two cars scraped together, but it didn't stop Remy. His car tore off down the driveway and toward the road.

I pulled my phone out of my pocket and dialed.

"Pick up, pick up, pick up," I repeated over and over.

But he didn't.

Luca watched the car disappear, then he reached up to touch the bruise forming on his jaw.

"Luca," Vaughn said, but Luca shook his head. "I need to get to work. Tell… tell whoever car that is" – he pointed toward the car Remy's had hit – "that I'll pay for the damage."

Vaughn tried to reach for Luca, but he shook him off and went to his car. "I'm fine," Luca murmured. "I'm fine."

I knew he wasn't.

Just like Remy wasn't.

Once Luca's car was gone, Vaughn put his arm around me.

"We should go after them," I said. "I'm worried about Remy."

Vaughn nodded. "Let's go say goodbye to your brother and Magnus, then we'll head to the city and check on him."

By the time we got back to the house, Magnus and Dante were already in the process of saying their goodbyes to their guests. Both men looked mussed and I couldn't help but smile. When Dante's arms went around me, I squeezed him hard.

"Take care of yourself, irmãozinho," Dante murmured.

"You too, meu melhor." I didn't wait for Dante to interject guesses as to what he was my best of this time around. I simply told him what I'd always known he was to me. "Meu melhor tudo," I whispered.

My best everything…

He kissed my temple, then held me for a moment longer. "I'll see you soon, okay?"

I nodded.

"And tell that boyfriend of yours something," he added.

"What?" I asked with dread.

"Tell him thanks for the wedding gift. Best present ever." He kissed me again.

"Wait," I said as I grabbed his arm. "What did he give you?" I asked.

"Ask him," Dante said with a wink, then he took Magnus's outstretched hand and they left.

My phone rang before I could say anything else. I sighed in relief when I saw that it was Remy.

"Remy, are you all right?" I asked. "Where are you?"

"I'm in the line for the ferry. I'm okay," Remy said. His voice actually sounded… normal. Which I knew wasn't possible.

"Remy, just stay there. Vaughn and I will come get you. You can come stay with us."

"Thanks, but I'm actually going to go stay with a friend for a couple days. I already called Dom to make sure it was okay."

Dom as in Dom Barretti, his boss.

As far as I knew, Remy had never missed even a single day of work in the two years he'd worked for Dom.

"Will you tell the person whose car I hit that I'm sorry and I'll pay for it?"

"I'll take care of it," I began. "But Remy…"

"Aleks," Remy said softly.

"Yeah?"

"I'm okay, I swear it."

"Please come stay with us," I repeated.

Remy sighed. "I'm going to stay with my sponsor. I'll call you from his house tonight when I get there and let you talk to him so you know I'm okay. All right? I need… I need to be with him because he'll know what to say to me."

I understood what it was that he wasn't telling me.

He was fighting the urge to get high.

"Swear to me that's where you're going," I said. "Swear it to me, Remy, or I'll camp outside your door all night."

Remy chuckled. "I swear it, Aleks."

I felt a little bit of relief because his laugh sounded pretty good. And he'd never lied to me before.

Because he was my friend.

"I'll call you tonight, okay?"

"Okay," I said with a nod. "Text me, too. Every hour."

"Aleks…"

"Every hour, Remy."

"Okay, fine, every hour. I have to go, the cars are being loaded onto the ferry."

I said my goodbyes and hung up.

"Is he okay?" Vaughn asked. I hadn't noticed him standing next to me.

"I don't think so," I admitted. "He says he's going to go see his sponsor and he'll call me tonight."

Vaughn's fingers went through my hair, then he pulled me close. "Let's go to the city and check on him," Vaughn said. "And if he's not at his place, we'll wait to hear from him tonight and see if we can't get him to let us come see him."

"We should check on Luca, too," I said.

"Yeah," Vaughn said. "We'll do that too."

I barely remembered to say my goodbyes to my family and friends. It wasn't until Vaughn and I were walking hand in hand to our car that I recalled Dante's parting words.

"Dante said to tell you thank you for the wedding present," I said as I glanced at him. Vaughn's thumb was doing that amazing thing where he rubbed it over mine. "What present? We didn't get them anything."

Vaughn smiled and looked at me. "Besides Magnus and Matty, what's the most precious thing in Dante's life?" Vaughn asked.

"Me," I automatically said.

When Vaughn didn't continue, I opened my mouth to ask him why that mattered. But the answer hit me all at once.

We hadn't given Dante and Magnus a wedding present.

Vaughn had.

He'd given my brother *me*.

Twice.

Once two years ago and again a month ago when he'd saved my life.

But he'd saved me in so many other ways too.

"Oh," I said with a smile.

A really big smile.

"Would you tell Dante something for me when he calls you tonight?"

"Of course," I said. My heart felt full as I realized my brother and Vaughn were actually going to get along after all.

But that lasted all of five seconds because then Vaughn said with a wink, "Tell him mine is bigger."

I began laughing and couldn't stop even once we'd reached the car. Vaughn opened the door for me and pressed me back against the frame of the car. He kissed me softly, then placed a piece of butterscotch into my hand. "Let's go check on our family and then go home, Aleks. Sound good?"

"Sounds perfect, James. It sounds absolutely perfect."

The End

Check out the next page for a sneak peek of the first book in my new Protectors spin-off series, "The Four." Book 1 is tentatively titled "Forgotten" and will be Luca and Remy's story!

Sneak Peek

FORGOTTEN (THE FOUR, BOOK 1)

Prologue

LUCA

"Yeah, he's fine, Aleks. We'll probably be talking long into the night, but I'll have Remy check in with you tomorrow for sure."

I didn't know what to make of the fact that the young man who stepped into the darkened apartment was talking about himself in the third person, but part of me didn't care as I drank in the sight of him. There was a light on just above him, but it was only enough to make out a few of his features.

But it didn't matter because everything about him was stamped into the deepest recesses of my brain.

Billy.

No, not Billy.

Remy.

I'd known him only as Billy the first time I'd met him when he'd been a kid. That moment was also etched into my mind, but for very different reasons. And it seemed like it wasn't just my brain that couldn't rid itself of every second of that dark day when I'd done something, become somebody, I never would have dreamed possible. *Every cell in my body remembered that day.*

The smells.

The sounds.

The feel of the terrified, crying boy who'd had to have the strength of an adult to deal with what I'd had to do to him to keep us both breathing.

They would have left him alone, you cowardly piece of shit.

The voice in my head was ugly and cold, but I knew it was true.

Billy... no, Remy, wouldn't have been punished for what had happened.

I would've been the one who didn't walk out of that house alive.

The kid had saved my ass by playing along with everything I'd told him to do.

And I'd fucking left him there.

"Yeah, Aleks, here's Remy. It was nice to meet you, finally, even if it was just over the phone," Remy said. He had a messenger bag strapped across his midsection and sitting on one hip. I could see his left hand fisted on top of the cheap-looking material. His right hand was holding the phone against his ear. He pulled the phone away from his face for a moment as if he were actually going to hand it to someone. I watched as he drew in a deep breath, then put the phone back to his ear.

"Satisfied?" he asked with what probably was supposed to have been a humorous drawl, but he didn't smile. The voice he used was the same one I'd heard earlier in the day right before he'd slammed his fist into my jaw.

His *natural* voice.

"Yeah, Joe's great," Remy said.

I knew he was talking to Aleks Silva, my brother's boyfriend. What I didn't understand was why he had pretended to be someone else... *Joe.*

Who the fuck was Joe?

I actually felt jealousy curl through my belly and that made me want to throw up.

Because no way in hell could I or should I be attracted to this young man.

Not after what I'd done to him.

"Yeah, I'm just going to stay with Joe for a few days... until he's sure I'll be okay on my own," Remy said, his voice a strange mix of confidence and certainty that, again, didn't match his expression. I willed him to turn around so I could see his face full-on.

I knew I should probably say something to make my presence known, but I needed these moments to take in everything about him. I'd already been through his apartment after I'd broken into it.

And breaking in was exactly what I'd done – and it had taken a hell of a long time considering the young man had four different locks on his door. Thankfully, he lived in a small building that didn't have a lot going on so late in the evening.

"I'll call you when I'm back in town," Remy said, clearly lying, since we were in town... downtown Seattle, to be exact.

I leaned back in the chair I was sitting in. It wasn't particularly comfortable, but from looking around Remy's apartment when I'd first managed to get into it, I'd already determined Remy seemed to prefer function to fashion or comfort. His furniture was the kind you could get from any cheap furniture store and while not exactly new, it hadn't seemed like thrift-store used, either. His bedroom had just a mattress and a dresser in it and his small kitchen sported only the basic appliances and a few pots and pans. His refrigerator was mostly empty.

Which might explain why Remy was so skinny.

"Yeah, I'll tell him," Remy remarked as he said his goodbyes to Aleks. From the expression on Remy's face, I could tell it pained him to lie to his friend.

So why was he doing it?

You know why.

I actually shook my head before I caught myself.

No, I refused to believe that. From the information I'd managed to pull together in the last few hours, Remy had been living a quiet, comfortable existence in the two years since he'd moved to Seattle from Chicago. He had a good job at a local security firm and from what I'd seen this afternoon, he was part of a large group of men and women who considered themselves family, despite so few of them actually sharing any blood.

I dismissed the fear that was going through me that seeing me had somehow set him back. It was just another layer of guilt I wasn't prepared to deal with.

But I also knew why I was really here.

It wasn't to apologize to him for what I'd done, because there was no way to apologize for something like that.

I'd destroyed his life.

My brother, Vaughn, had tried to convince me otherwise, but I knew the truth. I'd promised to save him, and I hadn't done it. I'd chosen another child to save instead of him.

And I'd ended up destroying them both.

I refused to let my mind shift to my son, Gio, because I just wasn't capable of dealing with that right now.

I couldn't even deal with the fact that Remy was Billy and that the boy I'd thought I'd never see again was standing right in front of me.

He'd been around thirteen or fourteen when I'd last seen him. The information I'd managed to have my private investigator pull together on Remy in the last few hours had been sketchy at best, but one thing was clear.

He'd never gotten to go home.

I only knew that because Remy's identity on paper had begun only two years ago. He'd been issued a new social security number and there'd been no mention of any kind of previous history in his records. His credit and employment history were only two years old, and there was nothing about parents or family in any of the little bit of a paper trail my investigator had managed to find. Normally, I'd have any one of my brothers do that kind of research, but I definitely hadn't wanted to explain to King or Con or Lex anything about Remy and why I was trying to dig up information on him.

Vaughn was the only one who knew what I'd done to Remy, aka Billy, eight years earlier when I'd entered a world I hadn't fully understood… one in which kids were sold and traded for sex.

Remy had been one of those kids.

My son, Gio, had been too.

I'd been trying to find Gio when I'd met Remy. I'd thought myself so lucky to have managed to get access to the sex trafficking ring that had stolen my child from me, but when I'd been led into an old farmhouse several hours north of Chicago, I'd known it wouldn't be so simple to find my son and bring him home.

But I'd been desperate, and I'd understood that my only chance of finding Gio had meant playing the game. Only, I hadn't understood the price I'd have to pay until I'd walked into a dirty, dark, nearly empty room with a single bed in it.

I also hadn't understood that *I* wasn't the only one who'd have to pay a price.

After hanging up, Remy merely dropped the phone to the floor. The entryway to the apartment was carpeted, so it barely made a sound. I could see the young man was agitated.

Really agitated.

He was shaking with whatever emotion he was dealing with.

I almost laughed at that… like it was a question or something. Like I didn't know *exactly* what the fuck he was dealing with.

He was dealing with having run into the man who'd promised to save him but had left him to his fate.

Do you know how long I fucking waited for you to come back for me?

I must have made a sound as I remembered the pain in his voice when he'd asked me that very question this afternoon because Remy froze, then turned to look in my general direction. The section of the apartment I was sitting in was dark, but his eyes landed right on me.

I expected him to say something or at least turn on the lights for the rest of the apartment so he could see me, but he didn't. Instead, he looked at the wall in front of him, then slowly eased the messenger bag off and dropped it to the floor next to his phone.

"You're late," he said softly. "By about eight years." He leaned against the door so he was still facing the wall. His voice sounded resigned and all the agitation just fell away until there was nothing. He pulled in a breath and said, "Actually, eight years, four months—"

"—three days, six hours, and thirteen minutes," I finished for him.

He glanced at me in surprise for the briefest of moments, then the emotion slipped away.

"Who's Joe?" I asked.

Remy let out a soft laugh, then turned so he was facing me. He reached out with his right hand to flip on the lights. "What?" he asked, his lips pulling into something of an amused grin. But it wasn't a natural one. "You worried I'm not quite right up here?" he asked as he pointed to his head.

The reference to his mental health hit a little too close to home considering what my son was currently going through, but I managed not to react. Although Gio had been rescued from the man who'd hurt him for so many years, my child wasn't okay.

Not physically.

And most certainly not mentally.

In fact, he was so far gone I couldn't even conceive of the fact that he was now even further out of my reach than he'd been when he was missing.

"Don't worry yourself about it," Remy said, the smile fading away. "They turned me into a junkie, not a psycho."

I knew who "they" was.

The men who'd taken him and forced him into a life no child should ever have to even know about, let alone face.

The confirmation that he was indeed an addict made something seize in my chest. My PI had found evidence that Remy had been enrolled in a Methadone program when he'd arrived in Seattle two years earlier, but I'd wanted to believe that meant his life had gotten...

What, Luca? Better? How the fuck does life get better after something like that?

I didn't have an answer for the question.

"So Joe is your sponsor," I said as stood. I saw Remy tense up slightly, but otherwise he didn't react.

"Was," Remy corrected. "He OD'd six months ago." Remy crossed his arms. "He'd been sober twelve years. Then his wife left him and he went in search of his old friend… they say it doesn't take much to have you wanting to reach for that needle," he added casually.

Like it was all some foregone conclusion.

"Could be something as simple as a smell that reminds you of the room you used to get high in… or someone who looks like your dealer… or something from your past shows up to remind you how fucked up the world really is."

I ignored the not-so-subtle message.

"And the voice?" I asked. "*Joe's* voice?"

Remy actually looked guilty for a moment. "I knew Aleks would come over here if he knew I was by myself."

"They were already here," I said as I motioned to the door behind him. "I was half expecting my brother to break the damn thing down, with the way Aleks was calling your name."

I didn't tell him that I also figured the hotel I was staying at probably would have been Aleks and Vaughn's next stop after Remy's apartment. My brother had messaged and called me multiple times, but I'd ignored his efforts to reach out to me.

I began walking toward Remy. With every step I took, he got more tense.

Other than being a little too thin, he was a beautiful man and I didn't recognize any of the child he'd been when I'd first met him. His hair was a lush brown that had lighter streaks running through it. It was haphazardly styled, like he was the kind of person who ran his fingers through the lush locks a lot and didn't realize it. His eyes were a deep blue color and he had full eyebrows, a straight nose, and a square jaw with just a hint of stubble on it. But it was his mouth that I was having the hardest time keeping my gaze off of.

His lips were a soft shade of pink and there was no other way to describe them than totally kissable.

I lifted my eyes and saw that Remy was watching me with what could only be called caution.

He'd undoubtedly noticed me checking him out.

"Nice trick with the voice," I said. "If I hadn't been looking at you, I definitely would have been fooled."

"I'm good at tricks," Remy said, his hard eyes pinning mine. My confusion must have shown because he tilted his head at me. "Oh, so he didn't tell you," Remy said softly.

I'd closed the distance between Remy and myself by at least half, but something in the way he said those last words had me coming to a stop. None of this encounter was happening how I'd envisioned it. I'd just wanted the chance to make sure Remy was okay and try to explain why I'd done what I'd done eight years earlier. Maybe we could…

What?

I didn't have an answer for myself. Well, I did, but they were all selfish ones.

Maybe he'll forgive me and I can stop hearing his sobs in my head every time I close my eyes.

Maybe he'll say he's okay and there was nothing I could have done differently.

Maybe he'll tell me he's happy and I can finally fucking breathe again.

Remy kept moving toward me, his eyes never leaving my face. I expected him to stop long before he reached me, but he didn't. He didn't stop until his body was practically brushing mine. His right hand came up to stroke down my chest and my cock instantly responded. I'd already felt like the lowest form of life on the planet for the fact that I'd been half-hard since he'd walked into the apartment, but now I just wanted to curl up into a ball of shame because I couldn't control my reaction to his nearness.

And my entire life was about control.

"Do you know what they do to you when you don't play by the rules, Luca?" Remy asked softly, almost seductively as he skimmed his hand down my chest. I told myself to step back, but I couldn't move. I knew how fucked up all this really was, but I just couldn't move. My body was homed in on his touch, but my mind was focused on his voice and his words, and I knew whatever was coming would just make everything worse.

But fuck if I didn't deserve worse.

So much worse.

My suffering was a drop in the hat compared to his.

"They let the pimps have you because you're too much trouble for the high-paying clients," Remy said softly. His fingers touched my dick through my dress pants, but my body was thankfully catching up to my mind and my flesh wasn't responding. But unfortunately, my cock wasn't deflating fast enough, so to Remy it probably looked like the whole thing was turning me on.

Which just made me more of a sick fuck in his eyes than I already was.

I let his words wrap around my mind as I accepted the truth of what he was telling me.

"I'm sor—"

The fingers of Remy's left hand quickly closed over my mouth to silence me. His touch was gentle, but his eyes were full of bitter, brittle anger.

"You owe me this," he whispered, and I nodded because I understood what he was saying, and he was right.

The least I could do was listen to what my actions had done to him.

"They first took me when I was eleven. I lost track of how many guys fucked me, but I never forgot the one who *didn't*," Remy said softly. "Even after they sold me to a pimp who shot me up with heroin right before he 'tested the merchandise' for himself, I couldn't stop thinking about the promise that help was coming... that *someone* was finally going to come for me. All I could think about was the gentle voice that had told me about the beach and dolphins and the promise that he'd take me to see them someday."

Remy dropped his hand from my mouth. My heart was pounding against my chest and my throat felt so tight I was sure I wouldn't be able to take even one more breath. I remembered all those things I'd said to him as if it'd been days ago, not years.

"I wish you really *had* fucked me in that room that day, Luca," he said, his voice husky with unshed tears. "It would have been kinder," he added.

I nodded because I knew he was right. I dropped my gaze. When Remy reached for my hand and pulled it to him, I let him. His fingers nudged mine open. Then he was putting something in my palm before he covered my hand with his.

"It's my turn to forget about you," Remy bit out, his voice incredibly even. "Take this with you when you go," he said as he pulled his hand back slightly to reveal a plastic baggie sitting in the middle of my palm. The bag had a small, black rock in it.

But I knew it was no rock.

"You're not worth losing two years of sobriety," he whispered as he closed my hand so it was fisted around the baggie. Then he was walking past me and I heard a door snick closed from somewhere behind me.

His bedroom door, probably.

Or bathroom.

It didn't matter.

It also didn't matter that he was wrong about one thing.

I'd never forgotten him.

And I knew now, more than ever, I probably never would.

I deserved no less.

About the Author

Dear Reader,

I hope you enjoyed Aleks and Vaughn's story. Up next in The Protectors series is the story of Matias and Sam who you met briefly in my Protectors novella, Protecting Elliot. And don't worry, Remy and Luca are getting a book, but it will be the start of a Protectors spin-off called, "The Four." Con, Lex and King will also be getting stories in that new series! So make sure to stay tuned...

As an independent author, I am always grateful for feedback so if you have the time and desire, please leave a review, good or bad, so I can continue to find out what my readers like and don't like. You can also send me feedback via email at sloane@sloanekennedy.com

Join my Facebook Fan Group: Sloane's Secret Sinners

Connect with me:
www.sloanekennedy.com
sloane@sloanekennedy.com

Also by Sloane Kennedy

(Note: Not all titles will be available on all retail sites)

The Escort Series
Gabriel's Rule (M/F)

Shane's Fall (M/F)

Logan's Need (M/M)

Barretti Security Series
Loving Vin (M/F)

Redeeming Rafe (M/M)

Saving Ren (M/M/M)

Freeing Zane (M/M)

Finding Series
Finding Home (M/M/M)

Finding Trust (M/M)

Finding Peace (M/M)

Finding Forgiveness (M/M)

Finding Hope (M/M/M)

Love in Eden
Always Mine (M/M)

Pelican Bay Series
Locked in Silence (M/M)

Sanctuary Found (M/M)

The Truth Within (M/M)

The Protectors

Absolution (M/M/M)

Salvation (M/M)

Retribution (M/M)

Forsaken (M/M)

Vengeance (M/M/M)

A Protectors Family Christmas

Atonement (M/M)

Revelation (M/M)

Redemption (M/M)

Defiance (M/M)

Unexpected (M/M/M)

Shattered (M/M)

Unbroken (M/M)

Protecting Elliot: A Protectors Novella (M/M)

Discovering Daisy: A Protectors Novella (M/M/F)

Pretend You're Mine: A Protectors Short Story (M/M)

Non-Series

Four Ever (M/M/M/M)

Letting Go (M/F)

Short Stories

A Touch of Color

Catching Orion

Twist of Fate Series (co-writing with Lucy Lennox)

Lost and Found (M/M)

Safe and Sound (M/M)

Body and Soul (M/M)

Crossover Books with Lucy Lennox

Made Mine: A Protectors/Made Marian Crossover (M/M)

The following titles are available in audiobook format with more on the way:

Locked in Silence

Sanctuary Found

The Truth Within

Absolution

Salvation

Retribution

Logan's Need

Redeeming Rafe

Saving Ren

Freeing Zane

Forsaken

Vengeance

Finding Home

Finding Trust

Finding Peace

Four Ever

Lost and Found

Safe and Sound

Body and Soul

Made Mine

Printed in Great Britain
by Amazon